# The Hills We Run From

ELLIS MAE

Ellismaewriting.com
https://twitter.com/mae_writing
https://www.instagram.com/ellismaewriting/

ISBN   979-8-9873106-0-1 (ebook)
ISBN   979-8-9873106-1-8 (paperback)

Book Design Kiia Kostet
https://www.instagram.com/kiiakostet/
Logo Design Diego Velez

# Content/Trigger Warnings

Hello reader before you begin this novel, I would like to let you know that it contains the following potentially triggering content:

> Drug/Alcohol Use
>
> Self-Harm
>
> References to Sexual Assault
>
> Depictions of Bullying
>
> Depictions of Negligent/Abusive Parenting
>
> References to Suicidal Ideation

Potentially triggering content has been kept relatively non-graphic. Feel free to reach out at ellismaewriting.com if you have any questions or if you feel a CW/TW has not been included in this list.

To my brother and his encouraging words of "It's actually not bad." Thanks for believing in me every step of the way.

# Chapter One

There is a house,
Covered in ivy
Thicker than sunbeams.
It is dark,
In this house.

There is a sliver of freedom,
Where the ivy does not crawl.
The cobblestone paving calls
And I place my pale, cold hands on the window
But I cannot open it.

There is a demon,
Covered in hatred.
Thicker than the ivy.
It is wild,
Tearing apart what I have made.

I stare through the window
As the ivy crawls over it.
If I were stronger,
I could shatter the glass
Before the demon tears me apart.

*Emmylou*

There's something to be said about rich, spoiled Americans traveling the world to "find themselves."

The smell of brewing coffee beans and the soothing indie music is designed to relax folks as they take pause in the hustle and bustle of the busy airport. I'm afraid, though, that the calm has been shattered by my grown mother throwing a childish temper tantrum.

I observe from a safe distance as she yells at the underpaid, overworked barista. If I tug at my sweater sleeves hard enough, maybe it'll swallow me whole and save me the embarrassment. Despite feeling empathetic for the young man, I'm glad it isn't me under the lash of her whip. Separating her from me by a whole ocean may not be enough to sever the small child she's built me into.

The barista glares at her with more defiance than I've ever mustered, but ultimately hands her a free drink. I give him an apologetic smile. He doesn't smile back.

"See, Emmylou," my mother starts as she turns around. If she'd just take a few more steps, we'd be out of earshot, but she's always been the type to kick someone while they're down. "That right there is why you go to college. Don't wanna end up working some dead-end job like him—too dumb to know what's what."

I sigh heavily and try to hide the grimace on my face; the last thing I need is to be on the receiving end of her tantrum. I pull the sleeves of my cotton candy blue and pink sweater down further and obediently follow those cherry heels through the throngs of people.

There's something to be said about teenage girls who still live under their mother's heels.

I chose the University of Edinburgh at my sister's word. We were laying in her room watching Outlander, her crushing on Sam Heughan and me pushing the thought of college applications out of mind. At the time, I had already applied to the colleges all my friends had applied to as well as the one my poppa wanted me to attend. In reality though, I was longing to leave Texas as far behind as I could.

"You should go to Scotland and find yourself a man with rippling muscles and an accent like him," she had said pointing to the screen. I only started searching for schools in Scotland out of curiosity and then applied when I saw what Scotland's scenery had to offer.

Looking for men, however, didn't seem exciting then and seems less exciting now as we pass through the streets of Edinburgh. There are drunk folks standing outside of bars smoking cigarettes and talking soccer, their beer guts protruding. The men are loud and sweaty. Not at all like the men Janey sent me to find.

I could have chosen a different school. I could've chosen a different country, but the one thing that did interest me about Edinburgh was its design. The rolling hills conquered despite their difficulty to build on. The leaning bars and houses as we weave through the streets. The cobblestone pathways that lead to my apartment and my school. Even a castle high up on the hill.

In Texas, it felt like everything was flat and covered in Long Horns. The heat was as suffocating as my mother's expectations. But here it's cool and gray, and in ten or so minutes, I won't see my mother again until Christmas.

The thought brings the first smile to my face since Janey visited with her fiancé this summer. Despite the company, my mother spent all of summer nagging me about what I was bringing to Scotland. Clothes were thrown out and bedsheets were shipped. I was only just barely able to hold on to my childhood sweater I'm wearing now. I thought mothers were supposed to be more concerned about majors rather than clothes, but when I brought this up to her, the answer was curt. She thinks I should be a nurse because it's "cute," but I have no desire to wait on drunken late night ER visits or clean someone's privates. My major is on hold for the time being while I decide between two contrasting visions.

As the rental my mother drives nears campus, I start to see more students laughing and goofing off just like the brochures. Maybe it isn't so outlandish to suggest I'll find myself here.


A very Scottish girl hollers a very Scottish "Oi" at me as she runs past. I shift the suitcase in my arms to apologize but she's already gone, her brown, curly hair flying in the wind behind her. The arduous flight has exhausted my defenses and I didn't even think to look before hoisting my sunflower-print suitcase from the trunk. Apparently listening to my perfectionist mother complain about not getting first-class seats can do that to me.

I look at her now, standing beside the car in those cherry heels. She lifts a perfectly waxed eyebrow at me.

"Emmylou, darling, go on and get your bags. I'd hate to miss my flight to Italy because you're slower than a sinner heading to church." I secure my backpack, being extra vigilant to not hit anyone as I swing it on.

About three times a year, my mother goes off with her girl-friends from college on an extravagant vacation. Unfortunately for me, my mother planned it a week after orientation. She deemed me too irresponsible to come to Scotland by myself and, thus, I'm already falling behind. I had to tell the school I had a family emergency, but hopefully this is the last time I'm dragged around by my mother.

I grab my other suitcase, a pretty lilac one that matches my flats, and throw a duffle on top of it. Before I grab the last backpack, I look up at my mother as she giggles typing out a text on her phone; I huff as I strap the backpack to my front. It'll be sure to put wrinkles in my dress that I specifically changed into after the flight so it would be presentable.

*You're always an unpresentable mess,* my mother's voice says in my head, and I bite my lip hard as I will it to shut up.

"Last time," I whisper as I steel myself to put on a pretty face for my mother. "Goodbye, mamma. I'd give you a hug, but I'm a bit outta hands as is," I tell her, fighting the urge to shrug; she says it makes me look pathetic when I shrug.

She waves a dismissing hand to me as she turns toward the bright red Mini Cooper and gets in. I watch her make a call before pulling away, her boisterous laughing visible in the rearview.

I spare her one last glare before I turn around to my new apartment that stands above me in looming, water-stained brick. I take a step toward my new future, my suitcase rattling along the cobblestones. The ringer for apartment 308 is covered in glitter pen drawings. I press it. I wait by the door, my stomach in knots—this whole idea could be the dumbest one I've ever had. I probably should have just gone to UT Austin like everyone else and kept pretending that I was the stereotypical blonde cheerleader filled with bubbly energy and no brains.

*They're not gonna like you Emmylou. You're too scrawny, too southern, too boring,* my mother's voice says as I stare at my reflection in the door.

"Give us a hand," exclaims a portly, pink woman, snapping me out of my thoughts. She brushes her hands on her apron before grabbing my suitcase with the duffle on top.

"You must be Emmylou! I'm Drew, the one that was texting you most of the time over the summer. You didn't hear as much from Kirsty because she becomes really absorbed in her work," she says as she starts toward the stairs.

"Sorry lass, we don't have a lift, but I already made my mates from the apartment below us carry up your furniture, so don't you worry." The stairs are covered in cement and I don't bother picking up my suitcase, choosing to let it slam against the stairs instead as we ascend.

"Oh, are we allowed to paint the apartment?" I ask, staring at the gaudy orange door marked with gold lettering proclaiming it to be 308.

Drew lets out a sighing laugh. "Not quite but, eh, Kirsty." She doesn't explain further as she opens the door and leads me and my suitcase toward an empty room. The apartment is actually really nice; shaped like an L, it has an open kitchen that leads toward what appears to be a dining table right in front of the main entrance and further beyond a couch and TV with a massive window backdrop toward the city.

My room is at the top right of the L and the walls are white and uncovered but the window in here, although smaller, lets in plenty of light. Drew delicately props my suitcase against my bedframe and mattress in the middle of the room.

"Well, I'm actually in the middle of evening meal but I can help you unpack or move around furniture once it's done. KIRSTY," she yells as she walks out of the room, startling me. Drew walks across the living room to a door across mine and raps her knuckles on a bright neon door adorned with an LSD vision of nature.

A pale-skinned girl with jet black hair comes out. She has paint on her cheek and basically dripping off every item of clothing.

"Sorry, was having me a wee painting session, you know how it is," she tells us before coming up to me. Her bright gray eyes peer over at me before she breaks into a smile. "You've finally joined us."

I stick my hand out abruptly as I watch her arms extend for a hug. She sheepishly smiles and takes it instead; I still manage to get just a dash of paint on me, but it's better than on my clothes.

Kirsty wraps her long hair in a bun and sticks a still-wet paint brush through it to hold it all together.

"Did you need help with your unpacking," she says absentmindedly as she sticks her nose up, inhaling whatever it is Drew has going on in the kitchen. Before I can respond, she whips back around and looks deeply into my eyes, her nose a few inches from mine as she crouches to look me head on.

"You have the most beautiful eyes; do you mind if I paint them sometime?"

I bite my lip, holding back anxious laughter as Drew comes back into the room with a wooden spoon. She conks Kirsty on the head once.

"No, you'll not be scaring our new flatmate before she's even completed her first day," she says with a huff, turning back toward the kitchen.

"Hmm, I suppose that is Finn's job," she mumbles before looking at me expectantly.

"Oh, uh, I think I'm actually fine with unpacking on my own. It'll help me settle a bit after the flight." But mostly I don't want her paint all over my stuff and her confusing accent further muddling my jet-lagged brain.

"Cor'," she says with a smile that grows before she finally turns back to her room and shuts the door.

Drew comes out of the kitchen and raises an eyebrow at me.

"Scran is just sitting on the stove if you actually want help from someone who doesn't look like they vomited a rainbow."

I laugh as a blush covers my face but accept defeat and lead her into my room.

"I guess I should have warned you more about Kirsty," Drew starts.

I laugh awkwardly as I grab the clothes she put on hangers. "Nah, that's all right. A bubbly personality never caused no harm."

"Eh, she's got bite when she wants to. I should, however, let you know now. My mates downstairs are a handful. Quite radge if you ask me."

She hands me the last hanger and I look at my desolate closet. I'll have to go buy fabrics to make clothes and fill it up. Better to think about that then whatever a *radge* is.

"They're coming for evenings tonight if that's okay," she asks, continuing the conversation.

"Yeah, that seems fun," I respond absent-mindedly, pulling out my sheets. "So what's campus like?"

Hearing the ins and outs of campus from her is more comforting than what I could find on the university website or Google Maps. Even though I'm exploring my major options I'm still required to take mostly gen ed's so I won't be running around campus much.

"Anything that's too out of my way I'm sure someone else in the group can walk you to," she says as she shoves my pillow into the sunflower-yellow cover.

"Oh, if it's not too much of a hassle I'd really appreciate that."

She nods once as if that's the end of it.

"Are you and the neighbors downstairs close?" I ask, now interested that they'll be walking me to class. I throw my duvet over the finished bed as she huffs out a laugh.

"Aye, we grew up together, so thick as blood. Or thieves I think is probably how two of them would describe it,"

I raise my eyebrow at her.

"You'll understand the dynamic soon enough. They're a radge bunch."

*Saatchi*

Adventure ends and I return.
A new year brings no promises.
I could trip right here and that'd be the end.

Edinburgh is blessed for its grey skies and cursed with its humidity. My feet pound on the pavement as I round off my tenth kilometer. Finn's playlist called *Summer Running to Meet Hot Chicks* is blasting through my headphones. It's paced for ten kilometers per hour, but considering it's my first day back, I'm taking it slow as I run through the streets, making note of all the stores I have to go to for scran. Germany doesn't have a good English brekkie and they definitely didn't have good meat rolls.

There are Irn-Brus on the corner and my mouth waters, aching for sugar, but I push through and take a swig of my water instead. I'm still about five kilometers from home, but I'm already emotionally tired from this run. If I pushed myself a little harder, I'd slide into that runner's high, but I have to let my muscles rest after the Berlin Marathon.

*I can't believe you made the times*, my brain whispers, and I slide my hand down to my short pocket to turn up the music. I'd like to make it through at least my first run back in Edinburgh without a mental breakdown, but my fingers are already jittery with pent up emotions, and I'm sure if I look at my watch it'll clock my heart rate as higher than average for my run.

Picking at my knuckles, I round another corner, barely dodging a dog and its walker. The bustling energy of uni starting again apparently has all the residents blind because that's the third person I've almost run into. I suppose I should have known when the first person out of the door almost murdered me with their massive suitcase. Had I tripped, I'd spend way too long healing a busted kneecap or bruised shins than staying in shape.

It's only September, and even though I'm well within the qualifying times for the Boston Marathon, I'm filled with nervous energy to stay in shape for April. I'm not sure if I'm running because I love it or because I'm running from that mental breakdown. Running used to bring me all the joy in the world. I remember racing Sai and Finn to the pitch before their practice and then still so chock full of energy that I'd run during their whole practice. Mam used to think I was going to have a heart attack after running for over two hours at eight years old.

Of course, running then was small sprints followed by laying in the grass looking for bugs. Now its music timed right to let me know my paces, hours of stretching and icing, extensive training programs, coaches, and the whole lot of it.

Everyone thinks I'll get my sponsorship this year and I may be able to quit uni to run professionally around the world. I want to get it because everyone wants me to, but I honestly couldn't care less. I run because I love it and now it's been infected by the fear that if I don't get a sponsorship I'll have to quit.

I can't keep my brain from vomiting on itself if I think about turning my passion into a career.

I reach the flat and hit my ending spot before slowing down, taking another cool down lap around the building before I finally walk to the door. My heart is in my neck and my lungs are begging to be remembered as they inhale deep breaths. Since I took it slower today, I'm not gasping, but the walk up the stairs still strains on my calves that worked so hard to push up the hills of Edinburgh.

I slam the door open hoping to startle Finn, but instead poor Anne Bonny nearly launches herself off her tower. I coo at her as I take out my headphones and pull out my mat to begin my stretches. I strip off my soaked shirt and throw a podcast on as I fold my waist, reaching past my foot.

"Howsit," Sai asks, coming out of his room, bowl of cereal in his hand.

"Aren't we having evenings at Drew's?" I ask before taking another swig from my bottle of water.

He nods through a mouthful.

"Run was fine. Make yourself useful and grab my notebook."

He rolls his eyes before going to the kitchen counter, grabbing my small green notebook, and tossing it at me full force while I'm pulling my ankle towards my ass.

"Fucker," I mutter before bending, still one hand on my ankle, to grab the notebook. My hamstring burns as the stretch extends, but I welcome it as I lean over my notebook and flip to the first page—all the others have been torn out and either placed on my walls or in my binder.

Anne Bonny saunters over and brushes her fur against my wet legs. At least the shower will wash off the deposited fur. She leans up and licks my nose and I nuzzle my head against hers, putting down my other hand to ensure I don't murder her with a mistimed loss of balance. Leveling back out, I take a seat and stretch my groin as I lean forward, pen in hand.

> Edinburgh is still grey,
> My fear is still toxic.
> Thank God at least I'm gay.

I toss my notebook at Finn as he comes into the living room. He runs a hand through his curly red hair while he looks down at it.

"You know how I always say your poems are shite?"

I nod, knowing where this is going.

"I really mean it this time. This isn't therapy, it's dodging feelings as if they're bullets," he says before going into Sai's room.

I'm sure he's going to try and steal some clothes from Sai to meet Drew and Kirsty's new flatmate. Sai doesn't notice from where he's sitting in front of the telly, laptop hooked up, watching a match—it's definitely in a different language and I don't think it's a European one. One of these days he'll download a virus onto that thing from stealing signal.

I look back down at my notebook. Feelings, therapy, other bullshit. I wasn't game when my therapist asked me to write about the trauma from secondary, but I did it. When they asked me to write about last year's marathon and the events leading up to it however? I don't see why I need to process any bit of trauma, period, when I can be processing what's on my dinner plate instead.

Still, habits.

The sky reflects the bird
But the bird flies away from the sky
It pumps its wings—ferociously
Burying itself deep underground
Here, the bird feels nothing

Well, that'll definitely be a long talk about how feelings are healthy if I show it to Sai, so I finish off my second bottle of water before I march to my room. I take a deep breath as I step into the bathroom and look in the mirror. The person looking back at me has strong eyes and a tough mug. They look ready to kill, all lean muscles and defined abs. I follow my dark skin to my right forearm. Wrapping my hand tightly over the phoenix tattooed there, I run my fingers over the scarred and gnarled skin underneath. Criss-crosses marking me, following the train tracks down the rabbit hole to hell. The phoenix does nothing but cover the weakness I've trapped within.

This time, when I look up, the person in the mirror looking back at me has blank brown eyes. Like a cow on a warm day, lost and naive. I'm not sure which one is the bigger lie, but I won't let myself see who is really staring back, so I turn around before locking the door and stripping down. Hopefully the water will wash away the tightening anxiety in my gut, even if for a bit.

# Chapter Two

I am not envious of the bear.
He wakes, hungry and alone in his den.
No one to gently wake him with bacon rashes.
Alone to his cold, wet chambers of lost Zen.

If I am not envious of him,
Why are our lives so similar now?
I am more alone than the bear.
He has the moss with Tardigrades.

The bear is surrounded by birds,
They chirp, like bells, for the new season,
And foxes as they burrow through,
The ground a recent thaw.

Unlike the bear, I am alone.
You left me as such
With your cruel eyes and crueler mouth
That have torn me down 'til I am just a vessel.

The South Asian girl I almost decked with my suitcase is sitting at the kitchen table when I finish showering off the muck and sleep sweat from the airplane. She's got her hands folded under her chin and raises a thick eyebrow at me when I walk in.

I feel my cheeks getting warm but of course I'm not surprised that one of Drew and Kirsty's best friend is the girl I embarrassed myself in front of—that's just my luck.

"Where's Sai?" Drew asks the newcomer, her back to me.

Saatchi smiles innocently before sweetly saying, "Probably polishing off his cock."

Drew tries to pop her on the back of the head but the girl dodges it, not without knocking over a cadmium green dining chair.

"I'm kidding! Fuck, it's not like Kirsty's fanny is all that clean anyways," says the newcomer with a teasing grin toward Kirsty.

She smirks before saying, in the same sweet tone, "At least after my partners have a taste of mine, they don't leave me."

I watch as the newcomers face falls and she mimics Kirsty before sticking her tongue out. Drew chooses this moment to turn around and lets out the most exasperated sigh before winking at me. Perhaps I should've saved my airplane nap for now so I could dodge the increasing feeling of not belonging.

"Emmylou, I'd like to say that they're only acting out because of you, but they're nearly always this vulgar."

Drew leads me to the table where I sit in the only chair that's white—every other one is adorned in art and doodles. Kirsty's is the most intricate; a sunset that becomes a starry night, and the legs are women scantily dressed with pointed ears and magic bursts flowing around them.

"Saatchi," the newcomer says across from me, extending her hand. Her bushy hair is now braided on the sides that lead into a giant ponytail of curls. I lean across the table to shake her hand and introduce myself. Her eyes widen.

"American," she proclaims, taking a once over of me as if expecting to find cowboy boots and an American flag after my accent so clearly gave me away. I'm glad I didn't change back into the sweaty dress after the shower. "Christ, Finn's going to go mad."

I watch as she bites her lip and squints her eyes at me. I try not to strain under her gaze. After all, she's got nothing on Texas cheerleaders.

"Honestly, what is taking those two so long?" Kirsty asks, looking toward the door. She pats my hands absentmindedly. "Don't be afraid to tell Finn off if he fancies you. He'll respect your no, just hardly ever gets it. Quite a looker that one." She looks back at me and smiles. There's still paint on her right eyebrow. It's bright purple.

I bite my lip. If she thinks he's a looker, then he must be a runway model because so far everyone I've met is textbook attractive. There's no way I can fit in with these folks. Drew has portly curves and the pinkest cheeks, her hair a fair brown that so far lives in a top knot. Kirsty is tall and all long, pale legs with long black hair that brings out her bright gray eyes. But Saatchi, who's leaning back in her chair to call to Drew for dinner, shows off her abs in a crop top, her jaw is defined while still staying feminine, she has tattoos on her arms and legs, and her hair is a monster I wish I had.

My hair has always been thin and pale blonde, making me look like a corpse and like it might start dropping at any second. I've always been too thin to have the curves Drew has, and my eyes are a vomit looking green, unlike Kirsty's captivating ones.

My mother always said I'd be lucky if I ended up engaged like Janey.

I watch as Drew tells off Saatchi for trying to sneak a bread roll and hands her a water instead.

"Why are all the chairs painted?" I ask Kirsty, speaking above Saatchi's laughs and complaints as I try to at least establish myself as someone in the room. Kirsty beams at me as if this is her favorite question.

"Oh, well I help everyone draw their personality on them. Saatchi is the least artistic one so hers is a wee bland but I like it still. I can help you with yours whenever," she says, easing some of my worries about making myself a part of their group. She stands and rotates her chair so I can see all of it. There's a heart with two blob-like people kissing on the seat of it.

"This one is Sai's, my boyfriend and Saatchi's twin brother," she says, turning the one at the head of the table. It's covered in soccer balls and jerseys. Some tickets are pasted on and little doodles of cleats. There's a painting of two boys with their arms over Saatchi. It's well drawn so I assume Kirsty drew that.

"He's a big footballer. He's on the team here at the university with Finn." She flips another chair and on the seat is an anatomically correct drawn heart, a stethoscope wraps around the sides and back, and a few drawings of soccer balls and vulgar doodles cover the rest.

"Saatchi kind of ruined it one day when she got drunk and drew all the penises on it," Kirsty mutters as Saatchi wanders back in from the kitchen with a bread roll and a water.

"I didn't ruin it! I think it gives it personality," she says with a fierce smile and Kirsty pats her cheek lovingly.

The back of Saatchi's chair has a poem in a black Sharpie. Most of her chair is covered in Sharpie and the base is that deep green Cadmium color. On the other side there are a bunch of numbers with apostrophes next to them.

"What are those—," I begin to ask as the door to the apartment swings open. Two boisterous men walk in holding a grocery bag and shouting.

"I brought the bevvys and the whisky, now where is my woman," shouts the shorter red-head with a nose piercing as he hands the bag to Saatchi and picks up Drew in a bear of a hug.

"Oh, I just despise when you call me that. Now put me down, ya oaf."

He does as he's told as the other darker skinned, darker haired man reaches Kirsty and puts his arms around her gently, resting his head on hers.

"I missed ya, bird," he whispers.

"He missed her tits," the red-head loudly whispers to Saatchi who is digging through the bag. He looks up from Saatchi and his eyes go wide when he sees me standing next to my blank chair. His smile changes and becomes exactly what I would expect from a poster boy.

"Well excuse my manners." He puts out a freckled hand and his eyes go softer; it looks genuinely practiced. "I'm Finn, best friend extraordinaire."

Drew bats his hand away and points her finger at him, close enough that he teasingly goes cross-eyed to stare at it.

"No, I will not have a repeat of the last flatmate," she says, and Finn drops his entire face and turns back to me.

"I'm Finn," he repeats with a pout. "I'm banned from talking to birds."

"She's American," Saatchi says as she pulls a beer out of the bag, which the taller man instantly grabs out of her hands with a scowl.

Finn gasps.

"An American?" asks the taller man, finally looking at me.

"Uh, hi, I'm Emmylou."

Finn dramatically pretends to swoon into Saatchi who pushes him to the floor where he lands with a thud. I hold back my laughter at their antics.

The taller guy holds out his hand and I shake it.

"Sai, and she's Saatchi."

"I introduced myself," she grumbles as she hoists up Finn.

"That's Finn," Sai continues stoically before letting go and turning back to Kirsty. His eyes go softer when he looks at her, but he still doesn't smile.

"Great, grand, we all know each other," Drew says. "So, Sai, why don't you set the table and Saatchi take Finn and grab the evening meal. You're about to eat it so don't steal anything. Emmylou, love, just have yourself a seat, as will I because I cooked everything." She plops into her seat and puts her apron on the back of it as the rest bustle around. Kirsty sits delicately in her seat until Drew scowls at her and she leaves to wash the remaining paint off her hands.

"Lord, give me the patience," Drew says, sighing as something crashes in the kitchen. I can just barely see, but it looks like Saatchi is staring down at a broken bottle that Sai slapped out of her hands.

Saatchi returns solemnly to the dining area with serving dishes of some sort of meat stew with potatoes. Finn carries in a plate of rolls looking smug as he takes a sip of his beer. Saatchi takes a seat across from me, Finn to her right, and Kirsty returns, sitting herself beside me.

"Here," Kirsty says, scooping the soup into my bowl and placing a roll next to my plate. I thank her as I watch Saatchi place four rolls on her plate. She takes a large serving of the soup and they all begin to dig in. All except for Sai, who bows his head and whispers a prayer before he begins.

"So, Emmylou, are you excited for your first day at uni?" Sai asks, blowing on his soup. Across from me, Saatchi shovels food into her mouth as if she's never had a bite in her life. Sai throws her a glare, but she grins at him with a full mouth and continues.

"More nervous, I'd say. I haven't actually seen the campus yet, so I definitely don't even know where my classes are." I try to keep my food down as I think about how horrible of an idea it was moving to a different country where I don't know anyone. The nausea rolls in my stomach. I'll look so lost on Monday.

"We'll take you to your classes. Let me see your schedule," Finn says, reaching a hand out. I stare at him but there's no flirtatious smirk or dreamy eyes. His genuine demeanor takes me by surprise. I had pinned him for any other boy I'm used to from high school. Everyone wanted something from me there, always surrounded by the expectations of being the popular cheerleader. People would want to be my friend for a popularity boost or try to get in my pants just to brag that they did. Even my mother wanted me to be perfect so she could brag to her friends at the country club that her daughters were the best ones.

I hand him my phone tentatively, wary of the cruelties of high school, but he and Saatchi only peer over my schedule.

"I'm walking her to campus Monday but I'm in class during her lunch," Drew says as Saatchi leans back in her chair to pat her belly. I'm not even halfway done and she's eaten basically half of what Drew made all on her own.

"Finn and I are off then, so you can find either of us. Then whichever of us can walk you to your next lesson," Saatchi says.

Finn types something into my phone and then passes it back. "There, now you have our numbers, so don't worry. Saatchi, Sai, and I are all logged on it." He goes back to his meal.

I nod my head in thanks before going back to my dinner, trying to chase away the discomfort at their blatant kindness.

Sai and Kirsty are cleaning the dishes when Finn shouts in the living room.

"Saatchi! We forgot to write your times!" He hops up from where we're gathered in the living room and goes to the kitchen, digging through draws until he successfully finds a black Sharpie.

"Mate, leave the times," Saatchi says with a groan, leaning away from the card game she and Drew are playing.

"Saatchi, we could get you a mad good trainer if you got well under qualifying times," her twin says from the kitchen. She frowns down at her cards. Drew tries to get her attention but Saatchi waves her off before standing and quietly telling Finn her times.

"Nasty shite you're doing there lass," Finn says as he leans down beside her chair and writes.

"What are the times for?" I ask as Saatchi returns with a pensive look. Drew drops a pair, much to Saatchi's chagrin.

"She's mad at running. Just finished up the Berlin marathon and her time easily qualifies her for the Boston Marathon this coming April," Finn says. He caps the Sharpie, grinning widely—obviously proud of his roommate.

"Well there goes that," Saatchi mumbles at her lost game.

"These are berry Saatch; they're just a few from Olympic qualifiers."

Saatchi looks over at her brother as he takes a sip from his glass then back at Drew and me. She smirks and shoots us a wink.

Her hand flashes out onto the table and she launches herself up. Drew exclaims beside me, but she's too late, and Saatchi goes crashing into Finn as she tackles him. Sai drops the glass in his hand in surprise and it shatters into the ground. Instantly, Drew is up as Saatchi and Finn roll on the ground wrestling. I stare with wide eyes, but Kirsty cheers them on.

Saatchi's obscenely short shorts ride up as she pins Finn onto his back. If I wore those my mother would send me to an early grave. It must by freeing to be like Saatchi and wear those shorts that show off her toned legs. I envy her.

I envy all of them.

There's a comfortability here that I'm not a part of, that even in Texas I've never known. Everything that happened within my group of friends, in front of my mother, with boys in the hallway—it all felt performative. It felt like a straightened spine and a polite smile, no matter the circumstances. I always had to be on for everyone. Not a hair out of place or a complaint on my lips.

Perhaps they're performing too but it's so different from my high school scrapbook that I don't recognize it. Even if they are performing, it's something I'd rather be a part of, and until I am a part of it, I'll be envious of them.

Even of Sai, who stares down at his roommates in resolute acceptance before lending a hand to his sister. She cackles before yanking him down so he falls on the pile with a big oof. Saatchi laughs maniacally as she does a barrel roll to stand up and puts one foot on her brother's chest with her arms above her head.

"The undefeatable Saatchi does it again," she yells, laughing like a rabid hyena, all wild and without pity. Finn groans from the floor and pushes Sai off.

"I think I've got glass in me," he groans, throwing his head back. Saatchi laughs at his words, but it appears I'm the only one shocked by this. Drew merely tsks before going to the kitchen to grab the first aid kit. Finn is standing with his arm clutched but still playfully swatting at Saatchi.

"How much glass is it?" I ask, walking over to them.

Finn looks down at me. They're all very tall. Drew is the only one shorter than I am.

"Eh, don't worry about it. Just a scratch."

Saatchi snorts beside him and pushes at his waist to turn him around. My eyes widen at the large piece of glass coming out of his shoulder blade.

"It's like half the cup, mate," Saatchi says, smirking. I look at Drew as she reenters the living room.

"I told you they were radge." She hands scissors to Saatchi who takes them to Finn's shirt. I didn't realize radge meant being unbothered by massive shards of glass protruding from muscle.

"Not squeamish, are you?" Drew asks as Saatchi cuts the last of the shirt. I shrug because I'm not sure if I am, and Saatchi looks into my eyes before helping Finn out of his sleeves. Finn picks at his fingers as Saatchi pulls away the bits of his shirt still stuck to the drying blood. His stomach is already visible and I remember Janey's request to find Sam Heughan.

Finn is well defined and his abdominals clench as Saatchi removes the last bit of shirt. My sister would be going crazy if she were in my position. She always loved the cut and chiseled men in shows.

"Okay, aye, that'll need stitches, but I think we can get away without a doctor's visit."

Finn snorts at Drew and sits sideways on the dining table chair, the back of it to his right. Saatchi leans down and grabs his free hand tight in hers.

"Why do you have so many freckles?" She asks him.

"I—argh," he screams out as Drew's steady hands pull out the piece of glass. I flinch and Saatchi looks over at me. She looks down at my own clenched hands before looking back at Finn.

"It looks like someone liquid shat on you and it splattered everywhere."

I snort in surprise, and Finn gasps again as Drew cleans the wound.

"What do you think it looks like Lou?"

I look down at Saatchi in shock. I've never had a nickname before, but I quickly move on from my shock as her expectant eyes search mine.

"Uhm, I don't know, maybe it looks like a bunch of little cows from, like, bird's eye view."

Finn grits his teeth and Drew inserts the first end of the needle.

"Have you ever had a finger up your bum, Finn?"

He squeezes his eyes shut. "What," he asks, half laughing, half crying from pain.

"That's where the male G-Spot is Finley. Ever tried it?"

Finn opens his eyes just to roll them.

"Sai has," Kirsty says from beside me. Both Finn and Saatchi snap over to look at her, their mouths open in shock.

"There, done. Good job with the distraction, Kirsty," Drew says as she ties off the stitch.

"It was just for distraction, right, Sai?" Finn asks, standing up. Pain already forgotten. Sai is halfway out the door, quickly throwing his coat on. "Sai," Finn calls. He looks down at his shredded shirt and then back up at Saatchi. They're pushing and racing down the stairs before I even have a second to blink.

"Radge, honestly, the lot of them."

Later that night, I sit in Drew's bed as she mixes a face mask.

"It's a good thing you're a nursing major."

She pokes her head out of her bathroom and laughs. "Told you they were radge. I actually learned most first aid before I even came to uni. I swear, I was patching one of them up every other night."

"Is it always that entertaining?"

She hums but doesn't respond. "How do you feel about Monday?"

"Nervous, I don't know any freshmen. At least you had all your friends when you started." Since I didn't even come to orientation, I had to live off campus. Drew and everyone else are all sophomores, so I won't even get to be in any classes with them.

"Well, not Kirsty actually," she says as she stands by the mirror. She globs on the blue face mask. "You'll make mates easy enough. In fact, you're so bonnie that I'll bet the lads will be dying to talk to you." She pauses applying the face mask and raises her eyebrow at my reflection. "Or lasses?"

"But I have to sit alone until I make friends." I groan and fall back into her bed. "Give me the scoop. Since you weren't friends with Kirsty before, how'd y'all become close?"

"Oh, well. It wasn't actually me who made friends with her first. It was Saatchi, surprisingly enough. Kirsty is big into activism and changing the world, and Saatchi is big into rebellion. Kirsty actually got Saatchi to sign up for a protest last year and when they got arrested that's when I met her."

I stare wide eyed at her and she smirks.

"I didn't warn you enough, did I? Saatchi didn't want to tell her brother. He can be a wee bit . . . protective."

"So you're saying I need to get arrested?" I ask incredulously, and she rolls her eyes.

"Course not. Hmm, I just made friends in my major. I'm not as close with them but they're still good to study with. I wouldn't invite them to live here or anything."

"Why'd you invite me to live here then? You barely know me." *She probably saw a photo of you and thought an ugly duckling in the group would make everyone else look better.*

"Oh, uh." She sits beside me and motions to the face mask. I nod and she slowly traces my face with her cold hands. "So, I guess before I tell you I should explain something about myself."

I hum, unable to move my face.

"My mam, she left my da and me when I was young. The only times I ever talk to her are to guilt her into something. Actually, she bought these flats as a graduation present so I would never have to pay rent. That's how come all of us can afford it."

I recall her saying there was no rent when we spoke over the summer, and I was surprised no one else had taken her offer yet.

"I just—I know what it's like to have a bad mam, and you seemed to have issues with yours?" She phrases it like a question and pauses to look me in the eye.

I bite my cheek, not realizing that had been clear from my intro message. "I mean, I guess. But she, no offense, she didn't leave."

"Aye, s'pose that's true," she says, going back to putting on my face mask. "Sorry, I just meant, it seemed like you needed support, especially when your mother's trip was interfering with orientation."

The air is awkward and I hold my breath as the mask hardens.

"Well, I appreciate it. She can be difficult sometimes, and I'm glad I could talk to you about it."

Drew grins at my words and her mask cracks. I burst into laughter at it and my mask cracks along with it.

The sound of our laughter fills the room and I feel bubbly hopefulness at my new home.

*Saatchi*

Finn's bright red hair glows under the streetlights as we sit on the swings at the primary near our flat.

Finn can clearly see the cogs in my brain turning.

"A time isn't going to help . . ." I pause, contemplating if this is too cruel. "It isn't going to make me stronger or invincible," I whisper into the night, thinking back to all those therapy sessions last year.

I want to stop feeling this constant fear in the back of my head—in my heart—and Finn and Sai's fixation on pushing me to be the best isn't helping. Their desire to see me successful after everything that happened is sweet but a constant reminder that something broke within me. I feel a tear slip out of the corner of my eye. Finn immediately scoots closer but doesn't reach out. I lean into him, pushing my swing closer to his.

"You're right," he says, wrapping his arm around me. "I'm sorry. We won't push you. I-I just . . . it's not the same. You used to be so carefree." He wipes at his nose, and I watch the streetlamp make his piercing glitter with the movement.

"Now it's like you run to get away from it all. We just thought if we helped you find a purpose, it could help." He looks down at me with his soft blue eyes and I break.

"I just miss it. I just miss it so bad," I say, voice cracking. "God, fuck, it was so good. It was so good to run and be free and now I feel like I can't ever be free again." He tightens his arm around me and I lean my head on his shoulder.

We're quiet as we reminisce about our races to his footie practice, our feet hitting the pavement and me breaking away in a landslide.

"I s'pose Laire didn't help," he asks without asking, mentioning my ex-girlfriend. A trainwreck of a human that I wasn't even supposed to talk to in the first place. I met her when I was in a bad place and she was in a worse one. She dragged me down with her and I still have the scratches on my heart from the slide.

But it was everything that happened before that still hurts me. And everything that happened after that pushed Sai from red alert to actively trying to hold my hand through life.

I'm letting my feelings drift away, forcing numbness, when Finn speaks again.

"I've been working on my rapping this summer. Poem?" he asks, grinning cheekily. I rest my hand on his cheek and smile sweetly.

"You daft numptie. I'm pretty sure a mute could rap better than you," I say before smacking his cheek hard. He splutters and pushes me away as I try to laugh again. I appreciate his efforts in helping me get out of my own head, but he is, honestly to God, the worst rapper.

"No, honest! Give me a beat, let's write a poem."

I laugh wetly before poorly attempting beatboxing. We're truly awful at this, and my lack of rhythm shows as Finn starts.

"Screw all this shite," he starts, off beat. "Nothing feels alright. I wish I could go back to before this made me want to inject myself with smack."

I gasp out a laugh and he shrugs bashfully. But we don't stop.

"Remember when Jenny Taylor, gave me a blowie behind the church," he continues when I pick up a beat again. I'm pretty sure it's a totally different one and it gets worse as I let out a snort. "Sai made such a good jailer, as you ran from your lookout perch."

I laugh and smack his arm, before falling to the mulch.

"That doesn't even make sense! How'd we go from smack to blowies," I hum in assent. "Aye, no that actually would make sense." I look up at him where he grins down at me. "I don't even think her name was Jenny Taylor though, ya prick."

"What? That was definitely it! And you were supposed to be watching to keep us from getting caught." I laugh again.

"I only ran from lookout because your mam and da were coming over so I had to stop them. How was I supposed to know Sai would find yous and rat you out?" We both laugh as we remember how serious Sai once was about the church. Of course, he still is a stickler for rules, which is why he isn't invited to late night shenanigans.

"Her name might not have been Jenny," Finn assents as he lays down next to me. "Hey Saatch," he starts, but I shake my head at him. He's done his job; I'd hate to revert his efforts.

"Okay but how about we go back home and watch a telenovela and gorge on tablets before bed," he says, wrapping his hand around mine. I run my thumb over his fingers.

"Sleep in my bed tonight," I ask, and he immediately breaks into a grin.

"You should be grateful I'm weak for some late night tablets."

We hop up, looking forward to the caramel munchies waiting in my snack stash under my bed.

When we were wains, everyone in town thought Finn and I would get married. I can see why they'd think so in a hetero-minded world. We spent every waking hour together. I spent, and still do, more time with Finn than I did my own twin brother. Glued to the hip.

Everyone thought that until I turned ten.

It had completely flown over my head that society had these expectations for men to be with women and women to put up with men. I'm glad it did because then I would have found it odd when the lass that sat in front of me in the pews suddenly caught my fancy. She had just cut her hair and it made me take a second look. Before that, no one particularly struck my radar—I was too busy playing on the pitch with the boys or causing problems in primary.

But I do remember her. I also remember it was that same day she got a haircut and was sitting in front of me in the pews that Finn leaned over and said he thought she was bonnie.

Maybe it was that comment that helped me realize it was also normal for me to find her a bonny lass. Finn and I hung to her after mass like leeches, and at the end of our recess, I leaned in and pecked her. Right there, in front of the town, the priest, God, and all the Saints, I kissed a girl. She blushed prettily and gave me a peck back.

I'm sure the performance had mixed reviews.

I know it did. Her mam gave her a scolding, and the next Sunday, she told me we couldn't be friends and I couldn't be her boyfriend, which I found weird because I was clearly a girl in my Sunday dress and long curls. But my mam was different.

She sat Sai and I down that night for dinner and apologized for never explaining to us anything about love and romance. She told us, our wee hands in hers, that men could like men and women could like women. I remember Sai frowning and telling mam that he had no plans on marrying Finn. I profusely agreed. Finn was family; it'd be like marrying Sai.

The point may have flown over our heads then, but we grew up knowing it was just as normal for queer folks to exists as straight. Eventually, when I saw the girl from the pews kissing a boy in the hallway two years later, we also had to talk about bisexual folk and how that was also normal. Sai looked at me, I looked at him, and we both agreed that men weren't for us.

Da bought me my first pride flag just as I was finishing primary and hung it in the family room. It's still draped there, crooked today. I suppose if he had hung it up straight it wouldn't be true to its calling.

It wasn't always guns & roses—Sai used to say sunshine and rainbows but that was too gay, even for me. There were harsh comments in the hallways, fights that broke out, and worse, but Finn was always there. So was Sai, of course, but he had to be; he's blood. But Finn never left, not even when someone dumped their tray of garbage on us at lunch. He even held me back as I tried to swing at them, juice dripping from my eyes.

I hate that word the school always used during their so-called "investigations." Bullying. I'm not a victim. They're victims to their own naivety, and I'm proud. I think about that as I sling my arm around Finn's waist. I'm proud to be queer, and I'm proud of this family I've created here in Edinburgh, and I'm proud of my family back home who would buy me cartons of eggs to throw at the shite heads at school.

"Finley," I say putting my face close to my best mates. "Finley," I shout loudly, and he jolts awake, barely missing knocking his head into mine. He's bleary as he looks over at me and I loudly snap a carrot between my teeth.

"Wha'," he grunts out as he rubs his eyes.

"We have to go get the receipts before mass."

He looks down at me and then stretches. "Did you already run?"

I nod at him. Got up at four to run seventeen kilometers. He closes his eyes and I snap another carrot between my teeth. He glares at me but slowly stands up before leaving my room. I hear him close his bathroom door just as Anne Bonny teeters into the room.

"'Lo, love," I tell her. Sai peaks his head in at that moment looking thoroughly put out.

"Christ, I was afraid you were being kind to Finn for a second there," he says looking down at my cat. He pets her on the head as Finn's shower turns on.

"Don't be daft." I look up at my brother. "How much do we have for books?"

He shrugs and pulls out a list from his back pocket.

"I've got what we can from hand-me-downs from the lads. Most of your lit books I luckily got from Aleksander. He says I owe him for them though at a discount. I got what I could of my books and one for Finn. No one wants to sell those on debt."

I exhale heavily from my nose and lay back in Finn's bed. "So?"

"So, I've got three textbooks that I can't afford and Finn has five. We've got enough for scran and the fee for kits but no money for boots for any of us."

"How do we get Finn's books? We can't let him get them—"

"I know," Sai says, cutting me off and shrugging. "I asked Kirsty for a loan."

I cover my face with my hands and he pulls them off quickly.

"I don' know what else to do. I'll pay her back once I can work the football practices or whatever coach says it is I do to give me a check."

I nod and Finn's shower turns off.

We're short on money because of me. I had to pull out of our fund to take a train to Berlin and then for a hostel while I stayed there. If I had just done well at the London Marathon last semester, we wouldn't be in this position. Reap what I sow, apparently, except it isn't even me who's asking for loans.

I keep the guilt off my face when Finn comes out and shamelessly dresses in front of us. The visible tattoo on his ribs is a twin to mine.

*Emmylou*

"You make your own clothes?" Kirsty asks, stomping in a puddle. Her flip-flops are sucked in and she stumbles out with a giggle.

"A bit. I'm not that good at it, but I'm hoping I'll get better."

"Did you make that dress then?" Drew turns away from Kirsty's antics and looks at me.

I nod and try to keep my hands from fidgeting in the fabric.

"Mad. I could never. Damn me for choosing to live with two artistic arseholes," Drew complains.

*She didn't compliment it because it looks atrocious. You never did fix that third stitch. Lazy.*

Kirsty finally stops jumping from puddle to puddle before ripping open a door on the campus. There are tons of students in the bookstore doing last-minute shopping, and I pull up my phone to look at my required textbook list.

"What's your major?" Drew asks from beside me. We've already lost Kirsty to a side room that leads to the art supplies.

"I, uh, couldn't really decide. I'm technically a fashion and history double major until I can declare one or the other."

Drew smirks at me and we walk to the freshman general education section.

"Those are two very different majors but good for you and all."

I pick up a textbook and Drew peers over at it. "Eh, I've got that one at the flat if you'd rather it second-hand." The credit card in my back pocket burns. I'm sure loads of students get their textbooks second-hand but that isn't really an issue for me.

"Sure, thanks," I say anyway.

Drew is a nursing major, so she doesn't have any of the history or fashion textbooks I need—not that there are many anyway. I'm not sure how I'm expected to know my major if I'm forced to take general education classes my freshman year.

Kirsty finally catches up with us with a bundle of new paints and canvases in her arms. Drew raises an eyebrow at her as she sets down her own nursing textbooks.

"This will be the best year yet. I feel it."

I wish I could share in Kirsty's enthusiasm, but I lack the confidence both older girls have. I'd give anything to feel comfortable in my own skin.

Once I've paid for the textbooks—more expensive than I had anticipated—we leave the bookstore and make our way toward the stores. Kirsty is much more reluctant to stomp in puddles now that she has new canvases strapped to her back.

"Emmylou," she starts and I look up at her. "I think it's berry that you came here for uni. I just wanted to say that." I stare at her in shock and she smiles. "Honest, I would never have the guts to do something like that. I just think it's cool is all. Very brave and all that."

I feel a blush crawl up my neck.

"She's right. I actually came to University of Edinburgh just because all my friends from secondary were coming here," Drew says before squinting at a group of boys. "Christ," she mumbles under her breath. Kirsty looks over and I'm saved from having to comment.

"Who are they?" I ask as the tallest boy looks at Drew. She grimaces and turns away, but it's glaringly obvious she's avoiding his stare. Kirsty waves and Drew smacks her arm with widened eyes.

"Are you trying to make this awkward for me?"

Kirsty smirks at Drew and tilts her head like a puppy.

"Yes," she says with an innocent smile. Kirsty laughs as Drew stomps away. I look back at the group and another boy with shaggy brown hair makes eye contact with me and smiles. Kirsty snorts out a laugh beside me before grabbing my arm.

"Oh no, lass. That isn't for you."

I laugh and follow her.

"Who are they?"

"Eh, I only know one of them. The biggest lad is obsessed with Drew. He's the football team's captain and they shagged a few times last year before he . . . well," she rolls her eyes. "He wanted a relationship and she didn't. You know how it is. It's uni, there's time to wait before being tied down."

"Aren't you dating Sai?" I ask to avoid telling her I know how it is, because, in truth, I've never had a boyfriend.

"Semantics," she says with a wink.

That night I put away all my fabrics and textbooks and think about what Drew and Kirsty said. Maybe I am a little brave for coming to Scotland. Just a little though because the rest is all stupidity.

# Chapter Three

The deer stands below my hills.
She is a miracle worker,
She breathes life as nature instills.

The fawn ears flick back,
The noise of the rolling hills new.
Her palpable fear of becoming nature's snack.

Everything is new.
Her legs, the rocks, the taste of the grass.
But who is she to you?

I check myself in the mirror again and adjust my braid. My mother always said my hair looks best down but I felt like I was constantly blowing it out of my face. It made me frustrated and anxious, and I definitely don't need that today.

It's braided in a strong Dutch braid right down the middle, the sides still loose and flowing. I found it on a Pinterest board under *Viking Braids* and that's who I want to be today. A strong, fearless woman ready to take on the world. Just like the women from Scandinavian who fought in wars to better their lives.

It isn't exactly on par with my dress that's ruffled at the hem and hangs off my shoulders. I secure the lace-up front and throw on my white sneakers before heading out of my room.

Drew looks me up and down before saying, "Freshers, always putting their best foot forward until midterms break their soul." She's wearing leggings and a large T-shirt that comes to her thighs.

Kirsty laughs from the kitchen where she's making tea.

"Don't listen to her, I still manage to get dressed up every once in a while," she says while doing a twirl, her bell-bottom jeans flaring around her bright red boots. "You look great, everyone will be properly impressed." She gives Drew a kiss on the head and then gives me a hug. "Good luck on your first day," Kirsty calls before throwing a flannel over her crop top and heading out, tea thermos in hand.

"She's right, you do look bonny but we have a schedule so grab your bag and let's get a move on." Drew stands from the kitchen table and we head out the door. The sun is, thankfully, out but I'm glad I decided to braid my hair because the air is clinging to my skin as soon as we're out of the building.

The walk to campus is unfortunately straight up a hill and I feel my hair sticking to the back of my neck.

"Is it always this type of weather?" I ask Drew as we huff up the hill. I should definitely start working out again.

"Oh lass, this is a nice day here. Normally it's raining," she says, smirking back at me as we finally get to campus. My first lesson is a gen ed for freshman and Drew drops me off with a kind smile.

"Don't be stressed. Everyone here is a freshman and you'll have everyone in the palm of your hand in no time." She gives me a pat on the shoulder—our bags too burdensome for a hug—before trotting away to her class.

Rooming with sophomores has put me at a severe disadvantage. Even with the two majors I'm taking classes for, I don't have a single class with any of my new-found acquaintances.

But the thought of deciding my entire life at eighteen seems too daunting, and I really want this to be my decision. Sometimes it feels like none of my decisions have ever been mine. My mother was so adamant about her reputation that everything about me was controlled. If she didn't like my outfit that day I had to go upstairs and change—sometimes up to fifteen times a morning. I had to keep my phone's location on for her at all times and send her pictures of what friends I was with so she could make sure I was hanging out with "people of quality." She even signed me up for cheerleading despite me wanting to focus on riding and maybe even competing with the horses on our farm.

She'd be foaming at the mouth if she saw me now. No one I've met so far would pass her checks of approval. Kirsty, who doesn't care about the judging eyes of others; Drew, with her healthy curves and flippancy toward men; Finn and Saatchi with their antics. But Saatchi would be at the top of my mother's shit list. Her tattoos cover her arms and legs, her words are vulgar more often than not, the multitude of piercings in her ears—it would all send my mother into a rage if she knew. Sai, being the polar opposite of his twin, would actually get the seal of approval from my mother. I'm glad to break free from her conservative thoughts, even if her voice still reverberates between my ears—a constant reminder of my shortcomings.

Getting to Edinburgh was the only fight I've ever had with my mother. Every other time I've kept my head down, never complained about changing a million times to have my outfit approved, or about not being allowed to go to parties where there was alcohol, or literally every little other thing about my life that was dissected and watched. I kept my head down for all of it.

When Janey said I should just follow my dreams, I did. I made sure to bring up the idea in front of my poppa. He's always supportive and mother never scrutinized me when he was around. Unfortunately, he was never around. I planned it just right, and now I'm standing in a classroom, in a historic city, surrounded by a bunch of people I don't know. More importantly, however, they don't know me.

I haven't opened social media once since I got off that plane. I haven't received any texts from the girls from high school who I'm sure are busy with their own thing. I haven't actively worried about what mother would think. Actively. Because her voice still echoes in my subconscious and right now it's telling me I should sit at the front of the class, back straight, innocent smile at anyone who comes in—attentive but unobtainable.

Plopping my books down in the middle row, I still need to be able to hear and see, I take a deep breath and lay my head down on the desk, notebook open to doodle, and wait for class to begin.

The boy I saw yesterday with the messy hair sits beside me, but I ignore him as the professor begins to speak. My stomach drops as I realize I don't have a single clue what he's saying—accent too thick and anxiety too high to comprehend his words.

It's syllabus galore my first half of the day and my stomach is aching with hunger. There's a small store with snacks and I'm honestly dying for a bag of chips and a coke. It's the small freedoms that help me remember that moving across the world to somewhere I don't know anyone was a good idea. I pop open my chips and pull out my phone.

Finn has kindly added me to their group chat named *Yer a thistle up my arse* and I shoot off a quick text asking Saatchi and Finn where they are and if they want to sit together to eat. I actually have about two hours before my next class where I can try to organize my syllabi and label notebooks now that I have a better idea of what the school year holds for me.

**Finn: In the business building hallway!! Loads of fun come eat here**

I pull up my campus map on my phone before it dings with another text.

**Saatchi: He means him and the footballers just so you know. I'm in the library. Take your pick.**

Easy choice. I trudge through campus to a rectangular building made of once white stone and windows. There are shelves upon shelves of books, and I shoot Saatchi another text asking where she is exactly; there's a few stories to this place after all.

Everything I've gathered about Saatchi's tough and boisterous personality is blown away by the image she paints when I find her curled up in a sofa chair, reading a book. She looks soft, her tattoos mostly covered by a sweater, completely at ease, no fire in her eyes or wrinkle between her brows. The little bit of sunlight streams through the window, and despite her combat boots and dark attire she still somehow manages to remind me of a cat curling up for a mid-afternoon nap.

"Whatcha reading?" I ask her. She slowly closes her book and raises an eyebrow at me. I can see the book says Chen Chen with smaller lettering underneath.

"Poetry," she says sharply. "No footballers for you?"

I shake my head at her. "No, I'm not really a fan of men."

I watch as she looks at me in confusion and sucks on her sharp canine before speaking again.

"Are you . . . not straight?" she asks, tilting her head. She's made of feral animals.

"Oh, no sorry I didn't mean that. I just . . . you know." I actually don't know. "They uhm, whatever, I just didn't wanna be around a bunch of loud boys I suppose."

She nods in understanding and picks up her book.

"I'm a lesbian you know."

The shock of her openness makes me flounder. One of the cheerleader's brother's shyly came out my sophomore year in high school. Unfortunately, the word spread and when it reached my mother, she made me promise not to speak with him. Exhausted from my ever-losing battle with her, I agreed. Despite that, she brought him up constantly to berate his "choices." She beat that dead horse until the day I left.

It's been silent for a beat too long before I say, "Cool, thanks for trusting me enough to tell me that." I cringe internally and watch Saatchi press her lips together hiding a smile at my awkward response. It suddenly makes sense why my roommate application asked if I was not just okay with the LGBTQ+ community but pro. Drew must have been making sure I wouldn't make Saatchi's life more difficult.

I pull out my notebooks because I'm definitely at a loss on whether or not I should say something else or just let her continue to read. I look up at her one last time, her large curls framing her face, the sun on her making her dark ocher skin glow, but she's enraptured with her book. I suppose it's time to try and organize everything for my classes.

I'm just getting done writing my schedule in my sunflower planner when Saatchi looks up at me.

"How was your first day, Emmylou?" she asks, highlighting a stanza in her book.

"Pretty uneventful so far, just getting my syllabi."

She pulls out a notebook and jots something down. I realize I have no clue what her major is. Kirsty's is art and Drew is going down the nursing track, but I don't know about the others.

"Haven't made any friends then?"

I shake my head before leaning forward in my seat. "Is your major poetry?"

She looks back down at her book before shrugging.

"That's more of a concentration in literature, but aye, my major is literature." She shrugs again. "Should probably pick a concentration soon," she mumbles under her breath.

"I'm surprised you don't choose something like physical therapy or coaching."

She grimaces before setting down her book.

"I don' know, not everything has to be surrounding my hobby. I'm not interested in being a career runner. I like competing, aye, but it's fun as long as it's on my terms." She picks at a scar on her finger absentmindedly. "How about you? What's your major then?"

I pout and she raises an eyebrow at me.

"You don't have to tell me."

"No, its just," I sigh and look away. "Promise you won't make fun of me?" I ask grimacing.

She leans forward with a smirk. "I make no such promises."

I roll my eyes at her, smiling. "Fine. I'm deciding between history and fashion design."

I teasingly glare at her to say something. Her mouth twitches as it fights back a smile, like a wild horse testing its reigns.

"Right, because those two are so similar. I don' know how you'll ever chose."

I laugh sarcastically. "It's just difficult to choose. I value both."

I look up at her, a blush painting my cheeks, before I say, "The things I hold dear to my heart are valuable, and it's frightening to let go of one."

*Saatchi*

the thing I hold dear
to my heart, is mine.
a bubble, I've created.
where my ecstasy
is mine alone.
independent of you.
determined by only
the sonnet my feet write
as they chew through the world

I take one last swig of my water bottle before closing the notebook and giving Anne Bonny a kiss atop her grey fur. She, of course, takes a playful swipe at me, but I lean in and let her rest her pink toe pads on my cheek.

Anne Bonny is the light of my life. She never expects to receive anything from me and is perfectly content with us laying in bed all afternoon. It's a wee bit of peace I don't get from anyone else. If I fall into a depressive slump, everyone has all these ideas of getting out of bed. Not Anne. She's satisfied to relax under the covers.

The sound of Sai banging around pots and pans disperses my thoughts. He's making evenings, probably some obnoxiously health conscious concoction of very non-Scottish scran. Us Scots aren't well known for our dieting.

"How was practice?" I ask walking into the kitchen. I rub my sweaty face on a kitchen towel; my shirt is too soaked to be of assistance. Sai glares at me as he checks the chicken baking in the oven. Gross. His chicken is always overcooked and thus, bone dry. I'd rather skip the cardboard even if it's supposedly healthy, although I have my doubts.

"Just regular preseason. Coach is trying to scare all the freshers into believing he's tough as baws."

I roll my eyes and grab a banana and two ice packs from the freezer. I lay down in the bare dining room and roll onto my stomach to rest my shins on the ice as I eat my banana and scroll on my phone.

"Have you started athletics workouts yet?"

I shake my head at him, thinking of the upcoming season. It will be relaxing as long as no one hyper focuses on me. Unfortunately, that can be a big asking price when I'm the talk of the town. Nearly hitting Olympic qualifying times for the marathon at nineteen will do that.

"Finn?" I ask, and Sai makes a flippant hand motion from the kitchen.

"The lads wanted to go out this weekend to start the season, so I think he's upstairs inviting the girls. He thinks he'll be the hero if he brings four lasses."

"Oh?" I scoff and try not to choke on my banana. "Should I put on my best bonnet and be prepared to wave around my fanny?" Sai puts his head in his hands.

"Aye, and while you're at it yous can bat your eyelashes and get the freshers to buy us a few free rounds."

A laugh escapes me and I choke on the banana this time having to roll up to cough it out.

Sai hums. "Definitely not built to be straight," Sai comments, and I grimace at him for even making me imagine something so disgusting. I tell him as much. All the older footballers know I'm queer. I pulled more birds than they did except for that whole relationship thing I did. Definitely should've stayed chasing skirt.

Sai dumps my meal in front of me. Chicken with some green looking vegetables on the side. I look up at him.

"You couldn't at least drown them in cheese?"

He rolls his eyes and sits in front of me as I begin to eat the bland, dry meal. I hate eating healthy. Give me a meat pie. Give me more carbs. Give me sugar and beer and nicotine.

"I don't want to run professionally," I tell him, looking up from where I'm still laid out. My shins are numb now, but shin splints are a bitch. It's a preventative measure because of the change in running surfaces.

He pats my head and swallows a bite of the cardboard.

"We've talked about this Saatch. Just . . . try and see if you can get your name out there. Get sponsored, make a professional team after uni, and if it's not all guns and roses then no biggie. Quit," He shrugs like it's no big deal and to him it isn't.

But for me it means starting now. It means healthy diets, an early bedtime, contacting coaches. All I want to do is run. I see no reason to make it a stressful beast that will nip at my heels every second I take a breath. I already don't like the pressure. But at the back of my head I'm afraid if I skip out on this opportunity, I'll regret it when I'm sitting in some stuffy classroom teaching poetry to shithead secondary students. Or maybe I'll regret it when the next Olympics come on and I know that I had a shot, no matter how small, to represent Scotland.

I eat my cardboard in silence, thinking of all the ways I should get serious after the Boston. I'll give myself the fall and then come spring I guess I can give this all a shot.

I'm lost in thought and Sai is lost in football stats when Finn bursts through the door.

"Lads, put on your best dancing shoes because this Friday we're gonna get mad with it." He holds his hands out expectantly but when neither of us react, he launches himself into Sai's lap.

"Just because you're in a relationship doesn't mean you have to be such a drag," he tells him, wrapping his arms around his neck, successfully dislodging Sai's phone. I watch it clatter to the ground.

"Mate, I was already planning on going. I may be captain next year, so I have to make sure I'm in with all the lads."

Finn pouts anyway and looks at me, missing Sai's eye roll.

"Yay! Bevvys I can't drink and rank lads. Exactly what I've always dreamt of," I sarcastically make jazz hands at him, and he frowns back at Sai who has accepted his fate and is holding Finn in his lap.

"Oh, aren't the Peterson twins just such a fun time? Maybe I'll have to go by myself. Only Kirsty there to keep me warm."

I snort out a laugh as Sai dumps Finn to the ground. He groans as he lands on his recently stitched shoulder.

"Mate, I said I was going." My brother stands with a huff and starts making a bowl for our resident carrot-topped, shit-splatted, prosexual roommate.

"You're going this Friday, aye?" Finn asks, rolling back up. I sigh and he whines. "No, Saatchi c'mon. Listen, you know the lads and they love you and everyone from upstairs will be there." He pouts before a mischievous smirk appears. "Emmylou will be there and you can get to know her a bit better." He winks as I roll my eyes.

"Come off it mate." I push his face away from me and turn to drink from my water bottle only to find it empty.

"Oh, but you know she's just your type."

He grins brightly as I scowl at my water.

He's not wrong. I've got a pension for overly feminine women. Emmylou's green eyes and bright smile are just an added aesthetic bonus. But no matter how attractive I may find her, the point still stands.

"She's straight, Finn," I say with a laugh.

Finn pouts again. He likes to live vicariously through me since he can't love, then instantly brightens. "Maybe, I'll make my move."

"She's straight—not suicidal," Sai says, chucking a piece of chicken at him. I'm left choking on raucous laughter as they begin to throw cardboard chicken at each other—my fears of running long forgotten.

Like any undealt with emotion, the anxiety surrounding my running floods my brain the next morning. I refuse to check my times after my morning ten kilometers and instead wander into my first class wearing my comfort clothes.

*Damn. Only week one and I've already hit a slump.*

I listen to Dr. Daly drone on about the benefits of modern versus classical literature. Sylvia Plath versus Rupi Kaur. History versus fashion in a sense. My hands itch to write. I turn to the lass beside me and ask if I can take pictures of her notes after class. At her agreement, I let my hands fly.

> This rock is older than my great-grandda.
> Yet it is full of wonder and mystery,
> Holding secrets that tickle my ears.
> Steady as it is, I cannot move or change it.
>
> The spring flowers however, differ.
> I created them with nails digging into wet soil,
> Spilled seed from my mouth into earth,
> Cried my tears to watch them blossom.

I stare blankly at the page before sliding it unfinished into my notebook, suddenly uninspired. After the lesson, as I'm taking a picture of the lass's notes, she looks up at me in awe.

"I saw your article on Twitter. You're like famous or something."

I thank her reluctantly and grimace as I walk away. It feels like Edinburgh is holding its breath in anticipation of my greatness. I don't want to let them down, but I ache for running to just belong to me as it once did. I used to play around with the idea of running slower on purpose, but when I bombed the London marathon unintentionally, I realized that wasn't really an option for me. I love competing, as long as it's on my terms, and my terms are haggis rolls and bevvys.

I plop down in my chair in the library and open Twitter. I immediately search the comments of the article because I'm a self-destructive sadist. It, unsurprisingly, doesn't take me long.

**Is an Indian really going to represent Scotland. WTF. Tell her to go back home.**

I glare down at the words as the familiar feeling of not belonging flows through me. Even being second-generation Scottish, born to a Scottish Da, doesn't allow people to see past the colour of my skin. India would consider me a foreigner, especially when I don't even know a lick of Hindi, and then the Scottish also see me as an outsider in the country I was born and raised in, purely based on genetics.

I keep scrolling before another catches my eye: **Fucking carpet munchers, probably going to bomb the next Boston Marathon**. I grind my teeth and start to type out a response I'll never post when Emmylou sits across from me.

"Have you ever had Dr. Daly?" Her green eyes look into mine, bright and searching.

"Aye, 've got him now for comparative literature and last year for fresher's lit."

She exhales heavily and drapes her arms over her knees dramatically. Like a puppet whose strings have been cut.

"Do you still have the notes? It's so embarrassing but I can't understand him."

I snort out a shocked laugh.

"No, aye, I've got them. Just swing by my flat sometime." I would normally poke fun at her for not understanding a northern Scottish accent, but after the comments, I just don't have the energy.

"Lou, have you ever competed in any athletics?"

She looks up from her shiny new laptop where she's setting a reminder to come get the notes. I'm envious of it. Sai, Finn, and I share a single dingy laptop.

"Sort of. I competed in cheer which, if it was an actual competition, they were actually pretty intense. I also did a little barrel racing when I was younger but that had to end."

In a moment of weakness, I was going to talk to her about my predicament, but, sensing a scapegoat to a conversation I regret starting, I grab tight.

"Why'd you stop?"

She frowns down at her mug before giving me an aborted shrug. I watch as she straightens up and tucks a pale, nearly white strand of hair behind her ear delicately.

"It just wasn't really my thing."

"Don't like horses?" I ask, trying to hide my excitement. All my mates think I'm deranged but I quite dislike the large bastards.

She laughs.

"No, who in their right mind would hate horses?"

I bite my tongue.

"We actually have a big farm with lots of horses. I know I've only been gone for about a week but I miss them so much. My horse, he's thirteen and a half hands tall—Bucky." Her eyes glitter as she looks off into the memories.

I stare at her in confusion, running my tongue over my gnarled canine.

"Wait, so you like the horses but you don't ride them? Or is it just barrel racing you don't do?"

She waves me off.

"Eh it's just . . . I don't know. I don't ride them . . . " she finishes like she isn't planning on saying more and I wait in silence. "Well, I'd ride them, just if the timing was right."

Leaving me further confused, she returns to her laptop after giving me a tight-lipped smile. From what I've gathered, there isn't really a wrong time to ride a horse unless it's raining or snowing too hard and, if American telly has taught me anything, that's not really a problem in Texas. But I let her dodge the question and pull out my notes from class.

Poetry's always been less confusing than people.

My brother is putting scran in a Tupperware when I get back from my afternoon run after lessons. It was only fifteen kilometers because if I run more than that, Sai will surely lecture me about rest. My own father's absence is never felt at uni as long as Sai is breathing down my neck.

"Let's go," Sai says as I finish my groin stretch, poetry notebook in front of me. I flip it closed and pat my grey cat on the head before following him out, bottle of water in hand.

It's drizzling outside as we trudge the cobblestone hills. I open the lid of my bottle and let the rain-drops fill it.

"Saatch," my brother starts with a laugh. "Ever heard of acid rain?"

I smirk at him. "Let's hope it melts my stomach."

That wipes the smile clean off his face and he frowns before pushing me. Before I can push back, he holds up the tub of scran in warning and I settle for a slap on his arm instead.

"How's your first week going?"

I shrug at him. "It's going. Have you seen the Rangers match?" He groans and buries his head in his hands.

"Aye, watched it while I was cooking. Fecking numpties are going to be impossible to beat this year."

I snort because they're nearly always ranked first. Sai decided long ago our football team would be the Hibs.

"Did you listen to it while you ran?"

I nod my head.

"I can't believe Lewis has the chance to play with them but wants to finish uni."

"Wouldn't you?" I ask with a raised eyebrow.

He scowls. Being on a football scholarship has allowed both Finn and him to go to university but, other than religion, I've never seen my brother passionate about anything besides football. It's a toss up on if he'll finish his pre-law degree or go play professionally. Finn, on the other hand, has gotten offers and turned them down. I'm afraid one day the Hibs will offer—that would break Finley.

"You could quit uni if you get Olympic qualifying times."

I'm the one scowling this time. "Is it a blessing or a curse to be this athletic?"

"Hard to know what the right decision is. A single injury could throw our future to shite."

We continue in silent contemplation before finally reaching the laundromat where Finn works.

Finn looks up from his textbook and grins so his eyes squint, his freckles just a Jackson Pollock painting with browns.

"Have I ever told you your freckles look like my toilet after shawarma?" I ask him, sitting on the front desk. A woman snorts out a laugh from the back of the store and I look up at her. She blushes prettily when I flash her a smirk. Sai slaps my arm when he follows my eyes. I stick my tongue out at him as he hands Finn the tub of scran.

"Getting tired of that joke, Saatchi."

I roll my eyes at Finn.

"Mmm, smells berry," he says, leaning over the counter to smack a wet kiss on Sai's cheek. "Thanks honey."

"I can't with the two of yous," Sai says, throwing his hands up in exasperation. Finn digs in as Sai leaves and we both watch as the door closes behind him.

Finn gestures with his head at the woman.

"Recently divorced," he mumbles between a mouthful. I grin before dismounting the counter.

Her brunette hair flips over one shoulder as she turns to me when I sit beside her. It looks nice. But it looks better that night with my fist wrapped around it.

# Chapter Four

These drinks bite heavy.
These drinks drown quick.
But if I stop now,
I'll remember the sight of you,
Body full of his dick

"What happened to y'alls last roommate?" I ask once Saatchi's mentioned "the incident" three times at the bar.

It's bustling with noise. The soccer boys have more or less edged us out, so it's just us girls and Sai. Well, us girls minus Saatchi, who is slamming back a shot with a senior, much to Sai's frustration.

Sai stares on with a scowl, his arm wrapped around Kirsty.

"Go easy on her. She's just having a wee bit of fun. She has loads of time before she competes again," she mumbles with a soft pat to his chest. He cuts his eyes from Saatchi and looks at me.

"She fell under Finn's charm unfortunately. It happens far and few in between, but when it does it never ends well."

"Christ, aren't we dramatic tonight," Drew tells him with a grin. "He's not exactly wrong though, love. Finn doesn't do well in relationships and . . . well." She pauses and pats her chin. "Finn's got that life of the party vibe everyone loves."

I look over at him now where he struts around in platform boots and a mini skirt.

"But he's also very sweet," Drew muses. "It actually isn't that uncommon that a bird will fall for him when they see that sweeter side. The issue is that, erhm, well, Finn doesn't feel comfortable in relationships. He prefers just a quick hook-up here or there and then that's it. It's how he's always been," she says with a shrug.

"He makes this clear of course. Raised quiet a feminist, that one, by our dear old Saatchi, so he's always honest. Tells them that he doesn't want anything more." Kirsty nods sagely, taking a sip from her dark beer, eyes on Drew. "Most of the time that's all they do until Finn gets—" Drew waves her hands through the air. "Caught up in something or another. But, gosh, sometimes some lasses think that 'oh, I'll be the one to change him' or 'maybe he feels the same since we've been together so long.'" She shrugs again. "Never ends well."

"Flatmate fell in love, Finn let her down, she left and didn't come back. Shite happens," Kirsty finishes up with a shrug.

I bite my lip trying to figure out if this is okay to talk about without Finn here, but I watch him arm wrestle a freshman and win before deciding it's probably fine.

"Is he just not looking in college?" I ask.

Sai looks back at me and scoffs. "No, Finn is never looking and won't ever be looking for anything romantic. It'll be easier for you when you understand that."

I blush hot when I realize that I sounded like another bleeding heart.

"That-that's not what I—"

"Of course not love," Drew says kindly, sending a glare toward the absent-minded Sai, who is back to staring at his friends.

"Just go," Kirsty says with a push, but he shakes his head.

"In a bit." He looks back to me. "Finn doesn't understand love, his heart is too small. It only holds room for one person and that person is Saatchi." He mumbles something else at Kirsty who shoos him away with a scowl. He finally separates from us and cheers loudly as he rejoins the group.

I look over at Finn and Saatchi.

"It must be hard for him to be in love with her considering the feelings will never be reciprocated," I say, and Drew puts her head in her hands and groans.

"Curse that man." She looks up and shakes her head. "You've misunderstood and that's all." She waves at Sai. "Finn *platonically* loves Saatchi." She emphasizes with her hands. "But Sai isn't exactly wrong when he says that Finn fills his entire heart with her. Sometimes I wonder if Finn was just a soul that got lost on his way to be Saatchi's twin and Sai got stuck there instead."

"Oh, ten o'clock, lost freshers," Kirsty whispers, officially ending the contemplative mood. A slim boy with scraggly brown hair is walking over to us, smile on his face. I feel like I recognize him but I can't remember from where.

"'Lo, Emmylou, right?" he asks, reaching a hand out toward me. I have absolutely no clue what his name is. "Uhm, I'm in your freshers English Lit. Monday morning." He slowly starts to lower his hand, but I reach mine out and shake it at the last second. I really hate when boys notice me.

"Sure. I'm sorry I didn't remember you, uhm."

"Harris," he supplies, grin overtaking his face. I give him a tight-lipped, awkward smile back before turning to my friends.

"This is Kirsty and Drew." Kirsty waves politely, grinning her kind smile at him.

"Sure, you're Sai's bird."

I watch as her smile drops.

"Actually, he's my bird," she responds in snark, sarcastic smile on her face.

"Oh, uh, of course. Equality and all that."

Drew rolls her eyes so hard I'm afraid they'll pop out, and I cover my mouth to keep my laugh from showing. Poor guy doesn't know who he's tangled with.

He laughs awkwardly. "Sorry that, erm, didn't come out right."

"No, of course not," Kirsty says meanly.

I bite my lip to keep from laughing at his predicament and wave my hand in a cut it out motion across my neck. I can sympathize with the poor guy.

Kirsty winks at me and deliberately takes my pleas the wrong way.

"Are you here with the intentions of trying to own our sweet Emmylou?" I blush hotly and avert my eyes from the train wreck. "She's a bonnie lass, sure, but I'll have you know she is part of the feminist club on campus and can't be bothered."

He gapes at her.

She isn't wrong, but Kirsty is the club vice-president, making it easy to be roped in.

"I-I really didn't . . . feminism is great," Harris says, defeated.

"Great," Kirsty says, back to smiling. "We have a protest in a few weeks. I'm sure you'd be glad to sign up." She pulls out her phone, JotForm already pulled up and grins at him.

"Uh, of course," he says, looking over at me.

I'm unwilling to throw him a lifeline and give him a shrug.

"Well, I'll see you in lessons Monday," he says, walking away backward once he's filled out the form.

"I'm his bird, huh?" Kirsty crosses her arms and leans her back against her chair. Drew laughs once more before grabbing her beer. "Sai," Kirsty calls and he gives one of the guys a pat on the back before coming over.

"Do you own me?" she asks as soon as he's at the table, and I choke back a laugh as I lean over my drink to take a sip. Saatchi got it for me when the boys were busy greeting each other like it hadn't been a few hours and Drew and Kirsty had gone to the bathroom to touch up their makeup. Even though

I'm drinking age, I actually have no clue what tastes good. It's clear and sweet so she definitely made the right choice.

Sai swallows and furrows his brows.

"No, of course not, what?"

"Do you get to tell me what to do?" she asks, still leaning back, cocking her eyebrow, lips pursed.

"No, what the fuck Kirsty?" he asks, mouth now agape.

"Good boy," she says, tapping his cheek. "Now go back to your friends."

He surveys her before turning his back and returning to the soccer boys.

"It's the hypocrisy for me," Drew says, snapping her fingers before raising her drink. Kirsty and I follow suit. "To smashing the patriarchy loves."

We clink and I start to take my sip before realizing Kirsty and Drew have upended theirs and are chugging it down. I follow suit and we all slam our cups onto the table.

"I know it's only been a week, but I love y'all," I say, my heart filling with fondness at this absolute change of atmosphere from my last life. They smile at me and we all reach across the messy table to hug.

*Forgotten your old friends already, Emmylou? I suppose it is easier to be sloppy and uncouth. I knew you'd always be the disappointment.* I grit my teeth at the resonating sound of my mother's voice in my head until Kirsty intervenes unintentionally.

"Awe, I love sappy Emmylou." Kirsty claps. "We're so glad you're here with us, lass."

I chase away my mother's voice in favor of my new blossoming friendships. The warmth of my new friends feels comfortable. I can do face masks with Drew and sign up for Kirsty's club without the constant stream of self-doubt and unwelcomeness that comes with my mother constantly over my shoulder. I'm already excited to join them the rest of the year in all of our crusades.

I haven't had to worry about any of the beliefs my mother drilled into me. I enjoy getting dolled up before classes but by my own standards and not for anyone else. The clothes I like and as much or as little makeup as feels right that day. I can even feel free to wear yellow no matter how much it clashes with my pale skin. No one in my group expects anything from me. I can go to protests and wear sweatpants—which I don't, but only because I don't want to. I can curse—which I also haven't actually gotten around to yet—and shrug.

Kirsty and Drew are the epitome of freedom here in the bar, clinking their glasses and loudly laughing without caring if they're being too loud or if any men are looking at them. Even then, Saatchi outranks them in freedom. She is so unconcerned by everything that even most of the soccer players are intimidated by her.

I look over at her and my stare must weigh on her because she looks up at me and grins. She raises a shot at me then winks before downing it in one.

I look over at Drew and Kirsty who missed the interaction as they laugh at something.

"Emmylou, any footballers you find fit?"

I look away from Kirsty and toward the boys. I shrug, nonplussed. They're all huddled around horse playing and loudly yelling to be heard over the live music. Sweat drips down, making some of their shirts cling to their skin, and I watch Finn buy a woman a drink after showing her some thigh in his dress, much to the chagrin of the other players.

"Not really. They're all kind of gross and immature." I'm not sure how Janey found a husband in college. I'm not sure why you'd want to. It seems smarter to wait until they've grown up and can fold their own laundry first. "Anyway," I start, uninterested in the hooting and hollering of the boys. "Are we going to yoga again this week?"

"If that's what you want. I know you wanted to try different things."

*Look at you, being so selfish that you'd ruin your so-called "'friend's" hobbies.* I bite my tongue, unsure of what to say now that my mother's voice has reared its ugly head on my night out.

"Oh no, that's fine. I don't want y'all to feel like you have to come with me." Unfortunately, that was the wrong thing to say because they start to profusely claim they also want to try new things. I can tell they're just being nice, but Kirsty pulls out her phone and starts reading off clubs before I can complain further.

"Archaeology Pals sounds good. It might help you decide between fashion and history." I make a mental note to check it out alone. "There's art, oh," Kirsty exclaims, slapping Drew on the arm, causing her to flinch and scowl. "A baking club. We should definitely go to that. Bridge," she says, continuing to read. "Beer, coffee, lots of dance, board and video games. Emmylou." She looks at me grinning. "There's a fashion society. Oh there are literally so many! How have I never paid any attention? Let's go to all of them." Drew laughs as Kirsty pulls up a schedule.

We're laughing again as we agree to make an appearance at the weekly Mahjong event when a soccer player comes over. Drew's eyes widen and she smothers a smirk.

"Oi, buy yous a drink?" he asks us, but his eyes don't leave Drew's. She tilts her chin up.

"Aye, can't see a reason to say no to a friend," Drew responds, putting emphasis on the word *friend.*

His smooth smile curves up on one side. "'Cor, don't have enough hands for us all. Give us a hand there, Burns?"

Drew rolls her eyes as he uses her last name and follows him to the bar. Kirsty snorts into her hand.

"The heck was that?" I ask, pointing back at her. "He didn't even look at us once."

"Well, that's her on and off again shag, that is. Lewis. He wants a relationship. She doesn't," Kirsty finishes with a shrug.

I look back at them again. Drew looks up at him flirtatiously.

"They won't be back but, well, if all our mates are gonna run off, we're not going to let that keep us from a good time," Kirsty says, grabbing my hand. The dance floor is empty except for the few tourists. Apparently having the entire soccer team here keeps the girls near their tables and off the floor.

I spin happily with Kirsty, laughter bubbling away the self-doubt and wild hair chasing away the night. Out of the corner of my eye, I spot Saatchi at the bar; arms propped behind her, eyes searching the dance floor.

*Saatchi*

Finn has one arm draped over my shoulders and another draped over Sai's as we walk up the hill towards the flat.

"I jus' love you lads. I wouldn'a been here in Edinburgh without yous," he slurs. I'm surprised he's still in those platforms, holding strong, after the amount he's had.

I can't stand heels. I don't even know if I've ever even worn a pair, but I'd have to be laying in my casket to be convinced to strap a pair on.

I'm glad Finn wore them though. He's been slowly embracing a new side to him since we came to uni. I remember the first time he came into my room and asked if I'd put eyeliner on him and here he is today, wearing platforms and a miniskirt.

All the lads were good sports about it and complimented his height and protruding leg muscles. Markus even hit on him, but Finley reassured the lad he was straight and ended up snogging a red-head in the corner.

"Aye, we're gonna be best mates for forever," Finn slurs as he wobbles his way forward.

"Of course we are lad, we're kin," Sai slurs back, and Finn begins to fake weep, making him harder to hold up.

A quick shoppe on the street still has its lights on, probably trying to convince drunk uni students to come in for water or, more likely, wee nips of drunken scran. Scran and water are exactly what my chosen kin need as they slur back and forth.

"You shouldnae go anywhere alone if you're drunk," Sai calls as I pull away.

I raise my eyebrow at him. "Think I'm alright mate," I say, giving him a pat on the back before turning away. Finn calls back belligerently as they walk away, but I ignore him as I jog over to the shoppe.

I open the door and it chimes at my entrance. Weaving through the aisles, I grab a few warm haggis rolls and two bottles of water. I turn and the items fall haphazardly to the floor as I make eye contact with the other person in the shoppe.

Her mane of blonde hair looks perfect despite the sticky, wet feeling of the night. She's looking straight at me, those hazel eyes calling me into the depth of her. I don't dare look below them for fear of what I'll see. Sensual lips, hips, and everything else.

I haven't seen her since I threw my future away.

"Saatchi," Laire starts, her voice a mixture of sweet sugar and ocean waves ready to crack my skull against the cliffs. I break and watch her bare legs take a step towards me and I think of all the times they were wrapped around my head, my torso. "I'm surprised Edinburgh's star athlete has time to go out."

Her hand cups my face and I lean into her softness.

"Drinking and everything? Have you given up on all that nonsense about running then?" Her snark is enough to keep me from letting my mind be dragged below the depths of the sea.

I take her hands off my face.

"Nah, barely had a nip," I say, pushing her aside to grab the items I dropped. "Have to keep at it and stay in shape."

"For what? You could barely finish the London Marathon after I left you."

I press my lips against each other in anger over her bullshit lie and lean in before snarling, "Don' not value yourself so much, lass; running always mattered to me more than you ever did." She may be anxious to drag me into the sea foam, but she forgets; I belong to the Scottish hills.

Her eyes fall and I feel a sting of regret. We weren't always toxic, but she wanted something from me I wasn't willing to give.

Even with the anger she's pulsed into me, I miss Laire. I miss her like an addict misses alcohol. I know she's bad for me. I know my life is better without her. But she's still a comfort to me in an unhealthy way. The way that when you finally feel at peace, a small part of you longs for chaos. She is the chaos I don't want to let go.

"Saatchi," Laire whispers before squeezing past me, shaking her head as she leaves. The chiming of the doors is the only thing left to fill the silence.

I detest feelings. Emotions. Specifically the bad ones. The ones you feel when you see your ex you met in therapy for an even worse traumatic event. Laire understood me like no one else, but that doesn't mean she ever made it better. She made it worse in fact, because Laire was always dealing with similar monsters as I was.

And, God, do those monsters howl in my head. They're currently begging to be heard and that desperate panic I feel to get away from them takes over. I don't want to disassociate and crawl into my bed, mindlessly watching telly until six in the morning when I get up to run. But I'm steaming mad. It's not fair. It's never been fair but, fuck, what I wouldn't give to just see Laire and not feel every bad thing that's ever happened to me crawling up my throat, choking me.

Screw these demons. Screw this brain I have and the past that marks my arm. I just want to feel normal. I just want to run away from this—this feeling.

I've got my mobile out before I've even processed it and I'm texting Markus. Taking another drag from the bottle of vodka I bought at the shoppe, I ask Markus about the party he mentioned at the bar. Markus has always been on Sai's shit list for constantly coming to practice hungover and still playing like a star. Their coach turns a blind eye as long as Markus keeps his defense up. He's been the hero of some very important matches and tonight he's going to be my hero.

I march towards the address he texts, determination set in my gait. I finish the bottle before I drunkenly smash it into a bin. Those pieces of glass could slice a pretty finger but right now that doesn't matter. Right now, I—I feel like I'm losing something. Some semblance of consciousness. The voice inside my head isn't there. It's missing and I let whatever instinctual drive for monstrosity overtake me.

I'll deal with everything later. When my brain is all together. When I can think. But now I don't want to think. Because right now, Markus is opening the door to his apartment and there's music blaring. I have to pretend I'm not losing connection to my body if I want to make it through this night without Markus calling my brother, so I plaster a smile on my face and greet him with fervor my brain doesn't process.

He hugs me and it tingles on my drunken skin. As if my body had forgotten I still had that sense and it's a shock to remember. He's yelling at me over the music and I nod along, but my eyes are glued to the table in the living room where a girl is doing a line of blow. The air has been sucked out of my lungs and I know that unless I want to suffocate, I need my own line.

With athletics looming in my future and a marathon, I should steer clear from it. But my brain is a gerbil running endlessly on a wheel, a carrot strapped in front of it. Dumbly running but incapable of pausing out of desire to get the fucking carrot.

Markus pats my back and walks away and I meander to the table, pushing past people's sweaty bodies, making sure to keep my hands in my pockets. They're shaking with adrenaline as I ignore what it was that was plaguing me.

The girl looks up from her conversation and grins at me.

"The prodigal runner falls far, huh? Want a line?" she asks. She knows me then, that isn't very surprising. I'm in the paper and the news frequently for running and I have an inkling that Sai and Finn make all the footballers brag about me any chance they get. Sometimes, I have the feeling that the entire campus knows me and I feel their eyes follow me. Waiting, waiting, waiting for me to fuck it all up.

Well. Here I am. I hope they're all happy.

The lass grabs her card to give me a line. She looks up in question and I nod before I lean down and cover one nostril and inhale. Hard.

My brain immediately clicks on like a bucket of cold water or an electric shock but calming. But my throat crawls with grime I swallow down before leaning in to thank the girl. She grabs the hand I hadn't realized I'd placed on her shoulder and pulls me down before placing her lips on mine.

"As payment," she calls over the loud music and I nod my head. She isn't what I'm looking for right now so I walk away and find Markus holding two cups full of alcohol. He cheers when he sees me and I holler right back.

I'm animated, like a puppet finally come to life. We cross arms and finish our drinks intertwined, my mouth sweating as the taste of alcohol stills in my numb stomach. I believe it was at my suggestion, but I can't remember over the pounding of my heartbeat what was said a second ago, only that now we're on a make-shift dance floor, jumping wildly and cheering on someone made of blurry lines.

Sweat drips down my temples, my hair curled with humidity. None of it matters. I'm having so much fun jumping. I love this song and I jump and twirl harder.

Markus screams into the crowd and I start to sing along, my body moving to the beat that thrums in my heart from the speakers. Someone else hands me a drink and I swallow it whole to prevent it from spilling while I'm dancing. My consciousness reels back too late, only in time for me to throw the empty plastic cup to the air, reminding me the drink could be spiked. I turn to see who handed me the drink but I can't make out faces.

"Markus," I yell.

He turns to me still jumping and laughing.

"What's'it?"

I'm panicking, but this is Markus, the party animal, someone I only consider an acquaintance. I can't talk to him about this, so I ask him if he wants another drink and he cheers as I leave for a drink.

Someone grabs my arm and I flinch hard, but I look up and recognize another footballer. Aleksander is a year above me but we've had a class or two together and I'm not surprised to smell weed in the air around him. He grins slowly at me, like a sleepy child before his eyes illuminate. He starts chatting to me about the class we share together and I realize he's absolutely right in saying we should demand an updated reading list. It's outdated. It's written by rich white men. I can't remember what was happening once he leaves, so I stand in the hallway before I realize I have nothing to drink and wander into the kitchen where I grab a plastic cup for myself and Markus.

I hold my hand over both our cups and make my way back to him. Shite, I wonder if there's still blow around here. I hand Markus his cup and drink mine as we jump and bang our heads to something loud and flashy.

Someone grabs my waist and I instinctively turn and swing my fist when they're too big to be a woman's hands.

Markus cheers along with other party goers and he leans towards the guy before shouting, "She's a fag, ballface!"

I bare my teeth in false showmanship at the guy as he scowls at me, holding his jaw. I show my bloodied fist to receive more cheers and make eye contact with a brunette who walks over and grabs my arm. I flinch again and pull it away but it doesn't stop her from leaning in.

I ache for personal space. I ache to be smothered.

"God, that was so hot," she says before she kisses me. There's more cheering around me but I don't pull away, instead wrapping my arms around her waist. She isn't my type. She isn't blonde. But she's here. Markus is in my ear yelling.

"Holy shite, she's fucking hot." Letting me know I'm at least pulling while I'm mad with it. I need a line. Her tongue opens my mouth, her skin is soft. I need a line. I pull back and see her pupils are blown wide. Maybe she knows where to find it or else I might boke on her; alcohol and despair already threatening to spew from the debauchery in my stomach.

I ask her and she responds, "That stuff is bad for you, Saatchi."

I'd forgotten I had a name.

She knows me then. I take a deep breath, trying to grant myself a few seconds of sobriety. Aye sure, she is definitely familiar. I think she does yoga with Kirsty on Wednesday, but I can't remember her name right now.

I throw a grin over my shoulder as I turn and shout back, "Whoever said I was good?"

I find the blow, not sure when I got back here, and do another line. Swallowing, I turn to see if she's still there.

She stares at me in shock before leaning in for another kiss. Her tongue explores me as my hands explore her and there's people around us but I'm not gonna boke and . . . and shit.

I was sad.

Why was I sad?

I pull back and rub at my head. Get the fuck out. No. No. Stop.

It was Laire. I think. Is that her name? I can't even remember her face. Much less why the memory of her brings the memory of something worse.

Stop. Get Out. Not here.

The lass grabs my hands and places a soothing hand on my head.

"I can help you forget if you help me?"

Ma once told me that the only people who partied past three were broken people looking to fill the void in their heart. They fill it with drugs and sex and alcohol. She told me this to warn me, but she never realized that I'd use it as ammunition to give myself a quick fix. So I take the attractive brunette to the bathroom where I prop her on the sink and stick my lips to hers.

After, when we're both panting on the ground, her arm covering her eyes. My phone starts to ring. I answer expecting Markus asking if I'm still around.

"Saatchi, where the fuck are you?"

Sai.

"Shite. Didn't mean to pick up your call," I say and I hear the slur in my voice. My stomach rolls and I can tell that in about five minutes I'm going to have to tell this lass to get out so I can shit my guts out.

"Saatchi, it's six o'clock and I came down to give you breakfast before your run and you're not home."

"Good God, did Finn not even miss me?"

I can hear Finn whimper through the receiver and deep down my sober self tells me I should feel guilty. Finn is delicate to my moods.

"Christ Saatchi, are you okay?" Sai asks.

I look at the girl who looks at me and smiles mischievously.

I hum a response at Sai because I can feel sobriety slowly filtering in. Sobriety feels like guilt and sadness and hollowness. I don't want to be sober ever again.

"Okay, fuck, we're going to come get you," he says before hanging up. Both of them demand I share my location with them. They say we should all share it with each other but I know that everyone in the group only really cares about my location.

Maybe one day it'll lead them to the woods and a rope around my neck. But most of the time it leads them to my last disastrous depressive relapse.

"So much for not being your sister's keeper," I whisper to the ceiling, head tilted back onto the bath.

I look up at the girl and smile. "Looks like I've got to go. Need anything?"

"A water," she says, leaning up to gather her clothes littered around the bathroom. Mine are still on. I leave the room and go to the kitchen. I spot Markus lying on the sofa, a backpack on to keep him from rolling onto his back and choking on his boke. Another footballer, some fresher I met last night but don't remember, is standing in the kitchen sipping on his own cup of water.

"How's it?" he asks, and I glare at him. He's got messy brown hair. "Well, it sounded like it went well," he adds, looking down with a blush.

"Don't worry, virgin," I say, patting his chest and grabbing a cup. "I'm sure one day you'll find the clit." I leave, cup full of water in hand, and reenter the bathroom.

"You sure you don't want me to walk you home or anything?" I ask her, crouching down.

"No, s'all right. My friends are still here."

I nod and smile at her before leaving.

The air outside is the most refreshing thing I've ever felt and I stand in the light drizzle, face trained upward. My head hurts, my mouth tastes like cum and booze, my joints ache with dehydration, and my hands are shaking with pent up anxiety.

Sai is going to chew me out, Finn's going to be all kicked puppy, and my run today is absolutely not happening. I might even lose my run tomorrow.

I feel guilty, but I don't want to. I want to turn back around and grab all the leftover alcohol and do it again. But I also want to go home and sit on the sofa and have Sai run his hands through my curls while we watch football with the windows open.

When we were wains, Da always left all the doors to the house open for the dogs to come in and out as they pleased. Sai and I would lay on the sofa watching football while Ma made eggs in the kitchen and Da made the toast. Finn would come in after breakfast and Ma would wipe the mud off his face and give him a change of clothes while she washed his.

There's a specific feeling around those times that I want back. That nostalgia of when everything was perfect.

Now everything is complicated and no one, not even me, knows if I'll self-combust or not. It's like carrying around the burden of being the black sheep of the world. Except my sheep is on fire and everything I touch gets scorched. I'm not sure how much more is left of Sai and Finn to burn before there's nothing left of us.

"Saatch," Sai says, standing in front of me. I look up at him and gauge myself.

I lean my head into his chest as a sob rips through me. I feel his arms encircle me as Finn comes over and puts his hand on my shoulder.

"F-fuck, it was supposed to help. I thought it'd help but I still—I still," another sob chokes out.

"Saatch," Sai says soothingly and rubs my back. "You're okay, everything is okay and you're safe and you can just run later this afternoon."

I push off him.

"No, no I don't want to. I want everything in here," I slam my palm into the side of my head, "to just shut up and just—I just want to be okay." I look at Finn. I'm not sure if he's a sympathetic crier or if we're just so connected, we always cry together.

"Listen, you are okay. You've been okay all summer. You like school, and life, and despite your grumbling to train better, you love running. So . . . what happened? Was it the drink?" Sai asks, bending his head closer to mine. Giants, the both of them.

I shrug.

"Saw Laire." I watch Sai's jaw clench and he blinks slow. He rubs his eyes in frustration.

"Sorry we weren't there for you."

I know he isn't only talking about last night.

"I—I just," I stop and take a deep breath. "Laire understands me."

Finn stands on my other side and gives me a sad look. "Doesn't mean she's good for you, dumbass," he whispers and knocks his hip against mine. "Is that who you fucked tonight?" he asks.

"Uhm," I wipe my mouth again. "No."

"Good, didn't think that shade would look good on her."

I laugh and nudge Finn.

I look up at the sky as Sai leads me.

"I'm sad, Sai."

"I know, Saatch. Maybe going for a run will help you clear out your head and get the alcohol out of your system?"

Finn groans beside me. "Maybe we should just have a relaxing weekend? Aye, Sai?"

Sai looks over my head and I can feel them having a silent conversation.

My therapist used to talk about making plans for short term happiness and long term. I think about short term as the lads bicker; short term is all I can manage at this point.

"Don't go to bars. Don't see Laire. Don't do cocaine," I say in a mumble, but both the boys stop abruptly.

They stare at me and I shrug in defense.

"Are we going to have to reinstate the buddy system?" Sai asks with a teasing frown. I roll my eyes. After I was hospitalized the second time in high school, Ma created a buddy system for me. It really sucked, but it was unfortunately necessary. I even had to sleep in the living room, but Sai and Finn brought the mattress to sleep there with me. Ma would even go into the bathroom with me.

"Fuck no, I'm not letting Drew watch me piss."

"Eh, who knows, maybe it's a secret kink you haven't unlocked yet," Finn says innocently.

Sai and I snort in laughter, and I push Finn who immediately pushes me into Sai, and before I know it, we're running through the streets of Edinburgh in the early sunlight, eyes red but laughter painted into the sunrise.

# Chapter Five

White Rabbit,
Down Fur,
Runs Left,
Sprints Right.

Smells Sweet,
Attracting All.
Come Here,
White Rabbit

Hunted Down,
She Hides.
Quick Zig,
Faster Zag.

Tell Her,
What Hunts,
Isn't Man,
But Herself.

The downstairs group was scarce this weekend but I'm not surprised to find Saatchi in the library come Monday with her boots propped up and a poetry book open in her lap.

"Whatcha reading?" I ask her like I do every day.

"Pablo Neruda, but it's all in Spanish so I keep having to translate words." She feigns nonchalance as she writes something directly within the book. "It's the only way to get the true effect of his writing."

"Oh, that's so cool. I love languages, especially the dead ones, like okay. Latin is really common and it has a lot to do with our current-day English but, oh man, I love trying to read things in Old English—like Anglo-Saxon, which was originally from England and the eastern and southern part of Scotland. Then it became Anglo-Norman and then all the runes changed to Latin letters so it's such a bummer cause now that language is hard to really understand in a modern-day context but so cool, nonetheless. Ya know?" I take a deep breath and look up at Saatchi who is grinning widely at me, her book forgotten in her lap. I blush hotly once I realize I've been rambling about something she probably has no interest in.

"No, lass, I have very little idea of the history of language if I'm being honest, but I'll bet the National Museum has some history of Scotland display up."

I smile shyly at her. "You think so?" I ask tentatively. "Maybe I could go Friday before the Mahjong game night."

She raises an eyebrow at me, as if Mahjong was weirder than being obsessed with dead languages.

"To what?"

"Will you go with me?" I ask, ignoring her.

"To Mahjong?"

"No, silly, that's a Drew and Kirsty thing. I can't ask them to go to a museum and Mahjong. I don't wanna bother them even more."

"But it doesn't matter if you bother me?"

I look at her smirk, waiting, but my head is empty of my mother's voice as I stare into Saatchi's dark eyes.

I return her playful smirk. "Nope," I say, popping the p. "You're rude enough that you'd tell me to hit the road if you didn't want me around."

She laughs; a barely there huff of a calm deer.

"Fair enough."

"So you'll go with me?"

"Aye, cause literature hasn't already made me enough of a nerd as is." I squeal in glee but she raises a finger. "Tell no one. I'll never hear the end of it."

"Deal, but if you're already embarrassing yourself, read me something."

She grimaces.

"It's all in Spanish, I barely understand it and have to look up words every five minutes." I wave her on anyway and she rolls her eyes. "No, they're all love poems. I'm not reading them to you," she says with a blush.

"Well, at least tell me what the one you're reading is about?"

"Uh, well it's called *Farewell* and its a poem about love and how he loves love because it's free to give away but that can have it's downfalls. Ya know, like, love could be forever but it can also leave and it's a divine thing that is flippant because it's free. Did, uh, did that make sense?"

I nod and she gives me an awkward smile.

"So, do you write your own poetry?" I ask, watching her eyes widen. She nods apprehensively. "Do you write other things?" She shakes her head at that and I deflate. "Nuts.

I have this paper due in two weeks for Daly but I don't really know what to write about." Harris had come up to me after the assignment and asked if I wanted to work on it together, but I'm sure he'd work on it in the business building with all the soccer players so I declined. Maybe I'll have to bite the bullet and ask him for help.

"You still haven't come to pick up Daly's notes."

I look up at Saatchi's words, grinning bashfully. "I didn't want to bug you this weekend. None of y'all ever came upstairs."

She laughs, head tipped backward. The sun is streaming through the window, lighting up the dark skin of her throat. "What just happened to bugging me shamelessly, lass? Just come by after lessons and I'll dig them up."

I smile at her, grateful, and she goes back to her book, brow immediately furrowing in concentration.

English Lit isn't the only class I'm already struggling in after one week. It's been made clear to me that science is not my strong suit as I struggle memorizing basic biology terms. Even algebra, which I thought would be an easy A since I've already taken it in high school, is giving me a run for my money. At least Ancient History has been exciting so far but I can't imagine I'll feel that way when reading quizzes begin this week. There is so much information to take in, and it seems like everyone else has it together while I can't even understand half my professors.

I feel my eyes stinging and I realize I've let my thoughts wander too far. I feel like I'm at the receiving end of the firehose but, instead of water, I'm overwhelmed with change, self-doubt, and the constant reminder that if I fail I'll have to go crawling back to my mother. I definitely can't cry in front of Saatchi, so I make the excuse of going to the bathroom. I pull out my phone to call Janey before realizing it's probably too early in Texas.

I lean my head against the stall door and shoot off a text instead. I can't afford to do poorly my first semester in school. Mother might make it a reason to drag me home and force me to enroll in Texas A&M or UT Austin. Or worse, maybe she'll make me go to community college and live with her so she can keep me under her thumb.

*You're not cut out for this, Emmylou. You're too weak and immature to do well in life without me there to guide you.*

I look down at my pinging phone and see an incoming text.

**Harris: Aye, for sures, I can help yous wit Algebra but I'm not in bio this time around.**

I ask him when he's free and scroll through my contacts for someone who could help me and land on Drew. Of course I should ask her because she's a nursing major, but I'm worried that I'm already proving to be the needy roommate. I've already invaded her free time once. I could probably just suck it up and talk to the TA. But I'm sure he's too busy.

Harris wanted to meet after class, but if I get Saatchi's notes first then I could maybe milk his assistance to extend to English Lit. I give Drew a curt wave before leaving the apartment; I've made it a goal to not be overly friendly in case I've been suffocating. Sai opens the door when I knock, barring the entrance with his body.

"You're not allergic to cats are you?" he asks as I hear a meowing behind him. I see a paw pop out from under the door and Sai scowls at it. "Sorry, Saatchi closed her bedroom door and now Anne is on a rampage. Anne gets antsy if she's left home alone too long."

I laugh and shake my head at him. He widens the door before quickly dropping to grab a small gray cat who meows angrily at him as he dangles her in the air. I reach out my hand so she can sniff at it with her pink nose.

"Saatchi mentioned you might be stopping by. Mind to take her the wee devil?" he asks, closing the door behind me.

"Oh, sure," I say, gladly taking the small fluffy from his arms and holding her as he directs me to Saatchi's room. Their apartment is much less put together, and the curtains are drawn, making it much darker. There are food bowls leftover on the coffee table and papers scattered everywhere, and I watch Sai take a seat in front of them as I knock on Saatchi's door.

"What?" she calls in a grunt.

"Delivery," I call back before opening the door. She's lying haphazardly on her stomach on half her bed. The other half is covered in what I can only hope is clean laundry. She must have just finished showering because the steam is still coming out of the shower and she's wearing sleep shorts and a sports bra, watching videos on her phone.

Anne launches herself out of my arms and onto Saatchi's back where she paces around and begins purring.

"Your cat is cute," I tell her.

She glares at it over her shoulder as it kneads on her back. "Oh, so we're sweet again now are we Anne?" she chides the cat in a patient voice. "No, Anne Bonny is a menace who wouldn't stop trying to attack my toes earlier." Saatchi slowly flips over, as to give Anne somewhat of a warning, and stands. "Here, I dug it up already." She crosses to her desk and hands me a white binder. "Sorry, my handwriting is shite, but hopefully it helps."

"Is this your poetry?" I ask, placing the binder back on the desk. Her walls are absolutely covered in papers with writing all over it. There's even back of receipts taped to the wall and one poem that creates a face.

"Well, yeah, but . . ."

I turn to her and see a light blush spread across her dark cheeks.

"Do you not want me to read it? I guess that can be pretty personal." I grimace and take a step back from the wall. My arm brushes hers, skin still warm from the shower.

"Uh, no Lou, it's fine." She walks to her closet and tosses on an atrociously bright, neon green hoodie with a shiver. "I guess, I write most of them after a run so some of them are sleep fogs after twenty kilometers."

"I won't judge you," I lie with a kind smile.

"Right, because a deep dive into someone's personal poetry is completely judgment free," she mumbles sarcastically, but she waves me on.

I run my fingers down one written in paint on a canvas. Kirsty's paint covers the edges, smokey hills blooming from the lettering.

A fog has descended upon Hillside.
I once called her home.
Cut fingers as I plucked at her weeds,
Grew callused as I tilled rows to let her grow,
Broke back as I sewed all her beauty.
I was prideful of Hillside.
Of her green youth, vivacious,
Of her curvy pastures, intoxicating,
Of her infinite promise, effervescent.
But she betrayed me.
For Hillside let the sky moisten her,
Wet until her reeds were soggy.

Rows I had tilled now creeks,
Hillside disgusts me.
I pour hatred over her mounds,
Long devoured roots uncaring.
She is brown with rot and still waters.
But I cannot move from Hillside.
I can only burn my house,
And with it, we both perish.

I take a breath, mind processing the feeling it brought on.

"Is it about Scotland? Do you hate it now or something?" I ask. I turn to find her over my shoulder, reading the poem. Even now, I can feel the heat from her. Maybe she feels a certain way about Scotland the same certain way I've grown to feel about Texas.

"No, I love Scotland even if it's pissing rain every other day. Some poetry is about a completely different topic than it sounds like it's about." She shrugs and I file that away in my head as I turn toward another.

This one is written on a napkin, imprinted with flowers.

"Wrote that one at Ma's house."

I peer up at it, having to stand on my tip toes.

Brown, Like the Effervescent Changing of the Seasons
Brown, Like the Scots Pine's Bark as You Dance Around it.
Brown, Like My Own Eyes.
For We Are One.
You and I.

"Oh, I didn't realize you had a girlfriend back home," I say, but she laughs awkwardly.

"Ah, no, it's for my cow. My Da has two hairy cows 'cause when I was wee I begged for one. Real junkie I was. I wrote it for her birthday and read it to her as I fed her top-quality grain." I gape at her and she laughs. "What?"

"That's actually super cute. I didn't realize you were such an animal person."

She scoffs. "You should meet my Da. He's worse. Brings home every stray dog he finds. Drives Ma mad. All I've got is Anne Bonny and two cows."

"What are their names?" I ask as I wander to a new poem written with a pink pen. This one is clearly about running, and as I skim the ones beside it, I realize most of them are.

"Neruda and Burns," she says, and I turn to her in question. "Poets," she says with a shrug. "Burns was a rebel. Neruda was a lover. It fits both of them."

"Do you have horses?" I ask her hopefully.

"Just a pony, but Finn's family has horses. Breeders." I move to grab the notes on her desk again.

"My parents own stables for racing horses."

"Like the racing you did as a wain?" Saatchi asks as she sits on her bed, her abs peeking out as she reaches back for Anne Bonny, who has created a hovel in the discarded laundry.

I'm shocked that she remembers such an insignificant thing about me and I avoid her eyes as I nod.

"Yeah, exact ones."

"Do you miss it? The racing?"

I walk to another poem as Saatchi rises from her bed, Anne curled up in her arms. She comes to stand beside me, not close enough to touch, but Anne Bonny eyes the distance pensively.

"Not the racing exactly. I just miss riding the horses."

Anne chooses that moment to crawl into my unsuspecting arms. She begins to purr when I adjust to make a nest for her.

Saatchi raises a single eyebrow as she looks down at her cat, arms now looking desolate as she still mimes holding Anne.

"Because it was never the right time?"

I bite my lip, now realizing maybe Saatchi pays attention more than I give her credit for.

"Well, maybe you could start an underground gambling ring to race cats," she jokes, slightly dispersing the tension. "Anne Bonny would clearly do anything for you." Saatchi smirks and I lightly elbow her with a laugh.

I ignore the butterflies in my stomach that blossom in fear.

*No one wants to hear you whine just cause your mother was looking out for you.*

*Saatchi*

It's pissing in Edinburgh when I run after class. Giant droplets of water mixed with sweat drop between my shoulder blades and, much less soothing, my arsecrack. I'm worried my headphones are getting water damage, but it's midday and Edinburgh is alive with bagpipes—for the tourists—and regular folk running to pick up the receipts or drink bevvys. On quiet mornings, I prefer running without headphones, but, right now, it's better this way.

Finn's favorite time waster before he deep dives into his homework on human anatomy is creating playlists.

The current one, *Running in the Rain,* is much tamer than some of the others he's made for me: *Running from My Problems* (lots of heavy punk and system breakers) or *Running Out of Sexual Frustration,* which I've embarrassingly used more than I'd like to admit. Those are better than the ones he made for Sai when he first started dating Kirsty last year: *Hot and Heavy Sex with Kirsty, Slow Sex with Kirsty, Being Topped by Kirsty, Five Minutes Before Class Fuck, Parent's are in the House Sex*.

This may be my most relaxed playlist but I'm pushing myself hard today. There are runners throughout the world constantly breaking PRs every race they compete in. Olympic qualifying times are getting tighter by larger and larger margins. For fuck's sake, even pregnant women are qualifying with new PRs.

I have a fartlek tomorrow and then I'm meeting with my athletics coach to discuss the new season. I've never really taken running this seriously, but if I want to get sponsored, or at least do well at the Boston Marathon, then I can't keep letting myself question if this is what I want to be doing. It's getting too competitive out here.

I'm not sure if it was the backslide that brought me to my knees or if a weekend without running made me realize there is no way this couldn't be a career path for me. I love running. I live for running. It's the only time I can just exist. Here, where the wind ruffles my curls and my legs ache with wanting, I am driven mad with the need to go fast. Mad with happiness as the hills roll by and Edinburgh can become a background noise in a world where I'm finally free.

I ache for folks who will never understand a runner's high, who will never know the true freedom your own body can provide you. Man was never made for cars and planes. We were built with sinuous muscle made for self-reliance, and, if I could have it any way I'd like, I'd get rid of the planes and trains and automobiles for the wind in my hair, the smell of Scottish hills in my throat, and the push of Earth below my feet.

When I run, I'm not some lost lamb of God but a breeze in the wind. No troubles behind me, no future ahead of me, just a heart pumping golden ichor and oxygen. I am my own God. I rely on no one but myself. Freedom is a breath away and I'm gone with it on the wind.

But, unfortunately, that freedom always ends and after a half marathon, averaging well under twenty-five kilometers per hour, I'm finally standing outside of the football stadium where I finish my cool-down laps and force my exhausted legs up to the gates.

The rain is pouring onto the field, creating a swamp as the lads warm up. I spy Finn's bright hair in the torrent and lean against the fencing. He sloshes over, already looking sour.

"I hate the rain," he says, placing his hand on mine where it rests on the fence.

"You're Scottish," I reply, leaving my hand so he can ground himself before the match.

"Aye, but it's pissing." His coach blows the whistle and he looks back. "Wish me luck?"

"You'll be needing more than luck to win. You're the worst footballer I've had the displeasure of meeting."

He looks back at me with a grin and I squeeze his hand before he's off.

Drew comes up behind me and holds an umbrella over us. I'm already soaked to the bone but I smile at her. She raises a duffle.

"Brought you something a wee bit drier."

"Aye, could really use it."

The stadium bathroom smells like the cleaner they scrub vigorously to get rid of the boke from uni students who can't hold their bevvys. Drew hands me the duffle and stands diligently outside of the stall as I undress behind the locked door.

I wish I didn't have to change in a public restroom.

"Better?" Drew asks when I step out.

"Aye, not sure for what. I'm gonna go sit in a puddle."

I stand corrected once I get to the stands; Emmylou and Kirsty are both holding umbrellas, shielding the metal bleachers just enough to keep them relatively dry. I sit beside Kirsty, who gives me a warm smile.

She grips my hand as the ball gets rolling, the other team immediately pushing for ground. Sai's kit is violently ripped back, and despite the jeering of the crowd, the ref makes no call. Kirsty worries her lip as the game continues. She's never been a fan of football, preferring the calmer things in life. Given this, I'm not sure why she picks me as moral support. I am an endless ball of flame as I yell across the pitch at Finley, anxious for a goal.

"Saatchi, what was that card for?"

I look down at Kirsty. It's odd seeing her this way, doe-eyed and unsure. Kirsty is a tempest of a personality but football always makes her feel foolish and confused.

I sit back down, having risen to curse at the call. "Finn slide tackled too late. When you tackle, you have to contact the ball before the player, else it's illegal. So he got carded."

"But you were shouting that it was clean?"

I laugh gently and rub her shoulder to take away the sting—she really hates being in the dark.

"He probably can't even hear me but, I don' know, you know Finn and I. Always have to defend the lads."

The rain lets up right as halftime starts. I lower the umbrella so I can use my hands to braid my frizzled hair. I zone out on Drew and Emmylou heading towards concessions when Kirsty speaks up.

"Can I draw you for classes?"

I look over at her as I tie up the end of the braid.

"Depends."

"Not a nude," she reassures me. Kirsty is all about body positivity and desexualizing the natural form—which is great and whatnot—except now I've seen nude paintings of my own twin.

"Aye, what's the theme?"

She looks away and turns back with her chin tilted high. I already know I'll hate it.

"Hidden emotions. Like each one of yous will represent one on your own, one that contrasts with the way the worlds sees yous."

I drop my head in my hands and groan. "Let me guess?"

She hums.

"Sai is anger?" She nods, and I think of my calm, mature brother holding a broom covered in blood. "Finn's is anxious." He may be the life of the party but he always seeks comfort in Sai and I. "Drew?"

"Loneliness."

"Fuck, Kirsty. You're bold."

She shrugs.

"Who have you asked?"

"Sai."

"And?" I look at her expectantly and she stubbornly holds my eyes.

"He said, 'Absolutely not.'"

"What am I?"

She looks at me pityingly, and my throat chokes as I look away. "Fear. Sorry, you're the most important. Edinburgh's Golden Girl, unafraid of coming out or competing against Olympians. They've even called you fearless. And yet . . ."

"And yet . . ." I remember the article. *Edinburgh's Finest Competes Fearlessly at the World Athletics Championship.* Post-secondary school bullshite, pre-Laire bullshite. I didn't place top ten for Scotland but I was mad close for a spritely seventeen year-old right out of the mental hospital. But the papers didn't know that bit.

"I'll think on it," I lie, and Kirsty deflates but squeezes my hand tightly in forgiveness.

The second half starts as Emmylou and Drew return. Emmylou smiles at me over Drew's head and I smile back. I wonder what her hidden emotion is. She seems to wear it all on her sleeve.

Finn gets taken out after his second goal as we lead 5-0. The second string comes in and Emmylou cheers.

"That's the lad from the bar, innit?" Drew asks.

"Yeah, I actually have a class with him too. That's Harris."

I look at the newcomer. His teammates pass him the ball frequently but he never gets near the goal, often losing the dribbling game. Nerves get the best of him and he ends with no points on the board.

I suppose I'm grateful nerves have never nipped at me. I've shaken hands with some of the best marathon runners but never felt fear on that rubber. I only cared about running, not winning. Not beating the best. Just putting one foot in front of the other. Pushing, pushing, pushing until the runner's high was all that was and I existed only on the track.

The match ends and we descend onto the pitch to congratulate the lads before they shower. Finely raises his arms out towards me, and I scowl as I take a step back.

"Don—" but he lunges and I scuttle away from his muddy, sweaty body. I'm dodging him when Sai wraps his arms around me. I go limp in his body, accepting my defeat as I'm covered in his muck from the pitch.

The lasses laugh at me as Sai rubs his dirt and sweat on my face. I fake gag once he drops me but I nearly do gag when Finn gets a little too close and I smell the sweat and grass on him. We're all three pushing and shoving when Lewis comes up.

"Oi Burns, nice to see you here."

Drew blushes and I sneak a look at Sai who looks away guiltily. I hide my snort at his discomfort; it's been over a year and yet he still sometimes shies away from giving Kirsty affection if Drew is in the room. Falling in love with your childhood mate seems like the worst way to go. I, of course, love mine differently and turn to Finn with a cheeky grin.

Finn grins down at me, noticing the same thing. His smile drops quickly as another footballer comes up. This one must be a fresher because I hardly recognize him.

"'Lo lads," he says familiarly and Sai's eyebrow goes up suddenly. Lewis turns and greets him kindly, as if they've been friends forever.

"This is Harris," Lewis says and Drew cocks up a hip.

"Aye, we've met." Harris laughs uncomfortably.

"Aye, that we have. I, uh, just wanted to say thanks for coming to the match." He waves his hands grandly as if he's talking to all of us, but he's only looking at Emmylou. I look over at her and she gives a tight-lipped smile.

"Riiight," Lewis starts, sensing no one else is going to speak up. God bless Emmylou for being so damn awkward. "I'll chat with you later Drew. Kirsty." He turns to me and playfully scowls. "Saatchi." Still upset I can beat him in arm wrestling then. I grin back, full of mirth.

"Right, guess we should go shower as well," Sai says, eyeing the freshman as if he's going to start spewing green space goo any minute now. Sai takes a step back and Finn watches, dropping his head to my shoulder. I nudge him with my shoulder and he taps me twice on the spine.

Finn and I don't have a solid gauge on Harris yet, but Lewis seems to like him. If Lewis plans on bringing him to the bars with us, we'll have to test whether Harris can handle the radge within our group.

That, and I don't like the way Harris looks at Emmylou.

Harris is already soaked to the bone and covered in grime so there'd be no pleasure in tackling him into the mud. He has, however, undone the laces on his boots. I nudge Finn's foot forward so he gets my idea. He moves it forward, nonchalant, to step on the undone laces.

"Finn," Sai calls, and Finn stops mid-step.

We must've looked at Sai with that look—he calls it our wee devil tell—because he just grabs Harris by the shoulder and turns him around.

"Damn spoil sport," Finn says before giving me a playful peck on the cheek and following the lads.

"What was that about?" Kirsty asks, grinning over at me.

I fake innocence and shrug.

"Did you want to go out for scran before Mahjong?" Drew asks once we're nearing the flat.

Emmylou glances at me briefly.

"Oh, uhm, no I think I'm actually going to, uhm, go do some errands?"

God damn Emmylou for being so damn awkward. I'm pleasantly surprised she's actually keeping her promise to keep our museum outing a secret. I had been joking in truth, but I appreciate her sincerity in the matter.

"O-kay, no problem," Drew says before she and Kirsty head up the stairs.

"Very smooth, Em," I say grinning at her once they've gone.

"I've never lied or snuck out," she says with a pout.

I laugh at her.

"That's sad. You should've lived your teens to the fullest, lass." She scowls, embarrassed, but I only roll my eyes. "Let me go clean up the muck from my face and I'll be back so we can go to the museum."

Anne Bonny calls to me as soon as I enter the flat, but I ignore her in my rush to get to the bathroom. She jumps up on the sink and paws at the water as I'm rinsing off my face.

"Dammit Anne, why am I feeling all jittery?" I feel like I'm sneaking off somewhere with Emmylou and the thought makes my stomach churn with nervous energy. I look down at my soiled green jumper and pull it off. I toss on a clean shirt and coat before rushing back downstairs to a waiting Emmylou.

"You're not wearing that ugly hoodie? That's good."

I gawk at her, impressed by her sudden ferocity. She has slowly started to open up to me, but every little thing feels like a shock.

"Cheeky," I tease, and she scrunches her nose at me before turning away. "What's wrong with it?"

"It's atrocious," she scoffs, and I raise my eyebrow at her. "No, seriously, it's the most hideous neon green. You never even match it with anything correctly." She pauses in contemplation. "Not that you really could match it with much." I silently vow to wear it more often as we keep bickering about my jumper; it's quite nice and warm for chillier runs.

The museum is relatively empty considering it's a Friday night, but Emmylou and I buy our own tickets and wander through. I don't have the heart to tell Emmylou this is probably one of the worst things I've ever had to do.

She stops at every single exhibit and reads the plaque, making sure to read it to me and give me further facts. I'm nearly brain dead from boredom, but I merely hum at all the right moments and fidget my legs when I know she isn't looking. Being still isn't incredibly easy for me and probably contributes a lot to my intense running schedule. I'm itching for a run right now, even after my run earlier, but I stand quietly and follow Emmylou around the exhibits.

"I'd give anything to have been the one to discover this," she says when we're standing in front of some runes.

"You could always be an archaeologist or whatever."

When I was a wain, I used to think archaeologists only found dinosaur bones. Dinosaurs seem cooler than little stick drawings on decaying paper.

"Ugh, don't confuse me further. I already can barely pick a major."

"Well, you seem to really like history," I mumble, thinking of the two hours I've spent of my Friday looking at items belonging to dead people.

"Yeah but, well, I really like fashion too." She shrugs and looks at me. "Did you just always know what you wanted as your major?"

I snort out a laugh. "I still don't know what I want as a major."

In reality, I didn't really think I'd make it this long through university. I thought I'd be long gone, and I'm now realizing my self-inflicted death may just keep getting put off, leaving me to not really know what it is I want from life.

"Well, what do you want from life?"

I look at her in surprise and then back at the runes. My life seems so insignificant. No one will ever put anything I've ever touched or created in a museum; no one will care about my life. I shrug.

"I just want to go back home and run."

"That's it?"

"Aye. I miss my parents and the life I used to have." I suppose she's earned enough trust to at least know that. I wonder if she'll be like Sai and Drew, never listening to what I actually want and only deciding what I should want.

"You don't wanna go to the Olympics?"

I shake my head. "Nah, it's expensive, and I don't really run for accolades. I just . . . run cause it's fun."

She nods, her curls—still frizzy from the Edinburgh weather—bouncing along with the movement. "That makes sense. But you don't know what you want to do? Did your parents ever tell you what you should do?"

I balk at the mere idea of my parents dictating my happiness.

"No, not at all. My Da's got a pretty shite head injury and he just kind of—," I make circular motions over my temple.

"Oh, I'm sorry."

I shrug her off. He's just a wee lost sometimes and can't work, but he's well. Except the migraines sometimes.

"Do your parents tell you what to do? Is that why you chose your majors?"

She looks away and, not for the first time, I realize something isn't right with her relationship with her parents.

"Or . . . guardians?"

"Uhm, parents. I don't know. My pa is pretty relaxed about me doing whatever I want, but my mother kind of makes me feel stupid for wanting to be a history major."

"What do you mean?"

She waves me off, but her shoulders are tight despite the practiced nonchalance.

"My da gets migraines and can't work," I offer, "so my mam has to work the farm and work in town to make money."

She looks over at me.

"Your turn now. What do you mean your mam makes you feel stupid?"

Her nose scrunches as she bites her lip, and I contemplate that maybe I've put her in a corner.

"Well, she just thinks I'm not really smart enough to get a PhD in history, so I won't ever make any money off of it," she says, looking away. I'm not really sure if Emmylou is intelligent, I don't know a lot about that, but school isn't for everyone.

"Money doesn't matter, does it?"

She looks at me then and shrugs.

I sit back on the ledge of an exhibit. "Sai and I aren't exactly wealthy as it is. We have a roof over our heads, aye, but we've never taken a family vacation and sometimes we had to worry about where food was going to come from. That doesn't mean we aren't happy." Or at least, struggling with financials wasn't what made us the broken pieces we are today.

"I guess you have a point," she starts, sitting beside me. "My family is really wealthy."

"Is that something you value?" Another therapy lesson. Running is something I value above most else.

"I value creating a comfortable life I suppose." She huffs out a sarcastic laugh. "My mother doesn't even work but," she pauses and looks up at me, her green eyes searching mine.

I hesitate while I think, or, while I process how her eyes make me feel.

"My mam used to think I was going to marry Finn."

She gives me a deadpan look. "I don't think that one counts."

I grimace and think more before finally deciding on one that hurts my heart a little.

"I'm afraid that I have to get a sponsorship or go to Olympics to provide for my family and to make my brother happy," I say, looking back at her.

"My mother doesn't think anyone will ever love me."

I suck my teeth and look away in shock.

"Shite."

"Yeah, she thinks I have to get a good paying job on my own because I won't ever be able to marry a rich man."

"That's the dumbest shite I've heard in a while," I say, thoughts running through my head. I can feel a rant coming on. "That, Emmylou, is so mad. Like, first off, you're an independent woman. You don't need to marry some bloke for money, you can be the rich man. It's the damn point of this century. Secondly," I look at her finally seeing she's more than I had previously thought. "You aren't unlovable. Everyone is worth love." If her bitch of a mother got married, then kindhearted Emmylou can definitely find someone.

She smiles up at me shyly.

"Thanks, Saatchi," she says, kicking her foot against mine.

"Just telling the truth," I say, sighing heavily. "Sorry that she's like that though. You don't deserve to be hurt by someone you should trust." Emmylou looks away and I feel at a loss. "You know, Drew has a white mam too, if you ever need someone to talk to about that specifically."

"Not you?"

I bump my knee against hers, then look at her again. This conversation has made me realize that Emmylou is more private than I originally assumed, and I search her eyes to see if they're any more open towards me.

"You can always talk to me, but I can't relate to you," I say with a shrug. "It might just be easier. But honestly feel free to tell me whatever."

She nods and looks away.

"I think that's the whole museum."

Thank the Lord. I stand, and she follows my lead. The sun is contemplating setting when we get out and I lead her to some shoppes.

"Where are we going?" she asks as I open a door.

I smirk back at her. "You really haven't ever lied before."

She shakes her head even though it wasn't a question.

"Well, there's an art to lying. For starters, have an alibi, which you do: you're going shopping today, not a museum with your radge downstairs neighbor."

She rolls her eyes at my words.

"The second part of lying, and this is the hardest, make it believable. And, you want to know something, Lou? It's damn impossible for you to go shopping without at least buying one piece of clothing. I've seen your closet. It's terrifying."

She purses her lips but follows me into the store.

"Well thanks a bunch, O' Sage of Lying, for that lesson," she says snarkily, making me grin.

"Maybe if you had learned that lesson earlier, you could've snuck away from your mam more often to ride the horses," I say, shooting into the dark. She blushes hotly, and I grit my teeth in anger knowing I've hit the nail on the head.

"Em," I start, sorting through some fabrics. "Your mam is kind of shite."

She groans and grabs one of the fabrics.

"Yeah, I guess she is a little but she was always there for me."

I raise my eyebrow at her but she doesn't catch it. Being there for your wain doesn't constitute telling them they aren't good enough to be married in my opinion.

"What other errands would I run?" she asks as we leave the fabric shoppe. The sky is greying.

"Scran," I say, opening the door to a pastry shoppe. It smells like haggis rolls and we buy a few.

"Meanwhile," she prompts as we exit. "What were you doing all this time?" She leans against me as the wind picks up, and I try to subtly lean away from her.

"Probably shagging a bird. I don't have running shoes on, so if I wasn't with Finn, just something self-destructive."

She looks up at me sadly, but not like she pities me. Just as if I make her sad, which is an interesting change in pace I slot away in my brain of *Things I Don't Deal With.*

"I don't think you're self-destructive, Saatchi."

I hum. "You just don't know me, yet."

She scowls at me and slaps me with the bag of haggis rolls.

"I thought we were prosexual in this house. Why is it different when you sleep with people than when Finn does?"

"Girls," I specify because it's important to me. She nods in agreement and I run a hand through my long hair. I ignore how my fingers tangle in the expansive frizz of it all. "I suppose it's 'cause no one trusts me."

"That's silly," she says, smiling. "I trust you. You make decisions for yourself and, well, honestly, I really envy that. I wish I could do that."

"You could always start," I say once we're at the door to the flats.

"Yeah, I guess." She looks over at me and smiles again. "Thanks for tonight. I had a lot of fun."

It sounds like a line at the end of the date, but I shake off the feeling and pat her arm. It feels like an awkward thing Emmylou would do so I blame her for my suddenly stunted social skills.

"Sure, Lou, that's what friends are for. Have fun at Mahjong," I say sarcastically.

*Emmylou*

Kirsty is sitting at her mirror doing her makeup when I walk in.

"Do you think it's just going to be a bunch of nerds?" I ask awkwardly. We had made jokes about attending the event, but now that we're actually doing it, I find I'm surprisingly nervous.

"Aye, I'll bet if they're playing this on a Friday night it'll be quieter, more introverted folk." I lean over her and watch her do her makeup. She offers to do mine but I shake my head and walk through her room while I wait for her to get ready.

Kirsty's room is painted black, which helps bring out her paintings even more. They're all framed in gold and I walk around to peer at all of them. Not all of them are of our friend group, but all of them are of people. She experiments with different backgrounds and lightings. Sai under the ocean. Finn in a cave. Saatchi in a jungle, Anne Bonny a gray jaguar beside her, looking ever the feral beast she is. Most are on canvas but she's used lots of different paints or whatever it's called. Crayons? Pastels? Not a clue.

There is a small collage near the bathroom I look over now and grimace.

"It was hard at first to get them to agree," she says looking up from the dresser mirror. It makes me kind of uncomfortable to see but they're all nude paintings. Finn is shamelessly sitting in a chair, legs spread, one arm on his knee holding up his head as he stares intensely.

"I wanted to capture the human body. Not necessarily sexualized. I mean, the human body is just a body. It isn't always something to be sexualized but there isn't anything to fear. It's just a body. It keeps us going and we have to treat it with kindness and love. They didn't have to be totally nude. Your body, your choice."

Sai is lying in bed, a sheet covering his leg but nothing else, his hair a mess. Drew is reclined in a bathtub, water clear, and her plumper body accentuating her hips and chest.

"Why didn't Saatchi get undressed?"

Saatchi is wearing a large sleep shirt and running shorts. Kirsty's paint shows she isn't wearing a bra under the shirt.

"Preference," Kirsty says with a shrug. Saatchi is nearly a professional runner and I've seen the cut of her abs when she wrestles with Finn, the sharp angle of her legs when she wears dresses, the defined muscles of her arms when she gets back from a run. I can't imagine she's ashamed of that.

"Do you want one?" Kirsty asks me.

"No. Maybe. Maybe," I finally settle on. "But tonight let's just go to Mahjong."

I only end up waiting for Kirsty for five more minutes before we're on our way to the club event.

Drew bumps her hip against mine as we walk and I think back to what Saatchi said about Drew's own parental issues at the museum. I smile at her in response, but I'm thinking about her mom. Our mothers are nothing alike. My mother is just nagging and trying to look out for me; her mom just up and abandoned her. It wouldn't be fair to bring it up to her. I would sound ungrateful just complaining about a few things my mother said, but in reality, there are much worse parents out there. My mother could be better, but every parent makes mistakes.

Drew has gone out of her way to show me that I'm not only a part of the group but also that my secrets are safe from the others. Saatchi is the only person I've ever told about my mother and she took it in stride, which I had expected from someone so strong and valiant as she is. But I can't imagine Finn, with his constant jokes and life of the party attitude knowing what to say. Or Kirsty, who is bubbly and kind, who'd probably look at me with pity. I'm not even sure Sai and I are that close, but I can imagine he'd say something along the lines of "tough it out."

Drew though? Drew is basically a maternal figure already. Always chasing Finn around for misbehaving or making sure Saatchi has a billion meals a day. But the words I wish to use to express the growing pains my mother inflicted on me stay lodged in my throat.

"Something on your mind, lass?" Drew asks me.

Kirsty does her best to look like she isn't listening in, and when I don't respond she walks a few feet ahead of us.

"I don't know. It's kind of whiny and embarrassing."

"Feelings can be embarrassing sometimes," Drew says, squeezing my hand. "Did you know, I lived in the same town as Sai, Finn, and Saatchi before uni?" I shake my head and she continues. "Aye, we all grew up together, but I wasn't really part of their group. They caused lots of trouble you see, and Saatchi and Finn often were kicked out of mass for one thing or another. But come secondary school, I had a few classes with Sai. And goodness. Well, I mean you've seen Sai."

I nod as a blush creeps up her neck onto her face and I realize she's calling him attractive.

"I just had the largest crush on him and, damn, everyone kind of fed into it. Or at least, they were in my head. Saatchi and Finn have always been calling me mam and since Sai is, like, this responsible father figure neither of them had. I just kind of had an active imagination of it." She lets out a breath of air before covering her face with her hand. "Once his mam even told me 'You take such good care of Sai when no one else does.' Either way, with my friends always telling me we made a cute couple and all that from his family, I guess I kind of thought we'd end up together.

"Obviously, when we moved to Edinburgh, he met Kirsty and it became so embarrassingly clear that he never even considered me. It hurt, and sometimes it still does, but what I'm trying to say here is, no matter what awkward or embarrassing, or even traumatic, past we have, we're all still close and have each other's backs. You can always tell me anything," she says, reaching out a hand and squeezing my shoulder.

"Come on, lass, let's go kick some arse."

I laugh as she leads me into the campus feeling lighter.

My mother can't reach me here.

# Chapter Six

Winter Breaks,
Sun beams onto Wet skin.

Happy, Are You?
In love perhaps.

Her skin glitters and dazzles,
And I run my tongue down to her navel.

Winter Comes,
Darkness fills reality.

I left summer behind in my dreams.
Except you and your wet skin.

There's a small coffee shop right outside of campus where Harris and I meet up at to work on homework together. I always end up waiting for him to get out of soccer practice, but I don't mind because the pretty cash register worker always gives me free refills. Saatchi's informed me that the store definitely charges for refills. Which makes sense, considering they also charge for water.

I'm sending a funny meme to Harris, we send them back and forth all day, when Saatchi barges in through the door of the shoppe, a tall blonde hot on her footsteps.

"Yer being a fucking shite head," the blonde yells and Saatchi cringes as everyone's eyes turn to stare. Saatchi continues to the register and orders something, earning a mean glare from the worker as the woman behind Saatchi continues to berate her.

"It's not like I'm asking you to dive back into everything. Just come to a party with me," the blonde says loudly, trying to wedge herself between Saatchi and the counter.

"Laire, for fuck's sake, I don't want to go, and I especially don't want to go with you," Saatchi says, fighting to pull her wallet out of her backpack. The blonde, Laire, reaches out her hand and grabs Saatchi's forearm. I watch, frozen, as Saatchi flinches so hard that she falls on her butt.

"Oh my Christ Laire, just fuck off," Saatchi whispers through the hands she's brought to cover her face. I start to get up, afraid that maybe this person Saatchi knows may have hit her in the past, but before I'm fully out of my seat, the girl starts to walk out of the coffee shop. I watch as she turns while pushing the door.

"If I get fucking raped, just know it's your fault for not being there for me."

I'm in absolute shock in my seat, and I can feel the tension in the room, but Saatchi just takes a deep breath before standing up and handing her card to the worker. With no idea if I should say anything, I watch Saatchi grab her coffee before turning toward the door. Our eyes catch and I watch her grimace and shut her eyes, quietly muttering out a curse as she leaves.

Awkward whispers fill the coffee shop, and I rush out the door. Saatchi is waiting for me, leaning up against the wall of the café.

"'Lo," she greets, taking a sip from her coffee.

I gawk at her.

"Hi. Are you all right?"

"Embarrassed and what have you."

I blink slowly at her and she raises an eyebrow at me.

"Erm, what . . . what can I do?"

She scoffs and looks down at her scuffed high-tops.

"Kill everyone in the shoppe who witnessed that."

"Did she hurt you? Who was that?" I look down at her arm.

"Oh, no. I just hate being grabbed but, aye, who doesn't? That's Laire. An Ex."

I brisk over the lack of information before repeating my earlier question. "Are you okay?"

She looks down at me, her deep brown eyes searching mine, and shrugs.

"She wasn't always like that," she starts, taking another sip. "I think that's what makes it hard. It was really good for a bit there."

I wait and she bites her nail as the silence grows heavy between us.

"I don' know, it was good until she decided it shouldn't be. Don't know why. Like she thought we were too happy or it was too easy or she didn't deserve it. So she spiraled. Drank a lot, partied, did drugs. And, I tried to make it work, you know? Followed her in but always held back so I could run the next morning. Guess it made her feel like running mattered more to me than she did." Saatchi shrugs and looks at me expectantly.

"My mother made me go to prom with a football—American football—player even though I didn't want to."

"Was he nice?"

I shrug because he wasn't not nice, I just didn't want to go with him. I wanted to go with my friends but they all had dates. My mother thought it would look embarrassing if I didn't bring a date.

Saatchi looks up then. I follow her eyes and see Harris loitering behind us.

"Oh, sorry to interrupt. Are we still . . ." He points at the coffee shop sheepishly.

"Yeah, sure, just give me a second."

He nods and he walks inside. I turn back to Saatchi as she raises her eyebrow.

"Should let you get to your date," she says smirking, canine glaring menacingly at me.

"Ha, just studying," I respond, but she's already turned away. "Hey, wait." I reach out my hand to stop her but don't, remembering she doesn't like being grabbed. I flex my fingers where they rest just above her arm—not touching but close enough to feel the heat from her body. Her eyes follow the movement and I pull back slowly.

"Listen, Saatchi. I'm really sorry that happened to you and I'm sorry it still hurts."

She turns back around.

"But?" she asks, raising that dang eyebrow again. It makes me feel something akin to envy but not.

"But nothing. Like you said, you didn't deserve to be hurt by someone you trusted. I'm just sorry it happened and I wish I could help."

She smiles softly at me and bumps her shoulder against mine.

"Come on, Lou, not gonna teach me to throw toilet paper at her house or whatever it is they do in those American movies?"

I let out an embarrassing and unexpected laugh, and she grins as I cover my mouth.

"Nah, we stick hard candies to car windows so when they pull 'em off it shatters the glass."

Saatchi's eyes widen and she laughs as I show her my best innocent smile.

"Christ, remind me to never piss you off," she says, pushing away my face with an outstretched hand. "But seriously," she starts softly. "Thanks, Lou."

I watch her walk away, her horrendously neon hoodie making her hard to lose sight of. Once she's gone, I turn back to the café and find Harris sitting across from my books.

Harris smiles brightly at me, placing a fruit tart from the café in front of me.

"Alright?" he asks. "You looked a bit stressed."

I nod and plaster an equally bright smile on my face. This isn't any of his business.

"Yeah! Ready for some peer reviewing," I say, and he pushes the fruit tart toward me again.

Harris has been so kind since we started studying and the fruit tart has become a staple for him that he buys for me, then I always buy him a to-go coffee before we part.

I absentmindedly skim his paper, twirling the rings on my fingers. He doesn't seem to mind though and happily distracts us from the topic of homework. I feel the tension in my shoulders drop as Harris and I discuss the few soccer players we both know, mostly repeating funny stories of Finn.

"I think you're using the wrong word here," I tell Harris once we've finally settled in.

"Am I?" he asks, leaning over the table. I feel his breath on my arm and lean back to give him space to read. "Oh, aye, looks like I did. Nice catch, Emmylou. You're so smart," he says, grinning at me.

"I'll bet you're an English major."

"Oh, no actually—"

"Then something smarter," he starts, cutting me off. "Engineering?" he asks, poking me in the arm. "Nursing?" Another poke. "Or, oh, pre-med?"

I laugh awkwardly, moving away from his third poke. I'm hesitant to tell him I haven't really decided a major and neither of them really fall under the STEM category.

"Still actually deciding between a couple actually."

"Well, tell me what they are. I'll bet I can help you pick one."

I look away bashfully, and he sighs.

"Not gonna tell me, eh?" he asks, back to grinning.

"I don't know. Guess it's a secret for now."

Harris leans back in his chair and squints across at me.

"I'm guessing your boyfriend knows."

I laugh; the insider knowledge of knowing I've never even had one making me gleeful at the incorrect assumption.

"Definitely don't have one of those."

He hums as he balls up his straw wrapper. "Tell me," he demands, flicking the wrapper at me.

I bat it away with another laugh. "Maybe next time," I say, standing from the table to pack up my stuff.

I'm all packed up and ready to go, anxious to check on Saatchi, when Harris tugs on my braid gently.

"I like your hair like this; the braid is nice. Suits you."

Finn told me this morning at breakfast that it made me look like a child, but I thank Harris all the same.

"And uhm." I refocus on Harris as he starts again, his cheeks red from the humidity pouring in from the open shop door. "I really like you, Emmylou."

I feel my smile broaden and my chest fill with happiness.

"I really like you too Harris. It means so much to me that you've really gone out of your way to help me feel welcome," I say as I turn toward the register to buy him a coffee. He has seriously helped with my homework and he's never been judgmental if I struggled with a concept. Between him, Drew, and Saatchi's notes—I'm going to ace this year.

"Ha, well, that's good to hear you feel the same. Maybe, we could . . . like, hang out. You know, outside of studying?"

I think of my friends back home, and of Finn and Saatchi teasing Harris every time they pass us on the way to classes. I asked Saatchi about it and she said it was "all in good fun between lads." I'm not sure I believe her.

"Just, like, you and me, right?" I ask guiltily. It feels bad to hide him from my friends just because I'm worried of what they'd do if I brought him along. Drew did say I could talk to them about anything. I might bring it up with Saatchi at lunch sometime.

"Aye, yeah, exactly," he says, oblivious to my intentions.

"Well, that sounds perfect," I respond—sounding overly relieved—and quickly hand him his coffee. I give him a wave and he grins back at me as I finally walk out of the store.

I immediately whip out my phone, but Saatchi hasn't texted me. I wish I had worn something other than nude suede heels today as I try to quickly trudge up the winding, cobblestoned hills to the apartment. The rain isn't helping, but at least I've got a raincoat that goes down to my calves. The heels might be soaked, but I don't care, picking up the pace. Sometimes, I wish I was as fast as Saatchi.

I finally burst through the brightly colored door. Drew and Kirsty are doing homework on the floor. I think of asking them if they've seen Saatchi, but I don't want to expose her if she was already feeling embarrassed at the café.

"How was your day, lass?" Drew closes her notebook and looks up at me.

"It was fine. I just went to classes and then studied with Harris." I take off my heels and leave them on the shoe rack by the door.

"Harris, eh? He's fit, innit?"

My raincoat drips on the vinyl flooring, and I'm thankful someone has already placed a towel at the door.

"Yeah," I answer absentmindedly as I take my coat to my room.

Saatchi is laying on my bed, hands under her head, smirking at me with one eyebrow raised.

"Fit," she mouths, silently. I roll my eyes at her and hang my coat.

"I'm just, uh, gonna study," I tell Drew peeking my head out of my room. She frowns at me and puts down her flashcards.

"You've been studying all day, lass. Why don't you come and chat with us?"

I look back at Saatchi who shakes her head, a devious smirk on her face.

"Sure, just let me, uhm," I glance at Saatchi again, who is now holding back laughter and being incredibly unhelpful.

"I'll be right out," I tell Drew and Kirsty. They look at me, questioning, but leave me to close the door.

I turn to Saatchi and raise my hands in question at her. She stands up and grabs my phone from my back pocket, handing it to me. I ignore the tingling sensation caused by proximity. Her fingers graze mine when we exchange the phone and I look up at her in confusion.

"Music," she silently mouths, so I tap on a playlist. She grimaces as my country playlist fills the room but quietly lays back on my bed.

"Huh, you really like sunflowers?"

I take in her cat-print socks and sit down beside her. I guess she hides a softer interior under those combat boots of hers. Like a domesticated beast.

"Yeah, they grow near the farm, and I'd take the horses running through fields of them when I got the chance."

She looks up at me finally, then awkwardly looks away.

"You didn't say anything to Sai or the girls."

I shrug at her statement, and her eyes pass over mine again before sitting up.

"Should I have?"

"Nah. I appreciate that you didn't. The 'Saatchi Protection Squad' has enough eyes as is. Can't be more suffocated than this."

I can hear the bitterness in her voice, and I cross my legs, making sure to cover my front with the dress before leaning toward her.

"Saatchi, they just care about you."

She shrugs, holding my eyes.

"I didn't call them because I thought you deserved privacy. I mean, I don't see why everyone needs to know; you seemed to handle it well on your own." I know a thing or two about wanting to prove to yourself you can handle life privately. "Don't look at me like that," I say teasingly, batting her cheek away. "I know you're the toughest person I know, but still." I shrug, unsure where to go from there. But Saatchi grins at me.

"You think I'm tough?"

I scoff.

"Yeah, of course I do! I mean, you're like the superstar of campus and everyone thinks you're like a God or something. Harris even told me some of the soccer team is scared of you."

She laughs, throwing her head back. It's my favorite laugh of hers. Not the unapologetically wild hyena she is with Finn, or the calming presence of a deer like in the library; it's something else. Something just for those she loves. A feral animal trusting me enough to show her neck.

"Football," she corrects. She's been getting in the habit of bugging me about it, and I've been getting in the habit of sticking my tongue out at her when she does. She reaches out and squishes my cheeks as I stick my tongue out. I laugh as I bat her away again.

Being with Saatchi is so carefree—like stepping into the sun after a long winter.

She sighs and rests her hands in her head.

"Well, I hope you still think I'm tough after that. God, it was so embarrassing."

"Seriously?" I laugh at her. "Of course you're still a badass. I mean, she was yelling at you, like who does that," I exclaim laughing, falling back onto the headrest beside her. "I'd have had a full-blown panic attack if that had happened to me. She seems like a headcase."

Saatchi laughs along with me.

"Sorry, I probably shouldn't talk crap about your ex."

"Ha! No by all means. I mean, like I said, she wasn't always like that. But aye, that was pretty radge, right?"

I nod vigorously and Saatchi laughs again. Then she sobers, looking forward, and I stare at her profile, taking in the typical signs that show the gears are moving in her head. She runs her tongue on her canine before finally speaking.

"Laire was always just getting so mad if I couldn't go somewhere with her and then she would start this grueling guilt-tripping process. Like, okay. This one time, Laire wanted to go get ice cream except she demanded that it had to be during one of the footie matches. I obviously said no and Laire just got, I hate to say this, but she got hysterical. Said I never put her first and that I was an awful girlfriend and like, fuck, all this awful shit, like no one would love me.

"I skipped the game. To go get some fucking ice cream and I pouted the whole time so Laire got pissed again. But by the next day she apologized and I thought maybe it was just a blip. But it wasn't. It kept going and sometimes I would say no and Laire would suddenly fall and cut up her knee or have her bike stolen or, God, just anything bad. Really helps lay on the guilt that way, I guess.

"You want to know the worst part?" Saatchi asks me, and I bite my lip, nodding hesitantly.

"I didn't even break up with Laire until I caught her literally shagging someone else. It was a party that she had dragged me to even though I was running in the London marathon the next day. I was supposed to be up bright and early to catch the train with the lads to the race. Instead, Laire guilted me into sneaking out and going to a party. And then she guilted me into drinking, and I mean, I know I could've said no—"

I stop her by putting my hand on her thigh.

"I get it, Saatchi. It's hard to say no in that situation, and it isn't your fault. I could've said no to my mother a million times, but," I shrug. "You just can't."

Saatchi nods and looks down at her hands. I look at the phoenix tattooed on her right arm. It traces up from her ring finger and covers the entirety of her arm.

"Either way, Laire dragged me out to this party and then shagged some dude. Makes ya feel like a right bampot."

I hold my tongue from asking what that word means and pat her knee.

"Well, she's the one who embarrassed herself at the coffee shop. So I think Laire looks like the bampot." Saatchi throws her head back again in laughter. My insides brighten at the reaction, despite her next words.

"You have no clue what that means, do ya?"

"Nope, not even a little."

She looks over at me and smiles.

"You're a bampot Lou, but I'm glad you're here."

"Anytime."

"Well, I should head out—leave you to it," she says, standing from the bed and going to my bedroom window. I give her a questioning look.

"I was kind of curious to see how long you'll keep my secrets. Besides," she says, opening my window and swinging a leg over the edge. "A runner always has to prove their arm strength." She gives me a menacing grin before lowering herself from my window ledge. I get up quickly, but she gracefully enters her own open window below.

She looks back up at me.

"Keep my secrets, Emmylou?" I put my head in my hands as I look down at her with a laugh.

"What, that you're secretly nice?"

"Aye, that's the one," she says grinning like a cheetah after a successful hunt before slipping away.

*Saatchi*

Finn joins me on my morning run, but I lose him somewhere on kilometer three as I listen to the *Battlesong of Scotland* playlist. I feel lighter today than I have in a long time, and I don't feel bad leaving him in the dust.

The air is humid and cold but I hit my runner's high and push through to the countryside where I run on dirt paths, surrounded by grasses now wilting as the seasons change. I hate the summer because it's too hot to go anywhere, but winter brings a lot more days on the treadmill. I always lose time on the treadmill, and running on the indoor track means chasing my tail like a dog.

If only it could be cold without snow. Then running season would be endless.

I end up waiting for Finn less than I thought I would, and I frown when I see him.

"Oh, don't feel bad. I did like ten kilometers less than you," he says panting, hands on his knees.

I laugh and finally check my time; I had been putting it off until Finn returned so we could check it together.

"Mad shite," he whispers as we look. I lock my phone and unlock it again, rechecking my time. But no matter how hard I stare, it doesn't change.

"That's impossible," I whisper back, looking at my time. It's well and easily an Olympic qualifying time. It even puts me as finishing in the top three from the last Olympic marathon times. Despite knowing the times by memory, I check them online then switch back to mine. It's still the same, my pulse is racing and I'm sure my stomach has fallen right out of my arsehole.

I look at Finn and he looks back at me, eyes wide.

There are tears in his eyes, and I breathe in deeply through my nose to keep sane.

"Don't tell Sai," I say, and he nods. We numbly walk back to get ready for lessons, neither of us wanting to jinx what this means.

Lessons go by in a blur. I continually check my time again and recheck the Olympic times. Nothing changes. I'm still third place.

Finn and I make eye contact and quickly look away in the hallway. Sai looks on at us, his eyes suspicious as he walks beside Finn. I know that slip up means Finn will be interrogated but hopefully he won't break.

I sit in the library and don't even bother opening my notebooks. I look at my times again. I hit the share button and send it to a few coaches and scouts. My hands shake for the next hour as I sip on my water. My phone buzzes with responses but I can't bear to look. Maybe it's an error and when I sent it, it recalculated.

Emmylou plops across from me and tilts her head to the side at my panicked expression. It's an exact copy of a confused puppy, and I mentally kick myself for thinking it's cute.

"Em," I whisper and she smiles, unsure. "I ran today."

"Yeah, Saatchi, you do that every day."

That technically isn't true; I take a break once a week to watch a telenovela with Finn that no one knows about but Sai, but I don't correct her.

"Em, you don't understand. I—" I stop and look back at my phone. All of the responses are excited, no times to correct or recalculate. They're real. It's real. I ran that fast. I ran that fast. I can't run that fast. There's literally no way.

I slide my phone to Emmylou and she looks at the time and looks back at me.

"Is that fast?" she asks innocently, and I try hard not to scoff.

"It would've won me third place in the last Olympics."

Emmylou's mouth drops open and she looks back at my time.

"Are you serious?" she asks gleefully and I nod my head, staring at the shelf of books behind her. My leg won't stop shaking. This is impossible. I'm not this good. This is ridiculous. There must be a mistake. I'm not an Olympic athlete. I don't even want to be one. I just want to run.

"Saatchi!" She places a hand on my fidgeting leg. I wish she'd stop doing that. No, I don't actually. Her nails are bright pink to match her shirt. "That's incredible. What's wrong?"

I exhale and toss my head against the plush chair.

That's the million dollar question.

"I don't know," I respond, grabbing my phone back from her. "Let's talk about literally anything else," I beg, putting my head in my hands.

"Uhm, okay, well. Today, Harris,"—I internally groan—"and I got assigned a partner project together. It's about the wars in Scotland which is, ya know, hysterical because I didn't even know there were wars in Scotland."

I bark out a laugh and look up at her. She smiles softly down at me, lips a lighter pink than her nails.

"How the fuck did you not know?"

"I don't know," she says with a shrug. "In Texas, it's just 'Remember the Alamo' and, uhm, the world wars," she says dismissively, and I laugh again.

"Come on Lou, you're like, obsessed with history. How do you not know more about this stuff?"

She looks at me contemplatively.

"I guess war just isn't the history I'm into," she says, blushing prettily.

"Well, I haven't really heard you talk about fashion like you talk about history." She opens her mouth but I cut her off. "Nah, goin' on about my jumper doesn't count." She pouts and I laugh at her.

"I like making clothes," she mumbles.

"Sure, and I like running. Doesn't mean I want a career out of it." I shrug. "But who cares what I want, right?"

"What? No, you should totally stand up for yourself and do what makes you happy."

I grin cheekily at her, knowing she's walked right into my trap.

"Aye, I should. Just like you should stand up to your mam and ride horses and date the lads you want." The last part tastes bitter in my mouth but I hush it away.

"Okay! New subject," she says with as much passion as she talks about the origins of Latin. I cock my eyebrow up at her and she waves me away.

"How's, uhm, Finn?" she asks pathetically.

"Well, you saw him yesterday. Still alive and all that. Still keen on cutting people open."

She grimaces.

"Is it bad that sometimes I forget he's smart?" she asks.

It's true though. Finn is the epitome of faking dumb to seem cool. The lad's one of the top of his class but you'd never guess it by talking to him. I always struggle imagining party Finn focusing on textbooks or anxious Finn directing an ER in an emergency. I tell Emmylou this and she agrees.

"But he actually is so calm during an emergency. Like a health emergency, I guess I should specify."

"What do you mean?"

I cringe at the reaction I'm going to get from this story.

"Well, so, you know how Finn and I sometimes egg each other on and get into slightly radge situations?"

Emmylou laughs, probably thinking of all the nights they've sat around in Drew's living room making bets on Finn and I's wrestling matches.

"Right, but sometimes, we egg on each other a bit too much."

"Jesus, what'd y'all do?" she asks, leaning forward excitedly.

"We, uh, well, we had been watching a movie or a show, I can't remember. Anyways, in this movie, they were playing this, like, game," I lay my hand flat on the tea table, ball my other hand in a fist, and make stabbing motions between my fingers.

"Five Finger Fillet?!"

I shush her as someone from a study table sends us a glare.

"Aye, sure whatever. Stab between fingers and all that. Except, well, we had been drinking a bit. Like, quite a bit. Like to the point that Sai and Drew didn't even think it was a bad idea."

That night we had all sat around mam's dining table, bellies warm with whiskey we took from da's cabinet—Finn had to put me on his shoulder to reach it. We were so mad with it that Drew and Sai didn't even blink when Finn and I grabbed a professional steak knife—mam likes to pretend she can cook but da's the only one that uses it.

"And anyways, at first we went slow, but, like I said—"

"You egg each other on," Emmylou says, covering her mouth, eyes wide with horror.

"Right, and I wanted to prove I was better, so I just kind of went for it. Anyways, I sliced so hard through my finger that it literally just—" I make a popping noise and pull at my finger to show it detached.

"You're kidding!" Emmylou grabs my right hand in her jumper-covered hands. I hand her the left one instead and she takes it, eyeing the rough scars that show where the stitches once barely held it together.

"Sai and Drew obviously started panicking, but Finn just got up and scooped ice into a bowl and grabbed my severed finger and placed it in there. Then he just like, in the calmest, soberest voice, tells Sai to go wake my parents and he grabs the med kit from the bathroom and just stops the bleeding like it's a normal occurrence for him." I shake my head at the memory.

"You're radge," she says, and I laugh as it comes out in her accent. Atrocious. I'm not even sure half the letters were used.

"Whatever. Shite happens. It's on there good now," I say, tickling at Emmylou's palm, maneuvering under her jumper sleeves.

"Nice jumper by the way."

She smiles and shakes her head.

"Nice subject change, but thanks. I made it myself," she says, looking down at it.

"That's balls. You did not." I look down at it. The body is white but each sleeve is a different color, like pink and blue cotton candies.

"Yeah, for real."

"When does anyone find the time for that?" I ask, and I watch her mouth open as she pales slightly. Huh, something interesting then.

"Oh, just here and there."

I raise my eyebrow at her and stay silent. My ma used this tactic on me—pregnant silence—when I got in trouble at secondary and would only tell her half the story. It's uncomfortable enough, waiting in expectant silence, that I'd always end up breaking and telling her the full thing.

"Saatchi," Emmylou says, batting my face away. Like she can't stand to look at me.

"I've never told anyone before," she says pouting, now pulling at her sleeves.

"Well, I'm your best friend so you can tell me."

"Don't be weird about it."

I make no promises, but when I don't respond she continues.

"I, uhm, I had leukemia when I was a kid."

My face drops in surprise and I instantly feel guilty about asking. I, of all people, should know some stories aren't easy to share.

"Shite, you don't have to keep talking about it if you don't want to."

"No, it's actually kind of nice to tell someone," she says, waving me off. "I just sat around in the hospital waiting for treatments and I knit while I waited. I was an outpatient, luckily, and I mean obviously I'm better now."

I nod, no longer asking for more but willing to listen if she's willing to give it.

"That must have been really hard for you. I'm sorry you had to go through that, but I'm glad you got through it. That can't be easy for you or your family."

She cringes and I feel my stomach drop.

"What?" I ask, and she grits her teeth.

"Well, not everyone knew."

"What?" I ask again, flabbergasted.

"My mother—"

I scoff and fall back into my chair.

"Saatchi," she reprimands, and I grimace, realizing this isn't my moment, and sit up.

"My mother wanted to keep it a secret. Like, from my pa and Janey, my sister. So I did," she says shrugging. "I was ten, but I guess that's not young enough to excuse my naivety. My whole world was, and honestly was for way too long, dictated by my mother, and I didn't think it was weird. She got me a wig and on bad weeks told everyone we went on vacation. I don't know what she would've done if it went on for longer or, ya know, if I'd died."

She looks up at me and I'm not even sure what to say. I can feel my hands trembling with emotion, and I keep them tucked under my knees.

"It didn't seem weird at the time. She told me we were making it easier for everyone else but—" She inhales deeply.

"My mother would drop me off for treatment so she could go to the country club. I remember sitting there crying because the pain was just absolutely crippling and, after a while, I just hated needles because they only meant feeling worse. Anytime I'd see one I'd just start sobbing. Everything was just a lot to handle for a kid. It was horrifying and I remember always feeling cold—gosh it was so friggin' cold because my mom would dress me up like it was any other stupid day. A skirt and a blouse or something like that. I'm not sure I even owned sweatpants until I got them through my cheerleading gear.

"The nurses were kind though. They'd sit with me as I cried and went through my treatments. I remember holding their hands and crying as the doctors would tell me I still had more rounds of chemo to go through. I guess they picked up on my misery because they started to reach out. One nurse brought me coloring books, another brought me toys, but one in particular sat me down and taught me how to knit in between my nausea cycles. She was my hero. It takes a lot of patience to teach someone to knit, and even more to clean up their vomit in between lessons.

"The first thing I did was knit myself a scarf that she let me keep there. Then a hat so I could keep my bald little head warm instead of that itchy wig. Eventually I had enough confidence to knit this sweater. Which, in hindsight, was bold. Obviously, it was way too big since I followed a pattern for adults, but it just ended up being a blanket sweater of sorts," she laughs with self-depreciation, and I cringe internally but let her talk.

"I should've hated my mother for leaving me to deal with that alone. Instead, I hated myself for getting sick and putting so much pressure on her and making her lie to my family." Her hollow laugh chills me to the bone, and I duck my head to keep my own anger from showing.

We sit there in awkward silence as I try to take calming breaths. I've hated people in my life. Genuinely hated to the point where I wished them dead at my hands, but I don't think I've hated anyone like I hate Emmylou's mam.

This isn't about Emmylou's mam though. This is about her having to keep her pain and fear a complete secret from those she loves the most.

"How did your da never know?"

She shrugs.

"He had just gotten a big job working on an oil rig. Janey was in her first year of college and wasn't around much. When she was, I'd conveniently be at camp or a friend's vacation trip when, in reality, my mother would squirrel me away in a hotel between chemo treatments. It's actually how my mother guilted me; she told me I'd ruin my pa's job and Janey's college experience if I said anything."

I chew the side of my cheek, foot tapping wildly as I try to compose myself before I speak.

"You still haven't told them?"

"No, who knows what they'd say."

I scoff, but Emmylou leans forward and buries her head in her hands.

"I just can't tell them Saatchi. I'm scared of what might happen." A tear rolls down her hands, and I stand from my chair and move to hers.

"Lou, you don't have to tell anyone if you don't want to," I say, sitting on the arm rest, hand hovering near her shoulders.

She leans into me before saying, "I know. But it was nice to finally tell someone. I wish I had the guts to tell more people."

"Uhm, well, you could tell the group?" She looks up at me and shakes her head before covering her face with her hand.

"Ugh, could you imagine the pitying look Drew would give me. Or, oh God, Finn would be so awkward." She's not wrong, and I smile as I think of Finn picking at his fingers, drawing his fists up to his head if she told him. Delivering bad news won't be his strong suit as a surgeon.

"What about a stranger?" I ask, gears churning. "Someone who doesn't know you or your kin?"

"What do you mean?" she asks as I start to stand.

"Aye, like someone you'll never see again."

"What?" she asks again.

I ignore her and grab our school bags instead.

"Trust me?" I ask, and she nods tentatively. I grab her hand and haul her out of the library.

This is the cheapest time of the year to travel to Scotland and there's a beer festival this weekend, so we're lively with tourists.

"Where are we going?" she shouts as we trudge off campus.

"To tell strangers."

She looks at me like I'm crazy, but I ignore her as I lead us to Edinburgh Castle. I pause near the gates and grab her shoulders, pointing her towards the crowds of tourists, "These tourists won't ever see you again."

She lets out a watery laugh.

"What? Do I just walk up to them and tell them I used to have cancer?"

I shrug.

"Do what you want, Lou. There's a first time for everything," I tease, and she squishes her nose before taking a deep breath.

"My mother hates causing scenes, and she hated even more when Janey and I would laugh or talk too loud in public. I wasn't even allowed to shout unless it was for cheerleading."

I watch her contemplative face before she whips around and grins at me mischievously.

"Fuck my mother."

I cheer her on loudly as the first curse word I've ever heard her utter escapes her lips. She rushes up to a tourist—poor hen probably thinks she's about to be robbed—and grabs her shoulders, shouting at the poor woman. I burst into laughter when it's clear that the lady doesn't even speak English.

"Well that sucked," Emmylou says, standing over me as I'm doubled over in laughter.

"Pick someone who isn't Asian, lass. I think you scared the shite out of her," I say between gasps of laughter.

"That was so embarrassing."

"Well everyone's first time sucks," I say teasingly.

She crosses her arms and kicks at my shin when she gets the innuendo. I kick her back.

"Go on, try again."

She takes a deep breath beside me and, with arms still crossed, leans her head back before yelling, "I HAD CANCER YOU FUCKS."

A Scottish bagpiper squeaks out an awful note in surprise.

She looks over at me with a grin, eyes sheen with unshed tears.

I follow her at a distance as she walks into the middle of the crowd and spins in a circle, shouting from the top of her lungs. Most people walk past her quickly; she looks insane. Her hair is frizzy and falling out of its braid and she stumbles around after getting out of her third spin.

But the sight of her still makes my heart beat loudly in my chest and I squeeze my arm in hopes of calming it down.

We prance around the entrance of the castle, her grabbing tourists, some that guiltily give her their money—I tell her to keep it; she, of course, gives it back—and others express their joy at her remission. I even watch one man start a blessing over her, tears streaming down my cheeks from laughter.

Eventually, a kind woman buys us tickets to enter Edinburgh Castle, cancer perks Emmylou never received as a child, and we stand on the highest point and she shouts it to the entire city, I can't help but feel an unwelcome longing as the sun sets behind her rosy cheeks.

"Thanks, Saatchi. This was actually really cathartic."

She leans her head against my shoulder and I ache. Like the air has been stolen from my lungs—stolen from the earth—and I accept my imminent drowning.

# Chapter Seven

Without Intention,
I began to see you.
The way you smiled,
Hair glowing like morning dew.
And it wraps,
And wraps,
Wraps
Around my neck.

You are my enemy.
You are my nemesis.
You are my end.
You are my love.
Stab me deep.
Cut me deeper.
End me here.
Let me suffer.

I cannot live without you.
Menacing Beast.
Darkening End.
Light of my Life.
Cut me,
And cut,
Cut,
'Til I bleed no more.

Emmylou's bed smells like honeyed apples and I shouldn't be laying in it, yet here I am. I'm not sure why she's going along with hiding our friendship anymore but it's to the point where Finn asked if I've even talked to her since the beginning of the year.

Ironically, I spend about three hours with her alone a day. Half in the library, where I mostly read and she mostly disturbs me to talk to me about what she's doing with Drew and Kirsty that day, and the other half in her bed, while she sews outfits.

"What do I wear to a protest?"

I empathize with the mannequin Emmylou repeatedly stabs. It's how I feel anytime she so much as looks at me.

"Comfortable shoes for running from pigs."

She rolls her eyes and I dig my grave a little deeper. I'm normally much better at not forming romantic feelings for platonic friends or even straight hens. In fact, I've never crushed on someone who was straight. This is a sick joke.

"I'm not going to be running from police officers. It's just a peaceful protest."

I don't tell her Kirsty is a shit starter or that I got arrested last year when I supposedly "peacefully" protested with her. Although, to be fair, "peaceful" isn't a word anyone in their right mind would use to describe me.

"Still. Comfortable shoes and something you could potentially run in. Nondescript," I add with a shrug.

She looks down at her mannequin. It gives me the creeps. I can't imagine waking up to it in the middle of the night. Not that I'm thinking about waking up in her room. Ever.

"Are you going? Drew said she isn't because she has an exam."

I hum in response. Kirsty told me not to scare her off from her first rally. She looks over at me and stabs the fabric onto the mannequin with force. It shouldn't be as hot as it is. I hate myself.

"No, do you honestly trust me to behave?"

She scrunches her nose.

"I don't think you give yourself enough credit, Saatchi," she says, sitting beside me. I wish so dearly to stab out my heart for stuttering even at that.

*Relax, heart. Platonic friend. Platonic. Platonic. Platon—*

She puts her hands on my thigh.

"You're a lot more responsible than you like to think. You know?"

I shake my head and shift, just slightly, so as to not make it obvious. She removes her hand and I breathe again.

"Like, you run every day consistently and still manage to do your homework. That's crazy, considering you run for like four hours. Sure, you're a little reckless sometimes, but isn't every college student? You've always been there for me and you're such a good friend to Finn." She looks at me. "I guess I just don't understand why no one will cut you a break, you know?"

I don't respond and she leaves me to go back to making whatever it is. I think it's for the Halloween party coming up, but I don't ask because my brain is reeling. The soothing folk music playing through her speakers and the twinkling sunflower lights do little to halt my brain, and before I know it, I'm standing from the bed.

"I think I'm going to go," I say, and she gives me a questioning look.

"You think?"

"Aye," I respond before slipping through the window. I drop my feet a few meters and land on my ledge, slipping through my window. I can hear the sound of a football match on the telly from behind my closed door.

I open the door so only my eye is visible and stare at Finn. He's hunched over a textbook in post-practice trakkies. Sai looks up at me but I don't open the door any farther. He squints at my antics but, used to them after nineteen years together, slaps Finn's arm and nods towards me.

Finn looks up from his textbook and his glasses wobble—he only ever wears them to study at home since they're an ugly pair from the second-hand shoppe. He laughs but stands, and I open the door enough for him to come in.

"Finley," I say, pulling him in quickly.

"Aye, gonna tell me what you've been up to every day in here for so long?" I give him an innocent look.

"Whatcha mean?"

He rolls his eyes and lies on my bed. I lie beside him and rest my head on his chest, something I only really do when I'm feeling a little low.

"Damn, and here I thought you were doing something good and not wallowing."

I pat his belly, hard, and he flinches with a groan.

"I haven't been wallowing. Honest. I just got to thinking." I hesitantly bite my lip and he waits. "Do you think I'm irresponsible?"

He snorts and I cringe.

"No. You're reckless, sure, but not irresponsible."

I sit up then and look down at him, but he shrugs under my inspection and starts picking his fingers.

"What do you mean?"

"Well, Saatchi. I mean, you're nineteen. Sure, we get into radge situations, and we can get a wee in over our heads but . . . shite Saatchi, you're the one who picks yourself off the ground every time something goes wrong. Not us. I'm gonna be honest with you, I wouldn't be where I am today if it weren't for you.

"I'm not just talking about realizing I wanted to do surgery after you sliced off your damn finger. I mean in the sense that you've always been so strong and so ferociously unafraid of who you are. You know? Your drive and your confidence, the lot of it, it's enviable. If I could even fill myself with half of your strength, I'd die happy."

I lay my head back on his chest, and we both stare at the ceiling in silence as I take in his words.

I've never thought of myself as a capable person, or even someone worth envying. I've felt weak and broken since I can remember. The depression that took over in secondary still looms heavily in the background, making it hard to distinguish success from failure, shortcomings from humanity.

"I don't see it."

"Aye, and I don't see myself as a surgeon. But here I am, top of my class. And there you are, Edinburgh's star athlete, and the best poem writer I've met," he adds, pulling my notebook from my bedside.

"Write anything interesting lately?" he asks me before I bring up running. "It's empty," he says, flipping through the notebook.

I shrug in response because it is, and I have nothing to say for it. Poetry is about feelings and I'm all consumed by an unwelcome, childish crush. I keep the poems tucked deep under my bed, far from the snack stash so Finn will never come across them.

"Write me something?"

"About what?" I ask him.

"Feelings," he responds, eyes searching for sadness in mine.

I grab the notebook and sit up.

"I hate my feelings."

"Then write about that," he says before patting my head and leaving my room. Anne Bonny slides in before he can close the door and, annoyingly, tries to lay on my notebook. She curls on it and begins to lick the hand holding it.

"You're supposed to be emotional therapy, Anne," I tell her before giving up and getting ready for bed.

I end up writing a poem the next day before classes and, unfortunately, the mind space I need for it is trying.

Cruelty.
It's what I've named my heart.
Beating Hard.
Feeling Harder.

Can I shut you down?
Make you drown?
You complex little bitch.

First you love,
Then you lust.
Feelings shut off
Where once they rushed.

It confuses me.

Cruelty.
What a wild child.
Immature in its own understanding.
I must nourish it to watch it grow.

Perhaps then, I will understand this show.

Love Once,
Anger Twice,
Sadness Consuming.
Pain is Looming.

Oh how funny,
To hate yourself.
But to love You.


*Emmylou*

Saatchi looks like she's planning a murder when I walk into the library. She has a far away look in her eyes and doesn't notice as I place my bag down at our spot. Her eyes are darkened from a fitful night and her brows are furrowed ferociously.

"You all right?"

She looks up and frowns deeper before shrugging. In the months I've known Saatchi, she gets in moods like this. When she's like this she isn't the fierce eagle, ready for a fight, or the scrappy hyena, cackling as it teases its peers, or the house cat, curled in the afternoon sun. Right now she's a snow leopard; alone in the wilderness—broken and afraid.

"You can talk to me, you know?"

"Aye, sure, but . . . I don't like nattering about inner turmoil."

"Then what do you want?"

"Distract me?"

I sigh but accept, hoping her feelings won't build up without proper expulsion.

"Kirsty's protest is today."

She hums but doesn't look away from her spot in the distance.

"I'm supposed to go help her get all the signs and carry it all to the top of the hill. Then we'll protest through campus."

"Hmm, good luck."

"Are you coming?" I ask her, picking up my backpack in preparation to meet up with Kirsty.

"Nah." She bites her lip like she has more to say and I watch the motion before I finally realize she isn't going to elaborate.

"Oh, kind of figured that'd be your thing." I hesitate, fingers pulling on my bag straps before finally stepping up to her. "Do you, uhm, could I give you a hug?"

She looks up at me in surprise and shakes her head.

"Okay," I say, accepting her no without question. "Well, I really hope you have a better day." She gives me a questioning look but I wave and walk away toward the classroom where Kirsty told me to meet her.

Kirsty is wearing joggers and a ratty pair of sneakers with paint on them. It's starting to get colder outside as October draws to an end, but she's only wearing a light coat.

"Hey, why doesn't Saatchi come to these? Kind of seems like her thing."

Kirsty snorts and looks up at me questioningly.

"Sorry, this is going to sound harsh, but I've literally only seen you talk to Saatchi like a handful of times. How do you know what she likes?"

I blanch at my slip up. Saatchi only ever asked me not to tell anyone about our trip to the museum, but I've had fun keeping our friendship private. I like having Saatchi's undivided attention, and I don't want Kirsty to feel like I've betrayed her friendship by bringing up Saatchi and I's friendship this late.

"We have lunch together in the library. We talk a little during that. Not much, obviously; she's quiet."

Kirsty nods, satisfied, but doesn't respond to my question, instead electing to grab posters from inside closets and off of desks to collect them all into one section.

I grab some posters from her hands as Tye, another member of the club, walks in, her long locs tucked under a warm beanie.

"Don't we look comfy? You don't look prepared to protest," Tye says, voicing my own thoughts. Kirsty shrugs and grabs a wheelbarrow for the signs.

"Here, yous can start putting everythin' in here. And feel free to put your coats in here once you're spent from walking the hills of Edinburgh," Kirsty adds with a friendly wink directed to Tye.

We take turns pushing the wheelbarrow, and by the time we're at the top of the hill, Tye and I have both taken off all of our coats, panting slightly.

"I hate these bloody hills," Tye says, leaning a defined arm against the stone wall where we all agreed to congregate.

I nod, agreeing solely through my heavy breathing.

She shifts so both of her arms can haul her up the wall to sit. Tye has stronger arms than Saatchi.

"Oh look, our first group is here," Kirsty says excitedly.

I turn to look at them ascend the hill. Without the weight to drag them down, they seem excited to be here.

Once the whole group has arrived, armed with posters and feminism, we begin to march down toward campus. Kirsty has planned this perfectly so that we are walking the campus right as classes get out. I feel a wave of pride as I hold my sign high above my head and chant with these people. I made the sign last week with Kirsty in our apartment, but I spent most of my time laying on the carpet thinking of what it should say.

Abortion clinics in Scotland are legal, unlike many places in the United States, but the Scottish Parliament is looking at creating buffer zones—areas where anti-abortionists can't protest—to protect woman in need. In the US, it's an easy sign: "My Body, My Choice." But here, where it's legal, it's different. I ended up with a sign reading "Keep Your Eyes Off My Body."

It has only been a couple months in Edinburgh but I know myself now better than ever. I care about things because I chose to. I care about women's rights, history, my friends—and there is so much more I have left to discover about myself.

I feel brave as I hand out fliers about abortion rates, safety, and buffer zones to the people on campus and Kirsty follows me, chanting out whatever Tye leads us in. Tye hoists a poster high above her head when we get near a group of boys. She must know them from other protests because they immediately start jeering. Kirsty glares and thrusts a flier into one of their hands.

"I don' want your flier, cunt."

It must be the electricity in the air, or the fact that Kirsty is yelling at him, or me asking myself, *what would Saatchi do?* It could be any of those things, but I think most of it is that Kirsty swings first, and when one of his friends goes to swing at Kirsty, I do the only thing I can think of and kick him square in the balls.

I only wish I remembered we had a police escort.

*Saatchi*

"No! It's those pigs! It was self-defense," Kirsty's voice blares through Sai's phone speaker. I look away from the shared laptop as I'm finishing the last bit of my essay before the Halloween party. Finn looks over at me, a secret smile on his face as he remembers my own arrest last year at one of Kirsty's protests.

"Love, I know, I heard you," Sai shouts from his room where he dresses with haste.

"When will you be here?" she asks him. "Oh, whist. I will not be hanging up," she tells someone else on her side.

"He's on his way, Kirsty," I tell her, typing my last sentence and saving the file.

"You gonna print that Monday?" Finn asks me as Sai leaves his room and grabs his phone, taking it off speaker.

"Aye."

"Can you print my worksheets too? I saved them under the 'Please Print' folder." I smile at him and nod. My phone begins to vibrate in my pocket and I pull away from the dining table to answer it.

"'Lo?"

"You're receiving a call from Edinburgh Police Station. Accept the call?" I snort to myself and tell the robot to patch her through.

"Saatchi," Emmylou starts in a watery voice.

"Oh, no. Don't be sad," I say, heart aching.

"They put me in handcuffs. Do you think they'll call my mother?"

"No, course not, Em. You're grown, so they aren't going to say anything to her, lass." She breathes out a sigh of relief and then starts to giggle. "Going mad already in prison?"

"Ha! No, it's just a little police cell. I guess I'm just laughing because I'm officially more of a badass than you."

I choke on a surprised laugh. "I've been arrested, Lou. Sorry you're going to have to go above and beyond."

"Yeah, I already knew but you never told me about it. I thought maybe you'd give me the win, since I'm in jail and everything," she whispers, voice hesitant again. "Can you come get me? I know Sai is coming but . . . can you just come? I'm kind of freaking out." I turn and look at Sai as he hastily puts on his trainers.

"Uhm, aye, I'll be there, but I have to go now cause Sai's nearly out the door. See you soon."

"Yeah, see you."

I end the call and walk towards Sai.

He looks up at me and motions for his keys that are on the kitchen counter.

"Want me to go with you?" I ask him as I hand him the keys.

He laughs and looks up in shock once he realizes I'm serious.

"What? Why would you want to?"

I shrug.

"I just . . ." *want to be there for Emmylou.* "Emmylou might need a second person to sign her out that isn't you. You know? Like if you can only sign out one person at a time."

This is a lie and Sai sees right through it.

"Are you planning something dumb?"

I bristle and roll my eyes. "No, never mind you ball face," I tell him, walking away. He scoffs behind me, and I hear the door shut just as I enter my room, eyes already on my running gear.

Fucking Sai. How am I supposed to prove I'm responsible and worth something if he doesn't even give me the opportunity? Everything I do is a cry for help in his eyes. I can't even try to help out a friend in need without him thinking I have some ulterior motive.

Although, I suppose in his eyes perhaps Emmylou and I aren't even friends.

I feel pent up and annoyed at everything. I'm annoyed at my twin for thinking I'm a child. I'm annoyed at myself for keeping Emmylou and I's friendship a secret. But I'm especially annoyed at Emmylou for being who she is.

She should be calling Harris to bail her out of jail. She should have him sneaking into her room at night. She should be making dumb eyes at him and asking him for hugs.

I walk out of the door to the flat, ignoring Finn's calls about the impending Halloween party.

*It isn't Emmylou's fault*, I realize as my feet start pounding during my warm-up. I reprimand myself for sounding so toxic and push myself harder.

I'm simply embarrassed. Falling for a straight lass is textbook stupidity, and I wish I had built an emotional wall towards her sooner. Even with a wall, I may have ended up feeling the same way. But it hurts. It hurts like a suffocating lung.

Every look, every touch, every flash of her smile; it all sucks the wind out of my lungs. The only thing that could bring them back is if she looked at me with intention, touched me with longing, smiled at me with love. The problem is, she never will, and so my lungs are forced to go without oxygen.

I accept this though. Just like I've accepted that this crush on Emmylou is growing and shows no signs of ebbing. Just like I've accepted I can never do anything about it.

With down-turned shoulders, I finish my quick run and trudge up the stairs of the flat. Finn is sitting on the sofa playing a video game. He looks up at me and nods his head, the skeleton makeup making him look less like my best mate.

"Alright?"

"Aye, just needed it. 'Preciate you waiting, mate."

He hums and pauses his game.

"The girls?" I ask behind a shut door as I strip quickly and hop into the shower.

"They left already. Emmylou actually asked about you."

He leaves it hanging, and I bite my lip in silence. She's probably fuming at me for not going to meet her at the station.

"Probably just wanted someone there who's been arrested before," I say lamely as I step out. My costume is easy, and I throw on a hooded black robe and grab my scythe before lacing up my combat boots.

"Ready?" I ask Finn as I walk out.

He grins at me and leaves for the kitchen to grab a bottle of whiskey.

"Aye, let's get mad with it."

Markus's flat is brimming with bodies. It's stifling and claustrophobic and at any other time it'd be a problem, but the whiskey sits in my belly and I'm just calm enough to flow to the music unbothered.

Finn leads us into the crowd, searching for familiar faces. There are lots of hands reaching out to stop us, desperate to bring us into their conversations. It's all the same conversation, however. They ask us how we are, ask Finn if he's dating that lass they thought he was, and ask me how running is going.

Finn knows all their names and they know all his conquests. In the past, before uni, I rather enjoyed doing this bit with him. Making everyone feel welcome and important. Learning their names and everything about them. Now, it's not only tedious, but I have no desire to let people know more about me than what they read in the papers: queer, runner, Scottish-Indian. That's all they get from me anymore.

My eyes wander away from the third group we've stopped at and I catch Drew's eye. I absently pat Finn on the back and push my way through the crowd towards Drew. Lewis waves at me as I join them.

"'Lo," I tell him, raising my drink when he offers me a cup of whatever he has. I learned early on that putting any form of alcohol in my water bottle will ruin the flavor of water forever. Now, I save a specific bottle for these occasions.

Drew's arm is wrapped around Lewis's waist, and I grimace but pretend it's the taste of my drink. He's a bulky footballer that is berry to have around the lads, but he's not exactly someone I'd pin Drew to enjoying having around.

"Where are the criminals?" I ask Drew. Lewis raises an eyebrow but we both ignore him.

"Oh, you know. Here and there. Probably stealing valuables and graffitiing feminist quotes on the wall." I laugh and she leans in conspiratorially. "I always thought it'd be you and Finn who were the criminals."

"The night's still young," I shout over the loud music.

"Are you planning on doing something radge?"

I look over at Kirsty as she appears beside me and grin down at her, even in her heels she isn't taller than I am.

"Only if the sun rises in the east tomorrow."

She rolls her eyes and my brother leans over her head and squints at me. I smile cheekily and he shakes his head before greeting Lewis.

"How are you feeling about captain next year?" Lewis asks my brother where he's attached himself to Kirsty, and I frown and turn away from the conversation.

Emmylou is standing next to a girl with dark locs. She throws back her head in laughter and I feel a pang of jealousy before I remember I don't have the right. I couldn't even pick her up from the pigs tonight.

Emmylou looks over at me and then over my shoulder. She waves me tentatively over and the lass she's with looks over at me. I break from the hens clucking about politics and make my way to them.

"Sorry, Sai wouldn't let me go. Said I'd do something radge," I tell Emmylou as soon as I'm close enough. She frowns sadly at me but doesn't say anything.

"You should've been at the march though, mate. She was bloody brilliant."

I look at the girl with locs and raise an eyebrow.

"Saatchi," I tell her.

"Tye," she responds in that same sharp accent.

"English?"

"Aye," she says teasingly. It could almost be seen as flirting, but I can't be sure yet.

"Where in England are you from," Emmylou says, taking a step closer to us. Her hair brushes my arm, tickling it but not setting my nerves on fire.

"Brixton, which is South London," Tye explains as I try to subtly lean away from Emmylou. She catches this and glances between us questioningly.

"'Lo! Oh, Tye, how's the party treating you?"

I look up at Finn who has draped himself between Emmylou and myself. Tye gives him a questioning glance as well and opens her mouth before closing it.

"It's bangin', yeah. What about for you, Finn? Shouldn't you be getting your date a drink?" she asks and I roll my eyes at her indiscreet prodding.

"Oh, Saatchi's gay. They're not dating."

I inhale sharply and feel Finn's head snap towards Emmylou. I'll have to have a chat with her about outing me while I'm surrounded by people I don't know. Sai, Finn, and

I can only fight so many people. Tye must sense Finn and I's hesitation because she speaks up quickly.

"I'm queer as well, so nothing to worry about." Her smile is carefree, as if we aren't both constantly assessing if it's safe to be ourselves or not with new people. I appreciate the gesture and nod slowly and wiggle free of Finn's arm. He drops it quickly.

"Well, got your eye on anybody here tonight?" Finn asks. I can feel Emmylou's eyes blazing into the side of my face, but I ignore the heat of her stare like I should've been ignoring Emmylou all this time.

"Just three," Tye says boldly, and I can't help but let the snort escape from my mouth.

Finn grins cheekily but Emmylou doesn't react. I look over at her and realize she hasn't even heard Tye.

"Or maybe just one?" she questions, and I look back at her and shake my head.

"Emmylou and I aren't dating. Well, none of us three are dating if that's what . . ." I pause as I confuse myself.

"Ha, well. Why don't we get refills and make our way to the dance floor," Tye says.

Finn follows her like a starving pup and I start to follow before Emmylou stops me with a hand in front of my stomach, not quite touching.

"That wasn't the right thing to do, was it?"

I grimace and look back at Finn who is slowly getting lost in the crowd.

"I'm sorry. I thought you were out so I thought it was okay."

I look back at her and her green eyes drink me in. They tug on my heart and I feel my chest expanding, making room for it. If I stare too long, I'm sure it'll begin to crack my ribs and puncture through my chest. Then, my heart will bleed on the ground at her feet, unless she catches it. But she never would.

"I am out. It's just," I look around at the crowd. "Not exactly the safest place to do it. Never know who's homophobic in a party this big."

"Right," she says, nodding sadly.

I groan inwardly at my own stupidity and grab her chin softly, tilting it up towards me.

"Oi, it's fine. You didn't know. Count us even since I couldn't come get you after you took down the patriarch." She laughs lightly at that, and I let go of her face, leaning back to remember what breathing feels like.

"It's fine," she says, her accent extra thick. I bite my lip and accept her words tentatively.

"Are you still worried? Your kin won't know."

She shrugs and then shakes her head, hands running through her loose hair.

"No, I know that. I just," she looks up at me and I try not to shy away from her eyes. They look the same green as the hills behind my farm. "You're my best friend. I kind of wanted you there."

A shite friend is what I am. The reason I wasn't there was because I've been keeping our friendship a secret. At first, by accident. I hadn't realized Emmylou wouldn't tell anyone about the museum but then everything was a secret because I was testing her; seeing how much of her I could truly trust. Now, it's because I'm embarrassed, because I'm sure it's clear on my face how I feel.

Before I can say anything, someone steps into the huddle Emmylou and I have created.

"Hey, Emmylou," he breathes out.

I sneer subconsciously. It's the grossest, breathiest thing, and I shiver in disgust.

"Oh, hey Harris. What are you dressed up as?"

He looks like a tart.

"Ha, I'm actually dressed as a cowboy." He looks down at himself awkwardly. "I guess I didn't really have the right clothes laying around. I just figured whatever boots would work."

Emmylou nods kindly.

"Yeah, I see it. It's just dark in here so I couldn't tell."

"An angel, that's cute. Suits you too." I roll my eyes. Emmylou must see it because she nudges me with her elbow. "What are you?" he asks me, and I fight the urge to roll my eyes again, or, better yet, slice my fake scythe through his fake face.

"A God."

Emmylou bites her lip and looks away but the guy just nods slowly.

"Right." He sizes me up and I flash my crooked canine at him. "Anyways, Emmylou, would you like to dance?"

"Yeah! We just have to grab Tye and Finn first and then we can all dance."

Harris looks crestfallen and I try not to cheer at Emmylou's oblivious nature. Emmylou looks at me expectantly and I begin to lead us to the kitchen where I imagine Finn and Tye must be.

I'm disappointed to find they didn't even make it to the kitchen. Instead, Finn is wrapped up in her, leaning against the wall, as they snog.

"Finley," I shout, smacking his butt. He jolts back and glares at me. "We're going to dance. Would you like to join us?" I smile at him innocently but Tye cheers and grabs Emmylou's hand, leading them to the dance floor.

"Cockblock."

"Could you even get it up, whiskey dick?"

A snort comes from behind us and we both look back at Harris.

"What are you laughing at? You look like you've never even seen a cowboy on the telly."

Harris frowns at my words and Finn laughs.

"You're supposed to be a cowboy? Oh shit, mate. Tryin' to impress our wee American?" Finn asks.

"Let's just go dance," Harris mumbles.

I roll my eyes at him and turn toward the kitchen to grab drinks. Finn follows behind me.

"I'm getting drinks," I tell him, wondering why he's so close behind me.

"Do you think that lass is Emmylou's mate? Should I ask her if it's okay?"

I snort at his panic and grab an unopened vodka, pouring half into my nearly empty water bottle. I'm not exactly a good party guest to invite.

"Go ask her," I say, taking a drink from my bottle. It goes down like water and I frown at the implications. Maybe I should slow down.

Finn looks away excitedly and goes to grab Emmylou. Harris is awkwardly swaying beside her and Tye who are excitedly shaking their hips. Finn says something and hauls Emmylou away. I send a cocky smirk and a wink at Harris before turning to follow them into the bathroom.

I really shouldn't pretend he and I have a competition. For one, Kirsty would skin me alive if she knew I considered a bird a prize, and, secondly, there is no competition. Emmylou is straight and I'm just stirring the pot. Or maybe I'm pissing all over it.

"What's up?" Emmylou asks, sitting on the bathroom sink when I close the door behind the three of us. I try not to think about how last month I had a different bird on that counter top.

"Would you be upset if I slept with your friend?"

"Given her consent, obviously," I add, leaning against the door.

"Aye, obviously. If she said aye, would it be okay?"

Emmylou laughs and shrugs.

"Sure, whatever. I mean, you're gonna tell her it's just a hookup, right?" He nods enthusiastically. "Then yeah, you're an adult. Whatever."

She glances over at me as I drink from the bottle. I hand it over and she takes it gladly.

"Oh my God, Saatchi, what if I can't actually get it up tonight?"

Emmylou coughs on the drink, but I'm not sure if it's the vodka or the comment. I take a deep breath, realizing I'm going to have to pull out my wee radge demon to get Finn's head on straight.

"Mate," I shout, grabbing his shoulders fiercely. "You are a fucking God. You've shagged half the birds in Edinburgh." Quite frankly, I'm concerned we should be getting him tested more often than twice a month. "You've fucked three lasses in one night and two at once—"

"Three, actually, that one time."

"Exactly!" I push his chest. "You're untouchable."

"Aye!"

"You're the best shag any girl's ever had!" I push again, harder.

"Aye!"

"You're gonna go out there! Tell her you want to hook up, get her consent, and rock her fucking world!" I push him once more and he pushes me back and we start to yell at each other. I can see Emmylou staring at us, eyes wide, from the corner of my eye, her mouth glued to the straw.

Finn pushes me back far enough and I back away as he does a roar of excitement. I follow his lead and join.

"Go Finn," Emmylou cheers.

"You got this, mate!"

"Hell yeah I do! I'm the best."

I can blame my slow reflexes on the alcohol. I'm a second too late in grabbing Finn's arm before he's swinging at the bathroom mirror. Instead, I grab Emmylou around the waist and haul her off the sink as Finn blinks owlishly at the shattered bits.

"Berry?" I ask her as I set her down. She nods slowly, and I turn back to Finn before bursting into laughter.

"Now you've done it mate! We'll have to go back to the flat and stitch that up. Tell your little lass goodnight and use your left hand tonight," I say through my guffawing laughter.

Finn stares at me in shock, clutching his hand before he slowly begins to laugh along.

"Oh, y'all really are a lot together," Emmylou says from behind me. I turn and look at her. She's still attached to the straw.

"Woah, slow down there, lass," I tell her, letting my laughter die down. She looks at the cup, surprised, seemingly having forgotten of its existence.

"We're a right mess," I say, looking around. There's blood on the ground and Finn is frowning down at his hand in annoyance.

"Finn. What are we supposed to do?" I ask, and he finally looks up at me and takes a deep breath.

"That's it. We've ballsed it up. I have to pick out the glass and clean it. Or we could pour that vodka over it and wrap it in a towel?" I smirk at him and shake my head at the prospect of his going around a party with his hand in a towel just to shag a bird. "S'pose let's go then."

I turn to Emmylou who is now leaning against the door, eyes slowly closing in exhaustion. I can hear the sink behind me as Finn rinses the blood from his hand.

"Em, you want to go with us? You're looking a wee gone."

"Yeah," she slurs, and I hold back a chuckle.

"Le's go home then."

# Chapter Eight

Night Falls.
Darkness Encompassing.

I hate it here,
My brain is cruel.

Dusk Breaks.
Darkness Lingers.

*Saatchi*

I watch the snow fall across my window as my alarm goes off. I feel unerringly numb while it blares under my pillow. It keeps blaring as I stare at the snow, limbs heavy from disinterest.

The alarm stops, and I look at my hand as it turns the mobile off. The body I'm in tries to register panic but my brain is disconnected; floating like a snowflake with no clue where it's going and no desire to know. The only thing I feel is the sweeping numbness that fills the crevices of my soul and covers me like the cocoon of my blanket.

My head is empty as I stare out the window. I let the hours pass, empty but heavy.

*Emmylou*

It's snowing today and I tip my head up as Harris and I walk out of the building.

"It doesn't snow where I live in Texas." Which is mostly true, though sometimes we get flurries that melt as they hit the ground.

"Don't get too excited. It's still early in the year, probably won't stick," Harris says, bundling his scarf tighter. He's just rounding the end of his soccer season and I'm grateful I won't have to sit through any more matches huddled under a blanket or an umbrella.

I start to walk toward the indoor gym where I'm meeting Kirsty for yoga. Harris trudges through the slush beside me as he heads toward practice.

"Emmylou, you remember when we talked about hanging out?"

I lift my eyebrow at him; Saatchi has good habits and I'm not ashamed to steal them.

He laughs awkwardly. "Well, are you free after practice?"

Since it's the weekend, I don't have to worry about homework, but I'm not sure if the group has plans.

"I'm not sure, let me check." I pull up the group chat, now named *The Chest Burster from Alien looks like a Penis*, courtesy of Saatchi.

**The American: Are we doing anything tonight?**

**Fuckboy: Aye! Always**

**Sai: No. Give me rest.**

No one else responds and I ignore the battle going on between Sai and Finn.

"I should be free," I tell him brightly before sending another message in a separate chat box.

**Emmylou Humford: Is everything okay??? You weren't at lunch**

I've already sent Saatchi two messages but they haven't even been delivered. I look up at Harris as he starts talking again. We solidify plans for hot cocoa and part ways.

Kirsty is rolling out her mat on the wooden floor as I walk in after changing. I roll out my own mat. I made sure to buy one that wasn't covered in sunflowers. If Saatchi caught me with another sunflower-themed belonging, she'd absolutely tear into me for it. This one has little cartoon highland cattle that I found at a tourist store. I think of Saatchi's cows, one red and one black, as I stretch.

I wish I could go see her farm. I miss the Texas heat, but Scotland has much more lush greenery. Besides, that farm is filled with bitter memories and a version of Emmylou that doesn't exist anymore. Now I'm a criminal and yell at strangers with Saatchi and get drunk at parties. Soon I'll be drunkenly getting tattoos with Finn—Drew insinuated that Saatchi and Finn have matching butt tattoos.

Scotland is giving me a better idea of what I want from my life. I think I'll pick my major for the next semester. I think I might block my mother from my social media accounts. It was scary leaving home, but, so far, it's been so much easier than I ever thought. It feels like nothing could go wrong.

"Sorry about making your first protest stressful," Kirsty says as we roll up our mats. I grab a towel to dry off my neck.

"No, it's fine." I bite my lip as I put the mat into my sling. "I was kind of stressed at first but, well, Saatchi actually made me feel better." *She does that a lot actually*, I think.

"Really? Saatchi? When did you talk to her?"

"Oh, just at the party," I say, lying poorly. She sizes me up but doesn't say anything.

"Are you and Saatchi friends then?" she finally asks once we're walking out of the yoga studio.

"Uh . . ." I'm saved from a response when my phone starts to ring with a WhatsApp call in my pocket. I awkwardly pull it out and motion to it, turning away from Kirsty. She smiles and waves goodbye, parting ways with me and heading toward the art studio.

"Emmylou! Darling, I was just looking at tickets to go visit you in Scotland."

I laugh at my dad's boisterous voice that I've only heard sporadically since being in Scotland. He's fibbing, of course; he knows I'm coming back for Christmas break. I tell him as much and he complains.

"It isn't soon enough. I just can't help that I miss you so much already! How are all of your friends? And classes? Have you decided to move back? You could go to Texas A&M and just be half an hour from your old man."

"Oh my gosh Pa, chill. My friends are good, I'm actually hanging out with Harris today in a bit. I think I've got an idea about my major—Saatchi actually kind of pointed it out to me."

"I always knew I liked Saatchi. You should bring her to visit during winter break."

I laugh again. "Saatchi? In Texas? Lord, I can't even imagine it. She'd dry up in that heat."

"Hmm, well as long as you know she's always welcome and so are you. You know that right? No matter what, I'll always love you and be proud of you." I bite the inside of my cheek as an unexpected wave of emotion envelops me.

"Sap, you're gonna make me cry," I complain but he just laughs. I can imagine him in his office, cowboy boots propped on his glass desk, fidgeting with his hat. He's so stereotypical but I love everything about him.

"Hey, Emmylou?"

"Yeah Pop?"

"I hope you're happy out there. I miss you a lot but I'm glad you're living how you want. Your hair looks cute on that picture app and so does that little friend Saatchi of yours."

"Christ dad! Don't hit on my friends!"

"That's—that's not what I meant. Forget it. I love you. Be safe."

I laugh at his stuttering and sigh to myself once he's hung up.

Feeling lighter on my feet, I head toward the apartment to get ready to hang out with Harris. Maybe I could convince him to go dancing afterward.

The cold bites at my nose and my duck boots stomp through the slush. I'm sure the curls I took time to do this morning are frizzy, but I find I don't mind as I look up at the snowflakes. My pa would love this. He had to visit Alaska a few times for business and he'd always bring Janey and I jars of water. "I brought you back snow," he'd say and we'd laugh as we sloshed around our jars of water.

My train of thought stops as I find Saatchi sitting on the curb in front of our apartment, cigarette in hand, fingers slowly trailing through the slush. She doesn't have so much as a coat on.

"Saatchi," I say quietly as I hunch beside her. "Are you okay?"

She looks up at me, her eyes distant. "God laughs at me." Is all she says before turning away and inhaling at the stick.

I turn and walk toward the apartment angrily. She can be such an idiot sometimes. I understand she gets in these moods. I've seen flashes of them at the bar or when she reads a sad poem in the library and ends up staring out the window for the rest of lunch. Eyes just as empty as they are now.

I burst into her apartment, startling poor Anne Bonny. I pat her gray fur apologetically before continuing to Saatchi's room. There's a bloodied knife on her bedside table and I feel a chill go through my body. Not a mood then. Maybe more serious than that. I grab one of her hunter-green hoodies and a black coat. I stop at the door, trying to remember if she had shoes. Deciding she does, I continue into Finn's room.

His room smells like any college boy's room, so I hold my breath as I open the bathroom cabinets, avoiding the lube, and grabbing the first aid kit and the bottle of hydrogen peroxide he keeps beside it.

I race back downstairs, hoping I won't have to call Finn to ask if he knows how to do stitches. Saatchi is still sitting there, but she's pulling another cigarette from a box. I angrily whip it out of her hand, expecting a battle, but she just stares at me before dropping her head to look again at her fingers dragging through the dirty slush. Shoot. I forgot gloves.

"Lemme see," I say, grabbing her hand so I can see her wrist. She hands me the right one instead, numbly, still looking down. There's jagged, bloody marks on it and I swallow hard.

Even with the first aid classes I took with Drew, my hands shake as I pour hydrogen peroxide over the cuts.

"Saatchi," I whisper as the blood clears from the cuts. Some are shallow, barely breaking skin but three of them make me cold to the bone. They're deep and I squeeze my own hands to steady them.

"I can't tell if they need stitches," I say, staring at the torn and battered phoenix.

"Do you see fatty tissue? It's yellow," she says, emotionless.

"No."

"Then it's fine."

I search her face but can't find anything. With shaking hands I pull out my phone and call Finn.

"'Lo! Howzit Emmylou?"

"Finn, how deep before a cut needs stitches?"

Saatchi lights up another cigarette and looks into the snow; almost like she'd face plant into it if she could.

"Is it Saatchi?" Finn asks, tinny over the phone. "I'll be there soon. If the bleeding's stopped she's probably fine but I'm on my way," he says before ending the call.

One of the deeper cuts is still weeping droplets of blood, so I fish out what I need from the first aid kit, hands still trembling.

"Saatchi," I start when she's all patched up, the hoodie I grabbed wrangled onto her and the coat thrown over her shoulders. "Why did you do that?"

"To see if I could still feel something."

"And can you?"

She shakes her head.

I grab the back of her neck, with weight but not to hurt.

"Can you feel this?"

She looks up at me, really looks at me. Her eyes having some sort of recognition. She nods.

"You're fine, Saatchi, you just have to come back. Just feel my hand, yeah?" She nods again and I look away. "And you feel the wet floor?" She shakes her head so I grab a pile of slush from the ground with my free hand and drop it down her back. She inhales sharp. "Feel that?" I ask, frustrated, and she lets out a hollow laugh.

"Aye, Lou, aye. I felt that."

"Good, cause I've never been in a snowball fight," I say, quickly standing up and grabbing a handful of slush off of a car and throwing it at her. She gasps and looks at me incredulously. I stare at her waiting, unsure if that was the right thing to do. But in a flash she's up, flinging straight slush at me.

"It's not even snow," she shouts at me when I pelt her with another slush ball, ducking behind a car. She doesn't laugh as she chases me around the car, but she's slowly coming back to her body; relearning her limbs and the way they connect to the rest of her.

I stand across from her, peering at her above the SUV, but she's taller and she pushes the slush from the roof across and it all lands on me. I squeak, and in my moment of weakness, she's moved around the car and grabs me around the waist, lifting me up. She gasps in pain, and her left arm quickly releases me.

"That's where I would've dropped you into a snow pile, but I'd just break your head."

Her breath is right in my ear and my chest aches at the lingering hollowness of her voice.

"Sorry," I say, turning around in her grasp. She's warm against the biting wind. "I don't know if that's the type of distraction you needed."

"Normally, Finley just makes me play video games, but next time I'll show him snow works better."

I let out a shocked laugh, surprised she can make jokes with the type of day she's had, and rest my forehead below her shoulder when I can't bear to hold myself up any longer.

A voice coughs behind us and I slowly turn, still laughing, to see Harris standing there. Saatchi's arm drops, but I nudge her with my shoulder and smile up at her.

"Sorry, Harris, I was a bit distracted by this hooligan. Let me go up and change real quick so I'm not soaking wet while we hang out." I turn to Saatchi. "Do you want to come with us?" I ask her but she shakes her head. "Would you like my gloves while you wait for Finn at least?"

"No your hands are too small, lass," she says, putting her hand up for proof. "'Sides, Finn will be here soon anyway."

"I could just reschedule," I suggest. She looks up at Harris and shakes her head.

"Okay," I say, turning slowly, reluctant to leave and walking up the stairs to change. My hair is a mess but I'm out of time so I just undo it from the braid and throw it into a messy bun. I change my wet clothes into something more comfortable. *Dancing is definitely out*, I think as I toss on leggings and comfy, faux-fur lined boots.

I'm surprised to see Saatchi and Harris still outside. Saatchi's tongue rolling around her canine and Harris's brow scowled.

"You sure you're okay?" I ask Saatchi one last time, grabbing her hands and stepping between her and Harris's face-off.

"Aye, things just happen sometimes."

I'm not sure if self-harm is really a "thing that just happens" but I squeeze her hands and turn toward Harris.

"Do you mind if we wait for Finn," I say, not actually caring if he minds. Saatchi scoffs behind me, but I ignore her petulance as Harris agrees. It's awkwardly quiet as I stand beside Saatchi waiting but, luckily, Finn's there in just a handful of minutes.

I hug Saatchi tightly but she shoos me away before I can say anything.

"Enjoy your date," she says, and I roll my eyes at her teasing.

"Let me know if you need me."

She lets out a quick puff of air but turns toward Finn and the apartment without another word.

I feel guilty for leaving, but I also know that Finn knows her better. Nothing I do will really be of benefit and she's probably better off without me.

I look over at Harris. He's dressed in a nicer coat than I've ever seen on him and his hair isn't in its typical messy fashion but combed back instead.

"Well aren't we dapper today," I say, patting down his hair. He laughs and rubs the back of his neck, cheeks red like a tomato from the cold.

The café is just kitty-corner from us and he only responds once we're across the street.

"I just thought I'd look nice for our—"

He's cut off right as I open the shop door and enter to the warm smells of pastries and chocolate. It's the perfect day for a warm drink and sugary sweet. I tell Harris as much but he smiles uneasily. I wonder if he and Saatchi exchanged words because he seems rather nervous.

"So, what's Texas like?" he asks as we stand in line. I'm peering over the glass counter like a child but I pause to look up at him.

"It's hot and where I live there are huge farms with lots of cows. There's lots of football, American football I mean, and lakes to swim in. Hardly ever gets cold." We step to the counter and he orders a hot cocoa and looks expectantly at me. "Oh! You don't have to pay for me," I say, but at his insistence I go ahead and order—still just a college student after all. I'll take free food where I can get it.

I grab my fruit tart and large hot cocoa and find us a booth. Harris, surprisingly, sits right next to me. I awkwardly stare at my fruit tart as I feel his arm brush against mine. I guess when we study at the coffee shop, he always sits in the chair next to me, but that feels different. I don't like feeling boxed in by him. Just a few weeks ago I would have taken it in silence, but now I've learned to put my foot down, thanks to the three strongest women I know.

"Could you sit over there? I don't like feeling boxed in."

Drew once told me that women should never apologize. She was raised solely by her father after her mother left them. Her father always needed to be taken care of because he worked so much—hence her maternal side—but he did teach her to stand up for herself and never let any man tell her what's what.

Harris looks at me with wide eyes before awkwardly shifting to the bench across from me and apologizing. I can't figure out what's suddenly changed between us but the air is stiff with a burdensome feeling. I wish I had stayed playing in the slush with Saatchi.

"Do you like the pastry?" Harris asks after I've bitten into it.

I nod my head, covering my mouth before responding.

"Yeah, I always love sweet things, and fruit adds a nice extra natural sweetness."

"Aye, any other favorite foods or local places you'd like to try?"

"Actually, yeah! Finn and I were talking about checking out this American burger place that opened up. He says he needs me there to see if it's legit. I doubt it will be because in the UK, and most other countries don't put sugar in their bread like we do in America." I know the history behind this fact but I bite my tongue. Finn says my history monologues are boring; I think Saatchi just puts up with them.

"I didn't know that, how come?"

I grin at him before going into the details of how WWII caused a bread demand and sugary bread was cheaper to make, then the corporations took over, and now Americans can't stand having low-sugared bread. It's all just about comfortability at this point.

After all is said and done and I've talked about bread for a while, our cocoas are empty and I go to stand, anxious not to miss out on whatever is going on tonight.

"Maybe we could take the longer route?" Harris asks as we exit the shop. I look back at home but agree despite the biting cold and growing concern for Saatchi.

"Have you started on the final paper?" I ask him as I huddle against my coat.

He gives me a tight-lipped smile.

"Uh, aye, I have. Are you stressed about it? Do your parents put a lot of pressure on you?"

I blink owlishly at him as we continue to walk the streets. It's out of left field and the probing question makes me suspicious.

"No more than anyone else's I suppose. What about yours?"

"Yeah, actually. Berry, that is. I've got an older brother and he's brill. Like, seriously a genius. My parents are pretty vocal about letting me know I don't live up to the bar he's set."

He looks away from me and I feel guilty for bringing up his family issues to avoid my own.

"Oh, I'm sorry. You've helped me a ton this year because you're really smart too, so don't let them tell you otherwise." He shrugs but smiles down at me. "Also, you're a hotshot soccer player. They've gotta be proud of that, right?"

"Eh, actually, that's part of the reason they're so disappointed. They thought I should've quit and focused on my grades. I hardly played this year so maybe they're right."

"No, don't say that," I start, grabbing his forearm. "You played this year and I'm sure next year you can take some senior's place."

"Ha, I kind of want Finn's spot, if I'm being honest." He awkwardly rubs his neck and I grimace. Finn's spectacular and I would rather see Finn on the field than Harris, but I don't want to rub dirt in the wound.

"I had a really good time tonight," Harris says, breaking the awkward silence as we walk through the hills, lit up by still open shops.

"Ha! Yeah, if by that you mean listening to me talk about bread."

"Nah, I think it's cute," he says, grabbing my hand.

I look down at his hand in confusion and watch him slowly intertwine his fingers with mine.

Then it hits me. It hits me all at once like a train rambling through College Station at the worst possible moment.

I, Emmylou Humford, am the dumbest person alive. This entire night, I've been on a date. Of course, the way he dressed up, the fact he bought my cocoa; Lord, he even sat on the same side of the booth as me. Now here he is, tangling his fingers with mine and I am struck speechless.

I'm on a date. He's holding my hand. I didn't know this was a date. I am an idiot.

As I panic, left hand gripping hard at my sweater, we quietly walk toward my apartment. He runs his thumb over my knuckles and I hold back a squeak as I internally flinch. I can't believe the situation I've gotten myself into, and I panic silently as we approach my safety.

Stopping in front of my apartment, I realize I have more to fear when he doesn't immediately let go of my hand. Where are my Drew super-powers when I really need them?

"Listen," he starts. "I really like you and I get the feeling you like me too—" I choke on my tongue. "But I think you should probably talk to Saatchi."

I physically reel back at the unexpected change of topics, suddenly too surprised to worry about our hands intertwined.

"Wait, what?"

"Well, I mean, you should let her know that we're getting serious. It's obvious she's pining after you."

Not only am I on a date, but I'm on date with a dickhead.

"Are you—what? Harris," I flounder. I pull back my hand and put my head in it instead. Maybe if I close my eyes long enough, this will have all been a bad nightmare. "What are you even talking about?"

"Saatchi," he says, hesitantly looking up at the apartments. "I just think she fancies you."

I stare at him aghast.

"I—we're just friends." I leave out that I only think of Harris as a friend as well.

"Well, aye, but does she know that?"

I laugh in hollow shock and shake my head at him.

"I'm gonna go," I tell him, backing away.

"Wait." I bite my lip and stop moving. "Sorry, maybe I shouldn't have said anything." It's an effort not to unleash my sarcasm. "But, uhm, I was hoping we could—well, there's this thing for football . . . maybe you could be my date. I mean, if I haven't sent it all balls up."

Men really do have the audacity.

"I should go. Drew's probably done with dinner. Goodnight." And with that, I shut the door to the apartment behind me.

*Saatchi*

I listen to Emmylou shut the door of the building and slam my head against the wall. I feel guilty for leaving my window open to listen when I saw them get back, but now I know I'm really fucked.

Of course Harris would pick up on it. And of course Emmylou thinks of me as only a friend.

I feel so disgusting. It's like this day will never end and I'll forever be in this cycle of numbness and self-hatred.

"Saatch," Sai says once it's clear Harris has left. He closes the window and sits beside me. "It's nothing to be embarrassed about. People have unrequited crushes all the time."

"Feels worse when your queer," I tell him, and he wraps an arm around me.

"Yeah, well, it shouldn't. Just keep being her friend and time will put you with the right person."

I don't know how to tell him that she feels like the right person. Someone who knows nothing about running but everything about color coordination. Someone who laughs like the sun and screams at the sky. Someone who patches me up with acceptance and no questions but knows exactly how to level me out of a slump. She's everything I wanted and didn't know I needed.

"Still sucks," I say instead, and he hums in agreement, rubbing my shoulder.

"I didn't even know you liked the bird. When do you guys even talk?"

"Lunch, in the library," I say, leaning into his arm.

"Oh, that's why," he mumbles. "I had no idea."

"Aye, well, felt like if I pretended I didn't, I wouldn't."

He exhales heavily beside me.

She means so much to me. But I'll never mean as much to her.


*Emmylou*

"Emmylou? You're not serious."

"Dead serious, Janey. Like a full out, full blown date and I had no idea."

My sister squeals and I land backward on my bed with a thump. It's easier talking to her now than it was at the beginning of my time here in Scotland. After I called her in the beginning to complain about loneliness, I dodged a few of her WhatsApp calls and resorted to texting. Janey never seemed to have any problems in college, and I'm still too ashamed to tell her how anxious I was at first.

"Well? Was it good at least?"

I pause, coming back to our conversation about my not-date with Harris and realize the thought hadn't even crossed my mind. I've never felt that way about Harris, never even thought to feel that way about him.

"I'm not sure. How did you know you had a crush on Eric?" I can imagine her looking at her ring now, feet propped in his lap in their apartment.

"Well, I had butterflies and he had me blushing. You know? All that stuff that made me feel nervous. But then, it was calmer. Like when you lay out in a field, the wind rustling the grass, sun hitting you just right. That homey feeling."

"Oh. Well I guess it felt awkward?"

She huffs out a breath.

"Nah, that ain't it. Guess it's on to the next man then. I'm sure there's some athletic man up there with tattoos and a bad boy personality."

I laugh; her fiancé is a nerd who likes architecture and anime. Even then, he's still up to mother's standards. I once told Janey, in confidence, that I would marry someone who was the opposite of what mother wanted. I'm not sure if I meant it—even being so far away from her I still constantly feel her influence on me even if her voice is now interrupted by Drew's and Saatchi's.

I hear her in the morning when I get dressed or when I decide on a muffin and a bag of chips instead of a salad. I hear her when a soccer player nods at me in passing through the campus and when my friends curse. But now I also hear Drew, always saying I need to eat more and eat with the intention of happiness. And Saatchi, her fuckall attitude giving me the strength to forego the coverup and instead wear the low-cut dresses I've always wanted to.

"Even if there was, I think Saatchi would scare them away. Also, speaking of her. Harris said the shittiest thing today after the non-date." She hums in question. "He said that Saatchi has a crush on me."

"Oh, well . . . I mean, does she?"

"No way! She's like . . . no, just, I don't think so."

We're silent for a beat, then two, then three.

"You should find out."

"What? How?" I ask, sitting up in my bed.

"Oh just, like, feel what vibe she's putting down. You know? Like, does she make a lot of eye contact? Or maybe, grab your arm unnecessarily? Does she gravitate toward you?"

"You're insane, Janey," I tell her, laughing off the idea. "If that were it, she'd have a crush on Finn; they're glued at the hip."

"Whatever you say, small fry. Hey, but listen, I gotta go. We're getting lunch with Eric's parents but I'll talk to you later! Love you lots."

My phone clicks, ending the call.

I wonder if Saatchi feels anything romantic toward me. Does she think about me throughout her day? Or right before bed? Does she get excited at the prospect of having lunch with me? Does she put on a specific outfit because she knows I'll tease her about it, or hope my eyes linger a little more than usual? Does she bring me up to her brother and ask what he thinks?

I can't imagine Saatchi lovestruck. Besides, none of those things mean anything even if she does do them. I know, because I do it all the time, and I don't have any romantic feelings toward Saatchi.

# Chapter Nine

Exhaustion creeps in so tightly.
I'm a swaddled babe
Tucked in nightly.

Give Light to the Anger then.
Mirrored in frustration—
a purposeful end.

"Have you been stretching?" Sai asks while rolling out my calves. I simply glare back. He watches me do it every day. "Shut it. Eating well?" I nod. "Sleeping well?" Nod. "Drinking water?" Nod. "No booze?" Nod. "Cigarettes?" I hesitate, then nod, but I know I've been caught when he bats me in the head with the roller. "Fucking idiot. How are your times?"

I look guilty over at Finn, who pauses studying to look guilty over at me. We still haven't told Sai or anyone—other than Emmylou. My slipup is enough to let him know something's up.

"Whassit? What don't I know? Are they bad?"

I shrug at Sai but he holds out his hand anyway.

"Nah, 'm not showing yous."

He impatiently wiggles his hand.

"Just—" I look at Finn and he grimaces. "Just don't freak out."

"Cor', now lemme see."

I hand Sai my phone. I watch him put down the roller and unlock it, immediately opening my running logs. His mouth drops and I feel my stomach drop with it. I might boke.

"Saatch. Christ have mercy," he lets out in a whisper.

The thing about my times is, they've gotten more consistent. I'm not sure if that one run unlocked something within me but ever since it feels easy to match them. Easier still to consistently get Olympic qualifying times. I'll never be the best, but I've never really wanted to be. I just want to run. And watching Sai double and triple check my times versus the Olympic times means I've lost this fight. I've already sent my coaches my times. They've already responded with training programs and requests to drop out of school. I told them I'd decide once the semester ended.

It's too close. If I drop out, I'll have to go to a training center. Maybe they'll stick me on a mountain where my lungs have to relearn to breathe. I'll sit in some room all day bored out of my mind thinking about my new diet and my exercises. I'll dedicate every second to training and then I'll qualify; realistically, that'll be easy. Then I'll compete. All over the world. All the time.

And probably, at the end of that, I'll be hundreds of thousand of pounds in debt. Maybe I'll win a medal or maybe I'll get injured and not even compete. Maybe I'll be away from my friends for so long that they'll be gone and graduated by the time I get back. But maybe, just maybe, I'll stand on a podium, on National TV, with a gold medal around my chest.

But, realistically, do that many people even watch the marathon event?

"What are you going to do?" Sai finally asks once he's stopped mimicking a goldfish.

"I don' know. They want me to quit uni. Can't even be bothered to think about how far in debt I'd be to have coaches." I bury my head in my hands. "Maybe Olympics are for the modern-day gods. Rich folks who haven't lived below the poverty line their whole lives and aren't scared to live there again. I can't bank on sponsors; nobody wants an Indian Scot with a crooked nose and gnarled teeth." I roll my tongue over the canine that never sits right to emphasize my point.

Sai looks back down at my phone. He knows I'm right. It will be hard on my wallet, but it'll be even harder on my mental health.

"Maybe when qualifiers come around we can think about it then," Sai whispers, and I look over at Finn. Ever since Sai gave up on his dreams, he's become too fixated on mine. Or at least, whatever he's decided are mine.

"This is exactly why I didn't want to tell him!" Finn watches me angrily type out a text back to Sai, telling him to sod off. This is the third coach he's sent me and he's even created an estimated cost excel sheet. It's over fifteen thousand pounds. A year.

"Do I look like I shit gold bars?"

Finn shakes his head and grabs my phone from me.

"Just take a breather for the opening of Kirsty's gallery, yeah?"

Kirsty, the goddess amongst our group of inadequate, has secured two weeks in the corner of a gallery. All on the human body in love. It was going to be contrasting personalities but it turns out none of us would actually let her expose our faults. Finn and I are skipping lecture to see it as soon as it opens. About ten minutes ago, I was excited for it. Now I feel like I might set the building on fire with my rage alone.

"Oi, Emmylou texted you."

I peer over Finn's arm. Sai said she'd come looking for me while I was out running. I'm glad I wasn't around to hear her talk about how great her date was. She'd probably blush prettily as she talked about how fit Harris is. I wish, so deeply in my soul, that everything she did wasn't so damn pretty. Or gorgeous. Or damn near breathtaking. I'm fucked.

"Eh, I'll see her later. Don't respond," I say, holding the door open to the gallery. Kirsty texted us earlier to let us know we could wear whatever, but I feel sorely unprepared in my double-socked Doc Martens and paint-splattered pants. Finn looks worse, wearing sweats amd an anime sleep shirt, two sizes too large, under a homeless-looking coat. Christ, did he even try today?

"I look like a vagrant hoping for a place to sleep," he says before looking over at me; I sneer impolitely at the lady at the front desk. "You look like an anarchist," he says as I turn away from her. After I was arrested freshers year protesting with Kirsty—a sexual assault case pushed under the rug—everyone banned me from protests. Apparently, activism can ruin your chances at the Olympics. Well, that, and I did technically tackle a pig and yell at him that he probably beats his wife. Mam says I'm just too heated for activism. Says I should stick to writing poems in blood and pushing them under the Dean's door.

"Maybe I should get back into that," I say, thinking of the rush it gives me to unlock full freedom. Finn grabs my shoulder and leads me towards Kirsty's corner of the gallery.

"Let's try not to bail anyone else out of jail this year," he says as we reach Kirsty.

She's made good use of her limited space, filling it up to the ceilings with sketches. Finn says something to her but I'm drawn towards the sketches. There I am, smiling as Anne Bonny licks my nose, laid on my back in our living room. The marker below it says *A Supporting Love: She sits with her emotional support animal as they both show their love and appreciation for each other's existence.*

Kirsty had asked me if I was okay with the details earlier in the year but seeing it now makes me long for the comfort of my cat, despite having cuddled her this morning under the covers. It's been about five hours since I've seen Anne but I miss her. I hope she's having a warm nap in the sunlight that streams from the window.

The sketches are all quick lines that create intense detail—from the shadow my bent nose creates to the finger that sits a little crooked since reattachment, as it's wrapped around a book in another sketch. I spot Finn and I fighting over a bowl of scran: *A Platonic Squabble for That Which We Love.* No further description. There's one of Sai, clearly lying in bed after a night with Kirsty. Finn grinning after a match of footie. Drew flirting with death as she flambés a dessert.

I barely withhold my groan when I find a sketch of Emmylou. I wish I could claw her out of my soul. Instead, there she is, smiling at something else Kirsty didn't sketch. Kirsty, God damn her, captured the soft twinkle in Emmylou's eyes and that soft smile she gives when she thinks no one is looking. I'd give anything for Emmylou to smile like that for me. But she never will, and I'm forced to starve off a demon growing in my chest.

"Oh Saatchi, it's written all over your face."

I turn around to see Kirsty looking at me sadly and Finn over her shoulder, fists coming together slowly.

"It'll fade," I say, looking around making sure none of our other friends have snuck in while I was distracted.

"No, it won't. You're in love."

"Hold yourself. 'M not."

"When," Finn asks, finally speaking up. The damn pity in his eyes makes me feel like I could spit a rocket. I watch his fists envelope him in a hug and take a calming breath.

"I don' know. It's like an illness. You think it's just a cold and you'll get better but then you're on your deathbed." Emmylou is like walking toward Death. I know Death will slash my stomach open with that scythe of his but, I just can't help it. I've fallen in love with her. Every damn bit. The shy bullshitty version that is scared of her mam. The nerdy version that drags me to museums to read every boring plaque under each exhibit. The strong version that took to Scotland all on her own and yells at the top of her lungs to be heard. I love her. I'll love her more tomorrow. I'll love her every second. And I fucking hate it.

Saatchi is unnaturally quiet when we go out to grab drinks after Kirsty's art show. It was to celebrate her achievements but she didn't even join us, saying she had to rehash her final piece. Instead it's just Finn and I making small talk while Saatchi tries to drown herself in a pint of beer.

"So, how's Harris? He never told me how the date went."

"Oh, did he tell the team about it?" Finn nods and I suppress a groan. "I didn't even know it was a date," I defend.

"Well, that's embarrassing."

I glare at him.

"For him I mean! Would you go out with him if you knew?"

I had ranted about it to Drew and Kirsty after I had gotten off the phone with Janey and they asked me the same thing.

"I'm not sure. I've never thought of him that way. It was just awkward. Is that what dating is supposed to be like because, if so, don't ever sign me up for that."

Saatchi snorts then and I look up at her but she's already looked away. I wonder if she's having another low day. She doesn't seem low, just quiet. Contemplative instead of dreading being here. Definitely present, just distracted. I follow her line of sight and catch what's distracting her.

There's a blonde at the bar. It isn't Laire but this one is tall and leggy just like Laire. I wonder if Saatchi's only likes dating people taller than her. I've always been short.

Finn says something but I don't hear because suddenly the blonde at the bar is looking back at Saatchi and I watch, almost as if in slow motion, as Saatchi stands and crosses the floor to talk to her.

"Sorry, what was that?" I ask him, peeling my eyes away from Saatchi. I have no interest in watching her ditch us for some random hookup.

"Oh, just that I don' think I'm the best person to give advice on dating." Finn smiles awkwardly. "But he definitely likes you." He shrugs.

"Did he tell you what he said at the end of the date?" Finn shakes his head and I take a sip of my beer. "He thinks Saatchi likes me." His eyes widen and he looks away.

"What a ballbag," he huffs, leaning back. "I hate when straight folk assume she likes any girl she's friends with. That is so aggravating. I knew I didn't like him for a reason." I bite my lip thinking of which bait to take.

"So, uh, you don't think Saatchi likes me?"

Finn turns slowly toward me.

"I don't think I've seen the two of yous exchange words if I'm being honest. Except at the Halloween party and I thought that was just being friendly." His eyes search mine and I look away nervously. Unfortunately, my eyes land on Saatchi just as she's tucking a piece of hair behind the girl's ear and I quickly look away.

"What was that anyways?"

"What do you mean?" I ask him, keeping my eyes pointedly away from Saatchi.

"When did yous become friends?"

"Oh, you know, just during lunch I guess; we mostly hang out then." *And sometimes we go to museums or she sneaks into my room.* She definitely won't be hauling herself through my window today though, because I catch her kissing the girl from the corner of my eye.

"Is she serious right now?" I whip around to Finn, who stares at me with wide eyes.

"What?"

"Like, she's literally supposed to be here with us. Can't she go one night without, I don't know, shoving her fucking tongue down someone's throat." I gesture at them but they're back to talking. And smiling. "Are we not good enough to talk to? She hasn't said a damn word all night but suddenly a fucking barbie doll shows up and it's all fucking smiles for her." I turn back toward Finn, who now has his mouth dropped. "Oh, don't stare at me like that. Saatchi curses all the time. And apparently can't be half-assed to spend time with her friends." I stand up abruptly. "I'm going to the bathroom. You better not ditch me too."

I feel like my skin is stinging with fire and, somewhere in my subconscious, I feel bad for snapping at Finn. But it's true. I'm so frustrated with Saatchi being in this crappy mood and then seeming fine and dandy as soon as she's away from us. She's supposed to be my best friend and I couldn't even talk to her today about the date. It was such a frustrating and embarrassing moment and the one person who's good at making me feel calm and normal won't even bother giving me the time of day.

I swing open the bathroom door and beeline for the mirror. Staring back at me is a red, puffy-faced version of myself. I know I'm vindicated in my anger. This was supposed to be a group outing with friends but only half of us came and then Saatchi ditched us and for some girl. What's the point of having friends if they don't hang out with you and can't tell you what dates are supposed to be like?

I wish I could splash water on my face but even with my waterproof eyeliner I'm afraid everything will smear and I'll look like I've been crying. I'm just about to do it anyway when the door to the bathroom opens gently and Saatchi walks in looking thoroughly cowed.

"Everything all right? Finn said you were . . . upset." I look at her reflection in the mirror as she stands behind me.

"Oh, I didn't realize you could actually talk tonight. Figured you were too busy either ignoring me or sucking face with some rando at the bar."

She scoffs and runs a hand across her face. I can sense her exasperation but all it does is feed my anger.

"Is . . . something going on? You've never been bothered by it before, lass."

"Yes! Yes, alright. Something is going on. You're my best friend. You're supposed to be anyway, and I had an embarrassing and crappy date last night and you never came over. I texted you and left my freaking window open all night waiting for you. I nearly froze to death."

She looks down guiltily but I've picked up speed and there's no stopping me now.

"You ignored all my texts today and now you're ignoring me to go hookup. That sucks Saatchi, so, yeah, of course I'm upset."

She quickly wraps her arms around me and I bury my wet face in her shoulder.

"You're right. I'm shite and I didn't mean to blow you off, lass." She rubs a soothing hand down my back.

"I-I hate Harris. I had no clue it was a date and I'm so embarrassed. I don't even know what I'm supposed to do."

She pulls back and wipes my face with her sleeves.

"What do you mean?" she asks with a soft smile. "If you like him, go out with him. If you don't, just tell him so."

"You make it sound so easy," I say, leaning my cheek in her palm. "I don't know if I like him. I've never even liked a boy. What's it supposed to feel like?"

"Well," she starts, looking down at me. "It feels like a heart squeeze, like they make you feel breathless, like you've never known happiness until them."

I look back into her dark brown eyes.

"Is that how you felt about Laire?"

She sighs and pulls away, resting her back against the door.

"No, not quite anything that strong. I don' know, it was smaller. Like an appreciation but not a longing." She grimaces. "Anyway, we should head back."

"So you can make out with that girl?" I ask bitterly. Saatchi turns back to face me with a searching gaze. I hold steady.

"Well, I don't have to . . . if it bothers you."

I scoff and push past her to open the door.

"No, of course it doesn't bother me," I say, huffing as I sit back at our table. Finn looks between us curiously but Saatchi ignores him.

"Well, what do you prefer?" Saatchi eyes continue their search but I don't respond and, to my joy, she sits beside me.

"So, the Hibs played well last night," Finn says awkwardly.

"The football team?" I ask, willingly taking the bait.

Saatchi turns to me, a grin spreading slowly.

"Did you just call it football?"

I feel my face heat up, and Finn lets out a shocked laugh.

"We'll make a Scot out of you yet, Emmylou," Saatchi says, smiling at me in a way that makes my chest tighten.

"So, what are you doing about Harris?" Saatchi asks later when we're both lying in my bed.

"I'm not sure. I don't think I like him but I'm so inexperienced about it." She hums in thought. "He asked me to the soccer banquet."

She frowns and I hold back a smile at her annoyance. I use football once and I'll never hear the end of it. She catches my smile and frowns deeper.

"So, you're gonna go with him?"

"Yeah, I think it'll help me understand a bit more."

"Aye, guess that makes sense." Her phone vibrates beside her. "I, uh, I'm gonna head to bed," she says, staring at her phone.

"Yeah, okay. Sleep well," I tell her, walking her to the door instead of the window for once—Drew and Kirsty are fast asleep.

"Night," she responds absentmindedly before shutting the door behind her. I lean my head against it and sigh. I'm sure Saatchi will stay up longer doing something with Finn. I know I've been a brat tonight, but I just wish she would've invited me to her late-night shenanigans.

I go to bed, thoughts of heart squeezes running through my mind. Hopefully the banquet will make everything clearer.

*Saatchi*

"Oi, how goes it?" I say once the door opens.

"I knew you'd be back," Laire says smirking before putting her lips on mine. It immediately feels like a battle— Laire trying to prove I need her; myself, unwilling to fall under her crashing waves. Her skin, once the smooth sea on a calm day, now feels gritty like sand under my fingertips as I trace her hips. She bites at my lips and claws at every part of me as she drags me down into bed with her. Once, I saw her as a goddess, her siren song luring me. Now, she's just a

Kelpie, and I'm the dumbass expecting to go for a ride without consequences.

Despite knowing she's here to ruin me, I still let myself drown. I drown in her because back home there is nothing but a different type of pain waiting for me. Laire is an old pain I can wash off, but Emmylou, she's a pain I'd have to claw at my chest until my skin rips, my ribs crack—spreading chips of bone into my lungs, and only then could I wrap my fist around my heart and pull it out. Only then will this pain end.

Laire keeps the pain away. Her hands in my hair and her lips on my neck as I pull down her trousers and shorts. Her sighs in my ear. Her legs around my head. But once she's spilled over my tongue and lit her post coital fag, it all comes rushing back.

I feel heavy disappointment settle into my bones as Laire rests her head against my clothed chest, smoke billowing around us. She isn't who she once seemed to be, and I'm not someone who deserves happiness. I'm disappointed in myself, and regret is a heavy thing to carry when the thing you regret lays in your arms.

"I can hear you thinking up there." She puts out the stick in the ashtray beside her bed. I notice it isn't empty. She only smokes after sex. "Why are you here Saatchi? We both know I'm no good for you." I lean my head in the warm hand that caresses my face.

"Do you remember when we first met?" I ask her.

"In group? Of course." She looks away. "I hated that thing. Sitting in a circle of strangers with the same trauma."

"They told us we couldn't ask each other's names or meet outside of group but you still came up to me that first day. Why?"

She shrugs and rolls off me before relighting the fag.

"You know why. I was—still am—in that phase. I needed a shag; one on my own terms."

"Then why'd you stay after?" I ask, looking over at her.

"Because you were sweet. You made love to me like you knew I could break. You held me like you cared. You made me feel like I could be everything you thought I was.

"So, I tried to be. But then I realized you weren't broken." I scoff and she looks over. "Or, at least, not as broken. And I needed you to fix me. Obviously, it doesn't work like that and I know that now. But, it was different, I was angry. I still am. I was angry you had a future when I felt like mine had been robbed. I was angry that you seemed fine. I was angry about what happened. I'm sorry about everything I did and keep doing. I wish it hadn't been you I talked to that day; you didn't deserve all the shite that I am."

"But I was."

"Aye, you were. And I'm sorry for that, but I still haven't gotten better. I'm still mad." She looks over at me and I search her blue eyes. They're filled with pain. "But, I'm guessing all that doesn't matter anymore."

"What do you mean?" I ask her.

"Well, just that, you've moved on, right? That wasn't making love. That was help me forget. Trust me, I know that one well."

I roll my eyes.

"Ha! So I'm right. Who is she?"

I drag my hands over my face. Peeking a single eye open, I finally respond, "Emmylou, Drew and Kirsty's new roommate."

Laire drapes her hands over my chest and rests her head on her crossed hands.

"What's she like?"

I rub my eyes.

"Oh, you know. Blonde, long legs. Oh! American."

"Saatchi," Laire says laughing. "You can't date an American. That's, like, blood-traitor or something."

"Eh, well that's fine. I won't date her. She's straight."

Laire gives me a pitying look.

"Well. That's berry. No wonder you're here, lass. But, come on, what's she like? Really."

My heart clenches as I think of Emmylou.

"She's, well, she's a lot of things. Like, she's really shy, but if you get her alone, she's something else. Like the hills, she's free and wild and she yells at tourists and dances at parties. She's not scared to chew me out for being dumb but she doesn't babysit me.

"She gets, like, that little twinkle in her eyes when she talks about something she's interested in—normally history. And she's brave. She's been through shit but she's taken on Edinburgh fearlessly."

"Shite like you and me or like Finn?" Laire asks.

"Eh, more like Finn," I say, running my hands down her spine.

"And you love her?"

"Aye." I sigh and run my hands through my hair. "Fucking sucks, Laire."

"Hmm, s'all right. Love hurts. Ours did."

"Aye, suppose it did."

We fall asleep, both in contemplative silence.

The next morning, I crawl out of Laire's bed and kiss her forehead.

"Bye, Saatchi," she says sleepily but her eyes speak of heartbreak.

"Bye, Laire," I say, and it feels like the last time.

The cold air nips at my skin as I walk back toward the flat. I'm glad it isn't raining but the sun is just starting to rise on the rolling hills of Edinburgh.

I wish my heart would rise with it, but I feel it slip down with the setting moon. Next week Emmylou will be at a banquet with Harris and I'll have to sit there as Finn's date, watching them flirt and hold hands.

Murder me, Emmylou. Grab my heart and rip it out of my chest. It would feel better than this.

I swing open the door to the flat and am surprised to see Sai and Finn seated at the dining table.

"'Lo," I say tentatively. Sai looks livid, teeth grinding, and Finn guiltily picks his fingers.

"Where were you?" my twin asks, and I clench my jaw.

"Out," I respond with a false blasé shrug.

"I checked your location."

There's fire in his eyes and I match it.

"Then why'd you fucking ask?" I snap at him and Finn's hands close into stress balls.

"Why?" Sai stands abruptly and the chair under him tips back. "Because you're an idiot, Saatchi. I feel like I'm constantly having to keep tabs on you—"

"Oh fuck off—"

"If it's not Laire, it's picking up your drunk arse from a party. Or, fuck, are you doing coke again? Jesus Christ, Saatchi. When are you going to pick your life off the floor? Cause I can't do it forever. Next time you take all your damn antidepressants I might not be there to take you to the emergency room."

My mouth drops and I lunge for him.

"How fucking dare you," I yell at him as I swing. My fist connects and explodes in pain as it crashes, bone against bone.

"Well that's where you're headed. You're so irresponsible," he yells, spitting out blood. "No one's going to take you to the Olympics like this."

"I don't want to race in the Goddamn Olympics. I never fucking wanted to but you never listen."

"I never listen?" He scoffs and rubs at his jaw. "I listen to all your bullshit. All the fucking time. But it's all just bullshit. You don't know what you want. You're so fucking dumb you're going to throw away your whole life and end up like da."

I wish I had saved my punch for right then.

"Fuck you," I say, walking away. "Oh, and next time: just let me die."

I slam my bedroom door behind me, and lock it for extra measure, before sinking to the floor as tears begin to fall. Anne Bonny comes and lies in my lap as I suffocate the sobs that threaten to break.

Sai doesn't know anything. He doesn't understand what it was like to hit such a low point that I tried to off myself. He doesn't get that tonight was good for me. He'll never understand because he's the perfect twin. The prelaw major who goes to church every Sunday and never makes mistakes. The only bad thing about him is me.

Anne nudges at me and I slowly stand up. My skin feels like it's crawling with stranger's hands and I move my dresser in front of the door. I scratch violently at my forearm as I fill Anne's food bowl. The darkness has just begun to fill my head but I'm already in the shower, the sins washing away like droplets but the memories unfading.

Anne Bonny suddenly stops weaving between the shower curtains as someone pounds on my door. I turn off the tap with shaking hands and they knock again.

"Saatch, I'm sorry." I throw on a sweatshirt and running shorts, body still wet and shaking. "I said some messed up things and I shouldn't have." I pull on my socks. "It's just, you have to focus on what's impor—"

"Sai," Finn reprimands as I lace up my running boots.

"Listen, I'm sorry. Just, can we talk after mass?" I push back the dresser and open the door.

"I'm not going," I say, pushing past my brother.

"Saatch—" But I've already left the flat. My feet pound down the stairs and I open the door to Edinburgh.

The world is just waking up and it would normally be a calming run but I press start to my least favorite playlist: *When Sai Fucks Up.*

I had felt closure after Laire, but of course Sai ruined the peace within me. But of course he wouldn't trust me. Why would he? I have a history of poor decision-making.

I've made my bed. It's full of sins. I count them every night. And repeat them when I'm lost.

"You've got some nerve showing your face," Drew says when I walk into her flat.

"Can I have a shower and a bag of ice?" I ask, ignoring her. My fist aches from hitting Sai. Drew rolls her eyes and stomps to the freezer. Kirsty walks out of her room and waves slowly.

"You mad at me too?"

She shrugs. "It's your life."

"Exactly," Drew yells, throwing the ice pack at me. "You only get one and you're ruining it. I cannot understand why you can't just try to get better."

"Oh fuck off, Drew," I snap. "I try and I try and I fucking try but it isn't enough for anyone. I have to prance around like this perfect little shite. The next fucking Olympian, pristine mental health, no need to let off steam. If yous are all just going to lecture me about every damn decision I make, then kindly fuck off."

"You know what you need?" I don't want to hear it so I turn away and head into the kitchen. "You need to stop hanging around Finn."

I whip around, venom on my tongue. "You're insane."

"No," Drew yells, poking her finger into my chest. "The two of yous always egg each other on. Go out with him to the bars and suddenly you're back on your bullshit."

"You can't control us like that! Don't involve him. My decisions are my own and I'll make them as I please."

"Right, cause you make the greatest decisions! I seriously cannot believe you fucked Laire last night!" The door opens then and Emmylou stands there, mouth drawn tight.

"God, smite me," I whisper. Drew looks guiltily at the ground as I push my way past her. Emmylou continues to stand by the door.

"Mind moving? Or would you like to tell me what a disappointment I am as well?"


*Emmylou*

I move out of the way and Saatchi stomps past me. Still sweaty from her run, smelling of musk and snow.

"What the hell happened last night?"

I shake my head in confusion at Drew's words. I'm saddened and worse to learn Saatchi left my room to go sleep with her ex, but I won't be part of this. I know how brutally she despises their babysitting and now I can see why. This makes me feel like my own mother is hovering over me. I understand they have good intentions but that doesn't mean it isn't suffocating.

193

"I have no clue how to help her anymore. She won't go to therapy. She won't talk to any of us except Finn. She's refusing to get better," Drew complains.

"Maybe she just wants you guys to trust her," I say with a shrug. I know I'm right. Saatchi's most at peace when they all leave her alone. She's always the most responsive to help if it comes nonjudgmentally.  It's why she always gravitates toward Finn. He's never looked down on Saatchi or held her to this standard. She just is who she is. Nuts and all.

"Maybe you're right," Drew says, looking at Kirsty for confirmation, who just shrugs. "I've always been monitoring my da. Making sure he eats enough, sleeps enough, the whole lot. Sai is the older twin, so he's always felt like he had to look after her and then Finn. Especially cause Finn's family is damn near negligent.

"I just don't understand how we're supposed to when she does this shite. Finn and Saatchi are always in trouble we have to get them out of."

I think back to that night Finn broke the glass and no one knew better. I wonder how many times they've been in situations where they can't ask for help because their friends treat them like this.

"Maybe if you leave them, they'd be able to get out of it on their own," I say.

"How can they grow up if we're always making decisions for them?"

I turn and Sai's leaned against the open door. He has a black eye.

"Saatch is mad. I made Finn cry." He shrugs and then walks over to slump against Kirsty on the couch. She runs a calming hand through his hair.

"We should probably talk to them," Drew says.

"And say what? 'Sorry, we don't trust you but we can try?' That's a load of shite and they know it," Sai says, throwing his hands up in the air in frustration.

"You've never really given them a chance, have you?"

Sai looks at me searchingly.

"Aye, maybe not enough. But, you seem to have given them quite a bit of attention."

My cheeks flare, but I'm not sure what he's insinuating.

"Don't start picking a fight with God next," Drew scolds. "Saatchi sticks to Finn the most perhaps because he doesn't . . . I'm not sure."

"Hover," I fill in testily. "Or judge. Or pressure."

"Okay, I've got it. Thanks," Sai snaps.

I cross my arms at him petulantly.

He looks down at the floor as Kirsty runs a hand over his shoulders. "Aye, I guess I can at least talk to her about what she wants from me."

"I'll go get them," Kirsty stands, giving Sai a kiss on his cheek.

We stand in silence, listening to Kirsty's footsteps. Saatchi finally opens the door after the fifth knock and refuses the talk until Kirsty tells her they just want to apologize.

Drew sits beside Sai as Saatchi walks in, hand already bandaged, and Finn slinks in, face red.

"Close the door. We've disturbed the neighbors enough as is."

Saatchi slams the gaudy orange door hard, glaring at Sai.

"Saatchi, I think it's time I apologized."

She cocks her eyebrow at that.

Finn goes to the kitchen. I hear him rummaging.

"I just don't know what you want from me."

"Oh, fucking berry way to start an apology," Saatchi yells, turning back to the door.

"No wait—" Sai starts and I reach my hand out for her arm, falling short. She flinches anyway but pauses. "I, uh, I meant I don't know because you don't tell me." Sai is also staring down at my hand and I pull it back and tuck it into my cardigan.

"I've told you before. I don't want to run in the Olympics," Saatchi says, turning around slowly.

"Aye, yeah, you're right. You have. I just never listened." He exhales and stands. "I'm sorry. It's just ever since Da . . ." he points to his head. "I've always, well . . ."

"Felt like you needed to suffocate me?"

"Saatchi," Finn reprimands, still in the kitchen.

"I'm just trying to say I'm not da and I shouldn't have been acting like it. You're an adult, Saatchi. You're going to make your own decisions."

I watch him hesitate. We're all thinking about Laire.

"You make your own decisions, and even if I don't agree with them, there's no need for me to express my opinion."

Saatchi slowly plants herself in her kitchen chair as Finn comes back from the kitchen with an ice pack he gives to Sai before sitting on his own kitchen chair.

"I've pushed you to think about running competitively, and I've pushed you to be in a healthy state of mind, but I can't make decisions for you. I want you to be happy. I thought I knew what that would be, but I've obviously just made things worse. I've pushed you away to the point where you feel like you can't talk to me. You're my best friend, Saatch. You always have been. I'm sorry I've been trying to be a father for you when I should have just been your brother.

"Can we work on it—together?"

I'm jealous of Saatchi for having a brother that even cares enough to reach out to her. Saatchi must not understand how grateful she should be because all she does is shrug.

# Chapter Ten

Does it feel like the first blossom in the spring?
Like a ripe mango straight off the tree?
Does it feel like a breath of fresh air?
Like the soil after a recent rain?
Does it feel like the sun after a storm?
Or like a breeze in the summer heat?
Then it could be love.
Perhaps, however, you're in the eye of the storm.

I clip back the last piece of my hair; I've put glitter in it and it shines pink. Finn helped me pick out my dress since everyone else is too busy trying to kiss up to Saatchi.

He seemed mournful. Like he was preparing me for a funeral instead of a date.

"Do you like Harris?" he'd asked me.

"No. Do you like anyone you ever sleep with?"

He shrugged as he hung up another dress.

"Not romantically. Are you going to sleep with him?"

"No."

Maybe it's obvious to Finn I don't like Harris. I wonder if it's obvious to Harris. I'm sure I could learn to like him. I'm sure I could learn to live with him opening doors for me and holding my hand. He's exactly as sweet as any other storybook prince you see on TV. It probably just takes time.

I twirl in my dress. It's marigold, with cut out sleeves and a low-back. I'll freeze tonight, but I'll look good as the cold Scottish air steals my last breath. My shoes are slightly more practical. Water-resistant heeled boots. My toes might still fall off. So be it.

I hear a knock at the door. I'm the only one still home. Kirsty and Sai left for dinner beforehand and Drew has taken Lewis up on his offer at a date.

Harris knocks again on the gaudy orange door, and I give one last twirl before grabbing my onyx peacoat and heading out.

"You look bonnie," he says smiling, holding his arm out. He's shaved his face and combed back his hair. His suit is the same shade of black as my coat and his tie nearly matches my dress, but even a shade off feels like a sham. I guess he didn't know what marigold was after all.

"Thanks," I say, taking his arm as we walk out into the cold November air. It's frigid as we talk about his season and I talk about the paperwork to pick my major. It's all small talk, I learn more about his older brother and tell him about my sister's upcoming wedding. I do well to avoid talking about my mother, and he eventually picks up on it and stops bringing her up.

It's all lovely, the small talk, but it feels stifling. Suddenly, I've found out that this man likes me and everything I do feels analyzed, as if I'm under a microscope. Nothing he does makes my heart squeeze or gives me butterflies.

The banquet is loud with the mating calls of soccer players. Harris aggressively hugs his teammates, testosterone practically palpable in the air. My eyes wander away from the mating ritual and I spy Finn across the hall.

Oh.

The ground has fallen from underneath me. I clutch onto Harris's arm to keep from toppling.

Saatchi is wearing a dress; it's skin tight and shows her toned arms, her muscular legs, her every little bit that she keeps under distressed jeans and the occasional baggy dress.

Saatchi's wearing heels. Her calves are so defined I'm sure sculptors make statues out of them. I'll bet Kirsty paints them every night. I would if I could capture the elegance of every dip; the definition of every line.

Saatchi's wearing lipstick. Bright red. And her lips.

Oh God. Her lips.

The realization that I want to kiss my way up her entire back does nothing to ground me. I want to kiss her lips. I want her strong arms to hold me. I want her. I want her. I've never wanted something so badly in my life.

She's a goddess and I have wanted her for so long. High up on her Olympian Mountain. I could never reach her from here. She's so distressingly out of my league.

"Are you alright?"

I turn toward the voice and am startled to see Harris. I'd forgotten he was here. I'd forgotten he existed. I turn back to see Saatchi, those lips of hers upturned in a smile. Laughing at something Finn said.

"Yeah," I respond shakily. He's thrown me back into reality, and reality is me on a date with this man and Saatchi having recently slept with her ex. In this reality, I'm straight. But, when I think of Saatchi's smooth skin pressed against mine, I can't remember why I ever thought I liked men.

We take our seats for the banquet, Harris pulling out my chair for me. He lays a hand on my shoulder and my spine stiffens at the unwanted touch.

He tries to make small talk with me but my answers are curt and humorless. I'm not trying to be rude, but it's difficult to focus, thoughts of an emerald dress on dark skin drowning out any coherent thought.

"She actually looks nice." I follow Harris's line of vision and spot Saatchi standing to go to the bathrooms. "You've told her aye?" I look back at him in confusion.

"Don't be naïve, Emmylou."

He says my name the way my mother does and, worse, it chokes on his accent.

"She's mad for you, anyone with eyes can see the way she looks at you."

My heart squeezes in my chest and I gasp out a choking laugh when I realize she makes my heart squeeze. Does she actually look at me a certain way? Is it possible to be with her?

"You think she has a crush on me?" I ask him breathlessly.

Harris looks at me, eyes searching.

"I think you should turn her down, if you know what's good for you."

"What do you mean?" I ask, feeling threatened.

"Please, do you think people on the footie team actually like her or anyone in her group? They're just a bunch of poofters. Fags. You don't want to be associated with them. Trust me. Next thing you'll know, Finn turns out to like a cock up the bum. He's already wearing skirts. It's like a contagion—a sickness."

I stare at him in shock.

"Sai's captain next year," I say, confusion at being blindsided by his sudden words keeping me from saying the right thing.

"Yeah, but I'll bet it was a pity vote for the charity case or some ploy to appear politically correct."

I look over at Sai. He's happily chatting with the teammates that surround him. One looks over at Saatchi and says something that makes her laugh.

Despite that Harris is clearly wrong about the team hating Sai and Finn, I can't help but feel that maybe he's right about one thing.

My mother always says the same thing. That liking the same gender is an illness. A disease that has to be corrected. A cry for help that needs fixing, caused by bad parenting and sexual assault and social media.

Maybe I don't like Saatchi. Maybe I'm just jealous of how good she looks in that dress or how athletic she is.

She walks back over to the bar to grab another drink and I watch her silently, gauging if this emotion is something I've been overwhelmed with or mistaken for something it isn't. But my stomach drops when she looks over at me as I realize it isn't a mistake.

Because Saatchi's lips are red and I want them on me. I always have.

As soon as dinner's over, I stand quickly. My dress feels too tight, my shoes too tall. I'm sure everyone is staring at me. I'm sure everyone knows. I have to get out of here.

Before I push back my chair, Harris grabs my arm. "Where are you going?"

"The restroom," I lie.

I do my best not to break into a sprint, but by the time I slip out of the doors, I feel like I've run a marathon. The sun has long set and the Scottish air bites at my bare arms that were once protected by the coat that now lays abandoned at the banquet. My heels stagger on the cobblestone. Wind whips my hair painfully against my face but I ignore it. I ignore all of it.

My feelings for Saatchi can't be real. Maybe if I didn't come to Scotland, everything would've been fine. I wouldn't have realized it. It wouldn't have been real. I could've gone my whole life without knowing.

*Saatchi*

I wipe the last of my makeup from my face and look up at my reflection in the mirror. I can't believe I wore heels, I thought it'd be a worse fate than death, but it actually wasn't that bad. It felt basically the same as running up a hill.

"Harris says Emmylou bailed on him," Finn says, propped against my door. He's still wearing his suit. His shoulders fill it out and I reluctantly remember why so many birds on the athletics team are always asking after him.

"Was he being a ball?" He shrugs and cocks his eyebrow. "Yeah, alright. I'll go check on her, I s'pose." He grins and I awkwardly pull on my trainers and look toward the window. "Uhm, don't tell Sai," I tell him before opening my window. Finn grins as I shimmy out of the window.

"Alright, even I'd say this is kind of radge," he tells me as I reach a fist up and knock on the window above me. "'Sides, weren't you going to start telling him stuff now?"

"Aye, but let's not start with dangling myself two stories above death for—"

The window above me opens and I look up at Emmylou. Her eyes seem hollow. Empty almost. I fear the worst and haul myself into her room before she can invite me.

"Are you alright?" I ask her as soon as I'm in her room. She's staring at me like I've grown two heads.

"Saatchi," she says breathlessly. I take a step towards her and she groans, dropping her head into her hands. "Everything is so confusing but it all finally makes sense."

"What? I don' know what you're on about. Did something happen?"

She looks up at me in confusion and I take another step towards her. She looks like she's about to bolt, so I reach out and grab her hand. "You can tell me if something's happened, Lou."

She stares at our hands before finally looking up at me.

"I don't want to be with Harris."

"Why? Has he done something?"

"No—you have." And then she's kissing me.

Not a thought. Not a single thought goes through my brain. I must be stark still because just as suddenly Emmylou is pulling away, a frightened look on her face.

It shocks me back into gear, and I'm wrapping my hand to cup her face and pull her in again.

She tastes like mint. Or honey. Or God.

She kisses like she's never kissed before; earnest and tentative.

She's every sonnet of love. Every moment of joy. Every sunshine that greets the Earth. I'd tear my heart out and give it to her, but, she already has it in the palm of her hand.

Love is so frightening, but as I wrap my arm around her waist and taste her against my lips, I realize I'd face the devil himself if I could have this every day.

She's pulling away and I feel fear before I feel her rest her head on my shoulder.

"Saatchi, I can't be gay" is all she says before breaking out into small sobs. I hold her tight to me and rest my cheek on her head.

I don't know what to say as her tears wet my sweatshirt. I rub my hand down her back and hold her.

"Is it cause of your mam?"

"Yeah," she whispers into my shoulder.

I kind of want to leave. I don't really want to deal with this. The gay guilt. It isn't a comfortable place for any queer person to be.

But I just hold her until she finally pulls away.

"I think I like you."

"Uhm . . ." I mean, she did kiss me. I should feel giddy, but I'm nervous; hands trembling where they hold her waist.

"You give me heart squeezes."

I groan sadly and lean my forehead against hers so as to not stare into her watery eyes any longer.

"So, what now?"

"I don't know."

The morning bird's call is like the baying of an ass,
The Swiss Alp's height is like the width of this sheet,
The French Riviera's color is like the grey Scottish skies,
The Icelandic Geyser's heat is like the tepid ice across Antarctica
All compared to you.
For your hair is the light, kissed by the moon,

Your hands are the warmth, engulfed by the sun,
Your eyes are the kindness, sent down by God.
And your lips,
Oh,
Your lips,
Are the reason I live.
The reason I breathe.
Your lips are a gift made for me.

Saturday morning I'm sneaking into Drew's apartment, knocking on Emmylou's door. I didn't want to pressure her into saying anything else last night and we left things unclear. But, in reality, I'm aching for her. I want to understand what it is I'm supposed to do to make her feel safe—like she can like me.

Does she even like me?

She kissed me, but I could just be an available woman for her to experiment on. She could regret it. Perhaps she drank at the banquet.

This is why I don't get involved with women who aren't sure of their sexuality. It's a tumultuous road of confusion and unclarity.

*You would've loved this a week ago*, my brain supplies. I shush it and knock again, hoping against hope that I won't wake anyone up. After a third knock, I decide maybe I can't even wake her up, and I sneak out again, deciding a text is probably more convenient. Perhaps I was too eager to see her in the morning.

Embarrassed, I crawl back into bed and squeeze Anne Bonny into my chest.

I find that when I take an inventory of my emotions, I'm more angry and annoyed than happy. Had Emmylou never confessed whatever it was she did last night, I could have accepted that perhaps she was just straight. I could have watched her find a man and get married and distanced myself from her slowly. But that's all over now.

By noon, text unread, I decide to go for a run. I feel pent up and thoroughly shamed. Of course she doesn't want to speak to me. She was never ready for that kiss last night and all she's done is drag me down into the turmoil and muck with her. I never realized Emmylou was so selfish, but of course she is.

I'm embarrassed not to have seen the signs of her being so focused on herself. Wasn't lunch always about her? Doesn't she always complain about her mother? What about me? She doesn't know my bags of burden; my cross to bear. She never bothered to ask.

The pace of the run calms me down, and I realize I'm being morally unfair and unrealistic.

She just needs time. It isn't easy for everyone and I should be more understanding, patient for her sake. Her family is clearly not supportive of her actions and it's my duty to pick up the slack—not just as someone who is interested in her but also as someone who is her friend.

But by the time I'm back from my run, the anger has returned. Still no text from Lou.

She can't possibly expect me to be supportive and someone to lean on if she won't even speak to me? This is exactly why I should have never gotten close to her in the first place. I should have just stuck with Finn and flirted with more birds at parties instead of making sure Emmylou was okay. Now here I am, in this predicament with a straight lass.

By evening, I'm fuming and contemplating lashing out by sleeping with anyone I may know. Instead, I go to bed, anger slowly puttering out with exhaustion and giving way to the real emotion: fear.

On Sunday morning, when I still haven't heard from her, I know something's wrong. And that something is me.

"What do you mean you've fucked up?" Sai asks as he sits down beside me Sunday evening when I still haven't gotten out of bed.

"I'm not coming back to uni. I'm going to live with mam and da. I've fucked up Sai."

He gives me a questioning look, and I shake my head so he stays seated.

"You have to tell me what's going on if you want advice. Or not advice. God, I don' know, but what's happening?"

"I kissed Emmylou. Well, she kissed me. And now she won't talk to me.

"Sai, I think I'm going to cry." And then I do.

*Emmylou*

After Saatchi leaves my room, I allow myself a few moments of joy. It finally happened; I've finally figured out why I was so drawn to Saatchi and, even better, it seems she was drawn to me for the same reasons.

She kissed me fervently, passionately. Exactly like what all the storybooks describe. My heart squeezed and fluttered so rapidly I thought I might suddenly stop breathing. It wouldn't have mattered though because she held me tightly in those strong arms of hers. She held me like I would disappear any second.

But I suppose she wasn't wrong about that.

It's still early enough in Texas that I could call my mother. I wasn't sure what I was planning to say, but I let myself build with hope. That little "maybe" that crawls deep into the chambers of my heart.

*Maybe she'll still love me.*

Family is supposed to be there with you always. I don't think my mother would truly cut me out if I told her. Even with everything I put her through while I was in the hospital, she was always there for me. She was there with me during every homework assignment and drove me to every practice and every friend's house. I put all my hope into my mother again, just this once.

She's the only one who needs to say yes to this for me to know it's okay. She's dictated so much of my life and if I could just get an ounce of approval here –just know she loves me enough—then I know it would be okay.

I rustle my head out from under the covers where I've been daydreaming about Saatchi and peek at my phone. I stare at it longer. She hasn't called me since I've moved here, but I guess we both knew eventually one of us would break.

"Yes, Emmylou?"

"Hi momma."

"Dear, I hope this isn't a social call. You know Jeanette's wedding is this summer and I swear there is no end to the planning."

I bite my lip as I figure out how to discreetly bring up the situation.

"How's that going?" I ask her instead, picking at my rose gold painted nails.

"I'm rearranging the seating chart. Unlucky that we've already sent out invites."

"Hmm, why's that?"

"Stop mumbling, Emmylou. Well, I was on Instagram this morning—no one uses Facebook anymore—and one of Jeanette's college friends was at some Halloween party with a girl. God, imagine?"

I choke out an ironic laugh.

"What do you mean?" It isn't surprising she brought it up on her own. It was dumb of me to feed the hope at all because she's always been vocal about disliking the LGBTQ+ community. If anything doesn't match her idea of an atomic family, it's always been vile spit on her tongue.

"Well, obviously I called her as soon as I saw it. Told her I couldn't have someone like that in my daughter's wedding. You know I hate cursing, Emmylou, but it's like those faggots are taking over the world. Changing every little girl and boy's mind into thinking they can marry anything they want—probably lawnmowers soon, for God's sake. And Lord, don't even get me started on those liberal snowflakes who say they don't even have a gender."

I feel tears streaming down my face.

"So, you'd uninvite anyone who was gay to Janey's wedding?"

I have to go to Janey's wedding. I'm her maid of honor. She's my sister. I can't pick Saatchi over my sister. But I want Saatchi. With every ounce of my soul I want her so bad. I try to choke back a sob.

"Of course. I'd even uninvite you." She pauses, and I bite my fist as the tears stream. "You know that, right Emmylou? You know you can't be a queer. You wouldn't be part of this family."

"Right," I say after a deep breath. "You don't have anything to worry about. I'm glad you got the seating chart fixed."

I hang up before I can hear her response, and I let the sobs tear through my body.

How can something so good as Saatchi be considered bad? Saatchi makes me so happy. She always has, and I was too blind to realize it was something more than platonic. I was so blind because of my stupid mother and the stupid way she talks and has ever since I was little.

I want to be with Saatchi and it feels like dying to pick between her and my own kin. It's not fair. It's not fair. *None of this is fair*, I think as I swing at my dresser mirror. The glass shatters and I feel my heart shatter with it.

None of this is fair. But I can't miss my only sibling's wedding. I can't risk being cut out of the family. I slowly lay down in the remnants of the glass, clutching my fist—I don't know how Saatchi does it—and let the tears flow.

I wish I could call Janey but maybe she's in on this with mother. She may just call me disgusting. My own sister might just call me a fag. I know my mother would; she just as well did. My father married her, so he can't be much different. I have no one now, and if I choose to let Saatchi into my life, I'll always have no one.

I don't fall asleep, instead watching the blood slowly trickle from my hand through blurry eyes.

I think I understand why Saatchi cuts. She says it's to feel something but maybe it's also to feel nothing. Right now, I feel so much. I feel like my heart is cutting its way out of my chest and crawling up my throat. It's gagging me and spurs on another wave of sobs that I try to keep quiet.

It tears through me religiously until I'm dragging myself to the bathroom, head propped on the toilet seat puking. I puke as tears stream down my face, and when I'm done, I just lay back down and cry some more.

My mother hates me. She may not know it. I'll make sure she never does. But she hates me. She hates me enough to cut me out of the family all because of who I love.

And I do. I do love Saatchi. I love her strength and her laugh and the canine she digs into her tongue when she's angry. I love her so much it hurts and all I feel is hurt. Why can't I love her? Why can't it be okay to love her? Why can't I just be happy with whoever makes me happy? She's everything and I've lost her before I could even have her.

I sob until I've got nothing left to cry and then I sob some more. My heart is wrenched with pain and my stomach sick with guilt. Saatchi must hate me now. Saatchi will hate me more come Monday when I can't even look at her. I won't be able to stand looking at her because I want her so bad but I can never have her.

I've never even gone on a date with her. I'll never hold her hand as we walk to campus. I'll never cook her breakfast after a morning run. I'll never cheer her on at races. I'll never wake up beside her in bed. I've lost everything just to hold on to everything else.

I feel lost and utterly broken as I slip into a fitful sleep.

I'm lying in bed, numb, when Drew pounds on my door.

"Emmylou, I swear to God if you don't open this door, I will tear it down and make you pay the repairs."

The sky is dark out and I have my last week of classes starting tomorrow. I was going to study for finals this weekend. Instead, I've just been crying.

"Emmylou!" Another fist joins hers and I recognize Kirsty's voice calling for me as well.

I drag myself out of bed, comforter wrapped around me, and unlock it. Immediately they're bursting in, but I've already turned around and covered myself in bed.

"What the fuck do you think you're playing at here, lass?" Drew rips the covers off of me. I must look a mess because she looks like I've smacked her when she sees my face. "Emmylou, what's wrong?"

It's the wrong thing to ask because I've burst into tears again and I cling onto her as I sob into her shoulder.

"It's not fair. It's not fair. It's not fair." I feel my lungs choke on themselves as I start to hyperventilate again. It isn't the first time it's happened this weekend but hopefully I don't have anything left in my stomach to vomit.

"*Shhh*, Emmylou, what's going on?" Kirsty asks, sitting beside me. She tries unclenching my hand and I wince. There's probably glass in it. "What happened, lass?"

"M-my mother. It's not fair." They both hold me as my sobs dwindle into tears and my tears dwindle into numbness.

"What happened?" Drew finally asks again, handing me a tissue. I blow my nose and throw it to the ground. There's already glass there and a plethora of used tissues.

"I called my mother, I don't know why. I thought maybe—" I thought maybe I could share my excitement about Saatchi with her. I don't tell them that, instead skipping to the meat of the call. "She uninvited one of my sister's friends from the wedding. Cause she's gay." Kirsty slowly closes her eyes, anger clear on her face. "Said that—that if I was a faggot like her," I spit out the word. "I'd not only be uninvited but cut off from the family."

"That's bullshit," Drew says heatedly, and I nod before crying again.

"I don't know what to do, Drew," I say, clinging to her again. "I can't lose my family. They're everything to me."

"What about Saatchi?" I look over at Kirsty. If they're knocking, it means they know, but I can't bring myself to say it. "You kissed her and now you're going to leave her?"

"Don't be an arse, Kirsty," Drew says, smacking her shoulder.

"I wasn't trying to be," she responds shamefully. "I just—she's upset too, you know. She thinks you regret it. She thinks you hate her."

"I could never hate her. I could never regret it. I hate that I'm hurting her. I wish I hadn't led her on knowing it could never happen. But . . . but I love her, Kirsty. It's not fair. I want both. I want my family. I want her. I want to love her every day with every corner of my soul. I want her to know she's worth every bit of love I have for her. But I can't. It's my sister's wedding. It's my family."

"We're your family, lass." Drew hugs me tighter.

# Chapter Eleven

E
N
D

M
E.

After my final on Monday, I've decided all I have left is my running career. There is no way I did well on it, and as soon as I get to the flat, I'm back out sprinting through the pouring rain. It's sleets of ice-cold rain pouring down on me as I sprint, my muscles begging me to stop, but I don't.

I don't stop because if I stop then I'll think. If I think then I'll drown in these pouring sheets of rain and tears and I'll take it standing because it's all I want.

So I run. And I run. And I run until my lungs are suffocating and my knee is screaming in pain, and I run until I fall.

The cobblestones, despite their smoothness, do cut. They cut deep and hard, but not as bad as Emmylou's absence. I roll over and let the ice rain cover me and drown me before finally sitting up. My knee's a wreck, the one that gave out. It's bleeding faster than the rain can clean it, and I watch as my thigh trembles. My hands flare with pain but my knee is fiercer. I go to stand and my stomach drops with fear; I can't stand on my right leg.

I lie back down. Maybe suicide by rain is a new way to go. Maybe I'll be a trendsetter. Or maybe I'm right outside of Young's shoppe and he'll come outside and drag me in.

"Saatchi! The fuck are you doing in the rain, lass?" Old Man Young yells at me outside of his shoppe door.

"Something's wrong with my knee, sir," I respond, tilting my head back to look at his wrinkly face. I ran his dogs last year. It was a good job I set aside in favor of longer runs and better times.

He scoops me up like a bride and I clench my teeth as a shiver of disgust pours through me.

"Let's call your brother then," he says, setting me down on a chair inside. I look down at my knee as he pulls out his cell phone. It's in the right spot, which is a blessing, but my thigh continues to twitch mercilessly.

"He's not answering."

"Must be in a final. Call Drew." I tell him her number by memory and he dials.

"Says she'll be here in a pop. Told her to bring you some clothes. And a crutch." He looks down at my knee. I look with him. "Whatcha gather 'appened?"

*Heartbreak.* "Overuse and not enough warm-up."

"Well, I'm sure our star athlete will be back in tip-top shape soon enough. Saw your article the other month." I wince, remembering the comments. "You're gonna make it lass." I hum and he takes it as agreement and walks away towards the back of the shoppe.

I lay my head back in the chair and stare at the ceiling, feeling like a failure. I pushed myself too hard in a moment of weakness and I may have lost my running career as well. It feels just like in primary when I'd wait for my mam to show up in our beat up Volkswagen to pick me up from detention. I remind myself that Drew and Sai have made a commitment to stop lecturing me, and it calms me just enough to tamp down my dread.

The door chimes as she walks in, carrying an umbrella and a plastic bag of clothes.

"Lass! Are you alright?" She must've prepared herself in the car to not yell at me because she's biting her lip as she looks down at my torn kneecap.

"Aye, just cold."

She hands me the crutches she has secured to her bag and I hobble over to the shoppe wash closet.

"Give us a hand?" I ask as I sit down on the toilet seat and shimmy out of my shorts, being careful around my knee. Drew pulls them down past my ankle and does the same with my pants. I shimmy into a pair of sweatpants and finally take off my soaked shirts in favor of a warm jumper.

I thank Old Man Young as Drew opens the umbrella and leads me to the car.

"Should we take you to a doctor?"

"Nah, let's give it a rest and see. I may just need heating and Christmas break off."

"Alright then, lass. Mind making a quick stop with me? I told Kirsty I'd see her final piece today."

"Aye, let's see it, then that way I can get it out of the way as well."

Drew shoots a glare at me and I wink back at her. We all secretly love Kirsty's art. I'm just not in the mood for love today. My love still aches, crushed in the palm of a girl who can't be bothered.


*Emmylou*

"What do you mean?"

"Oh, well, you know with Jeannette's wedding and your father's work I just think it's too busy right now for you to visit honey. 'Sides, Jeannette will probably just go to Eric's house the whole break and your dad will be holed up at the oil rig. So I'm just gonna take a nip over to France with the girls and you can have fun with all your little friends there."

"So, no Christmas?"

"Honey, you didn't listen. It's just not the right time."

"Right, I understand. I'll see you during the summer." My phone clicks and the line goes dead. It feels like I'm already losing my family.

I look out at the pouring rain and sigh. I guess if I'm not going to study, I may as well go to Kirsty's art show. It's not like I can lie in bed forever.

I toss on my rain boots, remember Saatchi referring to them as wellies, and try not to throw myself back into bed. I miss her. I know it's my fault but I miss her anyways. It's not like we can even see each other at the library anymore. I'm not even sure what I'd say if I could.

Bundled up, I leave the apartment, umbrella in hand to protect me from the cold rain. It's miserable out here and I know I deserve it. Scotland is crying buckets on me for hurting its most important resident.

The gallery is full despite the cold, and I slip in through crowds to the back corner. Kirsty is dressed professionally as she greets some big wigs. I avoid them.

The corner is no longer covered in sketches but one big piece. As I get closer, I feel my heart clench—ripped out again in a reminder of what I'm missing—because staring down at me is a large painting of Saatchi and me.

*Saatchi*

I've lost Drew in the crowd but I continue to unkindly make my way to the corner, sneering at people who don't move out of the way of my crutches quickly enough. I'm hobbling along and nearly fall as I see the one and only Destroyer of Hearts standing there. Her shoulders are dropped in defeat as she looks up and I follow her eyeline.

Dammit Kirsty. I could kill you sometimes.

I stare up at myself. But it's not a version of myself I've ever seen. I'm painted in rich browns and golds, sun streaming on my face as I sit in the library. I wish I could wipe that look off my face because I look so utterly and hopelessly in love.

Kirsty's painted my eyes so detailed that everyone in this gallery can see I'm hopelessly in love with the object I'm looking at. Emmylou. She looks gorgeous, but she always does. She's wearing her hair loose the day Kirsty decided to paint us and I remember longing to tangle my fingers in it.

The only thing Kirsty got wrong is that Emmylou is looking at me the same way.

"Load of shite, innit?"

Emmylou looks up at me and I'm surprised to see tears in her eyes. I look away abruptly. Not ready to see the guilt and regret. I hope Drew gets here soon so we can say we saw it and leave.

"Saatchi—"

"Don't."

We stand in silence, looking up at Kirsty's painting; she's called it *Loving Blindly*. She's right about that one. It was blind. So blind that I couldn't look at the facts when they were thrown in my face. Emmylou is straight and I'm just another college experiment on her road to self-discovery.

"Saatchi," she starts again.

I don't stop her this time. My leg aches but my heart aches stronger. If the last thing I hear from her is rejection, then at least I heard her voice again.

"Saatchi, I love you."

Not that. Wasn't expecting that. I bite my tongue. I heard if you bite it off you can kill yourself.

"Saatchi, please look at me." I shake my head. "Well. Well I do. I love you and you're so strong and I want to be as strong as you are."

I scoff and turn away from her completely. I start to turn my crutches but she keeps talking.

"I love you."

"Stop saying that," I all but snap. I will not make a scene at Kirsty's big debut, with everyone staring at us, the damn subjects of the painting. Not here. "If you want spew your platonic love bullshit, do it for literally anyone else but not me," I spit in her face before turning away again.

I hear Emmylou's footsteps behind me. I don't want to get wet again but I won't be trapped by her. I change my mind about the rejection. I think I'd rather die.

"Saatchi, you're gonna get wet." She opens her umbrella and looks up at me angrily. "I know I fucked up—"

"Look, if kissing me was such a fuck up why don't we just let it be?"

I turn away from her again but she grabs my arm. I don't flinch and the lack of reaction is so shocking I stop.

"No Saatchi. You're gonna listen to me. Kissing you wasn't a mistake. I'd kiss you every single day if I could." My heart aches and I turn my head towards her. "But I called my mother that night." I think she may be getting wet but I realize she's crying. I want to reach out but I'm holding my breath. "She uninvited my sister's friend to the wedding. Cause she's gay." She smiles without humor and I feel my shoulders sink on the padding of the crutches, realizing where this is going. "I asked her if she'd uninvite me and she said she'd not only do that but she'd cut me out if I ever kissed a girl. I wouldn't have a family, Saatchi.

"Saatchi, I can't ask you to hide who you are. I don't want you to hide who you are but I love you. Not platonically. Like, I really love you. I want to be with you. I want to go on dates and kiss you and love you every day and I want—" She lets out a sob and I can't stop my arms from reaching out, nearly toppling me over as I stay balanced on one leg. "I want that," she points into the gallery. "I want what we have but if—if you don't want it anymore, or if you can't hide who we are and what we mean to each other, I understand." I wipe the tears from her cheeks and she leans into my palm.

My hands burn where they hold her face. Even with tears running down her face she still looks beautiful. Even under the grey skies, she's still glowing. She's everything I've ever wanted and that makes it so much harder.

"I can't do this with you," I say, pain ebbing out with the words. She looks up at me but I feel disconnected as the next words come out from a body that isn't mine. "I understand you need time and to come out on your own terms, but . . . I can't do that. I'm not some puppet you can string along on your road to self-discovery."

I don't want to let her go. I want to believe this could work, but it's clear she's not ready for whatever this is. Between all the trauma her mam's dumped on her and her realizing she likes women, the last thing she needs is this. The last thing I need is a heartbreak I won't heal from.

I've been out since I was ten years old. I'm not ashamed of who I am and I won't be made to feel that way. I suppose it may be a bad time for me to realize that I can't keep self-destructing but, right now, the best thing I can do for the both of us is walk away. I'll give her time to figure herself out. I'll give myself time to focus on my own shortcomings. But I won't force her into something she isn't ready for.

So I turn away, letting go of her face, heart crushing into brittle pieces as I realize that will be the last time I'm able to, and trudge through the rain. I don't look back at her. There's nothing left to look back on, just empty dreams.

I understand the fear more than most. Coming out isn't an easy thing to do. But the attraction doesn't just go away with guilt or the fear of repercussion. You can't make the choice to be straight, but I won't be dragged into her turmoil. She'll drag me along in this mess if I allow her to.

No matter how much it hurts, no matter who I lose, I'll always be queer. I'm not going to shy away from the hateful comments, the rude gestures, or even the hate crimes. I won't be forced into the closet because of someone else's fear of who I am and who I love.

It isn't a choice, but if it was, I'd choose to love who I love every single day. I'll love Emmylou until my dying breath. I'll love her even if she decides she'd rather pretend she loves Harris. I'll love her even if she never lets herself have a taste of freedom. But I won't share in that misery with her.

I won't visit her parents under the pretenses of being just a friend. I won't hide my love life from my family and friends because she's scared word will get back to hers. I won't sit here, in ten years' time, unmarried, with no prospective for change because she's scared. Because I've been done being scared. Nothing scares me anymore except the thought of losing that freedom.

*Emmylou*

My bed has seen more tears this week than my childhood bed ever has.

I feel hollowed out but the tears keep coming. There's nothing I can do to make the tears stop because I'm mourning the loss of my heart. The hole in my chest aches and I clutch at my chest as I sob my way through the first half of finals week.

Drew is in and out, bringing me food and water, but I haven't seen Kirsty since her art show on Monday.

Drew sits beside me as I stare blankly out the window at the gray skies.

"Love, you should get out of bed today."

"I already took my final."

She runs a hand through my hair.

"When my mam left my da and I, he wouldn't get out of bed for nearly a month. It fades, Emmylou."

If I had enough energy that might make me mad but, as it stands, I say nothing.

"I'm sure some time apart during holidays will help you both. Maybe you can sort through your feelings or maybe you can just forget about the entire thing while you're with your kin."

"I'm not going back to Texas for break."

"That's a bit dramatic, don't you think? I don't think that would accomplish anything for you, lass."

"No, that isn't it." I finally sit up and take a deep drink from the glass of water on my nightstand. "My mother says they're all too busy for me to come down. Is it okay if I stay here if I pay the utilities?"

"Is it really worth it?"

I look up, surprised to find Kirsty at my door. She looks angry and I think of the painting probably still hanging in the gallery. "Is your mam really worth it if she's already dumped you here in Edinburgh?"

"Don't be a bitch, Kirsty. She's going through a lot," Drew argues heatedly.

"No," she yells, throwing her hands in the air. "I don't understand any of you. I mean, Christ, look at Finn. His parents don't even know he exists and he still goes home and sends money. And for what? To keep being ignored? To not even have a meal on the table when he goes home? None of you make any sense. Emmylou, Drew's visiting her mam this break. Did you know?" I shake my head and Drew's shoulders draw up to her ears. "She abandoned you, Drew! She could give a rat's ass about you. Why are you going to see her? What will that even give you? Closure? I fucking doubt it.

"Emmylou. Your mam dump you here in Scotland and didn't even help you bring your bags up. Sai had to beg his mother not to come clean the flat every weekend. I call my parents every night. Saatchi's parents have literally put a man in jail for her. But the three of you are ridiculous. Your parents are shite. They're absolute shite and I don't know why any of you fight to keep them around. To hell with them!

"Drew, your dad may have worked all the time but he worked himself to the bone to put a damn roof over your head and you can't even be assed to go pay him a visit? You're all mad. I would pick Sai every day if my parents didn't approve. Because he loves me unconditionally. But the three of yous, there's conditions that need to be met for your parents to even pretend to love you. It's bullshit. You all deserve better and I'm sick of seeing Finn and Drew break their neck to even be acknowledged. Don't be like them, Emmylou." And with that she slams my bedroom door.

"Well that sucked," Drew says, tears pricking at the corners of her eyes. She stands up and leaves, isolating me to the torrent of my own thoughts.

Kirsty just doesn't understand.

She's my mother, I can't just leave her. She brought me into this world and she clothed me and bathed me and, even though it wasn't what I needed, she still showed me love. She used to braid my hair and went to all my cheerleading events. One day she'll plan my wedding.

She could have been worse. My mother never raised her hand at me and there was always food on the table. Kirsty just doesn't understand. I can't leave my family for Saatchi. As much as I want her and as much as I trust her, if she were to leave me, I'd be left with nothing.

She's not perfect. But she could be worse.

# Chapter Twelve

Pain crawls into my heart.
There, she nestles into the hallowed cave
Chewing at the dried blood,
Seeking what I crave.

"Listen," Saatchi says, leaning against my doorframe. She won't look up at me, but I'm thankful Drew made me get out of bed to wash my sheets and shower. Even with the tense energy between us, I'm thankful to see her. Her curls are blossoming in the humidity and she's wearing shorts despite the cold. I look at her crutches and try to avoid staring at her muscular thighs but it's a lost cause.

"Drew told me about your situation for the holidays. I know she and Kirsty have plans but, uh, you're welcome to spend break with us." She scratches at the back of her neck, eyes still trained on the floor.

"With your family?"

"Well, aye. I mean Finn stays with us most of the time." She finally looks up and I catch her eye. "Friends are always welcome." My chest stings like she just impaled me instead of saved me. Friends. Because that's all we are, if even that. It's my fault that that's all we'll be. I guess my mother was right when she said no one would like me here. It would've probably been a better idea to just live down the road from my parents. At least then I wouldn't ever know what I was missing.

The problem is, I do know. I know what it feels like to have her arms wrapped around me and her lips against mine—it feels like I finally knew myself. I finally understood every piece of the puzzle that is who I am but as I put that final piece in, the whole thing flew apart and scattered. Now I can't find any of the pieces. Now I can't even find my voice.

I nod at her and she awkwardly pats the doorframe.

"Grand. We leave tomorrow after Finn's last final. I'll, uh, pick you for the train." And with that she's gone and I feel a fresh wave of tears overcome me. She looked great.

It's like the sun follows her wherever she goes because, even when we're indoors, her skin glows brightly and I just want to run my hands across every inch. It shines in her eyes so I can see the deep browns and, even though her eyes look at me with less light than they used to, they're still powerful and endless. Now she can barely stand to look at me.

Maybe, despite what I thought, I was just a fling to her. It isn't like Saatchi doesn't make out with random girls all the time. I hadn't even talked to her before I ruined our friendship. In fact, I went as far as practically telling her I was in love with her and she probably just thought it was a quick romp hidden in the corners of my bedroom.

I'm a fool for letting this semester build my confidence. My mother always told me my relationship would be like this if I didn't shape up. Of course one measly semester isn't going to be what makes me desirable. Saatchi still probably sees me as some dumb girl who can't grow up.

Why can't I grow up? Why do I need my mother's approval in my relationship? Would Janey truly uninvite me if Saatchi even wanted me?

I wish Saatchi wanted me. But I guess to her I'm just a friend who stupidly thought we were more.

*Saatchi*

"Wait, go over it again."

I sigh and look up at my brother from my place on the sofa. Finn snuck out a high-tech icing wrap from one of his premed courses that I'm using on my thigh and knee.

"She said she couldn't be with me. Cause of her mam. But that she wanted to."

"And you said you didn't want her back?"

"No, I didn't say that. You're being a pain. First off, she doesn't want to be with me. She's just found out she's into birds so I don't think she even knows what she's talking about."

He groans and dramatically drops his upper body so he's folded in half.

"Christ, whisht would ya? I'm not gonna go sneaking around like I'm ashamed I like girls for a girl who is on her 'road to self-discovery,'" I say, adding air quotes. "I'm not an experiment, Sai."

"I know that but . . . did you even talk to her about it?"

"What is there to talk about?"

"I thought you were in love with her, Saatchi?"

God, am I ever. Which makes it so much worse because either: one, she doesn't actually like me and she's just run rampant trying new things; or two, she does like me but she's ashamed of it. Either way, I'm not in. I'll just love her from afar and try to hold on to the little sliver of heart that's still in my chest.

"And now you've invited her to holiday with us?" Finn asks, popping his head into the living room from his bedroom where he's packing.

"Well . . . aye. I didn't want her to suffer."

"Christ, since when do you have a heart?"

I fling a sofa pillow at him but he's popped back into his room again before it can make contact. I stare at it, then at Sai before making grabby hands. He grumbles as he grabs it and places it back under my head.

"So, now what?" Sai asks.

"Nothing. I'll meet her outside of her final Friday, we'll go to the train, we'll all spend holiday in the Peterson household, and then we'll come back."

"Well, our holidays will sure be awkward. Don't ya think?"

I fling my pillow at Finn again.

Awkward is an understatement.

"How was your final?" I ask as she steps out of her last final carrying, of course, a sunflower suitcase.

"Fine," she responds in a near silent voice.

I turn away from her so she can't catch the roll of my eyes.

It's her fault she's gone and made this awkward. I didn't tell her to confess feelings she didn't have. It isn't my fault that suddenly our friendship feels nonexistent.

I'm a wee steaming when we finally cross the bridge and get to the station. Emmylou's suitcase rumbling on the cobblestone is the only noise between us. Even Anne Bonny doesn't complain from her bag strapped to my back. I'll bet she can feel the tension in the air.

Sai and Finn are already sitting in front of a sign reading Inverness. It'll be the same train Kirsty takes, but she left the day before. Drew would've gone the opposite way to visit her mam for holidays. Smart of her to visit in person for what she's got up her sleeve.

"Maybe we just stay on the train the entire way," Finn says when I sit down with my crutches underneath me, leaning forward so as to not crush Anne.

"Like we did in primary?"

"Probably won't get in as much trouble this time."

Sai scoffs beside us. "Mam will have both your heads if you run off to chase Nessie."

"Nessie? Like, the mythical creature?"

I look at Emmylou, surprised to finally hear her voice.

"Woah woah—" Finn starts, jumping forward.

"She is absolutely real," I finish, flabbergasted.

"No, it isn't," Sai adds, and little does Emmylou know she's rekindled a lifelong debate. "It's a dolphin that a priest thought was a mythical beast. You can read all about it if you ever go visit, Emmylou."

"So, you're saying the priest is a liar?"

Sai glares at me; I can nearly touch the steam coming from his ears.

"It's an honest mistake."

"Aye, like mistranslating the bible from saying pedophilia is a sin to saying homosexuality is a sin," Finn says and I high-five him as Sai grumbles, leaning back against his seat. The train rolls up just as Emmylou opens her mouth and she shuts it as we all stand to get on.

I'm more than pleased to see the train. Despite my love for Nessie, I'm not sure I'm ready to keep playing pretend buddies with Emmylou.

"You believe in the Loch Ness Monster then?" she asks from behind me, sending a shiver crawling up my back.

"Well, the Chinese once thought Giant Pandas were mythical beast. 'Sides, there are loads of things people can't explain in this world," I respond snippily. Lore is real and important to me and my da.

"Our da raised us on fairy tales he learned at sea," Sai says, throwing her a rope, as he takes a seat.

"Not fairy tales," I complain, handing my crutches to Finn and sitting across from my twin. I glare at Finn as he sits beside Sai, forcing Emmylou to sit next to me.

"You're really going to sit there and tell me you believe in Kelpies and giants and whatever other bullshit he says?"

"I was named after a giant," Finn says, pouting at Sai.

"Da says a Kelpie nearly got half his fishing ship once and that's why he moved inland and met mam. You're going to tell me it's not true?"

Sai covers his face with his hands. "Emmylou, at least tell me you're on my side?"

"Well, I guess it makes sense. No one on our farm is allowed to whistle at night and we're always worried about sending the horses further south cause, ya know, Chupacabras."

He glares at her but I soften my gaze in turn. Sai's disbelief has always raised my hackles in this debate.

"Do the Chupacabras," definitely not a word my tongue was made for, "hear you whistle?"

"No, the Skinwalkers do."

I frown at her. At least our beasts keep to the sea. Or Glasgow.

The rest of the ride is a series of Sai furiously searching the internet to disprove us and Finn increasingly getting anxious as we near his childhood home. Emmylou picks up on it at some point because she stops asking about the difference between Selkies and Kelpies and asks Finn if he's all right.

"Aye, I guess. Just hate going home."

"Not your home," I say instinctively, and he smiles gratefully.

"I shouldn't have spent so much money on bevvys at uni. Blair told me they've had another one. I'm not sure I can afford diapers and winter boots for the little ones."

"You're shitting me," Sai says.

"Who's Blair?"

"His sister," I say offhandedly to Emmylou. "She's married and she took some of Finn's siblings but she can't take the littles because they're too much and she can't take the healthy ones because they work the farm."

"So basically just John, mates sick every other week, and Sarah. Sarah lost a few fingers on the farm. Wouldn't tell me how."

"How many more are there?"

Finn looks up at Emmylou and I reach across the tables to grab his fists to keep his nails from digging in further. He lets me.

"There's fifteen total. Well, I guess sixteen now. We just work the farm and da drinks the money and mam pops out more wains. You'd think she'd be done by now."

"You'd think any of you have a brain and leave your parents to fend for themselves." Sai sounds more and more like Kirsty every day and I swat him with my free hand. Anne complains in my lap at the sudden movement.

"And go where?" Finn starts, frustrated. "Blair can't take all fourteen of them. 'Specially when one of them is still at the teet. Starve like the rest of us? No, we have to keep the older ones there to watch for the littles and Blair near to give them a bed if they need it and me in Edinburgh to try and send money when I can. It's a shite hand but the littles have it better than I did."

Sai and I are quiet at that.

The rest of the ride is silent as the three of us think about Finn when we first met him. Back then it was five of them. Blair's the oldest but Finn was only three when I first saw him in church. I didn't understand then, but the whole congregation was praying for a healthy pregnancy for his mam. He stood beside her at the front with runny nose drip clearing the muck on his face, the bones in his cheeks and hands jutting out.

The next Sunday, mam sent Sai and I to him and his siblings with sandwiches and helpings of soup to take home. The Sunday after that, Finn sat beside me in the pews and he's never left since.

Mam and da paid for him to play footie. They paid for him to go to school. They made sure he was fed. Maybe, at first, that's why he stuck around. My parents couldn't pay for all of them, especially when the pregnancies just kept coming, but luckily, we had Finn. One summer my parents built a bunk bed and Finn never went home after that.

That is, until one of his siblings died. The police called it natural cause. The town called it starvation. Finn started working at ten. Whatever he could find. Sai and I joined him but it was different. We didn't have the drive he did. He's always been a hard worker. He's always been behind a counter or shining shoes at the train station or mucking out stalls. I'm not sure how Finn found the time to do it all.

Taking care of his family under his parents' noses, studying hard to get a scholarship to uni, making it onto every football team just to be with Sai, spending all of his free time just to show he was my best mate. If I could see his soul, I'm sure it'd be wrinkled with wear. He's worked harder at nineteen than most men work in their lifetime.

It's no surprise that when he's at uni he's such a devil. He's never had a break in his life if it wasn't spending time with me.

I watch through the window, my hand still on Finn's, as we pull up to our town. It isn't much; there's a small town centre but beyond that it's mostly green hills and muddy farms. The snow has melted which means trouble for my crutches.

I hand Anne Bonny to Emmylou as I situate myself on the crutches. I watch with ire as Emmylou keeps her and Finn grabs my pack.

Grumbling, I follow everyone off the train and into the cold air. Sai leads us out and before I know it, he's being swaddled along with Finn by my very teensy, tiny mother.

"Lads! It's so good to see you. Lord, Sai have you gotten taller. Soon you won't be fitting in the car like your da." She turns to me and smiles. "Skinny Malinky longlegs the three of yous," she says, giving me my own hug. I bend to rest my chin on her head before she pulls back in confusion.

"What's this," she says, gesturing at my crutches.

"Got hurt."

"Well, what'd you do that for?"

"Didn't mean to, woman."

She frowns and turns away. "Oh, and you've got your guest carrying your bags. Lord, I swear I raised her better."

I raise my crutches to show my defense but she doesn't even look.

"Don't worry about it ma'am, it's really no problem," Emmylou says sweetly.

"She's a sweet bird isn't she," my mam says, giving Emmylou her own hug. Mam is so short that even Emmylou looks giant beside her. "Well, come on wains, haven't got all day. Your da's probably burning down the house making evenings." This, of course, is an absolute blasphemous lie, seeing as between mam and da, da is the only one who can cook. But we follow her, piling into the old Volkswagen beetle that's still kicking.

"Am I taking you to your parents' house, Finley?" Finn doesn't respond, eyes glued to the window. I stare at him through the reverse mirror.

"Aye," Sai says for him.

"Heard there's another one of them?"

"Mhmm, does that farm actually make them any money?" I ask.

"Lass, I wouldn't even know," my mam says, forlorn.


*Emmylou*

Finn's farm is so run down that I hadn't realized it wasn't abandoned until we got closer. There's children playing in the front yard and, despite the cold, one of them isn't wearing shoes.

Squished between Finn and Sai, I can feel Finn tense up, the nails from his clenched fists digging into the padding.

"Mate." Sai passes a wad of cash over me to Finn. Saatchi does the same from the front seat where she has a little more room to stretch her injured leg.

"Wish me luck lads. I'll be back for evenings." And then he's out, lumbering over to a bunch of children that squeal with delight when they see him. I watch him grab the littlest one and she clings to him as he wraps his corduroy jacket around her.

"There's sixteen of them?" I ask as we pull out.

"Should be seventeen," Saatchi says sadly from the front seat, still looking back to where we leave him behind.

I never realized how badly Finn had it. He always seems so light hearted and goofy with us. I didn't even know he worked, and yet there he is, prepared to go buy food, clothes, and diapers for a hand he never asked for.

My mother was never this bad. She may not have gone with me to chemo but she drove me to every session. She took me to every cheerleading game and friend's house. Bathed me, clothed me, fed me, and put a roof over my head. There are worse mothers out there, and I've been selfish to be the only one of my friends complaining over family problems. I'm sure everyone has them and, knowing Finn's story, I know some of them have it worse. Who am I to complain about a mother who was just over protective?

All she ever did was warn me that I wasn't good enough. She told me time and time again that I needed to work on myself or people wouldn't love me. And, as I stare at the back of Saatchi's head, I realize that my mother was right. She only ever had my best intentions in mind. I just didn't know how to listen, and now all I have to show for it is a broken heart and the looming fear of another holiday spent away from family.

I keep thinking about my mother as we drive through the center of the town. There's a church and a few shops. There's also a high school that Sai and Saatchi simultaneously turn their heads away from as we drive past. I stare at what looks like an office building and frown. These are made of cement and they stick out like a sore thumb in a town made of more cobblestones.

I miss Edinburgh already. I miss what it felt like before this last week—before I messed up Saatchi and I's friendship. It would've been easier to just pine from a distance than actually convince myself Saatchi felt the same way. Except, I didn't convince myself. I just went for it. Maybe, if I'd have just talked it out with her from the get-go, she could've rejected me then and we could've continued as friends.

But now everything is awkward and I realize it's only going to be more uncomfortable as we pull into a small blue home, where a large gray dog sits on the doorstep. It's barely a cottage, and I can't imagine it fitting Saatchi's family, much less adding Finn and myself.

"Oi, Grey," Sai shouts as he gets out of the car. The dog sprints up to him and places muddy paws on his chest. I get out and watch Saatchi's crutches sink into the mud. I can't hold back the giggle that escapes from me and she glares.

"Get your damn sunflower bag and whist. I'm going to drown here."

"You get her bags, Saatchi!" her mother shouts over the roof of the car. Her eyes barely peek over it.

The door swings open and the absolute largest man I have ever seen walks out. His arms are teed out and he shouts:

"My wains!" before a plethora of dogs are suddenly running from under his feet.

"Did I mention my da collects dogs," Saatchi grumbles as two yappy dogs bite at her crutches. A fuzzy Border Collie runs around my legs as I hoist my bag out of the trunk.

"How many are there?" I ask, and suddenly a man is grabbing the bag from my hands.

"Well, there's eight. That there is Blue," he says gesturing at the Border Collie. "Saatchi's friends are White and Yellow." I can guess which one is White but I'm at a loss as to why the other terrier is named Yellow. "This here is Green," I stare at an old dog behind Saatchi's dad with a little doggie beard down to his chest. "Purple." Another terrier. "Brown." I recognize Shelties at least. "And Pink." A small Chihuahua pokes his head out of the man's shirt pocket. "And I am Bram," he says slowly, as if his tongue didn't fit in his mouth, shaking my hand.

"Emmylou," I respond as he takes away all of our bags. Saatchi grumbles up the stairs, Anne Bonny on her back looking surprisingly calm despite the amount of dogs, and shakes out her muddy crutches before entering.

The house is warm and smells delicious as we walk in. The door opens immediately to a living room with lots of well-worn couches and a crooked pride flag under a Scottish flag and over a flat screen TV. The kitchen is to our left, filling the house with amazing scents, and a small hallway leads out of the living room.

"Boots as well," her mom calls from inside, and Saatchi and I take our shoes off and place them next to Sai's. White tennis shoes were not the right choice for this excursion.

"The bed's big enough, should I put both of your bags in your room, Saatchi?" Bram asks, exiting the hallway.

"Uh, no, I'll sleep on the sofa."

Guilt fills me, but Saatchi doesn't give me room to argue before she's wandering into the kitchen. I follow her in but before I can say anything I realize that all the dogs and Sai are in here as well.

"Stew," Sai supplies, peering into the pot.

"What type?" she asks before jumping onto the counter, letting the crutches unceremoniously drop.

"Don' know. Probably chicken with rosemary," Sai responds. I inhale the stew and Sai leaves the kitchen. I watch Saatchi eyeball her crutches, far below her, before stepping closer so she can't escape.

"I didn't realize you didn't have a guest bedroom. I can sleep on the couch."

She rolls her eyes. "It's fine. Just leave it."

"Saatchi—"

"Can we just," she exhales. "Can we just not? Can you just sleep in the room and eat the food and have a good holiday and not fucking look at me like that?"

"Like what?"

"Christ, like that. Like I've done something wrong." She huffs and forgoes the crutches, choosing to limp out of the kitchen instead.

I turn just as Bram walks in. He has to crouch to get under the doorframe. His height should be intimidating but he has this cloudy look in his eyes and a kind smile.

"Have you enjoyed Scotland then, Emmylou?" A large dog follows him in, and I barely have to lean down to scratch its side.

"Yeah, it's been a lot more welcoming than I expected."

He hums in thought and holds onto a bar jutting out from the countertop as he reaches above the sink to open a cupboard.

"I'll bet it's nice to be seeing the countryside though. Saatch says you're from the farm lands as well."

I look over my shoulder then back to Bram.

"I didn't realize Saatchi talks about me."

"Oh aye all—" He's cut off by someone coughing pointedly at the entryway. Sai looks at me with a smirk.

"Should probably take Saatchi her crutches," he says, eyeing them where they lay across the kitchen floor.

"Thanks for the chat, Bram," I say, swiftly grabbing Saatchi's crutches and taking my leave.

Out of the frying pan and into the fire.

Saatchi's sitting on the living room floor, aggressively stuffing a pillow into a cover.

"Brought these for you."

"Thanks," she says, without looking up. I grab the pillow and cover she hasn't started yet and start to arrange them. I feel her pulsing with anger beside me but I don't want to back down like I have been since this morning.

"I know you can do it Saatchi, I just—I don't know where I'm supposed to go or what I'm supposed to do. This isn't my house, so please, just give me somewhere to pretend I belong."

She finally looks up. "Aye, sorry," she mumbles.

I shrug in return and we sit there in silence.

Silence never used to be hard with her. Though it was few and far between, it always felt comfortable when it did occur. Now it feels like we've lost our once constant familiarity. The desire to be heard and seen now filled with aborted words and gestures.

"Uhm, your pa," her eyes snap to mine and I rethink the end of my thought. "He's really nice, I like him."

She smiles at that. "Aye, he's grand, innit he?"

Her smirk makes my belly flop, despite everything.

Finn sits beside me on the sofa once everyone's gone to bed.

"Blair is thinking of fighting for rights to the wains." I run my hands through his hair as a tear streams down his cheek. "Rachel ages out this year and we could split them in thirds."

"But you don't want to take a third of the lot?"

"No." I watch his hands run over his face. "Blair says she understands but it still makes me feel like a shite brother."

"It isn't your responsibility. One sibling would've been manageable but, what, three or four? Rachel deserves a life too."

"I know. Still." He leans into my shoulder and sniffles. "I've tried to help my whole life but I'm tired. I don't even want wains for myself cause I feel like I've had them my whole life."

My heart aches as I squeeze him tight.

"Just keep doing what you're doing. They'll make it out. Rachel did." I hold him as the tears begin to flow freely, both our minds on the brother that didn't.

The next morning, I wake to see Finn gone. I stretch my leg languidly and grab my crutches, making my way to the kitchen. Da is towering over the stove.

"Morning," I say, wrapping my arms around his waist, careful to keep my crutches up right.

"How's my wain?" he asks, leaning down a distance to rest his head atop mine.

"Missed you." I'm feeling especially grateful towards him after talking to Finn last night.

"Awe, lass, I missed you too. Are you happy in Edinburgh?" I look over my shoulder briefly but he catches it. "What's going on with the lass?"

I groan. Sai may think him dimwitted, but da's always been the most receptive with feelings.

"Where is she?"

"Porch swing with Finn."

I look out the window and there they are. Huddled under a blanket with a warm tea in their hands. I turn toward my da, white hair glittering in the winter sun, and tell him everything.

"Hmm, aye, that's quite the predicament."

"So, what do I do?"

He smiles down at me. "Well, if you're going to go the route of safety, then just be her friend. Otherwise . . ."

"What do you mean safety?" I ask, aborting an attempt to fold my arms. Damn crutches.

"You called it 'taking care of yourself,' which isn't entirely wrong, but you can't let fear keep you from giving something a chance."

I look out to the porch and frown.

"And if she's like the others?" I ask, thinking of this small town and its small-minded folk.

"You don't believe that or you wouldn't even be her friend."

After lunch, Sai is in the back playing footie. Neruda, sweet cow that she is, calls gently to me, and I wobble through the mud to her for the fifth time today. I mind her horns as I scratch her gently.

"Give us a hand with cleaning," I call to my brother. Blue jumps the fence and splashes mud on me. The sound of the football slamming into the lean-to makes our pony, Sally, whinny.

Sai exhales deeply behind me.

"Just pick up the poos with your crutch." I turn to glare at him but he's already grabbing a shovel. My crutches sink deeper into the mud and Blue makes Burns's ear flick as she sniffs it.

I don't respond, instead watching him toss the shovel over. We leave each other to our own thoughts as I brush the girls and he mucks their droppings. There's a peace to the silent winter afternoon and I lose myself in the familiar motions.

"So this is them?"

Neruda sniffs at Emmylou's outstretched hand as she leans against the fence. Sai makes eye contact with me across the lot and widens his eyes—I'll blame the winter sun for making my cheeks red.

Despite what my da said, I feel like I should stick to my guns. I mean, it hurts now, but won't it hurt more if she realizes it was just an experiment? Or if she leaves me because her mam disapproves? Or is the worst pain to always wonder what might have been?

I close my eyes tightly and take a deep breath of the highland air. I turn from my place against the fence and towards Emmylou.

"What happened to footwork?" Finn shouts as he rips open the backdoor. Emmylou turns away from me at the commotion.

Probably for the best then.

# Chapter Thirteen

Lover, I miss you.
Let me kiss you,
Hold you tight,
Never let you out of my sight.

The snow has melted,
You've been expected.
Yet you aren't around
And I'm digging into the ground.

Lover, you've killed me.
But you'll never see,
My hearts in its tomb.
Only you could help it bloom.

Finn and I sit on the porch swing watching the fog roll out. We've kind of fallen into this habit since break started. Sai and Saatchi sleep in and Greer, Saatchi's mom, feeds the pony and the cows before going into town with Bram.

"Why is Saatchi named the way she is?" I clutch my warm tea to my chest as I huddle under the blanket.

"Ask Saatchi that."

I let out a snort. This has been our morning ritual. I sit here beside him in silence for a while until eventually he finds a way to bring up Saatchi and I's tense avoidance of each other.

"Fine, why is Sai named the way he is?"

"Ask Saatchi that," he repeats.

"Finn," I start, exasperated.

"Emmylou. Yous both are gonna have to figure it out. We're a family. All of us in that junkie flat. I don't know what the hell is going through either of your heads, but you have to figure it out."

"There's nothing to figure out. I can't lose my family and I'll only hurt her more if I tell her . . . well that—"

"That you love her."

"Yeah, that." I take a sip of my tea and let it soothe my nerves.

"Do you?"

"Yes," I say without hesitation.

"Christ, I don't understand the two of yous. If I have to sit through one more awkward meal—" He's cut off by the ringing of my phone, and the pony in the run beside the house knickers at the noise.

"Sorry, let me just." I stand up, thankful for the dry pathway, and walk my socked feet away from him.

"Hi, pa."

"Hey, darling! How are your friends?"

"Obnoxious," I say loud enough for Finn to hear and he flips me his middle finger.

"Ha! Well, lots of time together can be like that. You know I hope you're having fun, but I'm sad you're not here."

"Pa, what in the world would I do on an oil rig during Christmas?"

He snorts. "Honey, don't sell me that short. I'm sitting right here in the living room in front of the fire. Janey's just gone to bed. Just her and I this Christmas I guess, but don't feel bad. We're happy you're happy. You know, hanging out with Saatchi . . . and Co." He keeps talking but I don't hear anything else. There is a notable absence of humming machines, and I must stand there silently gawking for too long because Finn is standing in front of me snapping his fingers.

I start before realizing I've completely dropped my phone and scramble to pick it up.

"Emmylou—"

"Sorry, dropped my phone," I say in a rush, cutting him off. "Daddy, you're at home?"

"Uh, yeah, it's Christmas, Emmylou? Are you okay?"

"And Janey's at home?"

"Yeah, she wanted to spend one last Christmas with us before getting married. Emmylou, we discussed this before you left. Did you forget? Like I said, we understand—"

"Wait," I say, stopping him again. "Where's mom then?"

"Uh, Spain I think. Or Turkey. Another girls' trip. She deserves it but I wished she'd plan it another time."

"Dad, did mom tell you I didn't want to come home?"

"Well, she didn't phrase it like that. I didn't want you to feel guilty and have to call me too. I understand you needing to go through your mother like that."

I clutch onto Finn who's still standing beside me.

"What did she tell you?" I ask in a whisper.

"Well, that you were spending the break with your friends. I just kind of assumed you were with Saatchi and uh, Sai is it? I remember Finn and Drew but not your other roommate. Christy? Nah, it was something more Scottish than that."

"Hey daddy?"

"Yes?"

"I love you. Merry Christmas."

"Merry Christmas, honey. Have fun."

I hang up with shaking fingers and Finn holds me as I cry into his shoulder.

I'm still there when Greer gets back and she walks us both into the house.

"Saatchi, get your arse up and make tea. Sai!" He comes scrambling from the room like a soldier ready for battle. "Make us a Scottish Breakfast."

Greer leads me to the kitchen table and sits beside me while Finn sits across. She hands me a tissue I graciously thank her for as I wipe my tears.

"What's wrong, lass?" she asks quietly. I make eye contact with Saatchi as she hobbles around. She's no longer on crutches but she isn't at full walking abilities yet.

"Just, my dad called. Guess I got a little homesick."

"Oh, well that's understandable. Well we'll share our home with you and give you a large breakfast and everything will feel better." She stands up and Finn looks at me sadly before following her. It's Saatchi's eyes that don't leave mine.

I'm thankful to Greer for the meal, but as soon as it's over I excuse myself and crawl into Saatchi's bed. Sleeping in it has been my own version of hell. It smells just like her and

I'm surrounded by everything that once was hers but isn't now. I'm just another discarded item to her.

I'm wiping away tears when my door opens and Saatchi slides in.

"What's happened?"

"Nothing."

"Don't lie," she says sitting on the foot of the bed. "What's happened?"

The full waterworks come and I reach for her in a moment of weakness, but she humors me and wraps her arms around me.

"My mother uninvited me to Christmas but everyone else went home. She—she told me not to come because my pa would be at work and Janey would be with Eric, but they're both at home and I miss them so much, Saatchi, and my mother lied to me." I shake with sobs in her arms and she runs a soothing hand down my back.

"Christ, Lou."

"It's like I've already lost them." Except I didn't even get the thing worth losing them for. Saatchi makes quiet shushing noises and I let my cries become small sniffles before I pull away.

I watch Saatchi as she stares at the ground, running her tongue over her canine.

"You won't lose them Emmylou. They're your family."

"You know that doesn't mean anything. Finn barely has a family and Drew's mom left her."

She sighs. "Looks like Kirsty got to you too. Listen, Finn's family is me and Sai and the rest of us. Drew has her da, and she's down in London trying to guilt her mam into paying tuition." She rubs the back of her neck. "Emmylou, I don't think your family hates you, or would leave you, and if they did . . . well, you've got us."

I look up at her. She looks sad, nothing like that painting Kirsty made. Kirsty must be delusional, but maybe I'm delusional too because I say:

"I don't have you."

Saatchi turns away at that and I watch her teeth grind.

"Emmylou. Look, we're friends. I—I care a lot about you, but I'm not your experiment."

"I'm attracted to you, Saatchi. I don't need to experiment to know that."

She turns back to me, chewing on her lip angrily. "Well," she hesitates and turns away again. "Well, I'm not ashamed of liking women and I'm not going to be forced back into the closet because you're scared."

I pause and think about everyone back home. Would every girl on the cheerleading squad never talk to me again because they thought I was checking them out in the locker room? Would every guy I was friends with think I was gross, or worse, sexualize me because of this? Would the students I sit next to in class every day at college sit farther away? What if the professors found out and didn't help me anymore? What if I lose job opportunities? What if my mother finds out?

I look up at her as she gets up to leave.

"Wait," I say, reaching for her arm but stopping short, she looks back at me, frowning. "It isn't easy. I haven't known since I was a kid like you. Can you just . . . wait?"

She looks at the door and I feel my stomach drop. Then she looks back at me. She exhales heavily before dropping beside me on the bed, both of us propped against her wall.

"Okay."

It's quiet and she keeps eye contact with the door. The need to get her to say something builds.

"Your room is small."

She lets out a small laugh.

"Aye, guess it is smaller than the one at uni." Her room only fits a bed, pushed up against the wall and a cat tree that Anne currently peers at us from. There's a door that connects to her and Sai's bathroom, but other than that it's empty. Not even a single poem on the wall.

"There's no poems."

"Emmylou."

"Just give me a second."

We continue in the silence. She's right. I don't want her to feel ashamed or feel like she has to hide. I don't like feeling ashamed or hiding. But it's hard. It's hard because there's not only my past friends and my future to think about; I have a family. They'll leave me if I don't hide.

"What would you have done if your family hated you for being a lesbian?"

"Well, I assume I would've been mad. I would've been mad for a long time but in reality, I would've been more hurt than anything . . ." She laughs bitterly. "Sai actually gave me a scare once." I look over at her in shock. "When we were wains, he wanted to be a priest." She swallows. "He hung out at the church all the time, soaking in information. One day he came home and told me it was a sin for me to like women." She rubs her eyes like she's trying to destroy an image. "We can sit here and make excuses like he was young and impregnable or that he was just concerned for me because he truly believed I'd be sent to hell to burn in a land without love forever. But none of that matters. It still hurt. Sometimes it still does actually.

"But I did what I do—got mad—and didn't talk to him for a week. Then he stopped going to church. Sundays and all. I guess he decided that his love for me was stronger than whatever God the church said they had. Course when mam got wind of this, she threw a fit. Said that God loves everyone and the church is a bunch of ballbags who know nothing.

"Sai started going to church again, but he never thought about becoming a priest after that. Leaves a sour taste in both our mouths. But the point is, Em, I wouldn't have talked to him again. Ever. I know that. But I also know it would've hurt so damn bad. He's my brother. He's my damn twin. I love him and that love doesn't go away just because of pain. I think that's what makes pain so much worse.

"I get it, to an extent, that you're scared of your family leaving you, but I also know I would've left Sai. I love him unconditionally. I deserve the same."

She turns to me.

"And so do you."

I lean my head against her shoulder boldly.

"But how will I pay for college?"

"Become a part-time student and work part-time jobs. You'll graduate later, but people do it all the time. Finn almost had to."

"What will everyone back home say?"

"Some won't care. Some will say 'you're so brave, I love you,'" she says mockingly. "And others will never speak to you again but you won't miss them. You barely miss them ,now. I haven't seen you talk to anyone from Texas the whole time you've been in Scotland."

"What if I get bullied?"

"Sai will beat them up. Trust me, even I've had my fair share of bigots."

"And what if the professors hate me?"

She raises an eyebrow at that.

"Emmylou, I'm openly gay and so is like a tenth of the campus. They don't give a rat's arse and the ones that do won't show it."

"And what if I lose my job someday because of it?"

"Then you sue them and if you can't prove it you move on. That's life."

"And what if I get uninvited to Janey's wedding?"

"Then Sai and Kirsty will just have to get hitched sooner than was planned and we'll throw a better wedding. All of Scotland will come. We'll get them to put it on the news."

"And what if my parents leave me and my family leaves me and then you leave me, what then?"

She looks over at me.

"Don't be daft."

And then she kisses me.

*Saatchi*

She still tastes like apple and honey and I want to drown in her, but I pull away.

"So, what's the verdict?" I ask tentatively.

"Yeah, I'm definitely in love with you."

I can't stop the grin from spreading on my face.

"Not what I meant," I say, pushing my nose into her hair to hide my face-splitting smile. Smells like apples and honey too. She's like springtime. I thought she'd be more like summer. Do sunflowers bloom in the spring?

"Saatchi, I need time. I need to do it on my own terms. But I'll do it."

I run my hands through her hair. "Yeah, okay then."

"Okay then?"

I look at her. She's trying to hide a grin of her own and I kiss it off her face.

"Okay," I say against her lips. "Let me take you on dates and beat up Harris," she pulls away to laugh at that one.

"And kiss you senseless." I lean in again and make do on my promise.

That night, at dinner, I quietly sit myself beside her. It mustn't have been as discrete as I was hoping for because Finn and Sai's heads both pop up and stare. My father grins knowingly and I contemplate stabbing myself with the butter knife when my mam sets the meat pie on the table.

"Are all the presents wrapped and under the tree?" mam asks obliviously. I tense as I realize my current present for Emmylou is probably not good enough, considering where we stand.

I look up at Finn and his eyes widen in understanding.

"Uhm, actually Greer. I should have a nip into town before we call it set."

"Of course lad, you and Saatchi can go in the morning." I nudge Finn's foot gratefully under the table.


"It's Christmas Eve Saatchi, what did you expect?"

I glare at Finn who raises his hands in innocence.

"Well, I can't just not get Lou a Christmas present." I stare back at the shoppes. Every single one closed. "The hell am I supposed to do?"

"Make her something?"

"Not helpful, mate."

"Oh, she likes horses, right?"

"What are we going to do? Steal one of your da's horses?" We both stand stiff as our rebellion runs with the idea.

"Will he be mad?" I ask Finn, gears turning.

"Not if we return it by the day after Christmas."

"Too drunk 'til?"

"Aye."

"Your mam?" I ask.

"Claims she can't even get out of bed after the wain." He stares at me and I stare back. "I'll just leave a note for the wains and it'll be berry."

And that is why on Christmas day, at midnight, instead of tucking into bed after mass so Santa can whisk presents under the tree, we're standing outside of the paddock, eyeing a Clydesdale.

"Really? You want the biggest one?" He's massive and he flicks his ear at us to let us know he hears us. "Why can't she just ride the Shetland?"

"The fucking pony?" I whisper scream at Finn. "She doesn't even like the pony." Poor Sally did not impress. I don't blame Emmylou, she's probably well used to race horses of high caliber. A little wagon pony made to bring hay from town isn't going to impress her. "We need the Clydesdale."

"His name is Beau."

"Oh is he French? Does he know he's from Scotland?" I ask, undoing the gate.

"It's whatever da can sell. Beau sounds more profound than like . . . well like Sally."

"Oh God, sure everyone gang up on Sally. 'S not like she's kept the cows fed and the house in one piece." She's a sturdy bitch and I love her. Everyone's opinions be damned. "Where's his lead? And saddle?"

Finn looks at me sheepishly. "Da keeps them locked in the house."

"You didn't think to mention that?" He shrugs and I can barely see him in the moonlight. "It's bloody snowing and you're going to make me ride bareback?"

"It's not for my girlfriend," he argues back. I ignore the title because he has a point.

"Gods be damned. Fine. At least get me a stool," I argue, pointing at my healing knee. He sighs but retrieves one.

I swing, rather ungracefully onto Beau's back and give Finn a hand up.

"He's tall," Finn says from behind me as he wraps his arms around my waist after checking in with me and I wrap my hands firmly in Beau's mane and urge him forward. Finn leans to close the gate behind us and we slowly leave the property.

Once we're out, I urge Beau faster and he canters across the town. Horses are not for me. I get too envious atop of one. They're strength and grace is something I can only dream of. Besides, running is much more comfortable than being tossed around, wind whipping across my face, in the freezing Scottish countryside. We pass the town centre when my phone starts to ring. I ignore it, knowing Sai is probably having a fit seeing as Finn isn't in the bunk above him yet.

I wonder what Emmylou is doing. She may already be asleep or she may be sitting in front of the telly with my parents. She's grown more comfortable around my family and has finally moved from ma'am and sir to Greer and Bram. She's nothing like Kirsty who immediately took to calling them mam and da and asking them their detailed life story. But she can't be blamed. Emmylou, that is—Kirsty can be blamed for everything. I have yet to answer her plethora of texts asking me if Sai's texts to her about Emmylou and I getting together are true.

Emmylou, unlike Kirsty, doesn't truly have a comfortable household. Or maybe she does. I only know what she's told me, which is that her mother is a controlling bitch who has never taught Emmylou love. Anytime I bring Emmylou a cup of tea or hold her hand she looks at me like I've shifted the earth. At first, I thought it was a gay thing, but when mam does it, Emmylou has the same reaction. She isn't used to being cared for or anyone noticing if she's cold and needs a blanket. No small act of service has ever crossed her path and it hurts to see. And I'm determined to make up for it, even if that means riding a giant across town so she can ride it for one day.

Is this illegal? Yes. Could I get in trouble? Potentially. But I have faith in Finn's father's alcoholism. I wouldn't care either way. If she wants a horse, she'll get the damn biggest most beautiful one I can find.

We stop outside the house and the horse whinnies at Grey who barely does so much as raise his head. A wolfhound does not make a good guard dog. Yellow, the Cairn Terrier, does better, but he's probably too busy chasing fairies in the pastures behind the house. Yellow can see them even if Sai can't.

I lead Beau into the paddock with Sally and we dismount.

"Think he'll be fine?" I look at Finn.

"He's got grain. It's just for one night."

We turn to the house and take deep breaths to calm the adrenaline of horse thievery.

The house is quiet when we come in, but I can see Sai's bedroom light is on. I wish Finn good luck before slipping into my own room. Emmylou is already in bed, her head poking out of the blankets as she stares at her phone.

"Where were you?" she asks curiously as I grab sleep clothes from my closet. I stretch out my thigh as I think of what to say. The physical therapy Finn has been giving me makes it feel worse than if I were to just hobble around on it.

"Out with Finn."

"That's vague."

I smirk at her before going to my shared bathroom to change. I lock both doors and stare at myself in the mirror. I'm not sure if she'll ask me to sleep beside her now that our relationship has escalated. She's difficult to read, because not even she knows what she wants.

It's like I'm walking on cracked pavement and I can't see my feet. I might hit a crack and land flat on my face, or she might take my hand and lead me away from every dip.

"Can I ask you something weird?" Emmylou asks when I return to the room.

"No hints about the present."

"No, not that. Uhm, it's hard to phrase. Why is your name Saatchi?"

"Oh, you mean why is my mother named Greer and Sai and I are well . . . Sai and Saatchi?" She nods and I laugh. It's a question I've answered to anyone who meets my very Scottish mam. "Well, my grandda was from India—married my grandmam who was from Scotland but my great-grandda didn't approve of their marriage. I gather he was racist, funny that. They had my mam, just my mam, before they died. Car accident or something. Anyway, my great-grandda took in my mam after that. She was wee wain, like three or something.

"Anyway, mam didn't grow up around Indian culture. He wiped it clean and she swore she wouldn't do the same with us. So, she named us Indian names or Sanskrit or Hindu. Not really sure. She tried, mind you, but it's hard when she didn't even have the culture herself. She used to buy us books to learn Hindi but we never picked them up. Think it makes it better that we also didn't bother to learn Gaelic even though da speaks it."

"Do you wish you knew more about it?"

"I don't know. I'm only a fourth Indian. Do you wish you had German culture or Irish or Sweden or wherever your ancestors are from?"

She shrugs and stares expectantly up at me.

"Why don't you have poems in your room?"

"Oh, are you trying to discover everything about when I was wain?"

"Well, yeah. I want to know more about my girlfriend." She blushes fiercely, eyes widening at her slip up.

I smile at her and sit beside her, resting my head on her shoulder.

"I didn't start writing poetry until I went to uni. Therapist thought it'd be good, and uni therapists are free."

"I didn't realize you have a therapist."

"Had." Something that bugs Finn and Sai to no end. But I don't want to go to therapy anymore. At least, not right now. It's too taxing on my mind to tear it apart bit by bit. Maybe someday.

Emmylou runs her fingers through my hair and I could almost fall asleep like this. Head tucked under her chin and her hands scratching at my skull. It must happen because I wake up sometime in the night when her hand brushes my bare stomach.

She's long asleep and I gasp awake at the feeling. Sitting up in bed, I scratch my forearm until it stings, fingernails scraping over the fading scars from protruding bone, and go to the sofa in the main room. The presents are stacked up under the tree and I eyeball them from the sofa.

There's one for each of us from each of us and an extra one my parents say is from Saint Nicolaus but we all know it's from them as well. I'm thankful we've had presents under the tree every year. I wonder what Finn's siblings do today. Finn will leave at evenings to make sure they're fed, but even he doesn't have enough money to buy fifteen siblings presents.

I sit in front of the tree and organize the stacks. It's peaceful and eventually White trots in and lays his head in my lap. I pet him in the silent hours and the sun begins to rise through the windows. I can hear the horse and pony nickering in their paddock and one of the cows moos loudly.

Standing, I walk to the backdoor, throw on my boots and coat, and enter the early morning, White on my heels. He yaps at the cows who pay him no mind. I enter their pasture and dodge Burns's horns as she begs for a scratch. I brush her down and grab the shears from her lean-to to cut off a matt near her arse. Neruda pays me no mind until she saunters over to the feed and trots right back over in search of hay.

They're spoiled because I've been buying them hay and grain but they're perfectly capable of eating the dry grass on the fields. Neruda watches me intently as I drop the hay and sprinkle grain on it. I dodge another horn as she goes to feed and turn to the sound of White's barking.

He runs excitedly to Emmylou as she steps out in that damn cancer jumper and a cable-knit hat. She shields her eyes from the sun as she walks over to the fence. I look at her sleepy face. She hunkers down further into the jumper, hands covered by the sleeves.

"Bit cold innit?"

"Yeah, saw the sun and thought a sweater would be enough." I fumble over the fence, something well practiced from games of tag with the lads but now a nuisance with a bum knee, and take my coat off, draping it around her.

"Thanks," she says with a sniffle and a smile. We turn back toward the cows and watch as they nose through the feed and eventually through the light dusting of snow in search of grass. White paws at my legs until I pick him up. He warms my chest and Emmylou warms my side. Even with the cold biting at my nose and throat, I don't want to leave the sun yet. It shines through the fog and illuminates the countryside. The hills look less hostile in the glow and I soak in the land I love.

"It's nice here." She drops her head to my shoulder and I watch White sniff at her.

"Scotland or my parents' house?"

"Both."

This would be a good time to tell her I love her. Here before God's shining light and the land that raised me, in the place I feel the most safe and comfortable, hot cups of tea probably already brewing inside. I'm biting my lip in preparation when the back door opens again. Yellow and Blue run out, and Finn stands at the steps.

"Presents, aye?" Blue runs past our property and Yellow follows. I drop a squirming White before I turn, taking Emmylou's hand, and enter the house.

It's warm in here and I blow hot air into both our hands, Emmylou's clasped between mine. In the den where mam has plates of gingerbread and cups of tea waiting.

"Some nocturnal beast sorted them so just sit in front of your pile and have at it," she says, looking at me questioningly over her cup. I grab a biscuit and sit beside Emmylou before reaching for my first present. Finn has already opened his and he nudges me in thanks as he finds a bookstore gift card. Medical books cost a pretty penny and I've worked a few odd jobs in preparation for the holidays.

My first present is a new pair of running trainers and I grin up at my da who smiles down at me. They're electric green and I'm about to stand to grab a pair of running socks instead of the wooly ones I currently have on when Sai speaks up.

"The thin package. It's not my only present but I'm tired of washing your holeridden socks."

I tear into Sai's gift, put on my new socks, and lace up my new trainers.

"You could probably get in a slow jog today if you keep it under a kilometer," Finn says as he opens a jumper from Sai. He squints at the design and adds, "They actually got the labels right."

"Better have. I looked at your textbooks to make sure."

Last year Finn got a shirt from Sai that had the muscle groups mislabeled and Finn only wears it to bed or if he knows he won't take his jumper off all day.

I flex my thigh before my mam swats at my head.

"Open the other presents first. No need to go running before dawn's fully broke." I stick my tongue out at her. She opens a cookbook and glares at the three of us. "Which one of yous got me this? I can cook without any damn instructions, thank you very much."

We all look away, admonished, but I'm not sure who bought it until da says, "I did actually. It's only Indian recipes." She glowers at him and we all quickly turn from the ensuing argument, opening presents in a haste of giggles.

I grab the smallest box, the only one that remains and open the hard cover to find a small silver chain with a wire-wrapped orange Highland Cow dangling off of it. I hold the cow between my fingers and rub his small horns.

"I wanted to get you something for when you miss home at college."

I look over at Emmylou and she smiles shyly at me.

"I didn't know they sold these in town," I say, handing her the necklace so she can put it on.

"They don't. I ordered it a while ago."

"Before . . .?"

"Yeah, before us and before the fight."

My heart squeezes in my chest, but I turn from her so she can clasp the necklace. My mam winks from beside me and I shoot her a scowl. No need for her to make it something embarrassing.

"That present is from me," I say, pointing at a round fluffy object. Emmylou smiles and reaches for her last present, opening a sunflower throw pillow. She tries to glare at me but can't hide her smile.

"Thanks," she says before stealing a quick peck from me.

"No fucking way," Finn says from beside her, and I look over to see him and Sai holding matching tickets. "Tickets to the Hibs versus the Celtic? Seriously, Bram, this is amazing!"

"Greer went ahead and bought you the train tickets to Glasgow." The three of us groan. Glasgow is not a place worth going and the Hibs are from Edinburgh, but I suppose they'll make the trek. Sai and Finn give my parents hugs and don their new Hibs kits I bought them. It now makes sense why my parents' requested that be one of my gifts.

"You think Boyle will sign my kit?" Finn asks and Sai swats at him.

"You blood traitor. Is his name on the back?" Sai asks. Finn flips his jersey showing us the name of the Australian player. "McGinn is where it's at mate," Sai says, showing the offending jersey, and they both put them on before wrestling to get to the backdoor.

We listen to them fall out of the door before my mam asks, "Did they even put their boots on?"

I shrug before turning to Emmylou.

"I've got one more present but it's outside. You may want to change." My mam raises her eyebrow and I smile innocently before following Emmylou to change into trakkies and a running jumper.

"What is it?" she asks, through the door as I change.

"You'll see. You didn't happen to bring anything you could get dirty in? Or . . . perhaps ride a horse in?" I hear her gasp, then knock to let me know she's dressed. I enter as she's tying her hair in a high bun.

Mam and da are already standing outside when we get there, staring disapprovingly at Beau.

Emmylou squeals before semi calmly walking to the Clydesdale and letting him smell her. She pets his snout as my da finally speaks up.

"Is that the horse from Finn's da?" I hum my agreement and both my parents exhale in exasperation. "Good thing that match is the day after tomorrow so the lad can get out of town."

"He'll return it tonight when he goes for evenings."

"And you?"

"Maybe we'll go back for Hogmanay." Emmylou looks back at me and I leave my parents to join her.

"You got me a Clydesdale for Christmas?" I laugh at her and gesture for her to get on.

"No, I got you a ride on Beau for a day," I grunt out as she uses the fence to leverage onto his back. I lean my head against her thigh. "I know you missed the horses back home. Sorry wee Sally isn't big enough to ride." She grins excitedly and looks for a bridle.

"You'll have to ride him bareback. We couldn't manage the saddle or lead and Sally's isn't big enough." Sally nudges against my palm as I speak on her and I run my hands across her head. Emmylou nudges Beau gently and I open the paddock to let them out. Sally whinnies beside me until da comes over and harnesses her. She'll probably just run with the dogs so she doesn't feel left out since there's nothing to carry on Christmas morning.

"Where can I take him?" Emmylou asks, looking down at me. She's a goddess upon his back and I smile up at her.

"Just up that road toward the first big hill. It's only three kilometers and I'll run it with you." She and Beau will probably run circles around me, but I'll finish the six kilometers eventually.

"Finn said you could only do one."

I wave my hand, dismissing her.

"Just go as fast as you want and I'll make my way to the hill. Turn back once you get there and you can go at that as long as you want."

She looks disapprovingly at me but finally pulls away. Beau trots gently, and I start a slow jog behind them, assessing my thigh and knee.

Once Emmylou gets comfortable, she starts to pull away and they're running gracefully by the time I'm anything near a jog. She blazes a trail forward in the grass and snow and I watch with envy.

I wish I could run like a horse. I can't stand horses because he's probably already on his way back by the time I'm bent over at half a kilometer.

My lungs burn and I stretch my thigh on the side of the road. I'll have to get on the bike once I'm on campus to bring my cardio back up without straining my thigh. It's disappointing how quickly my body depletes to an average sack of meat.

I'm jogging along slowly when Emmylou returns, panting, her cheeks red. Beau's breath steams in the bitter morning chill.

"I want a Clydesdale when I grow up," she says slowing him down beside me.

I try to hide my heavy breathing but her eyes search me as I jog with Beau at a walk beside me.

"Do you want to get on?"

"Christ, no. Hate horses." She frowns and I realize my mistake.

"You hate horses."

I take the opportunity to stop my pitiful excuse for a jog.

"Well, not hate." Yes, hate. "I just don't like riding them. Why can't I just trust my own feet to get there?"

She laughs at that.

"So do you hate trains and cars as well?"

Yes. "No." But she can see through my lie.

"My goodness Saatchi. Aren't you dramatic? What are you going to do when you go to Boston? Run everywhere you go?"

"Why not? I do it in Edinburgh."

She leans over her knee and grabs my face.

"Honey, the US is a lot bigger than Scotland. You can't really walk to places. It isn't built for that."

I move my face out of her hand petulantly.

"Well, I can put up with it for a bit. It's not like I'd ever move away from Scotland."

"Oh," she says sadly. I grimace. I hadn't even thought about where she'd want to live. I'm not ready to even think about that, so I start jogging again. She trots forward and tugs kindly at my hair before pushing forward again with Beau.

The sun glows in front of her, creating a halo around them. I ache for her to be near me again.

The steam from the shower relaxes my aching thigh just enough for me to limp out of the bathroom once I'm dressed. Maybe running this soon after an injury was too much hopeful thinking.

Emmylou is lain out on the bed when I step into the room.

"How's your leg?" I shrug at her as I toss my wet towel on the bed frame. She subsequently pouts up at me and I sit beside her.

"Kiss'll make it better," I tell her boldly.

She laughs but leans in.

Her lips are soft with the apple-flavored balm and I follow the taste as she tilts her head. I'd follow her anywhere. I'd burn forever if it meant I could hold her here in my childhood bed and everywhere that follows. But, the thing is, I won't burn. I know I won't because I love her so pure. There is no sin in a love like this.

And then her hand is on my waist and I remember, not every thought I've had of her is necessarily pure. I press myself against her and kiss along her face until I'm nipping at her neck. She lets out a noise that I shush because, even though mam and da are out with Sally, the boys are still probably around here. Honestly, I don't want her quiet though. I want her louder, but I'll take my time with her.

So I do, moving back to her face and running my hands along her thighs, but she grows inpatient. She crawls into my lap and grinds against me. I let out a gasp and, in that moment, she sneaks her hands under my shirt. She starts to pull up and my kisses on her neck stutter.

I should stop her.

I feel my shirt move along my spine and every nerve stands on end as my lungs pause their gasping.

All I have to do is say no. My heart beats in my head and in my throat and in every tip of my fingers as she starts to pull it near my chest. Subconsciously, or by her direction, my arms are angled so she can easily slip the shirt off.

She can't take it off.

And then the shirts over my head. It may be for a split second—I can't tell—but it's enough, because I'm suddenly blind and I'm not sure if I'm breathing and my arm hurts and I'm definitely not breathing and I should've said no because the shirt's in my face and the darkness holds the most painful memories.

I should've just said no.

Somewhere, she's calling my name but it's too far away from the blindness. I'm not breathing. Or I am. I don't know where Emmylou is. Is she here? Why didn't I say no? Or stop? Just stop. Just stop please, fuck please stop. Fuck.

*Emmylou*

"Sai!" He's in the backyard but at the look on my face he stops mid kick and sprints into the house. "I don't know what happened." I try shouting at his retreating back but my heart is choking my words and I'm not sure what comes garbled out. I try again, "She just started panicking." Finn rushes past me, following Sai, and I stop outside of Saatchi's room where she's still gasping for air, clawing at her arms. Small droplets of blood cling to the places her blunt nails have cut into.

"Saatch! Saatch, I have to help you." Her eyes are glassy and she shakes her head, but her brother moves closer, slow like you would in front of a stray cat. "I'm just going to put the blanket around you, okay?" He grabs the blanket we tossed to the floor and crouches to drape it around her shoulders, but she fights at it and grips her shirt tighter. Her gasps are raspy and shallow but there is no air being pushed in or out.

"Saatchi," Sai yells when she swings at him with full force. He barely dodges it and Finn takes a step into the room, but Sai raises a hand at him to stop him without looking. His eyes are trained on Saatchi, whose frantic, panic-stricken face seems to not see anything. "Saatchi, it's me. It's me. Look at me." He reaches out a hand but Saatchi shakes her head. She's trembling, or something stronger than that. She looks like she'll vibrate right out of her body.

Finn turns back to me and puts a hand on my shoulder, making me flinch at the unexpected contact. He looks at me and I realize I'm also shaking with panic, tears streaming down my cheeks.

"Sai will take care of her. Come on." He pulls at me again and I look at Saatchi, but she isn't looking at me. She's not there. It's like she's in a different world but I know I'd do anything to get her out of it.

"But, Saatchi?" I ask staring at him, and he nudges me out of the doorway, closing the door behind us. I can still hear her gasping, but it grows quieter as Finn guides me to the kitchen table.

"I don't know what happened. I didn't—I didn't mean to." He passes me the box of Kleenex that's still on the table.

It seems so far away from now, whatever I had cried about the other day. Saatchi had been there for me then, a quiet but steady figure prepared to listen to my woes and do what she could. I'm not sure how, but I've caused her pain. Again.

I am wracked with guilt at being the constant driving force behind her pain. I'm reminded that this moment isn't about my own pain when Finn finally looks up at me, his own eyes heavy with unshed tears.

"I know. I know you didn't mean to. She . . . she probably didn't . . . she should've . . . It's hard." His hands ball up and he grabs a Kleenex. "Fuck," he says and we both sit there crying.

"Finn, I should've—it's my fault."

"No." He reaches out and grabs my hands, tears streaming down his face. "It was mine. This happened before you.

"We were sixteen. We were sixteen and it was horrible and it's my fault. I was supposed to be with Saatchi that day. I was always with Saatchi every day, but that day I wasn't." He looks up at me and there is more pain in his eyes than I've ever seen in anyone. He hurts more than he did when he left us to go to his family. He hurts more than when he and Saatchi fight. He hurts more than my mother when she found out I had cancer. "Emmylou, it's my fault. It's all my fault. I was supposed to be there. I—I was—"

I cling onto him tightly as we sit there and cry. We cry until the sun is past its high point in the sky. We cry as our hearts bleed out for someone we love and a pain we'll never know. We cry until Saatchi comes out of the room, bundled in the blanket and wearing five layers of clothes despite the warmth in the house. She doesn't acknowledge either of us as she sits in front of the TV and turns on whatever happened to be on last.

Sai grabs a Kleenex and blows his nose before sitting teary eyed beside us.

"It's not your fault," he says, turning to me and then to Finn. He grabs both of us tightly on the shoulders. "It's not. It's none of our faults. It's their fault and they rot in prison because of it. It's not our fault." He says it like a mantra, and I look over at Saatchi. She stares blankly at the TV.

"Can I go?" I ask, pointing at her.

Sai nods.

"Just don't touch her right now. You can sit next to her, just don't touch her for a while."

"Like a few days," Finn adds through his tears.

I get up, grabbing a few tissues, and sit beside Saatchi. I don't say anything as we watch the soccer match on the screen.

"Did they tell you?" she finally asks, eyes blank.

"Not in so many words but," I swallow, forcing my voice not to crack. "I can guess."

"You didn't ask me what the worst thing about coming out was. I should've told you."

I wait, but she doesn't continue. I lean my head against her chair, just to be a little closer. The match finishes and Greer and Bram get home. There's whispering in the kitchen and I can hear Finn break out in tears again.

"Tell Finn to stop crying." I look at Saatchi. She's still swaddled, eyes still on the TV. "No, I'm serious Emmylou. Get up and tell Finn to stop crying or to leave." I get up silently and enter the kitchen. Greer has Finn wrapped in her small arms and he towers over her as he cries.

"Saatchi send you to tell him to stop crying?" Sai asks when I walk in. I silently thank him for saving me and nod. "Come on, mate. Let's go for a drive." Sai grabs Finn, leading him away and out the front door. I look guilty at Greer and Bram.

"No, it's all right, lass. Don't be upset. This too will pass," Bram says, hugging me. Greer wipes her tears on the kitchen rag. "We'll make evenings, you go sit with her." I thank him and return to my spot.

We watch the first half of a game before Greer hands me a plate. We normally all eat together in the kitchen but Sai and Finn aren't back.

"Saatchi?" Greer asks, offering a plate.

"No."

And so Greer leaves and I don't know where she goes because it's silent again except for the game. I finish my food and place my plate on the coffee table, unwilling to leave Saatchi's side. We watch another game and Greer and Bram go to bed. Then another and Finn and Sai come in, grab plates and go to their room.

Only then does Saatchi finally cry. I watch as tears silently stream down her face, wishing I could brush them away. Saatchi doesn't cry. Saatchi never breaks. But even as she does, I love her with everything that I am and I hurt watching as she hangs her head to let the tears roll.

"I didn't tell you the worst part was the bigots," she starts in a shaky voice. "Some of them are run of the mill—call you names and tell you you'll burn in hell. But some are worse." The tears fall freely and she pulls the blanket up to clean her face. "I was open and out and everyone knew it. Most people didn't care. Actually, before then, I thought no one cared. Stupid of me.

"I had just gotten done with field practice. Normally Finn and Sai get out at the same time so we walk together. But that day, a girl pulled Finn aside to flirt with him and the fucking newspaper president pulled Sai aside to interview him before their upcoming match. I used to take the longest to shower. You know, loosen up my muscles and all that.

"Didn't think anything of it when someone walked into the locker room until he was pulling me out of the shower. Slammed me so hard against a locker that it split my arm, bone out and everything."

Tears pool violently, blurring my vision, but I can still just make out her hand tracing a tattoo that covers the scars of a gruesome injury.

"He slammed me so hard against that damn locker. And then he raped me." She stops crying and leans her head back against the chair.

She's silent as she continues to watch the soccer game. She inhales one rattling breath and stops. Then two more before she finally speaks again.

"He said he'd fuck the fag out of me. Teach me what it is to like men." She laughs hollowly. "Suppose my screams were loud enough to attract attention. I think that was kind of the worst part though. Everyone knew about it afterwards. Word spreads when pigs have to get involved. It was just like reliving it over and over again. The questioning, the pitying looks—like I was broken. I couldn't escape it. It followed me everywhere and I was drowning in the memory. So, I tried to off myself. Ended up in grippy socks with no strings in my trousers." She finally looks over at me.

"I don't know why I bothered pushing you. This isn't a life you want. This isn't a life anyone chooses."

"But I'm still choosing it." I'm terrified for her, for my future, but I know the words are true and honest. Sexual assault happens whether you're queer or not and being queer isn't a choice, but the happiness I feel from Saatchi and choosing to be with her is and I'll make it every time.

"Are you scared?" she asks me.

"I've always been scared."

"But now?"

"But now I have someone who's taught me to be brave."

She pauses, her eyes searching mine.

"I'm going to shower, and then I'm going to put on five layers of clothes, and then I'm going to sleep in my bed with the door locked and you beside me and a pillow between us. It'll probably take me a few hours because I'll have to stop and cry and maybe have a panic attack or two. Do you still love me?"

"Every day."

"Fine."

We only make it to the five layers of clothing before Saatchi crawls back onto the chair and turns on another game. I wonder how many games until we run out. This one is in Mandarin but she watches without complaints.

My eyes are heavy, my head slips, and I wake up frightfully pulling away from where I landed on her shoulder.

She eyes me carefully.

"You're weird, Emmylou. I don't like it." I don't know how to respond before she's opening her blanket. "Come on, the feet come up. We can sleep here." I crawl into her lap and rest my head on her shoulder.

"Is this okay?"

"Yeah. Thanks for asking."

# Chapter Fourteen

World Cruel,
Bites, Bites, Bites
Cover Up,
Scars, Scars, Scars.

They're Coming,
Smash, Smash, Smash.
Not Safe,
Die, Die, Die.

I've decided Hogmanay is the loudest celebration I've ever been in and I've been in Times Square when they drop the ball and American football stadiums with jets flying over. Scotland, however, is on a whole different level. Everyone is exalted and drunk. Bagpipes are scattered throughout the crowd as I hold onto Saatchi's hand and Kirsty's arm as we move along.

I can tell Saatchi's thigh is aching but she powers on, and I drink my hot toddy from a thermos before reaching across Saatchi to hand it to Drew.

The girls came back when they heard our plans but the boys stayed in Glasgow after scalping more tickets to another Celtic match. Drew seemed in high spirits when we met at the apartment, but I wasn't able to ask her how it went before she was asking me for every detail about break.

Somebody thrusts a scarf at us. It's blue and white and Saatchi hands the man some quid before grabbing two. I can't hear her over the cacophony, but she places one around my neck and wraps the other around herself. Kirsty waves him away. I've never seen her wear anything that even says Scotland. Drew sometimes wears a shirt or sweater from places in Scotland she's visited but it's the downstairs group that makes up for it.

Saatchi is decked out in tartan and a green jersey for the Hibernians, the soccer team her family loves. She has a large top hat with blue lace and the Scottish flag pinned to it. I just know if Finn were here, he'd be wearing a kilt, even though Saatchi's told me they're only for special occasions like weddings.

We're a few blocks from the castle before Saatchi finally tugs my hand away from the parade. I pull Kirsty along and Drew follows as we weave out of the crowd toward a small restaurant that's open despite the hour and take our seats outside.

"How's your leg?"

She shrugs at me but pushes her knuckles into the muscle.

"How can I be sweating when it's so bloody cold out?" Kirsty says, ripping her beanie off.

"We should take a picture before the crowd leaves," Drew says, standing up. I offer Saatchi a hand up that she dismisses as Drew asks someone to take a photo.

"Do I look okay?"

I adjust Kirsty's beanie and tuck in some stray hairs before we both turn to the camera. We all smile with our arms wrapped around each other.

"Wait, one more," Kirsty tells the woman before turning to me. "We won't post this one but, you know," she bumps my hip. "At least try to look like a couple." I laugh at her antics. I suppose she's always been the one rooting for us to get together. It's only fair that she gets to see the product of her efforts.

I lean my head on Saatchi's shoulder with Kirsty's arm still around my waist and the last picture is snapped.

"Thank you," Drew tells her, taking her phone back. Kirsty turns to us mischievously.

"One of just the two of you?" Saatchi groans and rolls her eyes but I grab at her jacket before she can walk away.

"Yeah, that'd be nice actually."

Kirsty takes my phone and I turn to Saatchi who looks wholly uncomfortable. "It's just for us," I tell her before leaning up and kissing her cheek. Kirsty snaps a few more of us just standing beside each other, and when she's finally done I turn in Saatchi's arms.

"Thanks for this."

"Hogmanay?"

"No, just, you."

I watch her face battle between emotions and prepare myself for teasing before she settles on another one, one I don't know well yet.

"Anything for you," she says before kissing my forehead. I hear the camera click again and Kirsty smiles sheepishly.

"Sorry, it was just cute."

I laugh, taking the phone from her at Saatchi's insistence, and sit beside Drew to flip through the photos. The ones where we stand beside each other look awkward and I delete a few. I flip to the one where I'm kissing Saatchi's cheek. She looks embarrassed and shy but gives a wobbly grin to the camera. I can't stop staring at it because I've always pictured Saatchi so confident, but here it looks like I'm the one who has her wrapped around my finger and not the other way around.

The second one is even better. We both seem so comfortable in each other's arms and I smile gently up at her as she kisses my forehead. It's that same soft and quiet feeling from our time spent at her parents' house over Christmas. Like crawling into a warm bed on a cold day.

I look up at her as she orders snacks for the table. As always, her dark skin glows. Even from the store lights she looks beautiful.

I look down at my phone and set the one of her kissing my forehead as my lock screen and the shy version of Saatchi as my wallpaper. That version of Saatchi is just for me. I look up at her again and her eyes soften as we make eye contact. Maybe I have her wrapped around my finger just a bit.

A chair pulls up to our table suddenly, and I look up at the intruder. My mouth tastes sour as Laire sits down and turns to Saatchi.

"Well, not so straight after all."

Saatchi, surprisingly, laughs.

"Happy New Year's, Laire. Why don't you go be a shite somewhere else?"

Laire smiles softly at Saatchi. Against my will, I feel guilty. There is love clearly painted in Laire's eyes that I twist into blaming myself for taking that from her—no matter how illogical.

"Happy New Year's, Saatchi," Laire says getting up.

"That was—" Kirsty starts.

"Hold your whist," Saatchi complains as our food comes out. I wrap my ankle around hers across the table and she blushes.

"Oh, aren't you taken," Drew teases, seeing the action. Saatchi blushes harder, choosing instead to fill her mouth with food rather than acknowledge Drew.

"All right?" I ask her afterwards as we walk behind the girls in the biting air. I wrap myself tighter under her arm to steal her body heat. She nods her head, contemplatively. I squeeze her hand and follow her to the apartment. It's late when we get back and I pause at her door, but she looks at me awkwardly.

"Is it cool if I sleep in your bed tonight?"

Saatchi doesn't sleep well when we share space and I feel guilty as butterflies flutter around in my stomach.

"Of course, but won't Anne get lonely?"

She runs her tongue over her teeth and looks back at the door. "She'll be fine for one night."

"Okay," I say tentatively, leaning up to kiss her before leading her up the stairs. The apartment is warm and I unwind my scarf to put on the hanger along with my coat. Saatchi's hands shake as she undoes the laces on her boots.

When she finally stands, I stand beside her, unsure if I should take her hand or give her space.

"Tea sounds nice," she says quietly into her scarf. I give her a smile as I turn from her and get to puttering around the kitchen. I've seen Drew do this a million times but with Saatchi's eyes on my back, I suddenly can't remember what temperature to boil the water to.

Saatchi's arm reaches slowly over mine and settles around me as I lean into her.

"Here, it's this setting for black tea. Thought you'd know that by now, what with living here for so long and what have you."

I shiver at the press of her cold lips against the back of my neck. Her hands follow the curve of my waist and, it's with a feat from God, that I keep the gasp from stuttering out when her hands, finally rest, connected around the front of me.

"I'm nervous," I whisper to her in the dark kitchen, the sounds of Hogmanay still outside.

"Aye, can feel it in your pulse," she responds into my neck. "I don't have to stay over and we don't have to do anything." I'm already shaking my head before she's even done.

"It's not that. I just, haven't before." She pulls back and I turn in her arms. "But, uhm I-I want to . . . with you, I mean." She bites down a grin and I bite down the urge to melt into a puddle as my cheeks heat.

"Cute," she says before she leans into kiss me.

Saatchi wraps her arms around my waist again as I lean all my weight into her. I trust her wholeheartedly and, even with the anxious butterflies blowing a windstorm, I want to give her what I am and take what I'm given.

Her mouth is experienced against mine and I hold back an unwelcome sound as she bites lightly at my lips. But I can't help the sound that escapes me when she kisses my neck, and I'm fighting every instinct to keep my hands squarely on her shoulders.

She pulls away and I can't help the whine that's released from my own mouth.

"Bedroom," she says breathlessly, and I flush but eagerly grab her hand, pulling her with me.

She shuts the door behind us and puts a hand on my shoulder.

"Just, take a few steps back?"

I do as she asks and she presses her back against the door.

"You don't have to," I say as she takes steadying breaths despite the itch to feel every part of her against me.

"It's fine," she says before taking one last breath and pulling both her sweatshirt and shirt off in one. She stands there, unsure for a second, and I hold my hand out to her. Not close enough to touch her, but far enough that she sees the invitation. Just like trying to coax a feral cat closer. She truly is a wild animal.

She takes my hand and pulls me back in.

I chase her lips as she pulls my own sweater off and I chase her lips as she lays us on the bed and I chase her lips until I realize I need her mouth elsewhere.


The bed is warm as the sun streams gently through the window. I wake slowly to the feeling of Saatchi tracing small patterns on my back from below me. Our legs are tangled and I can feel the drops of sweat sticking us together.

"Sorry, I run warm when I sleep," I say, groggily pulling away, but she holds me in place.

"'S fine. I already knew that," she says before kissing the top of my head. I lay there and listen to her heartbeat. It speeds up when I run soft fingers along her side. At first I think it's from excitement until she lets out a snort and grabs my hand.

"Tickles."

I smirk before pulling my hand away and beginning an onslaught of fingers running across her ribs. She laughs uncontrollably before bringing her knees up in defense. A gasp of air escapes me as she flips me onto my back, and I don't recover before she's kissing me fiercely. I let my hands roam her skin and I'm lost in her when there's suddenly loud knocking on the apartment door.

"I thought the boys didn't get back until later tonight," I say, pulling away to grab my phone. I swipe through the Instagram notifications of the photo I posted last night to see it's already past noon. Even then, the boys shouldn't be here yet.

"Hi there, darling! I hope I'm not intruding . . ."

My blood chills to absolute ice and I gasp with the weight of a sucker punch. Saatchi's wide eyes look down at me and I squirm underneath her.

"Saatchi, get up," I whisper with panic in my face. Her eyes lock on mine, something I don't have the bandwidth to decipher staring back at me, and she rolls off of me before covering her eyes with her arm. I scrambled up and make sure the door is locked before racing to my closet to throw on an acceptable outfit for the day as I hear my mother's voice from the living room.

Kirsty can be heard obviously stalling and I yank a brush through my knotted hair with desperation. My reflection shows a love bite on my neck, and I pause to look back at Saatchi. She hasn't moved.

My mother knocks on the door.

"Be right there." I take a calming breath, frantic to keep the desperation out of my voice. "Just got out of the shower." I change into a turtleneck and throw on a scarf for extra measure before running to my girlfriend.

"Saatchi, baby, you have to get under the bed or the bathroom or something. Shit, if it weren't for your knee you could use the window."

She finally uncovers her eyes and all I see is pain. There's this endless world of hurt inside of her that she never shows, and right now I can't comfort her like I wish I could. I'll do the best I can.

I grab her face and press my lips to hers. "Saatchi, listen, I'll tell her, but not right now. Not like this. Please. I swear I'll tell her, just please get under the bed."

The hurt doesn't leave, but she at least gets up and tosses on her T-shirt and underwear before grabbing all the clothes and taking them both under the bed.

There's a sigh of relief and a threat of tears I don't let escape, instead turning to the door and opening it.

I swallow as I look head on at my mother. She's the exact same as I remember. Lips a cherry red, pink cheeks, motherly figure, and yet, there's this anger that fills me when I see her. Followed by hurt and pain and the bitter reality that my girlfriend is stuffed under my bed because my mother can't see past her expectations and find real, genuine love.

"Hi sweetheart," she says before surprising me with a hug. I blink and tentatively wrap my arms around her, but she's already pulling away. "I know how much you hated missing Christmas so I thought I'd pay a visit," she says as she goes over to sit on the bed. Thank God the duvet is covering the edges of it. "Smells rancid in here."

I bite the inside of my lip as I picture Saatchi below, on the verge of laughing. Then I bite it harder as I remember the pain I saw in her eyes as I wrangled her under.

"Yeah, probably. I was out pretty late and passed out without showering. It gets pretty sweaty being in a crowd to celebrate New Years."

She smiles at that.

"Looked like fun! I saw your cute little Instagram post."

That's why she's here then. It wasn't even the one of just me and Saatchi. I thought it was innocent enough to fly under the radar, but I guess even resting my head on Saatchi's shoulder is enough to raise flags for her.

"Are you hungry?" I ask, keeping my eyes from under the bed. "There's a really good breakfast restaurant just a block away." She grins at me, like she's preparing to grab at a mouse already stuck in her trap.

"Why don't you show me your apartment first?"

"Like you said. It smells bad. I'll clean as soon as we're back and you can see the rest of it while I vacuum."

She blinks slowly and tilts her head. I mimic her tilt and smile innocently. She knows. The room smells like sex, I'm wearing a turtleneck, there's a girl under my bed. She must know.

But just as quickly, she stands up and accepts my offer for brunch. As we walk out of my room, I see Drew and Kirsty trying to inconspicuously drink tea at the dining table but both of their ears are turned toward us.

"We'll be back later. Let me know if y'all want me to pick up any brunch." And with that, I turn my back on the apartment and let my mother see the city that has made me.

# Chapter Fifteen

I call a peach by her name
So that when I bite into her,
She calls me the same.
I bow and lay down my power
For I trust her to keep me above
To show me the meaning of true love.

The sound of the door shutting is quickly followed by Kirsty and Drew's footsteps into Emmylou's room. I have no desire to emerge from under the bed frame, but I sigh and wipe my face before crawling out.

"Holy shit, did she know her mam was coming?" Drew asks, and I shrug before thinking better and shaking my head as I throw my trousers on.

"No, she couldn't have. She looked just as shocked as I did," *if not more panicked.* I don't have time to process exactly how I'm feeling with her mam just outside. I start to strip the dirty sheets and Drew, God Bless, follows my lead as we throw all the proof of last night into the wash.

Kirsty turns on the vacuum as I turn to Drew and take her offered mug of tea.

"She manage to say anything before they burst out of here?"

"Aye, just, get under the bed," I tell Drew petulantly. I'm not willing to let her see I'm hopeful Emmylou actually tells her mam. If she doesn't, then I'll realize that I wasted most of this year fawning over someone who doesn't care.

"I'm sure there was more. Don't forget that trust the two of yous have built. Don't throw this away because you're a child in this."

I suck my teeth at Drew and then hand her my empty tea.

"Whatever, I'm off," I say back, already halfway out the door. The boys aren't back yet from watching football and I'm thankful to get the flat to myself.

Anne Bonny cries at me and I fill her bowl and scratch behind her ears as I continue to the bathroom. My body is still warm from Emmylou's caress and my skin smells of hers. I'm reluctant to wash her from me for fear it may be the last time.

I knew what I was getting myself into though. Emmylou isn't ready to come out and I'm not going to force her. Living in the bubble we created during holidays—full of openly cuddling in front of my family and kisses snuck in the wee hours of the night—lulled both of us into a sense of invulnerability. It's ironic that her mam would show up right when things seemed to be going well. Either that or she has a sick, innate sense of when to pull the leash tighter on her daughter.

The warm water flushes me of the night before, but, internally, I still feel guilt clenching my gut—that sort of fear when you haven't done anything wrong but someone else thinks you have.

Anne stares at me from between the shower curtains.

"Be glad I had your innards scoop out. No emotions or feelings for you."

*Emmylou*

When I was younger, I used to revel in days I got to spend with my mother. I didn't receive a lot of attention from my family when I was young, with my dad being busier than a bee in the spring with work, and my sister old enough that she didn't want me dawdling behind her. All I had was my mother. But I wasn't all she had.

My mother lived to be the center of attention among her friends and acquaintances. On the rare occasions I was brought along, I loved to see her in her element. Hair curled, lipstick shinier than the pearls on her neck, always smiling. I felt like I was standing in the presence of a movie star.

Most days, I'd only get a glimpse of this movie star since I was plopped in front of a television when I was too young for school and then tucked into a hospital room before finally being old enough to go off on my own. Whenever she did bother giving me the time of day as a child, our mother-daughter dates were my favorite.

She would plan these extravagant days where we would get brunch, mani-pedis, and I would try on dresses that she would pick out and then buy me. It felt like a day made just for me to be a movie star just like her.

I can't remember when her smile stopped reaching her eyes. I wish I knew what it was about me that made me a charity case in her eyes—a burden. She viewed my sister as perfect, let her have her way in life, and catered to her every need. At some point, I must have slipped up because, suddenly, every mother-daughter date became a collar around my neck. An inspection beneath a microscope. A day for my mother to nitpick and polish me off to fix whatever was wrong with me.

The pastry in front of me looks dry and the tea is too cold as I rub the sweat and sweetness between my legs together. I should be in the shower right now with Saatchi instead of sitting across from my mother, squeezing my legs together and covering the evidence of last night with my scarf.

"I could never stand to live in a place like this. It's so dreary."

I look up at my mother and her perfectly done makeup. She still looks like a movie star, but Edinburgh has painted her into a bitter memory. Now, she's the movie you get stuck watching after football season ends and there is nothing else on TV.

"I enjoy it. It's cozy."

She scoffs at her tea.

"Cozy is one word for it. Don't you miss Texas? Or, my word, at least the sun?" I shrug at her, feeling unwilling to play at this game. "You're getting so pale, and don't shrug at me. Emmylou, you need to get into a tanning salon if you're going to insist on continuing this—" She waves her hands around. "I'm not even sure. I was afraid this was your rebellious phase and I'd come to find you covered in piercings and tattoos." She looks me over. "None of those, right?"

"Nope, I just wanted to live on my own. I'm not trying to stick it to the man or whatever." I wonder what I'd look like with tattoos like Saatchi. She has a lot of piercings too. I should probably leave all that to her.

"Well, your room smelled like booze and sex. I really hope you're not doing any of that garbage. You know no man's going to want a used tissue."

I suck my teeth, then fight to stifle my smile as I realize who I picked up the habit from.

"No mother, I'm not having sex with men. I did, however, drink a little bit last night, it was New Year's after all and it is legal here at my age."

Her eyes don't leave mine as I give her a dead stare. This truly is a movie scene I don't feel like repeating.

"How long are you going to be here?"

"I was thinking of staying two nights, maybe three." Internally, I cackle at the irony. The child I once was would have given anything to have this much one-on-one time. Before Edinburgh, I would have happily bent my head and accepted anything from her.

"Why the sudden visit? We could've just been at home with Janey and daddy."

Her cup falters a hair before she takes a sip of it.

"Janey was with Eric and dad was at work. It's easier if you and I spend time here instead of flying to Texas to an empty home."

I tilt my head at her but she won't make eye contact. There's no point in her continuing to lie if she's already been caught.

There's no telling how much she's lied about to me. I've never questioned her. In fact, I didn't even question her now. It was an accident that I caught her.

I groan internally, impatience leaking into my bones. I should be lying in bed with Saatchi, but instead I have a headache and every inch of my body is demanding a shower.

"Yeah, guess this makes more sense," I tell my mother, rubbing my temples. "But classes start soon and I have a bunch of errands to run, plus I have to clean the apartment. Let's just head back and we can plan your time here better."
"If I didn't know any better, I'd say it almost sounds like you're trying to send me away."

The thought had crossed my mind.

"I could never, mom."

"Well of course not. You wouldn't know right from left if I weren't here to tell you."

I bite my tongue and lead us to the apartment.

Finn stands up abruptly as soon as I open the door. Drew puts her head in her hands and groans at Finn's guilty behavior.

"Hi, sorry didn't mean to disturb, was just," he looks down at Drew. "Getting notes for class." I narrow my eyes at him and he smiles innocently back before his eyes dart to my mother.

"Well, who is this young man?" my mother asks with sweetness in her voice. I look over at her and she looks expectantly at me.

"This is Finn. He's on the footba—the soccer team and he lives in the apartment below us with . . . the twins." There's a bomb in there I don't want to touch yet. "I presume you met Drew. She lives here with me and Kirsty."

Kirsty waves from the kitchen. "Glad you've returned to us ma'am."

I make a face at her changed accent, smoother around the edges and grating to my nerves. None of them should be going out of their way to play this game with my mother.

"I'm gonna shower. Feel, uh, free to make yourself at home," I lie before leaving the four of them in the living room. My room is spotless and I close the door before sinking to the floor against it. Biting the heel of my palm, I take in the vacuumed floor and changed sheets. There's folded laundry on top of my dresser. I crawl across the floor, pathetically, and reach for my phone still plugged in on my night table.

### Window Open?

I stare at my phone impatiently as voices filter in from the apartment.

**Busy,** her text back reads. I bite my lip as I try to think of something to reply but it dings again. ***Sai wants to "not lecture" me.*** I smile down as I think of Saatchi and Sai having another of their sibling parenting moments. They both need to learn it's just the way each of them is.

I respond with a heart that she reciprocates and then climb into the shower. The hot water eases my sore muscles and washes the stickiness from my skin. There isn't anything I can do for the marks that litter me, but that's my fault. It seemed like a good idea last night. Less so with my mother just outside.

She better have a hotel figured out.


*Saatchi*

Finn's feeding Anne his eggs when I get a text from Emmylou.

*My mother wants to see Edinburgh. Do y'all want to come with? If not I can sneak down tonight?*

I stare at the text, then turn off my screen before looking back up at the telly. England is playing. I hope they lose.

"Was that Emmylou?" my nuisance of a brother asks.

I grunt in response.

"Saatchi—"

"Aye, yes, I remember." Yesterday my brother and I had a sit down about feelings and all that rubbish. Her feelings, my feelings, the blossoming yet tumultuous relationship we share. I rather it have went through one ear and out the other, but my heart is stuttering in my chest with uncertainty. It feels as if my heart has been a stuttering mess since this all began.

The alcohol on top of the cupboards is looking more and more tempting. The knife, however, is not, and one always leads to the other in this state.

"Finn."

He looks up, like a puppy ready to be of assistance.

"Aye?"

"Eat your brekkie before you make my cat any damn fatter."

Sai glares at me and Finn smiles before feeding Anne another piece. He likes giving them directly to her, claiming her rough tongue is intriguing.

"Saatchi," Sai tries again.

I bite my lip hard and hold up a hand to him. We're trying to come up with this system where he shuts the fuck up when I ask him to and, in exchange, I listen when I'm not on the verge of pushing my fist through his face again.

"I'm gonna go for a run."

Finn looks out the window. "It's freezing out there," he tells me as I go to my room.

Thermals are life saving for a runner in the winter. They're also the bane of my existence. I have to fight myself to not strip them all off once I actually set out to running.

Finn's progressed to giving Anne tea as I leave the apartment. The snow fell again last night and there's a stillness in the air. Crisp air enters my lungs and I gasp in mouthfuls for fear of missing this when the city begins to move again.

I forgo my headphones in favor of listening to the crunch of fresh snow under my running boots. The snow isn't thick enough to sink into and it's cold enough that the ice stays away from my tread. Nature beckons me into its silence and I put one foot in front of the other.

The air bleeds my lungs dry, but I'm grateful for it. There is nothing like a snowy day in a big city without a single footprint. My steps outrun my thoughts and I go faster and faster. The muscles in my legs pump in perfect synchronicity and I can't even feel my hands sweating under my gloves.

Step. Another. More. Faster.

Run.

Run.

There is nothing but snow. Clean. Unsullied. Covering every blemish that these cobblestones hide. Every spot where the boke or blood were too deeply ingrained to clean out. Every tear that moistened these Scottish lands. Everything invisible in this blanketing perfection.

I gasp as a droplet of sweat lands on my nose from my headband and then gasp again as my run high burns off into typical exhaustion. My brain coughs blood along with my lungs, causing me to internally groan as my thoughts turn the corner with me and sit between my pounding feet and the pavement.

If only they could be crushed like the snow.

*What are you going to do about Emmylou*, my brain asks. The problem is, I'm not sure if this is an Emmylou issue or her mother or society or whatever bullshit. Maybe it's a me problem. Perhaps if I were a good person, I could just tell Emmylou "It's fine, take your time and come out when you can. It doesn't hurt me like a serrated knife plunging into my heart." If I were a better person, maybe I'd even mean it.

*What are you going to do about yourself?*

I stare down into the clean winter powder I'm trampling over.

The snow may be untouched and unsullied but it doesn't reflect my own soul. It feels impossible to be the kind of person Emmylou deserves. Someone who does little things for her like no one has done. Someone who listens to her prattle about history or whatever her fixation is. Someone who has patience to wait until she's ready to come out on her own time.

Someone who has a head on their shoulders that isn't full of cocaine and trauma.

I'm not that person. I'm afraid I won't ever be. I love her so much.

I love her.

I can't do this to her.


*Emmylou*

Saatchi leaves me on 'read' and I'm still pitifully gripping my phone, hoping for a response, when my mother comes into the kitchen. I've taken my time getting ready in Drew's room where I've been sleeping to give myself space from my mother.

Poor Drew and Kirsty are caught in the crosshairs of the awkward tension permeating the air. I'll especially owe Drew a home-cooked meal after this is all over. Saatchi will definitely deserve some quality time after my mother is gone. Hopefully tonight I can sneak down to her room for cuddles. That is, if she isn't mad at me.

There is some grounds for me to be upset with her as well. I do understand it isn't easy for my controlling, bigoted mother to be here, but she didn't have to completely hang me out to dry. Even then, I can't be mad at her.

I just miss her.

I miss her laugh where she throws her head back; the way she rolls her eyes at my antics or sucks her teeth when she's annoyed. I miss her crooked nose and the way the sun kisses her skin. I miss the feeling of her soft fingers wrapping around mine.

It's been less than forty-eight hours since I saw her last and yet I ache to even be near her again. To feel her warmth pressed against my shoulder, to hear her stifle her laugh in my hair, to taste her skin under my tongue. She's a presence that calms even the most tumultuous fears in me, and I've chased her away.

The glare on my face must be obvious as my mother sits across from me at the kitchen table.

"Don't look at me that way. I didn't take that long to get ready," she says when it takes me too long to paint a placating smile on my face.

"Yeah, sorry, I was just . . . lost in thought. It's pretty cold out there, are you sure you wanna go?" The snow is new and covers the city. The footprints are sparse since most people are still home from work and school for the holidays.

"Well, I suppose we don't have to, but I do want to meet those little friends of yours downstairs. Finn was a cutie.

Anything going on with him?" My mother's matchmaking is a little less harmless than my sister's. It presents a burden or some sort of expectation on how I should act, look, and behave. Whenever it's my sister, he's on trial; he's the one who's proving his worth. My mother always makes it feel like I'm the one who has to prove my worth to him.

"Finn is just a friend," I tell her, and she raises an eyebrow.

"He seems like he was looking for you yesterday. Maybe if you were a little friendlier with him or . . . you could try cooking him a meal? Are you still working out? You know the stories about freshman fifteen." She takes an analytical look at me and I bite back a sigh.

"Nope. We're really just friends."

"Oh, well. What about the other boys living there?" I start to shake my head and she instantly nods. "Yeah, I kind of figured. Sai sounds Indian so, what, he's like a nerdy foreign student. Same with Sasha I'll bet. Sounds like a . . . Russian maybe? Are they a studious bunch?" I hold my breath as I peer at Kirsty and Drew's bedroom doors but neither are open. Hopefully I've managed to scrounge up some luck and at least Kirsty is painting with headphones on.

"Uhm. No. Mom, you can't say sh-tuff like that." She raises an eyebrow at my slip up.

"Am I wrong?"

"Yes," I tell her, annoyed.

"Well then I hope those boys weren't the ones who went off and taught you to curse." I groan into my palm. "Don't do that, it's gross."

"Is everything gross to you?" I snap.

She presses a hand against her chest. "Lord, Emmylou. Run off to a different country and now you think you're all grown up enough to yell at your momma. Show some respect," she continues to press as I try to speak up. "You wouldn't even be here if you weren't so privileged, but at least you've never acted like that before." I want to scoff because all I've been thinking about is how to live without the privilege she's provided me but I hold back. "You would be nowhere without your father and me, so don't go treating us like trash now that you've got these so-called friends." She looks away from me and scoffs.

Guilt roils in my stomach when she wipes a tear from her eye.

"Your family is all you have, Emmylou. You think these girls would help you pay for college? You think they'd help you plan your wedding when the time comes? Or," she leans in and I prepare for the next punch. "You think they'd take you to every chemo treatment even when they have exams or dates or their own lives to worry about?" She wipes at her face again. "Don't you dare treat me like that after everything I've done for you."

"Sorry," I respond quietly, thoroughly reprimanded. She's right. I've spent too much time here hating her for something that she probably meant well. Not all people are good at communicating their love and maybe I just took her words and twisted them while I've been here.

Saatchi isn't good at explaining her feelings, maybe this is the same. Maybe I can take the same approach to it that Sai and Saatchi have taken and build better communication between us.

"I-I just—" she holds up a hand before I can continue.

"No, you've said enough. Let's just call a cab and *try* to forget this. This is my last night here after all and I'd hate for you to ruin it." She stands and I shrink behind her feeling, small again. It's probably better to wait for her to calm down before I talk to her. She's probably right though, and I'll just ruin her trip here. Maybe I should just leave it for the summer.

*Saatchi*

Emmylou looks cozy wrapped in that damn cancer jumper and my bed throw. I'm surprised to see her here and I squeeze the bag in my arm tighter to my side.

"Hey, hope it's okay that I'm here," she whispers quietly into the night. "You weren't picking up your phone—" she bites her lip to cut off what I can tell is a sad noise. Nothing can hide that heartbroken look on her face. She's staring at me like I might bolt or yell.

"Aye, course it's fine," I tell her, peeling off my winter wellies and outerwear. I can feel her staring as I strip to my shirt and pants, the trousers too wet from snowfall. I bite my lip and look up at her.

"Stay there?" I ask and she nods and averts her eyes, which seems a bit much but I let her have her uncomfortable moment. I pull off my sports bra and slip back into my shirt before grabbing the bag and sitting beside her in the bed.

She looks over at me, unsure, and I move the bag out of her eyeline, but her eyes track the movement anyway. I grip the bag harder as I try to arrange my thoughts.

I had this whole plan of coming home and spiraling as I decided what exactly to tell Emmylou tomorrow. There's something controllable, and therefore beautiful, about planning an argument. Although, the ideal is that my final draft isn't an argument. Her being here throws a wrench in those plans.

Tipping back in bed, I push the bag under my pillow and crawl under the blankets. Emmylou looks at me and I sit up before raising my blanket. She bundles the blankets around her, dismissing the throw, and sniffles with watery eyes as she puts space between us.

"Saatchi," she starts, and I can't stop the deep sigh that shakes my chest. I rub my face to avoid her eyes.

The silence is telling between us, but I have a feeling it's telling each of us different things.

I grab her delicate hand and slowly interlace my fingers with hers.

"I uhm . . . Finn and I went out today. Just to go for the receipts." I pick at her already chipped nail polish. It's Scottish Blue. She painted them for Hogmanay which now seems like so long ago. "I kept thinking about this, us," I tell her, gesturing with our conjoined hands.

"It seems silly to say it out loud." I bite my lip as I bide my time. "I'm not a good person to date, Emmylou. I'm volatile and at the first sign of trouble, my instinct is to duck out. It's taken everything in me to not . . . well, anything.

"I kept thinking about the snow. About how clean and precious it was. I thought about how I wouldn't have ever seen it had I not survived my suicide attempt. I thought about what Finn would be doing, or Sai, if I'd been successful.

"It isn't just that though. This isn't some moment where I have clarity that'll last forever. Even now, my teeth are aching with the need, the bone crushing desire, to be drunk, or take a hit of fuck all, or anything. I want to be high. Or dead. I don't want to deal with this and—and I don't just mean this: you and me this. I mean every day that comes after today.

"I'm terrified of everything. Tonight, I could dream of what happened and wake up with fear in my lungs and poison on my tongue. Tomorrow, it could happen again. Next week, I could get hit by a car and never run again. I'm so terrified of what every next moment may bring that I don't want to live it." I look over at her as she waits patiently with words sitting on her tongue.

I want to tell her I want to be better for her. Or some other sappy thing. But it wouldn't be true.

I don't want to be happy for her, or for Finn, or my brother and family. I don't want to be better for myself. But I'm tired; I'm so tired of living in this purgatory of half in and half out of this life that I don't have another option.

Today, I went to the stores with Finn. The snow wet my trousers and my boots. Folks pass us on the street. Nothing happened. Nothing out of the ordinary. Nothing that should make my brain so toxic, but just like almost every day, it was.

"Despite that, I do want to get better. I don't want to die. I want to run and I want to see my brother get married and Finn . . . well, fuck if I know." I look over at her. "And I want this to work. I want this to work because," I hesitate and look out my window at Edinburgh. "Because I love you. You make me happy and you make me feel like getting better for myself. You make me feel like I can't breathe and like I finally have all the oxygen I've ever needed. I went to get the receipts today and all I could think of is getting them when we're older and live together. I'd go for a run in the morning and you'd have breakfast ready when I got back and we'd eat it together as we started our day, and then when we got back, I'd make dinner, and you'd eat it with me before we'd crawl into bed together.

"So, uhm, I know you already said it, but I don't know at what level you meant it. The way I mean it is, I love you and if you don't want to tell your mam yet, or ever . . . that's fine. I'm not gonna lie, it hurts now, and it'll hurt anytime she's around if I have to pretend I'm just your roommate or a friend but," I look over at her finally. She's biting her lip as tears prick at her eyes. "Fuck it. Whatever. I'm happy. You make me happy and if you decide to tell her, just let it be on your time."

"Dammit Saatchi," she says as she wraps her arms around me and the real water works begin. "You can't always go around making me cry."

A small smile breaks through my melancholy.

"You got the part where I'm fucked up right?" I ask her, and she laughs into my shirt.

"Oh yeah, trust me I got that. But," she pulls off. "If you wanna get better, that's what matters. You just have to want it," she says, solidifying her words with a delicate punch to my heart.

She looks at me morosely. "I thought you were going to break up with me." I look away from her in guilt and she whines. "You were? Cause I wouldn't tell my mom?"

"Aye, no," I say, shaking my head. "Just cause it's hard to be in love. I'm scared. Don't you think it'd be easier if we just didn't?" She laughs and kisses my cheek.

"I'm not scared. I trust you."

"Horrible decision."

"Not at all, I've seen the way you care. It's all or nothing with you, so if you've decided you're in, I've got nothing to worry about," she tells me gleefully. I internally wither at feeling so seen. She must catch it in the look on my face because she laughs before tackling us backwards, further into the sheets.

"I can't believe my mother surprise visited," she says up to the ceiling as she adjusts her head on my chest. "I thought that shit only happened in movies."

"I thought you didn't curse, but you've been doing it more and more lately," I tell her back, avoiding the topic of the woman I hate so deeply.

"Yeah, I guess, probably when I didn't know I was a fag."

I snort and have to lean up to catch my breath as I choke on my own surprise. She giggles under me and I stare at her with wide eyes.

"Who are you and what have you done with my Emmylou?"

She laughs and pulls me down for a kiss. We eventually go to sleep curled in my blankets. Mouths tasting of apples and smiles.

# Chapter Sixteen

Heartbeat tangled to your lungs
Cover me in flowers pink with Spring
Ocean of love that makes me speak tongues
Beneath you is everything

I watch Finn flatten his hair with anxious hands as Sai knocks on the orange door. He's more nervous than I am even though it's my first formal meeting with Emmylou's mam. Finn's never been a big fan of meeting parents though, or, I suppose, adults in general. I wonder how our childhood fears work when we're suddenly adults.

Sai looks back at me lost in my train of thought and shoots me a stern word through his eyes alone. As we were scrambling to get ready, which for me meant peeling sticky sheets of cat fur off my only pair of jeans, Sai gave Finn and I a talking to about selflessness.

Someday, soon hopefully, Sai will pull that rod out of his ass and let Finn and I be general menaces to society, but until then, I'm subject to these lectures on the daily. That isn't to say they aren't somewhat beneficial to us. Sai probably makes a good point when he tells Finn and I to keep our heads down and refrain from causing a disaster.

This is already stressful enough as is for Emmylou and there isn't any reason to poke a still bear. No matter how much I may want to, because the thought of pushing Emmylou's mam to the brink of blowing a gasket appeals to the inner child I have no desire to chase away. Like being a rambunctious student in class just to get back at the professor who assigns too much homework in primary. I've never been known to be a still or mature child and I've taken that into adulthood.

But.

Love. Or whatever bullshit they call that anvil that sits over my heart in the shape of Emmylou's happiness.

They should have put a warning label on love.

Drew opens the door and her bright, fake smile pulls me out of my thoughts as the lads push on ahead of me. She straightens my shirt and I fight back a fidget. Sai wanted me to put on a dress shirt but accepted my choice of a T-shirt without graphic print or running logos.

I may be meeting my girlfriend's mam, but she doesn't know that, and part of making sure this goes well is going unnoticed. After all, if I've gathered anything about Emmylou's mam, it's that she's undeniably homophobic, and with that notion there tend to be other discriminatory feelings that would put me at the top of her shit list.

"Are you nervous?" Drew asks me quietly as she shuts the door. I hear the lads introduce themselves further in the room.

I shrug at her. "Why would I be? I'm just one of the lads from the flat below as far as she knows."

"Emmylou isn't going to say anything?"

I look down at Drew and see her confusion.

"Nah, she isn't ready. And that's fine," I tell her honestly before stepping into the room and plastering an awkward, tight-lipped smile on my face.

"Nice to meet ye. 'M Saatchi," I hold out my hand to Emmylou's mam and she takes it with wide eyes.

"I must have completely missed something. I thought the boys from downstairs were coming for dinner?" she asks Emmylou. I watch as Emmylou paints different emotions on her face before finally settling on innocence.

"I do live downstairs. 'M not a lad though, there must've been some misunderstanding," I tell her, finally letting go of her hand. They're soft and doused in so much fragrant lotion that the flat is overwhelmingly covered in her scent. Her manicured nails run against the back of my hand subconsciously as she pulls away, her long, fake lashes still fluttering in confusion as she looks back at Emmylou. There's barely a wrinkle on her; hair coiffed to perfection; smells American.

No wonder Emmylou has self-esteem issues when false perfection walks beside you with a blackened soul.

"Doesn't your mama worry about you girl?" Emmylou's mam asks.

"Every good mam does. That's why I live with my brothers," I tell her flippantly. Finn raises an eyebrow at her when she looks between both of us, daring her to ask, but she backs down. "Sorry," I prompt when she doesn't take the bait. "I didn't seem to catch your name."

"You can call me Mrs. Humford of course." She turns away and goes to Kirsty who is in the kitchen.

Emmylou looks at me pleadingly and I raise my hand slightly at my side to placate her.

The only way we make it through her mam's last night here is for me to keep my head down and mouth shut. It may be against every fiber of my being, but if I don't keep my head down, I'll have to speak to her. And there is no way I'm calling this calloused bitch by any honorable title.

Mrs. Bitch is helping Kirsty bring plates to the table and I follow Sai's lead and sit at the table. My chair is beside Sai's and as far away from Mrs. Bitch, for which I thank my lucky stars.

"Oh, you aren't going to help?" Mrs. Bitch asks as she sets a dish down, looking at me expectantly.

"I would only get in the way," I start innocently. "I don't know where anything is since I'm hardly ever in this flat," I lie. "Maybe Sai could help since he's here so often," I say looking at him. He nods agreeably but Emmylou's mother holds up a hand to stop him.

"That's alright. Women are strong in the kitchen, right? Feminism and all that new age ideas your generation loves so much."

"It's, uh, alright. I don't mind helping."

She shushes him and he tentatively sits back down. Kirsty glares at Sai as she sets down a dish.

"Actually, Tamara," Kirsty starts, addressing Mrs. Bitch by her apparent name. "The idea of feminism is that women can do anything men can do and that women deserve equal treatment. Ideally, Sai *and* Finn would be helping set the table." She looks down at both of them, annoyed. "Which you normally do," she says quietly to their defensive shrugs.

"See, that's what I don't understand about it all," Mrs. Tamara Bitch starts. "Women can't do everything men do. They're stronger and more suited for," she makes an aborted muscle flex, "all the manly things. Besides, with women getting these breadwinning jobs, who takes care of children? That's why this generation is so aggressive and rowdy. They were probably unmothered and ran around causing mischief."

Kirsty scoffs beside Sai, and I longingly stare down the tortilla soup Emmylou cooked. Kirsty is definitely rowdy and if she flips this table I will cry. I've put on my "supporting Emmylou" face, and now I deserve my reward of Tex-Mex food.

Emmylou sets my dish in front of me, startling me from my staring contest with the tortilla soup, and I look up into her soulful green eyes. Her hand brushes my shoulder as she pulls back from the plate and I trace the way her lip pouts as she pulls away.

It takes everything in me not to watch her walk away, instead opting for falling deeper in love with her cooking instead of the curves I have yet to sufficiently acquaint myself with.

"Let's just agree to disagree and sit for a beautiful bit of scran made by Emmylou herself," Drew cuts into the buzz that's been going on around me. I look away from the food to watch Kirsty sit angrily beside Sai. Emmylou sits beside her mother, nearly furthest away from me, and Finn shoots her a smile that Tamara's eyes lock onto.

"So Finn, right? We met just the other day." Finn nods at Tamara as plates are shuffled around. I dump a kind helping of soup into my bowl and prepare myself for the crisps to make their way to me. They're currently being blocked by Sai, his head bent in prayer as the plate waits beside him. "What are you in school for?"

Finn smiles up at her as he dollops a large amount of sour cream into his bowl. "Oh, biochemistry, part of the premed track."

Tamara shoots Emmylou a gleeful smile and I turn away to frown at my soup that no longer seems palatable.

"Well, I'm sure you're the talk of the town then. What with being a soccer star *and* smart; I'm sure all the ladies are trying to snatch you up."

Finn presses his foot against mine under the table. I bite my smile down hard and press back, permission that I shouldn't give—but even love can't erase my carnal desire for chaos.

"Actually, they are. In fact," he pauses to shove a large spoonful of sour cream into his mouth. "I've shagged as many attractive, consenting birds as this city has offered me. Birds, of course, meaning women, and shagged, of course, meaning fucked—in case you weren't aware."

Sai coughs violently into his napkin as Tamara's smile tightens and her eyes widen slightly. I appreciate her trying to put up a front of nonchalance—it makes it more obvious. Her front of non-judgement, of laissez faire about feminism and sexual freedom. But it's clear, there in her eyes, she's looking down at Finn and Kirsty and everyone else who doesn't fit her cookie-cutter ideals.

It's no wonder Emmylou still succumbs to her mother despite no longer being near her. A heel dug into your back long enough will leave not only scars but bleeding wounds if the stiletto is sharp enough. There is no doubt that Tamara Humford sharpens her stilettos every moment she's in the spotlight. She's a show pony, trotting in elegance perfected at the end of a whip. I wonder where she keeps that whip when she has to be on display as she is now.

Emmylou herself sits quietly, but not passively, beside her mother. She seems tired of this, one eyebrow peaked with tension and her lips more chewed than the meal in front of her. My eyes must weigh on her because she looks over at me and sneers playfully, like a child complaining about being at a fancy dinner. I subtly stick my tongue out back at her and she hides a smile behind her napkin.

Maybe she really is tired of everything her mother has put her through, or tired of who she was before. It's hard to return to a cage once you know what freedom tastes like. Like suffering through a debilitating illness, miraculously overcoming it, only to be struck with the illness again. It's harder to overcome something the second time and it's clear that Emmylou has no plans of falling back into her mother's cage.

"Saatchi?" Drew asks, startling me. I look up and realize that during the time I've zoned out on my own bowl in front of me, I have become the topic of conversation and everyone's eyes are on me.

"Aye, did you say something?" I ask Drew, but her eyes drift to Tamara.

"I was just asking what you were majoring in."

I tilt my head at her, surprised she doesn't know. My mam knows everything about all my friends, especially Emmylou. Even without knowing I'm dating her daughter, she must at least ask about her friends from time to time.

"English with a concentration in poetry."

She hums in thought and twists her spoon with delicate, perfumed hands.

"And what do you plan on doing with that major? You don't strike me as the type to go to college to find a breadwinning husband."

"Oh, I, uhm—" *don't plan on finishing university*, but before I can say anything, Emmylou speaks up.

"I wouldn't say that ma. I'm sure I'll make loads of money as a fashion designer to sustain both of us."

My mouth hangs open in an unfinished sentence as I stare at Emmylou. She nonchalantly takes a sip of her lukewarm tea.

"Ha, just kidding," she says petulantly. "I'm not a fashion major anymore. Hopefully Saatchi's running career can support me as a history professor, or whatever I choose to do with that, once we're out of university." She puts her spoon in her bowl decisively and looks over at her mam, whose distaste is clearly visible. "Isn't that kind of the idea though? Be like you and marry someone successful?" She turns to me and looks on innocently. "You'd be okay with that, right Saatchi?"

I flounder like a fish in response and look around the table to make sure I'm not hallucinating, but everyone seems in the same shell-shocked state. Finn finally looks at me and gestures with his eyes.

"No, aye, of course, I'll uhm, aye marriage," I say as I internally beg and pray for a snowstorm to rip through the flat and take me with it. I'd rather that than sit through this.

"Emmylou," Tamara starts, her smile tight on her face. "Don't tease your friends like that. I'm sure Saatchi wouldn't want to support you. Besides, she probably has a boy somewhere she's got eyes for."

"Actually, Mother," Emmylou starts, fastidiously tossing her napkin on the table. "Saatchi's a lesbian."

The sound that comes from me sounds so much like a pug dog taking its last breath that Sai turns to me to make sure I'm still alive.

"Well, some people choose to live that way and it's fine by me," her mother says, smile now frozen and eyes glazing over as she stares into the void of her soup.

"That's great because I'm gay too." Hook, line, and sinker.

I should be proud. Kirsty should be jumping for joy that Emmylou stuck it to the man. Sai should be happy that I'm not dating a selfish prick again. Drew should be beaming like a deer watching its baby take its first step. But we're all silent. It's only Finn that raises his pint and says, "Hear, hear, atta girl Emmylou," before her mother finally resets.

"That isn't funny, Emmylou," she says. Her smile is now gone, replaced by cold eyes and pressed lips.

"It isn't a joke. I fucked her just last night."

I now, officially, know what it's like to breathe like a pug dog. It's a lot of choking on air and death rattles.

Sai pats my back aggressively as I choke on air and Kirsty rushes to pass me a glass of water while Emmylou and her mother have a stare down. The tension is thick in the air until Tamara finally secedes with folded hands and a painful smile.

"Well, we can talk about it away from present company." Emmylou looks displeased with that but says nothing. Finn's spoon hitting the bottom of his bowl is the only sound, and it, once again, spurs the rest of us into action as we rush to finish our food and leave this meal behind.

Emmylou looks at me from across the table.

I know I'm in love, because when I look at her, all the tension goes away. It feels like when you get home from a shit day and you take off your bra knowing there are no plans for the rest of the night. She's home. So when I look at her, all the air leaves my lungs and my shoulders unclench and I smile across at her. Because I love her. Even if she's suddenly decided to be a brat and put all of us in the crossfire of this battle. It isn't like I wouldn't have ridden it out with her anyways; I only wish she would've given me warning so I would've at least not been caught with my pants around my ankles.

"I love you," I tell her across the table, throwing the metaphorical glove down beside hers.

"I love you too."

*Emmylou*

Sweat drips down my back as I close my bedroom door behind me. Saatchi is stubbornly washing dishes in the kitchen with Drew, unwilling to leave me too far out of her reach after dinner, but now I feel disconnected from her as I close myself in with my mother. My hands shake as I let go of the doorknob. Everything in me wants to run, or roll up into a ball at my mother's feet.

She stares at the wall away from me, silent. I bite my lip so hard it stings to keep it from wobbling. The last thing I want to do is back down, show my weakness after standing up to her, but all my adrenaline has left me. Now, I am nothing but a trembling mess. All I want to do is cry in Saatchi's arms as she runs her hands through my hair and kisses my forehead.

Everything about Saaatchi is so overwhelming. When I walk into a room and she's there, my whole chest contracts, overwhelmed like a child at Disneyland. I want to cheer and scream and dance. I want to tackle her and bury myself inside her chest cavity, build a home there, wrapped in her arms and lay in the jungle that is her soul.

That's why I couldn't stay quiet today when my mother started talking about "college youth" during dinner. It burned me when she spurned Kirsty and looked down on Finn, but that burning turned into flames when she spoke to Sai. Saatchi's eyes had glazed over when she finally heard firsthand how my mother felt about us after Sai spoke about his future career. I felt foolish for not knowing about Sai's dreams; for not realizing that Sai was so passionate about his sister that he dreamt of becoming a nonprofit lawyer fighting for the rights of LGBTQ+ and victims of sexual assault. It humbled me to hear him speak about his dreams to make changes in the laws so it's easier for survivors to be heard and respected. Scotland is more advanced in it's LGBTQ+ acceptance than the United States, but even then, Sai sees so many changes that can be for the better.

But all of this was for naught in my mother's eyes.

"Why are you even concerned with those people anyway?" she had asked. My eyes never strayed from Saatchi as she stared at her bowl in sorrow. "You're a nice young man who doesn't need to worry about those types of things."

"Well, we should all support the LGBTQ+ community," I had said quietly—naivety had me hoping that would be sufficient. That maybe she would agree. But instead, Saatchi sighed quietly down at the table.

I would not be part of the millions of heartbreaks she's already had. I refuse to burden her any longer. The passion I feel for her was the only spark I needed to ignite my anger.

I finally look up at my mother, as we both now stand in my bedroom, and realize that the anger is still roaring brightly inside of me. It's built of from eighteen years of being under her heel and it's about to snap the taught tightrope I've been balancing on to be perfect in my mother's eyes. But then she opens her mouth.

"You need to come back to Texas."

I prepare myself for a battle, but I stumble as my mother turns around with tears in her eyes.

"I know you know dad was home for Christmas but I swear he wasn't supposed to be. He really was going to work but . . . dad's sick, Emmylou. I guess you got the cancer gene from him."

"What?" I ask her numbly. "What, no, we . . . what?" We were supposed to be talking about something else. Saatchi's outside. I spoke with dad over Christmas; he would've told me. Except, maybe mother convinced him not to, just like she convinced me not to so long ago.

"I want to talk to him," I say instead. This could be a ploy. My pa could be fine. He probably is fine.

"You can call him on our way to the airport. I already bought you a ticket," she says, holding up her phone. The flight is for tonight.

"No, I—I can't go," I start, hands now shaking violently.

"Emmylou. You are not staying here while your daddy is sick. We'll send for someone to come pick up all your stuff but we need to go. I didn't want to say anything while we were with your friends. I wanted you to enjoy your last days with them but this was always the plan."

"But," I look behind me, beyond the door where my girlfriend is probably pacing. "Saatchi," is all I say before a slap rings out across my room.

It's weird—the way it takes me a second to realize my face hurts. Heat wells up against my cheek as my mother's hand rises again.

"Emmylou, you will not be choosing some college rebellion over your own kin. We need to go home and see your daddy."

I press my hand against my face as I hear someone call for me outside my door. In my numbness, I nod at her and she turns with authority to scour my room for something. I turn away from her ransacking and open my door.

Saatchi is standing outside my door, looking ready to break it down.

"Em, what the—did you fucking slap her?" she yells above my head. I'm still holding my cheek as I fall into her chest. Drew is standing beside her and looks at me with concern as Saatchi wraps one arm around me. "What the fuck is wrong with you?" she demands from my mother again, still rifling through my things.

"Saatchi, my daddy might die," is all I say as I slowly wrap my arms around her. She looks down at me in confusion and shakes her head slowly, but I pull her in tighter as numbness fades to fear and pain.

"The fresh hell," Drew questions. "Mrs. Humford, what is going on?"

"Her daddy has cancer," my mother all but yells from behind me. Something hits the floor as the sound of clothes hangers fill the air. "I don't have time to explain these things to children like you. Y'all are all too immature to understand any of this. It's the entire reason I came here and I wanted to give Emmylou a few last days with her college girl . . . *gal* pals, but you all had to make this some debacle." Saatchi tries to step forward but I hold her tight. "This is what I get for being kind," my mother grumbles as she huffs around my room.

"I don't believe you," Saatchi says from above me. "Have you called him?" she asks me, lips pressed against my hair.

"The flight is tonight. I don't have time for your lies and grooming." My mother pushes past us, my suitcase in hand. "I don't know what lies you've put in my daughter's head," my mother starts, hand reaching out to dig her nails into my arm as she pulls me away from Saatchi. "But family comes first. I'm sure she'll have plenty of time to put this experiment behind her as she watches her daddy die in the hospital."

I take the suitcase handle thrusted into my hand.

"That's bullshite," Saatchi says but she doesn't grab me. I look back at her and she says, "Just call him, yeah? Find out for yourself and then I'll go with you." I bite my lip at her and nod.

As my fingers fumble for my phone, my mother meets the boys at the door.

"You can't just rush her out of the flat like this. This is insane," Finn starts, but she stamps her foot and his head rears back in shock. "Jesus fuck, you're a child."

"No," she starts, pointing a finger at him. "You are a child who is clearly motherless if you're talking to me like that and whoring around." She turns back and snaps at full volume. "Emmylou, I am done here. We are leaving now or you can wait to see your daddy in heaven. If you ever get there," she finishes, glaring at Saatchi.

Saatchi ignores her and looks down at me.

"Anything?" she asks but the phone has gone to voicemail against my ear. I shake my head and, with trembling hands, redial.

"Of course not, he's in treatment or being sick all over himself because I'm here to get you and here you are being selfish."

I turn to my mother just as she stomps across the apartment. I'm too late to stop her as she grabs the phone from my hand.

I watch in horror as she flings it across the room and straight into a wall where it shatters.

"This is insane," Sai says from where he's blocking the door. "Let's all calm down a wee bit and Emmylou can fly when she's ready and plans ahead a bit." My mother turns back toward him, her nails digging into my skin as she pulls me.

"I am her mother and I say she goes now."

"She's an adult," Sai says back with as much force.

"I—guys I have to go," I say quietly. "Even . . . if he doesn't die tomorrow, I don't want him to be alone for chemo. It really sucks," I finish as my voice breaks. I look back at Saatchi. Her eyes are squeezed shut and she runs a hand through her hair.

"Right, just, call us when you land and . . . uhm," she grabs a marker from a kitchen drawer and eases my mother's hand away from my broken skin. Saatchi squeezes the bleeding wounds softly and looks at me. "I'll buy a ticket and meet you there?" I nod, silent tears streaming down my face and she writes her number on my arm in green.

"Okay," she says as she steps back, hand lingering in mine. "I love you." There's an air of finality in it that has me surging forward. I grab her face in my hands as I press my lips against hers. I won't let her go. I won't let her end it because of this. She's where I'm supposed to be. She's my now and my forever. She's carved her soul into my heart and heaven or hell couldn't erase it away.

"I love you. I'll see you soon."

# Chapter Seventeen

The morning bird's call is like the baying of an ass,
The Swiss Alp's height is like the width of this sheet,
The French Riviera's color is like the grey Scottish skies,
The Icelandic Geyer's heat is like the tepid ice across Antarctica
All compared to you.
For your hair is the light, kissed by the moon,
Your hands are the warmth, engulfed by the sun,
Your eyes are the kindness, sent down by God.
And your lips,
Oh,
Your lips,
Are the reason I live.
The reason I breath.
Your lips are a gift made for me.

Saatchi's number is scrolled on every inch of paper I could find in my childhood bedroom. Guilt and fear and regret are an ice-cold brick in my stomach as I stare at my locked door.

When I was a child, my mother turned the lock of my bedroom door the other way around for when I was grounded. My daddy turned it back once I was thirteen or so and I stopped mouthing off the way children do. It's turned back around now, and I'm once again a child trapped in my room.

Unsurprisingly, there are no payphones in airports anymore. I had walked off that plane and immediately started scanning everywhere for them to no avail. I hadn't thought it was necessary to ask a random stranger for a phone, but when we got to the car, my mother claimed her phone was dead.

I didn't think anything of it, anxious to see my father. I'd call Saatchi when my mother charged her phone, or at the hospital, or from Janey's phone. There were options. At least, I thought there were, until I was showering off the airport sweat in preparation of going to the hospital and I heard my door lock click shut.

"It's for your own good," my mother had called after I pounded against it in panic. "Your dad's on his way and so is Janey. I told them—I told them that Saatchi hit you when you rejected her and that's why you're back."

"What? She would never—"

"Emmylou! I'm protecting you. Just like I always have, child. You don't wanna know what your daddy will do if you tell him about—well, about what you've been getting into at school. I want you to be with Janey when she's walking down the aisle. I'm just protecting you; this will fade with time."

"You're crazy, let me out," I had yelled, fists pounding the door.

"Think about it, Emmylou. You're going to get yourself kicked out of this family for a girl you just met four months ago? Don't you see how silly that is? You don't even know her. This is just a phase, Emmylou. Some girls have those and it's probably my fault for putting so much pressure on you as a girl. I knew I wasn't as good a mother as you wanted, but I didn't expect you to lash out like this."

A phase. Lashing out. Experimentation. I can't help but scoff at the words as I cradle my legs to my chest. My bed feels foreign to me now. The drapes over it, a design by my mother, now look like a naïve child's. Everything in this room is glittery and polished. It could be the cover of a magazine or an Instagram post by a verified interior designer.

I miss Kirsty's room, dark and witchy. Covered in paint and splattered in personality. I miss the smell of Drew's; essential oils and self-care products surrounding the air when we studied. I miss Saatchi's room. Covered head to toe in poetry, written on anything within reach with whatever made a mark. I miss running my hands over the words she wrote about me as she talked to Anne Bonny laying across her chest.

I feel foolish for coming. I hope Saatchi didn't buy a ticket. Would she even know where to fly to? She'd just type in Texas and end up sixteen hours away. I'd still drive to get her if I could.

I hear the door close to the main foyer and I look up from my bed. There's no point in looking out my window. It's late at night and too dark to see whose car just pulled in. I don't want it to be Janey or pa. I'm not ready to see either of them or tell them.

Mother may be right; it is foolish to throw away my family for someone I just met. Saatchi and I may not work out—no matter how badly I want us to. But I'm not doing this for her. I have to do this for me. Because sitting in this room that means nothing to me now has made me realize I can't play this role I've outgrown.

I am gay. I am a lesbian. It may not be Saatchi, but someday it'll be someone. I won't hide that because, despite being scared out of my mind and mourning a pain that hasn't even been hammered down yet, this is who I am. And just like the ground under my feet and the sky above me, it is natural and unchangeable.

Janey's voice reverberates from downstairs and I bite my lip in preemptive tears. I'm too far to hear what's said but I sit quietly, ear to the floor as I try.

I fall asleep like that and only wake up when the foyer door slams shut. I have no idea what time it is, but I hear daddy's voice come barreling in. He sounds heated, in an argument. I've heard him yell over the phone at billing companies, I've heard him yell at farmhands when they make a dangerous mistake, he's even yelled at me every once in a while. But none of it amounts to his level of anger right now.

I look up at my door and realize my handle has been switched while I slept. Bookmarking my mother's manipulation for later, I quietly crawl across my room. Janey's room is across from mine and I can hear her downstairs trying to calm down my dad. If I'm lucky, her phone is in there. If I'm not, her laptop is and I can use that.

My suitcase is still packed and my wallet is tucked into my jeans. I can easily book a hotel and call an uber. Once I'm out of here I can figure everything out from there. Saatchi's number is ingrained into my brain and a hotel will have a phone to call her, I'll pay the long distance fee. She can help me schedule a flight back.

I pull my door open slowly and my father's voice increases in volume from two stories below. I hold my breath as I crawl across to Janey's room, weight distributed along the floor  praying the floorboards don't creak. I've done this enough to have it down to a T.

Janey's door is cracked open and I ease my way into the dark room. I don't dare turn on a light as I continue inching forward. Her bag and suitcase are at the foot of her bed but I ease my head off the floor to see if her phone is charging on her night table.

I internally groan at my bad luck and continue toward the bag. It's still unopened which means I'll have to put everything back once I'm done. I'm not sure when I'll have a chance to sneak out, maybe in the morning, when everyone is sleeping off the eventful night. I can schedule an uber for then, but if Janey sees her stuff has been disturbed, I might be found out.

The voices are still loud downstairs and I send up a quick prayer to a God who may or may not hate me and start to open Janey's stuff in search of my key to escape. My hands tremble and sweat as I delicately place things on the ground beside me. I wish I had my phone to take a photo, but if I did, I wouldn't be in this mess.

Just as I'm easing out her laptop, a foot creaks on the first step of the stairs. My head whips around and I scramble to set up my escape. This may be my only chance to get out of here unscathed. If I can guarantee leaving tomorrow morning, I can tell my family and then book it out of here.

I don't know my mother. I never have. It makes me fear everything I've ever known. I thought she loved me, but when that lock clicked on my door, so did the realization that I was fighting a losing war. She will never love me. I will never be what she wanted.

There's no way I can trust anyone in my family now, so I rip up the laptop screen and nearly cheer when it shows a full battery. More stairs creaking have me furiously typing away at the screen. I've only pulled up the screen for an uber when I hear my dad's voice at the top of the first flight. He's giving me no choice but to call for an immediate uber.

Hopefully Janey will forgive me, or at least not notice, the charge on her card as I order it quickly, too panicked to take the time to type in my own card information. I could risk getting a reservation from the driver's phone but that opens the possibility of something bad happening. I realize I should've booked the hotel first but it's too late. The driver is on their way and I'm not even sure if the hotel I put in as a destination has availability.

I'm just typing in the name when my dad swings open Janey's door. In my haste, I hadn't realized how much noise I was making, or the fact I had started trembling and sobbing in desperation.

"Emmylou, what the fuck," he says as he looks down at my sobbing face. I shake my head at him and pull my hands away from the laptop, tucking them into my chest. My sister stands behind him, peering in from under his shoulder. "What is going on?"

"I told you she's a mess," my mother starts as she pushes her way into the room. "I have no clue what lies that girl from school has been feeding her, but she's a mess. We need to get Emmylou to a psychiatrist; she's been abused and taken advantage of."

"Now, Tammy, hold on." My dad kneels in front of me, edging his way in front of my mother. "Emmylou, what's going on babygirl? Why are you crying?" He looks over my shoulder and frowns. "Why do you need a hotel baby?" I tremble as he reaches his hand out slowly and pulls me forward into a hug. My dad always gives the best bear hugs and I can't help the way I melt against him.

"Jeanette." My mother's voice is harsh and final. "Go get my phone and I'll call the hospital to let them know we're on the way."

My sister looks at my mother in surprise and turns to leave.

"Wait," I call out to her, voice breaking. "No. No mom, I'm not doing this. I don't care anymore, just let it happen."

"Emmylou—" my sister starts but she's immediately cut off by my mother.

"Remember what we talked about? We can get you help but you can't keep believing those lies."

I shake my head at my mother, cheek rubbing against my dad's shirt. He smells like his cologne and hay. He couldn't have been at the farm today with how long it took him to get here though. It's just his natural scent at this point.

"No." I push away from my dad and scootch backward until my back hits Janey's bed. Now at least I can see all of them and see what's coming. Whatever it may be. "I don't know what mom told you but, I'm just gonna tell you the truth.

"Saatchi's my girlfriend." My mother immediately scoffs and starts to open her mouth.

"Emmylou, you don't understand what was happening—"

"Ma, stop. Let her talk."

I smile at my sister in gratitude. Hopefully this isn't the last time.

"We . . . started dating during Christmas, just a few days before the day of," I pause and look at my pa. "I'm sorry, pa, I didn't stay because of that, I—I, uhm, anyway. I'm sorry if that's bad but, I really love her and I like girls," I shrug, a habit I've never been allowed to show in front of my mother, but it doesn't really matter when I have snot and tears covering my face.

My mother bites at her acrylic nails and storms out of the room.

"Emmylou," my dad starts, brows pinched as he blinks down at me. "Honey, I've known you were gay since you were in diapers, but you can find a girlfriend somewhere else baby. It doesn't matter how much you love someone; they should never hit you."

I wonder what the chances are of being struck by lightning. I wonder what the chances are of realizing that your life is a lie and that your mother is insane—abusive. The word has bounced around silently in my head but now it's screaming. Screaming against my temples, against my joints, into my heart. My mother is abusive. She knew. Daddy knew. They know I'm gay.

"What? You knew?"

My dad scoots closer and Janey sits beside him.

"Yeah baby, you used to talk about how you wanted to marry your kindergarten teacher. Which was normal until you talked about how much you wanted to kiss her. Then, well, we kind of got the memo. I just . . . figured you'd tell us when you were ready. But—"

"No, hold on," I stop him with a hand up. I wipe my face with the other hand. "Y'all all knew?"

"I mean, I didn't, but shit Emmylou, I don't care. One of my bridesmaids is lesbian. You know her, Olivia? We even made extra room for seating arrangements so her girlfriend could come."

I look at Janey and a new wave of tears pool at my waterline.

"But you and mom knew?" I ask my dad.

He nods slowly. "Baby, yes. We're fine with it. I tried to make that clear when, well, when you were with Saatchi over Christmas. I kind of figured y'all were already dating and you were too scared to say anything. I mean, she's why you stayed in Scotland, right?"

I laugh humorously and let my head land against Janey's bed.

"You're *both* fine with it," I say sarcastically. My mother steps into the room again.

"Emmylou, you didn't finish the story. You didn't talk about what Saatchi did to you and how you called me to go rescue you. About how she hit you."

I grind my teeth and close my eyes, willing this nightmare to dissipate.

"That isn't what happened."

"Emmylou, tell the truth."

"That isn't what happened," I repeat, my voice getting louder.

"Do not tear this family apart with your lies," my mother yells back.

"Tamara, what the fuck is going on here?" My father looks between us and Janey grabs my hand in hers and squeezes tight. I let a final sob rip from my chest and let numbness fill the rest.

"Saatchi didn't slap me so hard it bruised. Mom did. Mom came to visit –a surprise visit—because she must've seen my Instagram post with Saatchi. I thought it was innocent enough because," I look up at my dad, painfully resolute in my hand reaching for his. The truth might break his heart. "You see, daddy, mom told me since I was a kid that it wasn't okay to be gay. So I tried to hide it. Mom even called me to tell me that Janey had to kick her friend out of her wedding because she was gay, and that it was a good thing I wasn't gay because I'd get kicked out too.

"The full story, dad—is that mom came to Scotland and berated my friends to the point that I *had* to come out because I was tired of watching her hurt Saatchi with her blatant homophobia," I say, words spitting. "The full story, dad, is that mom is a liar. She convinced me to come back and leave my supportive and wonderful girlfriend behind because she told me you had cancer. Just like I did." I look at the ground. "Just like I did when I was younger—and that you were hiding it. I believed her because she *made* me hide mine because, God forbid, my cancer got in the way of your promotion or Janey's first year of college. So I went to chemo alone while mom went to the country club and I didn't tell anyone.

"I figured you were doing that too. You know? When you suddenly came home for Christmas, for chemo, right? Because you weren't supposed to be home for Christmas. That's why I didn't come. Mom called me and said you had work and Janey had Eric and for me to stay in Scotland." I finally look up at my mom's face. The tears streaming down her face do nothing to thaw the ice in my chest. "Bet that bit you in the ass though, huh? Since I spent it with Saatchi. Cuddled up in her bed. Gay and shit."

My dad turns slowly to my mom.

He's silent and she looks at him and shrugs.

"She's lying. I told you she's been lying since I got her on the plane. Trying to take it all back. We need to get her help." I push my nails into my palm. This wasn't an option I had considered.

"Call the hospital then," Janey says, eyes still on me. "Call the hospital where you stayed at, Emmylou."

My mother's head snaps over to glare at my sister and my dad shakes his head.

"No need. It's there. The truth, written all over your face Tamara." He stands up and looks away from her, hands clenched beside him. "Get out, Tamara."

"John—"

"Get the fuck out," he yells. I watch as my mother retreats into herself before turning.

The room is silent, my sister's tears hitting the floor, as we wait for the sound of the car turning on. My dad waits until her car is out of the driveway before turning to us.

"I'm so sorry," I tell him, but he's kneeling and gathering both of us in his arms.

"No. No, I am so, so, incredibly," his voice cracks and my throat tightens, as do his arms around us. "Beyond sorry that—"

"It's fine now, daddy," Janey says, tears staining both of us. "Emmylou's okay now, right?"

I nod against them and my dad begins to sob. My heart breaks deep and completely at the sound of my giant bear of a father sobbing into my hair. It's my fault that he's in pain.

She was right. I was going to tear this family apart. Just not in a way I expected.

I cling to my father as our cries fill the room.


My eyes are crusty with sleep dust when I wake up next to Janey. Pa's still sleeping on the floor on my mattress that he brought in. Another beep rings through the room and I realize Janey's phone is ringing. I scramble up and answer when I see Saatchi's name lighting the screen.

"Saatchi?" I ask, voice already cracking. My pa shifts and I silently sneak out of the room.

"Lou, fuck. Fuck. Are you okay?"

"No, but yeah. It's a lot." I sigh and sink to the floor in the hallway before I start telling her everything.

Eventually Janey comes into the hallway and drapes a blanket around me.

"Coffee?" she asks, yawning, dragging her pink slippers across the floor. I nod at her and she goes down. My pa comes out to find us both huddled under the blanket. The worst has passed, and Janey laughs at the screen as Saatchi's smirk projects across the ocean to us.

"That your girl?" my pa asks, groaning as he sits his old bones beside us.

"Yeah, this is Saatchi."

She waves across the screen at him and he waves back before taking my sisters offered mug of coffee.

"You should go, Lou," Saatchi says.

I frown at her but nod.

"Yeah, probably. I'll call you later—" I look at my pa. "When I have tickets back to Scotland?" He nods and smiles tiredly at me. "Yeah, when I have my flight back. Uhm, okay, love you, bye."

She smiles at my blushing face, still inherently embarrassed to say it in front of my pa.

"I love you too, Em," she says back and I smile at her video.

"Nice jumper, by the way," I tell her before hanging up. I'll ask her to send me a photo of her in my cotton candy sweater once I get a phone again.

When I hang up, pa and Janey both look at me, amused.

"Jumper? So gone for this girl that you've gone and snagged her words," my pa teases. I blush hotly and hide my face in the blanket. "Next you're gonna tell me you like soccer more than football." It takes me a second to process that he means American football, and he mistakes the confusion on my face for confirmation.

I squeal as he chases me around the house, threatening to make me watch football reruns all morning as Janey cheers us on from atop the dining table.

*Saatchi*

I hate airports. They have planes. And planes are untrustworthy beasts. I might just skip the Boston marathon this summer and only race in walkable countries. No cars, no trains, no planes, no damn horses.

Finn pops his knuckle beside me and I frown over at him.

"Why are you even here, bawbag?"

"I just want yous both to know I'm claiming dependent in this relationship. Designated third wheel. Whatever. Just don't leave me." I scoff at him and bump my shoulder against his.

"You? Nah, you're like a tumor attached to my heart. We're stuck with each other until we die." He nods in approval and I tighten my hands in the jumper. He's being kind by being here. Emmylou ended up staying a whole week in Texas, which is grand for her, even though she missed classes. But it's dug a seed of fear in me, like maybe her family isn't supportive and they've been slowly convincing her to stay there and leave me. Or come back and leave me. Or maybe she just wants to stay with her family now that her mam is out of the picture. Or maybe she just wants to leave me.

My spiraling stops when Finn gasps beside me and I look up to see Emmylou. She spots Finn, tall fuck face, before me, but when she sees me her face brightens and I ache to both look away and be blinded by it at the same time.

It takes everything in me to stay still but, of course, she doesn't take note of that and comes sprinting at me. I huff in surprise as she jumps into my arms, legs hoisting above my hips, and squeals in my ear.

"Saatchi," she coos as she squeezes the little remaining air from my lungs. I cling tightly to her thighs as I hold her up.

"Hiya bird," I whisper.

"Hi Finn," she says, still perched on top of me. "Is that my sweater?"

"Jumper," I correct.

"Aye, she hasn't taken it off since you left really. Might wanna wash it. Or throw it out honestly."

"Shut the fuck up, Finn," I tell him. Emmylou still clings to me and he kindly grabs her suitcase, bigger now than when she left.

I look up at her and she pulls back to peck my lips.

"Welcome home, love."

# Epilogue

*Emmylou*

Boston is wet against my skin and I try not to groan as Kirsty leans against my arm.

"Why are we here again?" I ask her from our place on the ground. My dad chuckles beside me and pats my back.

"Young love is stupid," he says, only to receive a playful slap from Janey. Drew hands me a water and I smile over at her gratefully.

"I should've gone with the guys," Eric says, frowning over the crowd from where he stands. "You think they'll get lost or confused?" Eric is an only child, but it's been endearing to everyone to watch him adopt Finn and Sai as his younger brothers. Even Sai, sensing a new and responsible party, has let loose a little since meeting him.

"Honey, they'll be fine," my sister drawls, tugging his hand. "Sit down, you're making me anxious."

"Oi!" All of us pop up quickly to join Eric as we hear Finn in the crowd. "She's in fourth, she's in fucking fourth." I still don't see him but the crowd is starting to increase its volume. Apparently, the news is traveling and we're all pressed against the barriers to see the runners make their final stretch.

People begin cheering as the first runner appears. I hold up my sign and Kirsty nearly jumps on top of the barrier screaming ferally beside me. Sai grabs her before she can as Finn steps up behind me.

"She's mad close to third though. I wonder if she can pull it off?" I fight the urge to lean over the railing as a cop walks past us. Kirsty glares at him but Sai holds her steady.

The second racer crosses the line and I spot Saatchi, and suddenly my dad is holding me back as I scream my lungs out. She truly is neck and neck with third and I beg my screaming lungs to give her power while, somewhere in the back of my mind, I process that she barely looks out of breath.

Each pace closer to the line has all of us going rabid and Sai fights to hold his phone steady so his parents can see over Face Time—Bram can't fly because of his strokes he had when Saatchi and Sai were little.

"Come on baby," I howl over the crowd. I hold my breath as Saatchi crosses the line a little ahead of us and push beyond my dad to rush over to her. She's cordoned off in an area where the crowd can't reach her, but she doesn't even bend over to breathe when she finishes. She shakes hands with the other finishers and I look around to find results.

"Fourth." I look back to the finish line and see Saatchi has now wandered over to me. I try not to drool as she slowly walks over to me. Her muscles glean with sweat, every ridge tight with hard work, and almost everything visible in a tight bra and running shorts. I watch her neck move as she upends a water bottle into her mouth.

She wipes her mouth on the back of her hand and looks down at me, chuckling.

"You didn't even hear me bird," she teases before reaching over and pushing my chin up, effectively shutting my mouth. "I said I got fourth. Guess I'll just have to train harder for next year."

"Yeah, and run in more races. You know?"

She laughs and shakes her head. "Don't look so thirsty, the cameras are watching."

I arch my eyebrow at her. "What are you—scared?"

"Never," she says quietly, dipping below the tape. She wraps an arm around me and pulls me into a hot, searing kiss.

She tastes like sweat and cold water, but I still whine as she pulls away before resting her forehead against mine.

"I love you, Emmylou."

We find out later that afternoon that there were definitely many cameras pointed at us and, despite not getting first, a picture of us ends up on almost every news article about the Boston Marathon, and I make sure to collect them all.

I stare up at them, framed on the poetry-covered walls in Saatchi and I's bedroom in our shared apartment with Finn, and look down at my sleeping girlfriend tucked into my arms.

There's a part of me that feels like I should think about my mother right now, but I can't find myself to care. I think of my dad instead, who now demands I illegally send him haggis and who Face Times Saatchi and I weekly. I think of my sister, who, despite the wedding stress and by the grace of God, made enough space at her wedding for five whole new guests. I think of Greer and Bram, their small house with a dog tucked in every corner, and their hugs every morning when I'm visiting. I think of Finn, a constant and welcome third wheel in Saatchi and I's relationship. I think of Drew and Kirsty, our weekly yoga sessions and daily activities just to remind ourselves we're still loved. I think of Sai, who now calls me for updates on Saatchi in a compromised, and slightly false, show of space for Saatchi.

I think of Saatchi. Everything she is. Everything she's given me. And I finally understand what love means as it bursts from my chest and calms me at the same time.

Anne Bonny looks up at me as I go to flick the nightstand light off.

"I was right, Anne. There's a lot to be said about rich, spoiled Americans who run off to find themselves."

# Acknowledgments

Thanks to everyone who joined me on making my ADHD gremlins real. First and foremost, to my editor, Carmen Riot-Smith, for her ability to make a compliment sandwich and knowing where the hell a comma goes. My agent for believing in me and taking a chance on this book. To Kiia Kostet for bringing my characters to life and taking a chance to work with a first time author and Diego Velez for creating a logo toward my future.

Thanks to everyone who read the 13th draft of this pipe dream: Ryley, who was just as excited as I was for the bullshittery; Ellie, who still hasn't sent me any haggis rolls; Maddie, despite it not being a fantasy, and of course my mother and father, who are incredibly supportive of my queerness.

Special thank you to my cat, Calico Jack, for always lying on my computer at the worst possible times.

Ellis Mae is an author, tea enthusiast and sports coach.
They've lived in over 17 different cities and lugged their cat,
Calico Jack, and two dogs Koda Blue and Copper
Montgomery with them to every spot.